PSYCHOPATHS & SINNERS

Don't... Book Five

JACK L. PYKE

CREDITS

Cover art: Adrienne Wilder https://authoradriennewilder.blogspot.com
Formatting: Joseph Lance Tonlet http://josephlancetonlet.com/
Proofreading: Archer Kay Leah https://archerkayleah.wordpress.com/

(Ver. 28.05.19)

ISBN: 9781072352235

DEDICATIONS

TO THE BEST OF BETA READERS: You're awesome!!

TO MY KIDS: I know, I know. I'm not supposed to mention that I play *Fortnite*, but I do, and I love that I make you grin under all those protests.

Love you, kids, always,
Mom

CONTENTS

HEARTFELT ACKNOWLEDGMENTS

TO MY CONSULTANTS:
I have the best with me:

Elaine (my computer and MI5 technical guru!),
Vicki (my dark content edit go-to lady!),
Katerina (my medical-and-everything-else stunner),
and Dilo Keith (as always, awesome conceptual guidance into Gray's
world!).

It wouldn't be the Don't... series without you all!!

TO MY PRODUCTION TEAM:

Adrienne Wilder: your cover art is amazing!!
Joseph Lance Tonlet: thank you, thank you, thank you!!
Archer Kay Leah: your proofreading is still so frickin' awesome!!

SHARED-WORLD NOTE

The Society of Masters: two-worlds, one BDSM universe.
Don't… series & Deliver Us series.

The Don't… series is part of a shared-world project with Lynn
Kelling and her Deliver Us series. Huge thanks to Lynn for allowing
me to use her guys, and her skill for portraying Jack, Jan, and Gray in
hers!

Please check out Lynn Kelling's website at:

http://www.lynnkelling.com/

"Don't bend; don't water it down; don't try to make it logical; don't edit your own soul according to the fashion. Rather, follow your most intense obsessions mercilessly."

Anne Rice, with Franz Kafka.

CHAPTER 1
FEELING BLUE

THE BREAK OF bracken and twig under bare foot left a light trail of blood on forest floor as Johnny Shipman walked naked through the woods. Cold sweat moulded like a condom to his body, no doubt giving a clear view of his pale skin, wrinkled fingertips, and how he walked doubled-up like an old man. Naked wandering aged him decades older than his twenty-four years. Full moonlight kept him company, helping to sheathe the cold sweat in a silver that glistened and shifted as light might skate and shimmer across a frozen lake. Albeit a lake surface ready to crack.

Johnny snorted a chuckle: even tough ice eventually cracked, right? But he couldn't figure out why his laughter carried on and bounced off the trees. His hair lay damp, matting to his face, and sweat lightly ran down his chest and stomach, trickling intimate touches through his pubic hair and down his shaft. Occasionally drips would fall from the tip of his cock as he walked, adding a soft beat to the quiet of the night.

Everything about tonight should have bothered his soul: the black pit of darkness around him, trees crowding in as wind ruffled leaves and left them raising a brow at which restless soul walked the path tonight, right down to the boldness of his nakedness and the buzzing going on inside of his head and body. Hands felt thick, heavy; footsteps too, but nothing mattered.

Soft laughter again echoed about the trees, and this time he paused and glanced around, hoping to catch which tree hid the culprit. Maybe they all did. Trees were good for that. Hide and go… something.

A fresh kiss of air made him shiver, mostly in pleasure as it tickled around his body. He felt good. He'd never been more comfortable with his body than tonight, never more willing to take a chance to lay with someone and not to have to worry about wearing that larger T-shirt to help cover up the puppy fat. It had been hard, taken so many years to glance down, like tonight, and watch the sweat glide over the bumps and ridges to his abs. To walk more than ten paces without heat rising to his cheeks from the effort.

Heat burned his soul. He'd turned his first head a few months back, a lovely looking guy he had bumped into at the factory, and the shy smile that came his way because of it…? He'd seen that same shyness in his own mirror over so many years for that young man, that *what if he looks back and catches me looking?* And going back those few months, that was the first time the young man had looked at him like that. God… it had felt so damn good.

These last few months, then today, finally fitting into that denim jacket that Chase and Ash had clubbed together to buy him, the backpacking trip in a few weeks—it was meant to make him, make all three of them. Life was worth living. Worth loving.

Do it, mate. Do it, do it.

The whisper carried on the night's soft exhale, or maybe from somewhere deep inside his mind. He tried to shake it off, even added a rub of his palm into his forehead to see if he could push the cobwebs away and find the owner of the voice, but it just forced spiders to crawl free and race down his fingers to his toes.

He stumbled into the clearing, and the weight of the rope he held in his other hand became clear in the moonlight as it smacked into his thigh. Rope? Why the fuck was he carrying rope? The ridges and rough grooves played under his touch, and for a long while Johnny stared down at it. A killer's love bite, one that would circle around him and come as full cycle as much as the history behind this place. Where they'd met, where they'd finish, all the friendship, regret, and panic choked free into the night.

Do it. Do it, do it....

Oh... Yeah. Do it, do it. He tossed the rope, wrapping it around the thick branch of an old oak tree.

Before he'd been forced to stumble away to take a piss, his clothes had been folded neatly over by the ruins of a den, a fresh roof of fern over the sticks keeping them dry. He'd lost his denim jacket, didn't know where—didn't care. But trainers that had seen him take many a late-night run kept his boxers and track suit off the floor. His mobile had come last, and occasionally a ringtone would break the darkness and quiet the wildlife.

The screensaver that came alive caught three men mid-hug. He smiled, still feeling the kiss on his cheek off Ash, the brush of those wild auburn curls against his eyes, then smelling the beer on the breath off Chase as the England colours painted their faces from the England v Wales Euro match that had gone down a year ago. They'd just about pulled through two goals to one, the last coming in the ninety-first minute, and the photo immortalised their reactions forever.

Do it. Do it, do it, mate....

As the rope burned his hands, no creaks and groans came from the old oak he now climbed up. Strange how the rope looked set to take his weight, the knots and tension already tested... perfected. But the tree had taken the weight of three kids over the years, and the oak seemed happy enough to help take the strain now too. The wind played and stirred the thickness of the rope as he automatically set the knot in place on the tree. He should smile now, right? How even the length of rope was catered for, how toes wouldn't quite touch wooded floor.

A ringtone cut through the night for real now, or maybe it had been calling all night, and this time he caught the flare of light, knew whose friendly faces touched the screen. For a moment panic cut through the mugginess clouding his brain. *Stop. So wrong.* This was so wrong. This wasn't him. He couldn't have grown this far without them. They'd hurt, so fucking badly, especially Chase. But something inside him hurt too, didn't it? Something was sick about life. That's why he was here, doing this?

No. Fuck this.

"Shush, shush-shush." Someone came through the silver moonlight breaking through the trees, a will–o'–the–wisp with big broad shoulders, yet a body on the whole that barely seemed rushed to come over. It seemed odd, how the distorted features stopped there just by him, head tilted slightly, watching him.

The man held a large rugged log. "C'mon, Johnny. Do it, do it."

The whisper bit deep in his mind, sending shivers all

over and—

The thud came softly in the night and this time the old oak cried against his own weight. Again the wind picked up as he danced, for a moment a burst of fight kicking in as he scratched and twisted against the rope burning into his throat.

Panic. He didn't hurt—he panicked, so fucking scared now, despite the voice that hummed softly, despite the man's—

"Flutter by the butterflies—" Someone brushed his stomach, a light flutter, like a turn of stomach on first meeting someone. "—dance on scent and air...."

As the log thudded heavily to the floor, kicked under his toes, his wrists were grabbed and bound tight behind his back. Johnny kicked and fought against the whispers— against the hands that traced his hips; he couldn't focus long enough on either. Cold foot cuffs wrapped his ankles, long enough to snake around the log and still most of his struggles as the man weighed it down with his foot. The stretching of Johnny's neck eased a little as his weight was taken, the pressure on the rope eased.

Saving. He wasn't here to be saved. Not by him.

"Shush, shush-shush, mate. Just... flutter by those butterflies—" Johnny jolted as the log snapped forward, forcing out a grunt and a new kick against meeting nothing but air as he tried to reach the log again. The man smiled, keeping the blood-slicked log away from Johnny's cut and grazed bare feet with a work boot that made sure the log played the hangman's game to the full. "—they dance no worry, stress, or care. You know that, Johnny?"

Johnny choked. Another touch traced his stomach as he fought, then the moonlight caught the glint of a knife one moment yet buried it the next with a light cut into his stomach. He grunted against the pain and the feel of blood just as something came from the man's pocket.

As the log was pushed back under his toes, taking his weight a little, he wanted to laugh at how his own body and the butterfly's danced their cry for freedom in twisted sync. His from the rope and cruel play with the log; the butterfly's against the tube and how it kept it captive.

And blue…. The wings offered such a startling blue contrast to the dark night. Yet… dark…. Colours shouldn't be seen in the silver and dark of a forest like this, but blue… those wings were so fucking blue. Odd how he thought butterflies didn't come out at night either… only…. Only….

The butterfly struggled between tweezers as it was tugged free of the tube. Thin glass hit the forest floor, and for a moment insect legs and wing tickled over his hip, his stomach, then—

The butterfly had its wing pulled off, stopping any play.

The log snapped forward, away from him, and Johnny danced his struggles as the butterfly's faded to nothing. A touch went to his hip again, then a brush of something else against his hip, against the cut. The fingering inside the cut came slow, pushing… tugging… something stuffed inside his hip as Johnny fought and kicked.

A sigh drifted over. "Flutter by the butterflies, love on coloured wing. So flutter by those butterflies…."

The log chuckled its way under the tips of his toes again, and Johnny ate up air as his weight was taken, a touch now brushing at his stomach.

"They're attracted to sodium in sweat, did you know that? It's why they flutter close by, those butterflies."

Both butterfly wings were nowhere in sight, and Johnny tried to push the attack away, stop more insects crawling inside of him. But with a wry grin given off the man, the log snapped forward again, making him fight for air.

As he danced and kicked, a groan came, then this time a mouth took his breath in a whole new way. Now standing on the log, the man crushed a rough kiss against his lips as his body pushed in close to Johnny's. Hands went everywhere: Johnny's ass, hips, back… then the man pulled back slightly, his groans filling the night as he stepped down and kissed a trail to Johnny's stomach. The log underfoot saw Johnny keep his breath, but now he squirmed and cried out at how the man licked down his body, tonguing around the cut—in the cut and playing with something else in there—then through his pubes. Finally a warm mouth took his cock down to the root. Hands gripped his hips, and even the blowjob carried a rough violation of its own: teeth, tongue, being sucked down the back of a throat that only pulled him deeper, harder, faster into the heat.

"Well, well, well." The man gave a chuckle, his breath playing along the dampness of Johnny's cock. "You sick fucker. You want this." He smacked the head of Johnny's cock, the hardness there, and Jonny danced again, this time trying to close his legs. But rough play came up and down his length for a second time.

"Nice. Very nice." The man bit his way up to a nipple, twisted the other, all the time fisting harder and faster down Johnny's cock as a body played bump and grind against him, another hard cock rubbing, moving, shifting into his thigh. "Fuck, yeah. We like this."

This… this was sickness, but it left him gurgling a cry into the darkness as the log was tugged from under his feet again. Heat fought the death-coldness, and his body jerked and forced itself into a corner, then cried *fuck yes* to the first stream of come into the fisting going on with his cock.

"Fuck. Perfect. Just fucking perfect, our Johnny." The man's breathing peaked, held, then suddenly calmed as come hit Johnny's thigh. A finger traced through the twin lines of release, focusing more on Johnny's, then a heated breath played over his bicep as tugging came at his hip again, at the cut and giving everything already stuffed in there a white shroud.

"Butterflies." A groan came. "Flutter by those fucking butterflies."

Life seemed to calm, go quiet. Cuffs were removed from Johnny's hands and feet, the log tossed to the side, dirt ruffled to leave behind no trace of extra footprints.

And all fight slipped from Johnny's body...

From the distance, sounding as though it came down a long tunnel to Johnny, the ringing of his phone came. Then a crush through heath from the opposite direction the man had walked filtered over, along with shouts and cries that should have hurt more than rope. Yeah, this was the place they all came to when life hurt, or when life got a little... cruel when Ash and Chase decided to play; he should have known they'd trace him here now. But nothing mattered anymore, not even the hands that touched his nakedness, swearing they were there to help, to just hold on, to just—

"... hold on, Johnny. Hold the fuck on, mate. Please, please, please, mate...."

CHAPTER 2
DON'T... LISTEN

GRAY TURNED HIS ear towards the bedroom door as it came again. Over the shift of blind that the last hold of winter-morning chill breathed into the bedroom, dull thuds, followed by muffled voices, filtered through.

The alarm clock seemed to yawn into life almost in answer, and although its voice was set to hush, another tap off Gray saw it simmer down its whimpering and settle back into sleep. The Wednesday-morning chill drifted across his bare shoulders as he stood there by the bed, and he glanced down, envying the warmth found within the sheets.

Life looked so tempting there.

Jan stirred, just slightly, enough to shift his hips under the light covers, his arms searching to hug the pillows a little tighter. No tenseness filled his body, and the fading grumble at nearly being pulled from dreamland was soft, halfhearted. The roughing up from the pillows earned Jan a few morning cowlicks to his longer strands of hair, and Gray half-smiled, gently running a touch over a few stray strands sleeping on the back of his neck. Jan almost—almost—had Jack's wilder look about him, yet the angle to his body was less Jack's *the bed's all mine, fuck you, mate*, and more a quiet *I'll take the other side because something's still missing here, bud.*

At 5:00 a.m., the alarm seemed content enough to let Jan sleep in a few more hours. He didn't have to clock into the accounts department over at the Masters' Circle until nine o'clock, and now that sleep came a little less troubled for him, Gray was content enough to let Jan sleep too.

He glanced back to his shirt and jacket hung neatly on the wardrobe door. He had a meeting at eight this morning, the scent of amberwood and body wash whispering that he'd been up an hour already. After giving a final brush at the crease to Jan's arm, at the fading puncture mark still bruising the skin there, Gray shifted back over to the mirror.

Hung close by, the black mélange waistcoat jacket matched the fine cut of the black trousers already sculpting his hips, both coming with Vivienne Westwood tags and showing a more formal appointment at his MI5 office with the director-general and Andrews, Gray's own elite operation's officer and manager. The necklace that slept around his throat wouldn't touch the cost of the suit in any lifetime, though, and could be found on most Italian markets. The black cross that acted like a little brother to the larger silver one stayed right where it touched around his throat, eventually finding a natural home under his shirt as Gray took the shirt off the coat hanger next to the jacket, then slipped it over his shoulders. As he tried to bury the chesty cough that came, he let the shirt rest unbuttoned as the tie came next. The tie wrapped the back of his neck, but he let it fall loosely down his open shirt as he turned his ear to the door.

Again a run of soft thuds. Again those mumbled voices.

This time Gray couldn't bury his cough, and a body pressed up close behind. Gray distractedly glanced over his shoulder as hands grazed down his hips, around his waist, one to rest against the flat of his abs. The other stroked just beneath the shirt, at his right side now where the blue moon rose tattoo with the silver collar wrapping around it was just about visible over the trouser waistline. The touch was nothing sexual, just—

"Morning." It sounded so sleep-filled, husky. Jan briefly rested his head against the back of Gray's shoulder before a kiss brushed his cheek. "So... sleep. Did you get any last night?"

Gray eased around with a deep sigh. Jaw tensing slightly, he rested his head against Jan's and lightly feathered a touch at Jan's naked hips. "Some."

Jan traced inside Gray's open shirt as he closed his eyes. "You're a lousy liar, you know that, Raoul? Life's spent listening nowadays."

"Hmmm?" Gray eased into a smile. Jan mapped the ridges and curves to his abs and sides in the gentlest of ways, and it really wasn't helping with how naked Jan shifted against him. "I'm no lousy liar."

"Maybe." Jan took a deep breath, dragging his nose along the curve of Gray's throat and leaving Gray shivering a little against it. He added nothing else, and Gray waited as Jan pulled away slightly and started on the lowest button of his shirt. The moves were slow, each button fastened with careful fingers, and coming with a shift off Jan, a slight hint of Jan's sleep-ruffled scent that had Gray looking away.

Jan, he wasn't lost, wasn't lonely, he just waited for that

third piece of the jigsaw puzzle to slot back in between them and take its natural, if somewhat kinky place. Those eyes held the confidence that said *It will come*. Even though Kes had only been buried a few weeks now, and Martin still lingered around like the bad proverbial… everything, they'd seen it over a month ago back at Christmas, how although Jack had been buried since then in Martin, Jack was still in here. In the scent of the sheets, in the private smile Gray caught on Jan's lips when Jan thought he wasn't being watched like now.

Again Gray calmed his breathing. Jan. All his nakedness. He came with an energy, maybe the wrong energy, or just slightly wired wrong with not having Jack here, because although Gray knew tender, how Jan needed tender, when Jan shifted slightly, his hip digging more into Gray's suit trousers to stop any mark of Jan's hardness into the material, Gray forced himself to back down with how he wanted to trace up Jan's nakedness, stroke, touch… rough up….

"Don't…." Jan gave a wry smile as he gave an extra light tug on Gray's tie.

"What?" Gray breathed into his ear, pulling him a little closer with a touch on his ass. Yeah. Jan had a damn good ass.

"Look at me like that…." The brown to his eyes lit with the differing shades of spring, injecting that need to get up and taste the day when his body hinted at something entirely different. "It's a Jack look, when he's ready to say fuck to getting out of bed and just getting downright dirty instead. And we agreed. We touch when Jack's back, nothing more, nothing less."

"If it's a Jack look, then saying don't isn't a wise word to use…." Gray rested his head against Jan's and loved running the curve of his ass. Yeah, that was a damn fine ass, as soft as the soul that cuddled up into him.

Jan stroked at Gray's right hip, at the tattoo marking his skin, maybe to calm, maybe to tease. Gray couldn't quite figure out which. Although he got the feeling that if he gave Jan some felt-tip pens, Jan'd rather sit quietly in the corner of Jack's cell, colouring the mirror of Gray's tattoo on Jack's hip in order to try and win Jack's attention over Martin's, now that Jack had been locked away in the manor since he'd taken to hiding away in Martin. Unlike Gray's, Jack's tattoo remained uncoloured. It would stay that way until Jack was back to see his own hip painted.

And Gray would watch, as much drawn to wait out and watch Jack's kink as he was to watch Jan's patience and calm.

Four soft vibrations came from Gray's phone, then went quiet. Jan stiffened slightly, and Gray stroked a gentle touch at his ass to settle disturbed waters. Waiting for the four vibrations to come again, Gray took the phone from his suit trousers.

"*Shw mae*" came the male voice on the other end, the South Welsh barely traceable, but there nonetheless. North and South Wales never really mixed, but here—

"*Sut mae.*" Gray kept Jan close, a tug making sure Jan came into the curve of Gray's throat. Jan responded, kissing at Gray's neck, sometimes nibbling, and for a moment Gray forgot about the call as the light kisses sent shivers down his side. This tender business... Jan's... he had Jack's decadence, but with an innocence that said he'd still see more beauty and pleasure in a painting full of buttercups over any BDSM scene.

"There was a death in the West Midlands a few weeks ago that should interest you."

Now Gray focused on the call. "Over a few weeks ago?" If it was of interest to this man and ultimately Gray, the delay in being notified was… unusual. When it came to handling domestic and foreign business beyond MI5/6 control, his orders came from the British military and… beyond, the former from the field marshal and chief of the defence staff: a call to business that the director-general for MI5 himself had no jurisdiction over. By the time a call like this was made, there was only ever one order: catch and cull. In government and Crown circles, Gray and his two other peers were known as the cullers, and they were usually called in on a scene within twenty-four hours of the incident.

"I'm passing over the details." Quiet. "This isn't a contract unless circumstance dictates otherwise."

Gray stilled a moment, and so too did Jan, as if sensing the change. That meant no interference and observation only, but also meant some time away from Jan… from…. He tensed his jaw. "Priority level?" He'd push for reassignment on an obs assignment like this. Andrews came to mind. It was about time he picked up on how to work outside of MI5 restriction.

"There's a sense…" Quiet again; the second time now and Gray caught the unease. "Psychological profiling suggests a potential for more victims."

Now that got his attention. Profiling suggested a killer, but the potential for more suggested a whole new ball game altogether with steps into serial-killer territory. Gray eased away from Jan, just slightly. He shouldn't have let that turn him away, but….

"*Nos da.*" That let the caller know he'd take the cull, and when Jan looked at him, it was full of a knowledge he shouldn't hold. By now, Jack would have turned his head away, given Gray his space, and in turn denied Gray's existence beyond Jack's comfort zone, and that had kept them close over the years. Jan... like now, Jan didn't look away, and having that softness of his gaze stay with him, on him... a conflict of emotions disturbed his own calm.

He pulled Jan back in, kissing at his throat and burying what bubbled inside. "Look after Jack for me, please."

A return kiss came, but Jan's cock had lost some of its fullness. Gray's hadn't. "You have to ask, then we have a problem, Gray." Yet the look in his eyes said they didn't.

Another round of soft thuds and muffled voices came, and they both pulled away at the same time, their looks finding the door.

"You get off." Jan shifted back to the bedside unit and pulled on his pyjamas. "I'll take this turn."

Straightening his collar, then slipping on his waistcoat and jacket, Gray headed for the door. "Get back to sleep. I'll see what's pissed him off this morning."

Jan looked over his shoulder just before Gray left. "No. I'll be there in a minute."

Gray smiled briefly. Jan told him no so easily, so unconsciously at times, even though he knew where "no" would take most others in Gray's world. "Catch me up when you're ready."

~

Gray closed the door behind him, burying his own heat, and looked down the hall as he pulled out his phone. They'd kept Jack's detainment and seclusion room close to theirs, mostly for extra support with overnight surveillance.

Looking like he was just clocking on, the main psych-nurse, Craig, stood talking to two orderlies.

Gray checked his phone as he went over. He stopped for a moment, re-reading the detail he'd just caught. A verdict of suicide by misadventure and drug abuse had been publicly given, or autoerotic asphyxiation, according to the headlines from the local paper. Yet someone somewhere suspected murder with Johnny Shipman. Gray agreed. The police report highlighted evidence of a Holly Blue butterfly inserted into the man's body along with two sets of semen, and it had been done when oxygen levels had depleted, near-death. Clotting of the blood and the life cycle of the sperm would have given a rough indication of when the semen was ejaculated and inserted into the cut, and as hands had been bound during the attack, that couldn't have been done by the victim. Those details hadn't been covered in the papers. Neither had the zero results with the DNA search.

Entomophilia, sex with insects… it wasn't exactly a new kink, either: to love the feel of bites off the likes of fire ants when you orgasmed, but it sure as hell was damn rare to kill the insect, then insert it inside the body with semen.

That was emerging psychopath territory. And it made Andrews his next call.

"Here," a voice answered. "I'm at home now. Do you need anything from the team for the meeting?" Home was a simple code for MI5 offices in London.

"I'm on business in Nottingham for a few days." Andrews knew what Nottingham meant. "I need some travel arrangements, also some photo ID for those surrounding the case. I'll email the exact location through now, along with details of the victim."

"On it. I'll get Rachel to cancel the meeting too.

Anything else?"

Gray looked back over his shoulder as a noise came from behind. Jan came out a moment later, slipping on a T-shirt now he had his pyjamas on. "Take charge of the Kenner case and stay close by the phone," he said to Andrews, then cut the call.

Gray eyed up the plain design of the pyjamas. "Your *Spider-Man* ones in the wash?"

Jan snorted as he finished pulling down his T-shirt over slim hips. "Turtles, they're *Teenage Mutant Ninja Turtle* ones in the wash, and Jack got them for me. Next time I'm out shopping, I'm getting you a pair. *My Little Pony* ones, for your lip."

Gray buried a smile. "Pony-play, hmm? Interesting."

"Oh, what? No…." Jan stared at him, and Gray could have pushed him back up against the wall with the disgruntled purity on offer there. "I grew up watching a lot of those shows as a kid."

Gray cocked a brow. "You watched *My Little Pony*? Seriously?"

Jan tried a few different faces, then settled on a laugh. "Stop perverting my life." He elbowed Gray discreetly in the side. "Last warning, Raoul."

He'd kept his tone light but quiet, yet Craig still glanced over, then carried on talking quietly to the night staff. Gray buried the bubbling irritation. He missed his home being his home, where he could fuck when and where he wanted without spies in the halls. Even his grandfather knew when to disappear.

But then Ed wasn't on watch with what lay locked away at the end of that corridor. Craig was. Since Kes's murder in France, Jan had argued that Jack needed Craig and the

MC's psychiatric team to oversee care with Martin. Free-range with Jack wasn't a good idea, and it was downright suicidal with Martin. Him being here now, under MC handling, was compromise agreed to on all sides. Along with detainment and seclusion rooms, Gray had had an obs and separate staffroom furnished close by. But for now, the door that opened to the detainment cell via a little hallway stood ajar, the seclusion room just down from it, closed, with one of the orderlies casting a glance every now and again in its vicinity. Gray tensed his jaw. "Problems?" It looked like there'd been more than a few this morning.

Craig offered a trained, albeit *Christ, I thought he'd gone to work* look up from filling in his touchscreen, then softened his glance a touch catching Jan. He offered a smile before he patted one of the orderlies on the shoulder. "You get off. But show Baz the staffroom first, okay, Paul?"

Next to Paul, a stocky man with a look that fitted a noir detective picture movie struggled to find something to look at. He was new, and it showed. Paul nodded and shifted his head the opposite way Gray had come. "Baz?" said Paul. Saying nothing, Baz only gave the seclusion room a quick glance, and Paul tugged him away.

"How's he holding out?" Gray watched them head off towards the office.

"Baz is ex-army and new to the MC." Craig didn't sound happy as he tapped something else into the iPad. "Which means he's catching up with what we're about, plus—" He thumbed behind him. "—Princess Peachless in there."

Gray raised a brow as Craig put his iPad on the table. The nickname was new, yet…. Peachless? Yeah, that could work. He buried a grin.

"Paul is top class, though." Craig ran a hand through his mucky brown hair. He'd been on five minutes and already looked like he'd done a full shift. "We'll get Baz there. I've got a good team in general here now: two for the day shift, two for the night, and I work half of each." He offered a tired smile. "But I'll be honest and say I'll be glad when Peaches is back. I kind of miss my papers being pilfered, over threats of slowly burning Baz with thin strips of bacon wrapped around him, true pig-in-a-blanket style, any day. I swear something about him has Martin on edge."

"Can I get you a coffee?" Jan went over and picked up the iPad and had a look over the report.

Craig relaxed as he joined him. "Ed's promised some decent sausage and egg around ten. He's a damn good cook."

Jan nodded, and Craig looked him over, maybe deliberately not looking at the puncture marks on Jan's arms. "How you doing, kid?"

Jan's smile was a little forced now. He was used to Jack being there for the methadone injections, Gray, but anyone outside of that? "Getting there. Just." He didn't like the intrusion.

Craig patted his arm, then rested back against the table. He understood.

"So you think Baz has got Jack unsettled?" Jan refused to use "Martin" outside of the detainment room. So had Gray. That was Jack in there. Martin only borrowed residency for a while, however much he tried to fuck everyone up with that residency.

More thuds came from down by the seclusion room.

Craig sighed hard. "He smelled fresh meat with Baz, no doubt, but it high-wired his synapses and got him all excited and on edge."

"Any injuries?" Gray came and took the report.

"No... just. Martin decided to dig through the wall to some wiring and piss on the electrics to get Baz's attention. Paul was forced to sedate Martin via the electronic tag on his ankle." Two more thuds came from the seclusion room. "That's Princess Peachless waking up and not being impressed with a padded cell now we have to spend time getting his room fixed." Craig folded his arms. He was a big man, not exactly on the attractive side, and could probably scare someone into being quiet, but his voice came with a calmness to it, and a professional touch to his big hands that knew how to calm as much as offer a restraint to a psychiatric patient without any drama. But besides all of that, Jack trusted him, and that's all that counted in Gray's book. "Martin's all up here." Craig tapped his head. "Bloody vicious and cocky with it too, but he doesn't have Jack's loveable side or his skill with Shotokan." He paused. "I just don't let him near sharp objects in case Martin blends personalities and suddenly finds himself Kung-Fu fighting."

Gray scowled. That was the ultimate concern: a blending of personality, but with Martin being the dominant side. They needed that dominant personality to be Jack. But Jack still hid, leaving behind the certified psychopath.... "Have you made a call to an MC electrician?" He kept business in-house because the Masters' Circle kept his business private. And he liked that privacy at all times.

Craig nodded. "He's coming out today, but to be honest, it looks like the room will be out of working order for a while."

"You'll need to relocate?"

Jan looked up at Gray, sharply. "He stays here, in this manor." It was there in his eyes: the promise that called out how they'd make damn sure Jack would wake up in his own bed, not locked away behind psychiatric doors with strangers and used beds.

Craig nodded. "Just to another room, nothing more. I noticed a storeroom downstairs that could easily be made Peachless-proof."

Jan choked a laugh and Craig nodded, happy.

But it had fallen silent in the seclusion room, and it had the quiet effect in the hall too as the door caught their attention.

Gray eased the iPad over to Jan without looking. He was aware Craig watched him too. "Time to say morning to Jack."

Craig paused for a moment. "Two minutes. No more. Don't wind him up."

Gray threw him a look, not exactly sure what it said himself, then rubbed at Jan's arm before moving off.

CHAPTER 3
DON'T... PLAY THE GAME

SWEATING, MORE THAN aware of how his body steamed into the padded cell, heat swirling and staining the air, Martin slumped on the floor and wiped his forehead on his arm. Dampness moulded his jogging pants to his hips and legs, and the manhandling that left bruises to his arms and chest only streaked the sweat. He needed a shower, needed to hit someone, maybe needed to fuck someone more, but his head and body didn't know which, and he groaned, his head falling back against the padded wall.

It was there under his skin, scratching, itching: the need to clean, fuck, clean, fuck again, and routine... fucked-up routine... and Baz....

"Baz what?"

The voice came so quiet, so calm, irritating something inside even more—had he spoken Baz's name then? Martin clenched his fists into his jogging pants.

"How about you fuck off, Gray." His voice wasn't as calm, as quiet, and he hated that weakness, that.... He scratched at his tattooed hip, at the burn and scar that the uncoloured tattoo hid, then groaned realising he'd done it. "Most men get a fucking dog as a pet." He pushed up, feet a little unsteady because of the sweat, head fuzzy from the sedative and, and something else that itched... just fucking itched under his skin, his hip, the uncoloured rose and collar tattoo staining itself with blood and deep scratches this morning.

Why the hell did Jack have an uncoloured tattoo on his hip?

"Fucker... his cologne...." Martin rubbed at his head, then frowned finding Gray there in front of him. People kept shifting into place one moment, disappearing the next, and Gray, he was in close now. He wore a suit, so finely goddamn well cut to his body that the brush of it against him infected Martin in different ways. Goddamn good ways....

Gray watched, waited, seemed to breathe him in. And that only rattled him more.

"What about Baz's cologne?" Gray's voice stayed so soft, so fucking calm, and those eyes, those fucking eyes. Concern tilted Gray's head slightly, and Martin focused on that, played on that. Yeah, he should be fucking playing on that. Right?

"Same cheap brand as Vince." He didn't realise that was what itched under his skin until he said it, and the slight frown off Gray only irritated him more. It asked how he knew Jack's past, just how close the memories were to the surface, just how close Jack was, and itch... everything now just fucking itched. Hurt—burned.

He snarled, pushing Gray away, but a grip at his own throat pushed him back. So fucking pathetic. Just there for the—"Tuh-tuh-touching." Christ, he'd said that? What the fuck was going wrong here? Where the fuck had his fight fucked off to?

Gray pressed in close, body against his as Martin's world swam. Then Gray's scent, that simmer of amberwood during a spring walk....

Martin eased his nose along the curve of Gray's throat and smiled at how Gray didn't pull away. Familiar, everything about Gray was so fucking familiar now. Calm. "Back in France...." He licked his lips. "Us killing Kes... the Funder. You still feel it?" He slipped a touch under Gray's jacket, just light, and fuck... something burned through Gray as much as it seared through him. "The need to fuck in that stained stillness?"

Gray shifted his stance, but to shift away from Martin and discourage contact, or to heat it all up, was anyone's guess. Martin grinned, running with the latter because... Christ. The heat that dug into Martin's own hip had him groaning. Something had Gray on heat this morning. And now he really needed to—"Fuck."

Martin added a hard drag of fingernail down Gray's abs that threatened to tear shirt and dig deep into Gray, bleed all that heat out. "After what you did to the likes of Kes... you'd come home and rough-fuck Jack, hm? Really fuck it out of your system and fuck me out of Jack's." Martin smiled into the perspiration that started to line Gray's throat, the salt lining his lips no longer just a taste of his own. "Missing him, hmm?"

A multitude of muscles kept tightening in Gray's jaw, and Martin nicked and licked at each one. Blue eyes were now screwed shut. Yeah, Gray hid it from most, but he slipped here. The fullness of his cock said he missed Jack. He missed him in so many wrong ways.

"Who's left to take care of you now, hmm?" Martin dragged a rough path of nail between them, along Gray's shaft, hard into material, then licked at his throat, all curve to jawline. Gray's heavy breathing said Martin could play just for a moment longer. "One day you'll get sick of playing gentleman with Jan. You'll miss Jack a little too much…." He grinned into his neck after he bypassed Gray's lips. "And where will you go, my lovely, hmm? Who will you drag to the floor?"

Gray didn't flinch as Martin bit at his throat: hard, rough, enough to take Gray back a pace.

"I know where you'll go to," he whispered heatedly into his ear. "I know who you'll fuck."

Now he went in for a rough kiss, tasting that sweat, forcing everything of his into Gray's world. And for a moment, one brief moment as a hand came up and gripped hard at the back of his hair, Gray chased it, forcing Martin back one, two paces, three—

"Gray." It came so softly, but Gray instantly pulled away, following Martin's look to the door as Gray's grip went from the back of Martin's hair to resting on the wall.

Jan stood leaning against the frame, arms crossed, gaze not leaving Gray's. "Work."

Martin sighed heavily but didn't release his hold on Gray. In fact he made a point of palming the fullness in his cock. "Don't you have a life yet, Janice? Or better still, a maid's outfit that fits a little better around those tits?" Then he grinned. "Or maybe you're hanging around, watching in case you learn something about taming this fucker."

"Yeah? Gray." He still didn't look at Martin. "Work."

Gray shifted, stopping over by Jan and gently running a hand distractedly over his abs, then whispering something in his ear before leaving. Whatever it was, Martin wished he knew because it caused a cock of brow off Jan that eased away any tension between them both over there.

Jan looked back at him as Gray left. "All taming done and not a single touch needed."

Oh that smugness there made Martin want to strip his balls with a cheese grater and add a huge side order of vinegar into the cuts.

Jan quirked a smile. "And Jack still says you're welcome, Mart. Get well real soon." He started to head out.

The remains of the sedative hit hard, and Martin eased to the floor, wiping an arm over his forehead. "Talk on art history and accounts keep your other boyfriends close, did it, Janice?" he mumbled more to himself, but it stopped Jan for a moment. "It'll get under his skin sooner or later. Hopefully later when it will fucking hurt you more, Janet." *Or is it Janice? Who the fuck cares anymore?*

The door closed behind Jan, and Martin grunted a smile into the quiet that Jan left him with.

Jan first.

He'd work on Jan first. Easy pickings whilst the master was away. And Gray was wired in a different way this morning that said he was dressed for doing just that: playing away. Wasn't fair that Gray got all the fun lately now, was it?

∾

Gray ran a hand through his hair as he stopped by his Mercedes. He kept an overnight bag in his car for emergencies, and he'd take from the source location if he needed anything else, but that didn't distract from everything else running under his skin.

A hand dusted his back, and he turned slightly, more flinched.

Jan offered a raised brow, an unsure smile, and Gray let out a heavy breath before slipping a hand to the back of Jan's neck and drawing him in for a soft kiss. "Whatever he says—"

"Yeah." Jan came in closer. "Ignore the psychotic fuck."

"Yeah."

"And you?"

Gray frowned and closed his eyes as Jan ran a discreet touch down his inside thigh.

"Really missing Jack, hm?"

"You heard that, huh?" Christ…. He hated how close Martin dug to the truth. "Martin's more prone to talk if he thinks he's drawing you in, and I needed to see what had worked him up."

Jan nodded, then pulled back a little. "Yeah, I know. Just keep focus on who's hidden back in that cell, okay? We play Martin's game, but by our rules. We let him hurt, we let him deal with what's going through his head and heart, but we back away when it gets to us too much. We don't feed it too much, right?" The warning was clear, so too was the knowledge that Gray could hurt when he really started to play. Jan had been hurt enough, so too had Jack, even Martin in his own right. So Gray knew if Jan called enough, it was enough because…

When he's stripped bare, when you've taken everything he has to give, when he has no mouth, no complications over his disorders, just quiet—he's been under your touch, he's lying next to you. And that's Jack when there's no roles, no playing, just him, just you—just us. If you see that bare honesty as pretence where you're concerned, Gray, then you're right to call for a time out, but not for Jack's sake here….

Gray briefly closed his eyes as Jan's words from the night before he'd lost them both to Vince hit hard. For all of Gray's world, his directorship of G-Branch at MI5, the culling outside of that and on contract with the British military and Crown, the hardcore BDSM and Masters' Circle, Jan and all of his softer world of paint life through numbers saw life a lot clearer than he did at times when it came to Jack, when it came to… life without them both and taking a step back for his own sake.

Gray nodded, then all the tension dissipated, and he kissed at Jan's cheek, loving how Jan chased it so lips tasted lips. "I shouldn't be long. A week or so, tops. I should be back by next Wednesday."

"I'll take it that no communication means you're good, so don't worry about calling."

Gray took out his keys. "You have Rachel's number and Jack's emergency code. Rachel knows how to get in touch with me safely. Let me know if there's any trouble."

"There won't be. We can handle Martin. I won't call Rachel, you know that."

That confidence had always been there with handling Jack, and it naturally seeped into looking after Martin now. Gray was no fool, though. He knew just how well Jan hid his own hurt in doing just that: looking after Jack. So this was Gray quietly saying that code was there for him, but trust… Jan would always have it, no matter the faults and flaws.

"What did you get from Martin?" Jan opened the car door for him, and Gray buried the echo of Jack there.

"Have a word with Craig about asking if Baz can change his aftershave. It was his trigger this morning, and knowing Mart, he'll be unsettled for a while." Jan frowned and Gray explained.

The unconscious rub at Jan's arm didn't go unnoticed. "I hadn't picked up on the cologne."

"Good." And Gray meant that, more than. He didn't want Jan triggered either. "Keep Martin's unsettled mindset in focus when you're with him. Don't get close. You get Craig to do that. Martin looks ready to fuck about."

"It still bites, how he reacted to my cologne. That doesn't go away." And the hurt was there in the fullness of brown eyes. "But it might be a good sign that Martin picked up on it too?" That high intelligence kicked through the hurt. "He's processing what happened and Jack's surfacing? That's Jack's disorders talking there." It seemed to give Jan that push away from Vince, his psychological reconditioning and rape, that Jan needed. "Okay, I'll talk to Craig. Might be worth also seeing if we can add upping Martin's meds as far as his—"

"—Sexual drive—"

"—need to fuck about is concerned."

Gray buried a smile. "It touches close to Jack's," he said as he let the window down and put the Merc in reverse. "Jack plays it just as dirty."

"But in a lover's way, with a lover's soft heart. That's not Jack in there. So slow. Easy. You don't return the fucking about too much."

Gray heard the sense, his own words, hated how he bit out a rough cough now, but it didn't stop just how much he wanted Jack back.

Jan crouched by the driver's side, concern filling his eyes. "That's three times today."

The cough hadn't gone away, but at least he didn't cough up blood anymore. Gray took that as a good sign. "Just stress, Jan. I'm okay. Honest."

Doubt kept Jan silent, but he stood, hands going in his pockets. "Get it seen to, Gray. Otherwise I'm telling... Ed."

Gray winced. "Don't pull the grandfather card. Not my grandfather card anyway." He managed a smile. "Ed gets damn scary, even for me."

"Good and more than noted. Book an appointment with the doctor, otherwise I'm playing informer."

"Does that mean I'm interrogations officer in the bedroom too?"

"Not funny, not at all." But his eyes said otherwise, something along the lines of: *fuck, no, that's Jack's dirty kink, but I maybe—maybe—wouldn't mind watching.* "You drive very carefully." Jan took a step back, and Gray couldn't resist the hard grind of gravel under tyre as he pulled away.

"You'll piss Jack off, Raoul," he heard Jan shout, and Gray buried a smile. He'd give anything to have Jack here, fighting anger as a mechanic who'd seen enough accidents, but mostly as someone who was scared of Gray's harder handling of a ride.

∾

As the gate opened, he pulled alongside the security gate as Ray pulled in from off the road.

"Morning, boss." Ray leaned over now he'd wound his window down. He looked conscious of how long the gate was open.

"I'm away for a week." Gray checked the roadside behind Ray as a text came through. He thumbed through it, and two photo attachments came up. One caught three men mid-hug. The man in the middle looked the eldest and matched the photo fit of Johnny Shipman. Painted faces hid the other two men, but the second photo didn't.

Again all three men were pictured, but this time in a nightclub. In the background and almost out of shot, Johnny sat alone at a table, his glance on something going off in the distance of the club. His smile was easy, his factory coveralls and the grip on his drink looking relaxed enough to suggest a quick pint after work had turned into a Friday night's drink fest.

But the other two men?

Both tall, both slender, both in factory coveralls rolled down to their waist to expose the supple abs and that finer slipstream of muscle that came with youth. In the heat of the club and coloured light that made a kaleidoscope of the dark, one had the other pinned against a wall. But where one lad had brown hair, cut a little neater into the nape of his neck, the dark, wild auburn curls and severe sea-green eyes from the other young man stole the shot in every way going.

The combination of darkness to the auburn curls, the unusual light hiddenite eyes, and the soft blush to cheeks on olive skin should have been awkward, especially on such a slender frame, but that's what made the young man so striking: how everything that shouldn't go together, did. All harsh shades of crimson lake mixed with a Northern-Lights haunting in those lighter-than-light eyes. In all honesty, both young men looked like cupids who had long since shed any tie to childhood, said fuck to sharing the high from the arrows, then gone straight for feral and got high on the fix themselves. Which contradicted everything about what hiddenite crystal was supposed to represent: how the sea-green aided those lost in addiction. These, they egged the addiction on. Both young men were MC material without a doubt, perhaps more so with Sea-Green there. He pinned the other young man to the wall, holding back a lick at his jaw with a hand in dark waves and a look into the camera that told the cameraman to fuck off. Now. Or that's the look that had been caught in that moment. Whether Sea-Green voiced that threat or not wouldn't ever be known.

Two names came up next: Ash Thomas (known as Red); Chase Palmer. The images and names had been pulled from Shipman's phone, which would no doubt still be in police hands. But Andrews wasn't known as Konami for nothing. His way in and around technology and the dark web were... partly why Andrews was Gray's elite unit manager. But only partly. Andrews had other talents that belonged on the dark web, let alone hunting down the terrorists, murderers, and rapists that hid below the surface web.

Gray filed the information away for a moment as Ray drew his attention with a tap on the steering wheel that said he wasn't happy with the gate being open for so long. Again. It was why Gray hired him: he took no bullshit. "So nobody in without your consent even by security clearance," Gray said eventually. "You vet everyone, even if Jan gives the all clear. Jan leaves, surveillance stays with him." Jack hadn't been the only one raped and hurt back then.

Ray nodded. "Understood." He fumbled with a radio attached to his belt. "Comm through the usual if there's any glitches."

Gray nodded and pulled onto the main road. As he did, a call came on his hands-free.

"There's a safe house in Milton Keynes for car and clothes changeover." Andrews sent through an address and Gray set his satnav. "The big boss wasn't happy about the cancellation. I've let him know I'm on the Kenner file. His comment was the usual too many wannabee chiefs and not enough intel on the ground."

Gray snorted. It was the age-old argument within MI5 and MI6.

"Something else too. A new case."

"Hm?" said Gray.

"Analysis of data sets picked up a potential bomber, a potential PI(b), across three encrypted social apps and sites. Each communication only comes with a familiar stated pattern, a date, time, location, in this case a library in Croyden, and the numbers sixteen and twenty. The date's been set for two days from now over at the library. All signed by 'Igniferae.' The concern for me is that they're not going to great lengths to hide their internet footprint on details."

"And there's no mention of a known cell mentioned either?"

"No."

"So either it's an idle threat or someone wants this information found."

"Yes. I'm with our team over at Croyden today. If 'Igniferae' intends on planting something, my guess is that they'd get on scene before the note was sent, or it's a dud location. I'll know in a few hours if we need to upgrade them from a PI(b) threat to PI(a). We're already on the encrypted apps."

"Okay. Have Rachel draught a warrant for the home secretary and have her agreement and paperwork ready in case you need to move on the target's email and phone interception. If you upgrade from PI(b) to PI(a), let me know ASAP. Look into the Latin the target's given you too: *Igniferae*. The suffix in use can either be nominative or vocative case, but both with plural feminine declension. Fire carrying is the literal translation or bearing fire." Never a good sign, not for a potential bomber, Gray knew that.

"Could be gender related, then, with the feminine declension? Maybe the bomber is female?"

"Unknown at this point. If the location is a dud, then gender relations could be too. Depends on your target. Draft in whoever you need." Andrews had already unofficially taken this on, but if the home secretary needed to be contacted, then Andrews needed clearance to act.

"On it."

"What about the West Midlands killing, besides those images?"

"Oh…." Some taps at a keyboard came. "Johnathan Shipman, age twenty-four. A Jennings is heading the case, with a profiler from Scotland Yard."

It was a plus in Jennings's direction that he'd not waited and sat on his instinct, but it meant unfriendly surveillance would be tight in the area. "Who does know about the murder?"

"Close family: mother, father. No siblings. Both parents have watertight alibis."

Gray would check their home out anyway. "Who found the body?"

Quiet, then another click of a key on computer. "The other two men in those images: Ash Thomas and Chase Palmer. Close friends and co-workers. They've been told it was suicide due to… hm… concerns regarding their profiles from the police."

Gray headed onto the motorway and raised a brow as Andrews explained. "Okay. Comm blackout from here. Reach me through Rachel if needed."

"Likewise if you need anything."

He cut the call, knowing it was a good while to Milton Keynes, but even longer to the West Midlands. A behind-the-scenes look at people in Johnny's life it was. And there was nothing stranger than other peoples' lives, especially when they thought no one was watching.

And what better place to start than where the body had hit the floor, and just whose footprints had supposedly been found there, and why.

Ash Thomas… Chase Palmer.

CHAPTER 4
ASH THOMAS

RED.... WHERE YOU at?

Sat at the kitchen table, darkness kissing at his body, Ash Thomas swiped his thumb over Chase's text message for the third time as it etched its way across his iPhone.

C'mon. It came again. *It's Saturday night, for fuck's sake. Where are u?*

Yeah. Where the fuck *was* he? Dishes sat drip-drying on the sink, the radio played low off to his left, singing in his ear about having kids through one-night stands, and from next door, glass muffled how Dumb and Dumbette's Saturday night's rumble already saw their kids shoved outside into the cold to avoid the fight-night shrapnel. Slightly burnt bacon still stained the air in the kitchen, his dad's chair sat pushed away from the table, and the usual quiet sigh off the house now his dad had left for... whatever he and Miles got drunk over on a Saturday night, played right along with normality too.

He sat in the kitchen, sense told him that, all the white noise around him told him that, but... but.

Ash distractedly swiped a stray curl away from his eyes.

Three weeks. He'd been back at work three weeks now, and the funny looks and stares over Johnny's suicide hadn't eased.

None of them had been into hardcore kink, not the sort that left him hiding in the darkness; left a friend hanging by a noose with come over his stomach and cuts on his hip. Johnny was....

The last few hours of Johnny's life had defined him in the public eye, but it didn't show the kid who'd thrown stones at other kids as they'd ran Chase into the tunnels and tried to video him putting sparklers down his pants on Bonfire Night. Nor the young man who'd gotten further up the ladder than Ash or Chase at their factory, and who had clocked on for Ash when Ash had been running late. Johnny was smart, funny, always the one to buy the first round, mostly because he had more goddamn money now than they earned.

So those last few hours of his life? That wasn't Johnny. Not the Johnny Ash loved. Not the Johnny who had Chase keeping so quiet lately.

The phone trembled in his hand again, and Ash brushed his thumb over the message.

C'mon. Come play with me, Ash. Burn it out. See where I'm at?

A picture came through, telling tales on how Mack's pub looked busy, with a very good-looking barman serving the local-yokels: a barman who seemed vaguely familiar.

Red... Fuckin play with me.

The pull to respond, to find where life lingered (although Chase seemed too angry, too eager to play tonight) was so much stronger now. But... but.

Johnny would have come, Red. You know that. Don't fucking

ignore me anymore. I'm tired of ignoring you.

"Fuck." Ash rubbed at his head and closed his eyes to the near-blackness of the kitchen. *Low, Chase. Really fucking low.*

The ticking off a clock filled the kitchen.

Yeah. But he would have, Red, and you'd have followed. We both would have followed.

Ash looked around the kitchen, at the light filtering in from the hall.

C'mon, Ash. Do it. Do it do it.

Shit. He thumbed hard at the phone. *I need a drink now anyway, you cunt.*

Rubbing at his wrists and the fading echo of a burn, Ash eyed up the keyholder nailed to the sideboard, the keys, and how his dad hadn't taken his car tonight.

Just a ride to the pub, nothing more. No trouble. Fuck that he didn't have any insurance anymore, he'd be back before his dad got home, before his dad remembered he had a car, and Ash knew how to jack a car when no one was looking. Well, mostly.

He eased to his feet, but a long look went out the window to his dad's greenhouse and shed. Ash frowned, then looked away, his heart falling a little more with it. Nothing was different about either: the doors to the greenhouse were shut, the shed keeping just as mum regarding contact with the outside world but....

But.

Always a fucking but where Raif was concerned. Always replace what you use, or leave it looking untouched....

∾

Dressed in jeans and V-neck T-shirt, Ash headed over for his dad's Ford Fiesta, opening the door and getting in a lot quicker than intended. He wanted to look back over his shoulder, to the line of houses sat opposite and how black windows blinked a dark alien landscape. He couldn't get used to this, no matter how hard he tried. There must have been a dozen pairs of eyes staying at home to catch whatever passed as Saturday night fever nowadays: *Big Brother*, *X Factor*... so he couldn't pin down what felt wrong.

The swaying of the trees over the road maybe called it for him, how an echo of a body shifting in the breeze offered a sick piñata, and Ash shut the door and pulled off the drive, burying that unease over being watched. He hated how Johnny's death had made his normal landscape so alien.

He found his way to Mack's ten minutes later, and a shiver ran his spine to echoes of darker times, better times. He shook it off but let a smile creep in with it.

The pub never changed. Sat opposite a primary school, Mack's wasn't much: an old Victorian ale house with a small car park and a small grass verge for throwing up on, even offering a large oak tree to lean on as stomach contents were lost. Chase caught a quick cig outside, and Ash eased the Ford in next to him.

"Fuck." The cigarette in Chase's mouth slowly danced through his pause as he took his time coming over. Shirt... black trousers... hair swept away from his face to deliberately clothe sin in youth and a suit, he dressed to take someone down, but something in Chase's too-slow smile said he didn't want to be here either. Not yet. "You fuckin' suicidal with 'borrowing' another ride?" He winced at how that slipped out. "Sorry." Hands dug in his pockets, Chase shifted about in the cold to get some warmth through a thin jacket before Chase found it within himself to poke his head inside and wrinkle his nose. "Being a Rolls Royce, the last ride was more classy. More us, less… old fart in a bucket. I'll stick to my efforts with a car, thanks."

Ash pushed out, and Chase flicked his cigarette off as he stepped back. "Last car was our boss's, Jim's, and, yeah, a Rolls. One I had permission to move, you cunt."

"A few feet. He said you could move it a few feet, not come here for a pint." Chase winked at him. "And I doubt your dad knows about you fondling Old Busty up against the pub wall here too."

Ash gave a shrug. It had led to strange things back then with Raif that Chase knew nothing about. Maybe good things. Maybe bad. Jury was still out on that one. Front door still locked. "Just help me to turn the mileage clock back on this when I go home." He'd learned the hard way over not doing that with the Rolls, and besides, his old gaffer knew exactly what use he got out of a car when it came to petrol and mileage.

"Whatever, bud." An arm dropped roughly around Ash's neck and pulled him in. "C'mon, let's go find us again."

≈

The same creak always seemed to come from the old double doors, and Ash winced as they pushed through to Mack's. Smoke instantly choked the air out of his lungs, and he twisted away a little to escape the choking. Mack's didn't do background music either, and "Don't Let Me Down" blared in the foreground. The only reason they came here was because this was one of only a few places that still allowed smoking in a booth over in the corner. It also meant it was busier than most, making it a fight to get to the bar. Twice he bumped into people huddled in the crowd, and twice he grumbled *fuck you*. He got a grunt off the first, a woman, looking like she shaved more often than he did with the amount of chin hair sprouting free. Yet the second person he bumped into, knocking his drink—

Fuck. Ash stilled.

He couldn't offer anything, not with who stood in front of him, not with whose drink he'd just spilled. Greying hair gave that distinctive touching-fifty feel, and yeah, the man could easily toss a rugby player or two. Jeans pulled tight over thick thighs, showing everything the man had in the crotch area, then a thick waist led up to a chest Ash would need rope, grapple hooks, and a strong will to scale, because, fuck—this man was more than built to push trucks. A butterfly was again sewn itself into the pocket of a shirt that was worn to deliberately show the heavy move and shift of muscle underneath, and with it, the need to turn away came quickly, instinctively, purely because he looked so… out of place in the public and daylight.

A smile came, something that said "Like this, is it, boy?", but the aftereffects of a stroke pulled at one side, turning the smile into a sneer. But it was there. Ash felt the hard tug at how he knew it was a smile. Eyebrows didn't arc gracefully, but went for a rigid vertical drop, shaping a flat nose that had been broken many times over the years. The man was far from pretty, in fact downright *Five Nights at Freddy's* scary came to mind at the moment, along with all the natural jump-scares and FNaF music. Lips had the same rigid drop, giving no soft contours to an alien landscape and… and….

Ash felt grief hit hard and went to say something, but a shove from Chase sent Ash towards the bar, almost as if Chase thought he needed help getting away from Jupiter's gravitational pull. Chase pulled him into the bar, but Ash didn't feel better in the flow of moving bodies.

"What the fuck was that?" Chase offered a chuckle as Ash slumped on the barstool and tried to bury a smile at Chase's nudge into his side. "If I knew you were still into scary-fucker sex, our lad, I'd have set you up with Mad Malcolm in storage. Nobody goes down there."

"What?" Ash looked at him. "He's your pet. I specifically remember this conversation at the factory, how you use him to scare Jim out of there."

Chase shrugged, barely hid a smile. "Like I said, if I'd known you were still into scary-fucker sex. You've been off it long before Johnny's.... Joh...." He couldn't finish that, and Ash knew why.

Ash managed to catch the barman's eye. "Pint and an orange juice, please." His conscience was bad enough. He wasn't drinking tonight, but knew Chase would, despite driving, and it was Ash's round. The barman pushed his orange juice over, his fingers straying a little too long against Ash's. He ignored the fuck because he couldn't for the life of him shake free how he knew him and sat looking down at his drink instead. The prick needed to get the hint quickly that tonight wasn't about fucking about.

Chase fell quiet too.

"Old friends." Chase held his pint up, then just as quickly downed half of it.

Not lifting his head, Ash barely tipped his glass. "Old friend," he mumbled under his breath. Johnny sat between them; he always would, and... fuck.

Now he recognised the barman. Fucking Peepshow. A few months back, Chase had pulled Ash over to the wall, and Peepshow had been there then, taking a photo and catching a fuck about that had meant to play with someone else in the pub: Sandy. It hadn't been for Peepshow. Sandy had sat close by them, and his look always cried out for a domming in all his old and lonely ways, so they'd pissed about with what he'd never be able to have, forcing Sandy to grip just a little tighter on his beer and look away as Ash jokingly played Chase against the wall: as a Dom paraded his bratty sub. That hadn't been the only lousy trick they'd pulled that night. A young lad called Freddie from their factory had played grass and gotten Ash, Chase, and Johnny separated for the weekend…. So Ash had made sure Freddie's boyfriend had cried out extra loud outside the pub as Ash fucked him. Chase had been the one to make sure Freddie had needed to be outside at that exact moment too, all more than innocent, like. None were their finest moments, but pissing around with BDSM? Ash briefly closed his eyes and set his jaw tensing. They'd destroyed a few people's lives that night. And Peepshow had decided to catch it all on his camera as Ash pinned Chase up against the wall. That… that had pissed Ash off more: wrong time, wrong two friends to try and catch in the act.

Okay, Ash had pissed Raif off that night too, someone who had later taught Ash a lesson he'd never forget, but Johnny had been the one to deal with Peepshow that night, coming in and telling the barman to back off because of the photo Peepshow had just taken.

The photo had also caught Johnny isolated in the background, and Johnny… he'd always been left behind in the shadows, still fighting in their corner, but still always left in the shadows because of how he thought he had no right to a lover's hold when he carried all that weight. Ash had hated that photo.

It was almost as if Johnny only really saw the beauty in his soul after he lost his weight; that he only had a right to look for love after he lost his weight. And Peepshow had ignored the fuck out of Johnny that night too, until Johnny had really grabbed the guy by the balls for getting close and making Chase hide in Ash's neck.

Had they done the same as Peepshow? Kept Johnny locked in the background? They'd only ever played with Johnny in the shadows, watching. Had they forced him there? Kept him there in that role and condemned him to being nothing but a ghost to the cold machines. And he broke?

"Stop it, Red."

Ash glanced at Chase.

"You didn't put Johnny there." The bitter chill from a dead friend seeped into Chase's tone. "I didn't put Johnny there. He did that himself."

Ash looked away, back to the corner where Johnny had sat when that picture had been taken.

"Fuck." Chase downed the rest of his pint and waved Peepshow over again. "I don't want this shit tonight. Three weeks…. Three fucking weeks. We should all be backpacking around Europe now." He let his fingers linger on the barman's a little longer than was comfortable, and Ash scowled.

Yeah. The trip across Europe would have been their first time away from the cheap UK holidays that Chase's and Johnny's parents had taken as they'd all grown up, money always too tight. Ash had been lucky there. With the backpacking trip, everything had been paid for, but it hadn't felt right. After Johnny's suicide, Chase looked sick every time he'd mentioned backpacking, to the point their drifting apart couldn't be stopped, so Ash had been the one to call a stop without asking. It hadn't felt right to leave Johnny behind for a second time. It didn't fucking feel right to see Chase play Peepshow now, either, because Ash knew Chase's look: he was about to take someone down and leave them bloody in the aftermath.

A very deliberate, yet sweet blush danced on Chase's cheeks. Game play tuned and set fully to play as it had been when Peepshow had stolen that photo.

A free beer came Chase's way, an orange juice too, and Ash felt a tug on his arm as hollowness hit his stomach.

"Pool time." But something darker played in Chase's eyes. He pulled Ash off his stool, sliding up close in the same moment, beer held out to the side. Then a kiss brushed Ash's jaw, a bite at his neck, and heat bruised his lips in the next, nearly pushing him back over the stool.

What the fuck? Ash gripped under Chase's jaw, making him back off, but Chase let his free arm drop onto Ash's shoulder as he ran with the grip on his jaw. Pissing on BDSM again: the supposed disciplined sub told to cool off and not touch, but a smile and gaze on Peepshow that said this was all for him now, no camera needed to catch the moment. He could have the real thing.

Bastard. Ash stared long and hard at Peepshow, then pushed Chase off him before turning away. He couldn't stomach playing tonight.

Chase had long since grown up. Long gone was the skinny kid with glasses who spent most of his time trying to keep his trousers from slipping off his ass. Now trousers were left to deliberately slip over his ass and offer a view of his most-wanted possession. That and those soft hazel eyes that caught more light now he wore contact lenses. Ash didn't know exactly when the change came for most others; he'd always liked Chase. Then when he'd caught on and realised people had started to look at Chase a little possessively, Ash had played it, used it a little to get them to the front of the beer queue. Chase played it just as much too with him and those who came on to Ash. The untouchable was always more of a draw, so they'd play their tag-team games sometimes just to see who they could leave out in the cold first. But tonight, of all nights? With that fucker? Ash put his money down on the pool table, then bit down sickness.

He flicked a look at Chase. "What the fuck's wrong with you?"

Chase put his beer next to Ash's on a table, holding up a card. Ash snorted. He'd won the barman's number. Already?

"You don't recognise his name."

Ash took the card. "Should I?"

"It's why Johnny rough-handled him so much a few months back when he took that picture." Chase took the card back and pulled out his phone. "I fucking loved the pic. Damn glad Johnny made the barman send it to our phones before deleting."

"And?"

The look that came up was so dangerous. "You didn't see it with Johnny back then, did you? That's Bitch Face's boyfriend."

So that's why Chase had chosen here specifically. Bitch Face Kate, who, on a good day, only spat bubble gum in Johnny's hair so he'd have to cut off chunks to get it out.

Bitch Face "gonna go clubbing the seal" Kate. Everybody always had someone who made their life a misery. Bitch Face had been Johnny's. "Leave it. The fucker's not worth it."

Chase grinned, that spark back now but for all the wrong reasons. "Oh, he is." Chase handed Ash his phone, his thumb brushing between Send and Camera. "Bitch Face has just had a kid. Let's see how she likes life in the cold, alone and left holding the pup after dad plays away."

Something slipped in Ash, and he moved in close, a hand on Chase's hip. He thought Chase would pull away like he'd shut himself down emotionally from Ash over the past few weeks, but he didn't, instead resting his head briefly against Ash's.

"Not tonight?" Ash closed his eyes. "We've had enough shit with Johnny's head games. It's not worth taking someone else down."

Chase sought his hand, or more the phone he held, and a button was pressed: Send. Place and time had been given for some fun with Peepshow.

"Johnny's worth it." Chase shoved away. He was trying to compensate too, to sort through every wrong done to Johnny, all to understand just why Johnny had left the way he did. Had Kate twisted her way back into Johnny's head? Got her boyfriend to do something? Those questions flat-lined Chase's eyes. Maybe even a thousand or so more unanswered questions tumbled around in there too.

Ash stared down at the phone. He could stop all the trouble in the making, let Peepshow know Chase could play dangerously and the barman would be the one to end up hurting.

Only he didn't. Part of him never would. Not when it

came to Johnny; not when it came to Chase hurting. Not when it came to driving through his own hurt and grief. Ash didn't like this part of them both, didn't understand where it came from or when, but at times, some dark and twisted times, it felt so damn good to see other people hurt instead of them. And he'd had three weeks of the worst kind of hurt.

At the bar and that brush of the barman's fingers against Chase's....

Yeah. Peepshow just about pissed him off on so many fucked-up levels now.

CHAPTER 5
SCORPION RING

A LIGHT RAIN started to fall as Ash rested against a wall, away from the pub's arched doorway but close enough to the huge tree to still be mostly hidden from view. Chase knew where he'd be.

Almost on cue, Chase came out, pulling Peepshow in close now it was his break time, and already seeking out Peepshow's warm mouth as he took him over to the tree.

Chase never let his gaze fall from Ash's as he pushed Peepshow up against the rough bark. The drinkers inside were lost to the music—the need for booze—but the dark kept any passing cars blind to what Chase started.

Peepshow had the wind knocked free from him, eyes startling a little as Chase shifted in for a rough kiss. Then that startled flare turned heated as Chase tugged the barman's belt free, going for the zip, and exposing his cockhead to the cool of the night. Peepshow bucked and hissed as strokes ran the length; then he fought to get Chase free of his jeans too. Kisses heated in the chilled air, exposed cocks in a bump and grind that left Ash breathing hard and denying the need that hit his own body and mind.

But… up against a tree…? Christ.

Chase forced Peepshow around, face-first against the bark, and taking the man's hands high above his head, he pinned them there with one hand. Then he pulled a condom from his pocket, tore at it with his teeth, covered his cock, and made damn sure Peepshow cried fuck yes as he pushed in deep, forcing the barman up to his toes.

Chase's fuck into him came hard, brutal, but he dropped his head briefly onto Peepshow's shoulder, rough-biting at the man's neck. Dampness glistened on Chase's cheeks, yet still Peepshow stood there and fucking took it: cried *fuck yes* to each hard fuck into him, loving Chase's roughness.

He didn't see Chase. How Chase tried to fuck through his own hurt. Peepshow hadn't seen either of them a few months back when he'd taken that photo, only wanted to steal an intimate piece of them as a keepsake. And he damn well hadn't seen Johnny at all, that hurt over being stuck in the background, forever now a watcher over how two friends touched, but never allowed to feel it for himself.

Taking out Chase's phone, Ash went close—over Chase's shoulder close—and with the glow from the pub windows lighting the way just a touch, he pressed Record. Fuck pictures. Bitch Face would get Peepshow's whole damn porn fuck.

He kept Chase out of the picture, but Ash made sure the cock fucking deep into Peepshow's ass shone through, and all his cries; then when Chase grabbed Peepshow's hair and pulled his head back to expose just who was making all the cries, Ash caught that too. Peepshow was too caught in coming to care. He'd gone past worrying about being caught in that one moment.

And as Peepshow came, Ash leaned in, tugged Chase's head back, and kissed him roughly, his tonguing deep as he stroked at a sweat-damp hip. Chase sought that moment of... forgetting too, and Ash made damn sure he found it in a friendly touch.

Grief shook Chase's body more, that glistening on his cheek dampening Ash's and salting his kiss. All too quiet for Peepshow to feel it as anything other than a man in mid-orgasm, but not too quiet between friends; between ex-lovers who knew each other like no other in this heat.

Just... Christ. Ash bit down his sickness and pulled his kiss away as the wind caught the leaves of the tree, rousing the porn show watchers. Christ, Chase. A tree...? Why the fuck up against a tree?

Chase's breathing started to ease down along with Peepshow's, and head resting down on his shoulder, Chase tossed the condom away and tidied himself up. Peepshow did too, and as he started to glance back, looking a little startled, Ash put the phone away.

"Fuck." Peepshow's eyes settled to smutty. "Well hello there, Red. Not so fucked off now and unwilling to share this time, are we?" Breathing came heavy. "Give me a minute, you can suck me off, if you want."

Ash snorted, turning away and flicking a look at Chase.

Chase stopped him with an *easy, pal, easy* touch to his hip, but Ash had had enough. "I'm out." Ash pulled away. "You're finished here, right?" That meant he better be finished.

Peepshow turned around and tugged Chase in close. "Nah, he's not finished." A kiss. "Chase by name and fucked-up by nature, aren't ya, bud?"

Chase's gaze didn't leave Ash's, even as Peepshow got a

return adulterated kiss. The smile there was too hard. "No. Not finished yet. Want to really fuck the point home."

Ash glanced briefly at Peepshow, then nodded at Chase. "I'll upload your homework later for you, mate."

A breeze caught branches, causing a rustle, a ruffle of applause for the show, and Chase didn't manage to say whatever he meant to then.

Back in the woods, the den they'd built as kids had still leaked, wetting Johnny's clothes and shorting out his mobile phone eventually. They hadn't really noticed how the moon disappeared and a light rain began to fall. A deep, weighted swing and pull of rope on branch saw the twisted piñata figure sway lightly against the breeze, and Johnny...

Johnny.

Ash stilled too.

Johnny had been brought up a latchkey kid: always caught out in the cold. He died in the cold that night.

Ash still heard it when he lay still, trying to sleep: Chase's cry. He'd cut the rope, tearing off his own jacket to cover how bare-chested Johnny had been, a nightmarish reversal of how Johnny had always handed his clothes down to Chase to keep Chase warm, and... and—

"Hey." Ash shook it off. "With me, Chase." The walk back there needed to stop before they became locked in swinging from trees too, their memories the rope and noose.

A shiver raced through Chase, face too pale to be healthy by any standard, then he eased away from Peepshow, took Peepshow's hand, and brought him over. "Thanks for being here tonight, Red. You gonna be all right? I'm gonna head off home."

Ash mumbled a *yeah* as he searched for his keys. He

found Chase's phone first and offered it over.

Chase stared down at it as Peepshow fastened his jacket, mumbling something about the chill and getting home too after his shift.

Home. Life. Wife... baby. It all played in Chase's look, and his fight filtered to nothing. "Your call," he said gently. "Maybe Johnny's more."

Yeah. Where Johnny had rough-handled Peepshow a while back for fucking with them, Johnny wouldn't think twice about calling him and Chase cunts for doing this shit. He'd have made sure content was deleted before it caused too much hurt. What happened here belonged to Johnny. Ash frowned. He'd delete when he got home.

Ash grabbed Chase gently by the neck, this time the touch not so rough as he pulled him in for a long kiss. Fuck. He tasted good. Chase made it last longer, yet they pulled away at the same time when Peepshow came in to touch. "Give you your phone back tomorrow, yeah?" It's why Chase had given him his phone: Ash had been delegated to film maker tonight.

"Don't lose it, 'kay." Chase held up Ash's car keys now he'd pinched them. "I'll nick your car for it. I know where you live, bud."

"Fucker." Ash took them back, pressing the key fob, but when no sound came from his dad's Ford, Ash frowned and glanced around.

"Red, you all right, bud?"

Fuck. The strangest wave of déjà vu washed over him, of the last lesson he'd been taught that had started here, over playing about, and—

A hand rubbed at his shoulder. "Red?"

Ash stared blankly at Chase. "My... not my dad's car

now."

Chase glanced around the car park. "Again?" He wiped a hand over his mouth. "Dude, you… someone's really got it in for you. I'll… you…. Don't piss about this time. You need to call the cops. You need—"

Sickness hit heavy, enough for Ash to stumble over to the wall and throw up. He'd not touched any beer, but the world and all its fucked-up life spun as though he had. Some memories were just too painful, how the last time this happened, Johnny had been alive, Johnny….

"Fuck." Someone stroked at his back, then tried to shift his hair out of the way. "What the hell, bud? You all right?"

"Fine. Shut the fuck up, okay? It's fine. Just caught me out."

"Ash, you didn't fucking tell me what happened last time with Jim's car, when that was stolen from here. Dude, you gotta call the cops. This is twice now."

Ash shook him off. "Shut the fuck up. No cops." He knew what this was. Christ, he knew *who* this was and who had the car now, and he couldn't involve the cops.

"Ash—"

"Fucking leave it alone. It's okay."

"Fine." Chase pushed him off. "Fuck off alone, then. Sadistic Red, always up for playing the game but so fucking secretive lately. Yet still always the coward when it comes to getting the fuck away from what's just made you throw up. I mean, how fucking relieved were you when Johnny died so you didn't have to take that trip?"

The fuck? Ash shoved Chase back. "Like you've moved on, Chase?" Anger snapped, and all that was left for them was to turn on each other now there was nothing else in between. Was that why they'd stayed away from each other for a while? "The only reason you're here now is because you can't leave Johnny out in the cold alone. I know where you've been going most nights after work, drinking by his graveside. We've all got our ghosts that we can't leave behind no matter how much we want to, so fuck the coward in you too, you cunt."

Chase went to fight back, to speak, but then dug his hands in his pockets and glanced away. He looked back a moment later, but like wind failing leaf, all fight faded. "Yeah, I know we've all got our ghosts. But, Ash, I look at you sometimes and...." He seemed so sad as he came closer. "I swear I see Johnny in your eyes, only you don't know why. I can't lose you to a noose and tree too."

"Chase—"

"No." Chase took a step back and ran a hand over his mouth, shaking his head. "Ah. That fucking trip." He found Ash again. "It was meant to make us all. Get us the fuck away from all this shit."

An accidental tear slipped free from Chase, and Ash stepped in close, head resting against head. "It's okay, bud. I swear. I'll handle this, but I need to do it my way." He'd pissed off someone else tonight, someone he hadn't meant to, and that scared him more.

"Yeah, like I've ever left you alone to face the shit... imagined or not." Ash got a kiss to his head, a cup of hands to his jaw, but then a brush of thumb against the faded burn to his wrist came. "So you'll do what?"

Ash tried a smile. "Go home and hope it turns up."

Chase pulled back slightly. Peepshow had disappeared as soon as the trouble kicked off. "Ash, you believe in getting through the work week to fuck about. Goblins leaving you gifts in the night...? Nah."

Ash snorted a laugh. "I heard night and something about being gobbled—"

"Goblins."

"But," added Ash, although he lost his humour and the sting came with how easily it was to fall back into the black, "I've got a little faith in humanity lately."

Chase checked around his eyes, literally pulled at the lids and got in close enough to climb in and check his pupils. "You're stoned, mate. Seriously stoned. Or something's got you sniffing your dad's meds lately." Then he sighed. "Okay. Come on, Cinders, let's get you home again before someone nabs your glass slippers to match the dress they took last time." He lost his smile, then nudged Ash's shoulder. "You're fucked now, bud. You know that, right? That's your old man's car."

Yeah, he knew that. More than. But some control was still better than none. Some faith in humanity was still better than none at all, right?

~

Chase set his window down as Ash got out and went around to say goodnight. "You sure you're gonna be all right, bud?"

Ash stayed longer on the house across the street as he stopped by the driver's side. "Yeah," he said eventually, then shook off the chill. He smiled down at Chase. "Glad you called tonight, bud."

Chase shifted into reverse, the white lights lighting up the path back down to the road. "Fucking liar. But I'm glad you got your head out of your ass long enough to reply. And, listen, what I said earlier—"

"Don't sweat it." He dug his hands in his jeans pockets. "You're a cunt, but I love ya."

"Right back at ya, fucker." Chase looked him up and down, staying long enough on Ash's cock that Ash almost felt like going cockblock with his hands. "Need something to help there, Red?"

"Coffee, mostly." Ash thumbed back to his house. "Fancy skipping getting laid and going for morning after, where you go domestic goddess and do me one?"

"Yeah, right. Fuck that." Then Chase went *Grand Theft Auto* and high-tailed it off the drive and down the street, leaving Ash rubbing his arms against the cold and heading back in.

As he slipped his keys onto the kitchen table, he glanced at the clock. Half eleven. His dad wouldn't be back yet; the night-blackness of the kitchen told him that, as did the lonely tick of the clock. That meant he had a few hours to try and sort this shit out.

Strange thing being, he knew shit would find him out probably a lot sooner. He closed his eyes, letting a sad smile creep in with how thoughts on that kissed and teased over his body.

When had life gotten so... dark...? So goddamn... strange?

A last look at the door, leaving the kitchen in darkness, Ash headed on upstairs, trying to bury the taste of sickness and nerves. The car would find its way home. He knew that.

CHAPTER 6
NIGHT WRAITH

ASH RUBBED AT his head, padding into his bathroom and tugging the toothpaste and brush from the holder to help wash away the bitter taste of vomit. Tiredness pulled hard, the need to sleep but knowing he'd spend hours chasing it already kicking in. He'd gotten too used to night, to not sleeping, or at least he thought he had. He stripped down to his jeans as the water ran in the sink, then he washed up.

He stifled a yawn as he flossed.

Yeah, sleep. Fuck another stolen car, he needed to get his head down, if only that meant his head hitting the pillow as he watched shadows dance across the walls for a few hours.

Endeavour played in silence from his TV as he found his way to the bed. Habits. That was his: re-watching a familiar TV series so he didn't have to focus too hard on new content. It used to get him to sleep in the past, but now?

He fought another yawn as he pulled the quilt back.

"Shit."

Something fluttered up into his face and he ducked. Blue

wings brushed his shoulder, then seemed to shift and try to fly the fuck away from him as quickly as he tried to dodge.

"Christ." His heart settled seeing the stress. The butterfly fluttered away in blind panic, constantly hitting the mirror, or more the reflection of the light.

"Okay, okay... easy, mate." Ash grabbed a glass from the en suite and gave the butterfly a room with a panoramic view, his hand as the carpet. Slight flutter of blue wing against glass came, and Ash held the glass carefully as he made his way over to the open window.

"Stay away from my old gaffer's plants down there, okay? Don't break into the greenhouse. You won't like who you find in there." He held the glass out and gave it a light shake. It took the butterfly a moment, but it escaped happily enough. "And get your own fucking room next time."

Ash checked under the covers to make sure there wasn't a butterfly rave going on under them, then climbed in, throwing an arm over his eyes. The rumble of his phone fucked any chance of that.

Giving a sigh, now watching the chase of wind over blind, he cradled his landline phone between shoulder and ear.

"Hey, Red."

Chase. "Didn't we say fuck off twenty minutes ago?"

"You've still got my phone." Tired... Chase sounded as though he fought sleep too.

"You told me to keep it, remember?"

A soft chuckle drifted on through that sounded as playful as the wind outside, taking Ash back to old times, better places. "Just wanted to see if we were still good."

"Fucking liar. Try again."

"Fuck, okay. Just making sure my phone got back safely and stays safe. I forgot how you tend to kill phones in temper."

Ash winced. He did? Yeah, he did, although in the heat of the moment, that never registered. "Bullshit, try again." But he could see that probably was the main reason.

"Ohhhhkay, just wanted to know if you're tossing off and filming yourself on said phone you're keeping safe for me."

Ash laughed but didn't fight a yawn this time. "Glad to know you called it a night and went home, bud."

A long sleepy sigh came through. "Big bed... I like my space. I've gotten lousy with sharing lately."

Yeah, Chase liked to stretch out, share. Or he'd liked to share for a while; they both had.

"You know, considering your dad's car's been stolen, you're... sounding nothing but sleepy, Red." A pause. Chase seemed to take a drink of something. "You still a little high from filming earlier? How about I talk you through getting off, release some more of that tension?"

Ash relaxed, his arm coming off his eyes. It was an offer of play between them. For them in the aftermath of games. The winner was always there to give release to the friend who came in second.

Ash let a hand trace down over his stomach, body stretching into the covers. "I like playing alone, no cameras."

"Yeah. Me too." Chase's breathing was deeper, more distracted. He was still in playing mode and the breathing cried out where it was taking him again. But then they'd grown up playing like this. "You miss us, Red?"

"Sometimes." There was no lie there to the sleepy reply. But the burn in his body, Chase didn't own that, and Ash wouldn't ever hurt Chase by telling him.

Heavier breathing. "Only sometimes?" Sadness tinged the reply, but Ash let a smile creep up as he flicked the clasp to his jeans.

"Nice try, Chase. You're not thinking about me. Who are you thought-fucking?"

Quiet, the play of shadow on the walls, then a distracted chuckle came. "So little trust, Ashy...." A deeper sigh came, likely a slow play of hand down cock, then that sadness crept back in. "I missed my chance, Red...." He gave a groan. "But, Christ, I can still fuck about with him here... thought isn't a crime?"

"You finished with the guy you were seeing too?" Ash frowned. Johnny's death had hit them both so hard, but he wished he hadn't been so lost in his own grief to see Chase fall further into loneliness. Ash had kept away because he thought Chase had something—someone—good in his life to hold on to. "Christ... so sorry, bud."

"Not your fault, Red...."

Ash stretched into his own touch as he slipped into his boxers, his own shift to play with echoes, with who haunted his head.

A chuckle came. "Fuck, you sound up for it now, Red." A pause. "Who's got you touching yourself so quickly lately, hm?"

Ash stalled, his touch paused between his thighs.

Chase's breath hitched, then—"Shit." He sounded good mid-orgasm. He always had. A moment later there was a grunt, then another "fuck" as he came down, more exhausted.

"Christ, Red." A smile came through in his voice. "Wish Peepshow was here to lick this off."

Ash managed a smile despite life cooling for him. "Tosser. There's wipes in your drawer for that."

"Oh yeah." Chase made no move away from the phone to get anything. "Y'sure you don't need a hand over there?"

"Your hand's over there, playing with you. Clean it,

Chase."

Wipes were pulled from a box by the side of Chase's bed. "We still gonna be sad enough to be doing this when we're fifty?"

Ash shrugged as he watched the shadows. Sex over the phone had started as a joke, but then most things did when you're a kid. They hadn't had the courage to face each other and test their bodies out back then, so calls on mobiles that ran up their pocket money had come in.

Ash wiped tiredly at his eyes again. "Maybe it's all we have left, mate. All we deserve."

The line fell quiet, then a hard sniff came through. "You know I love you, bud?"

"Yeah, love you too, mate."

"Bullshit. If you loved me, you wouldn't be there."

Ash let out a smile. "Likewise, you prick. Now fuck off for good and let me sleep."

A laugh. "You're buying breakfast on Monday, by the way."

"Oh, you're back to sitting with me, huh? So hell yes." Ash snorted a chuckle. "I know where your hand's been."

"Okay, okay, fuck off then, and stop calling me, stalker. No matter how much you beg and plead, you just can't have me. I keep telling you that."

"Twat." Ash let the handle rest back in the cradle and threw his arm back over his eyes. The other found a natural home resting on the flat of his lower abs, just under his boxers.

Heat simmered, keeping his cock half full and caught in the same sleep-can't sleep limbo Ash lay in. Pubic hair tickled his fingers, the roll of his cock not far from that and drugged enough to mistake the kiss of wind from the window as though it were a lover's.

But sleep… neither of them were going to find any

sleep. Not tonight.

A sweep of light cut under the rim of his arm, like the sweep of lighthouse light over a cliff face left chuckling at how it had blinded the falling man to the cliff's edge, and Ash stilled.

Breath held, he waited.

It came. Three hard revs on an engine. Long… slow… each ending with a flash of a yellow indicator.

This wasn't any pass-over from a dream this time. It wasn't any mistake how a second "borrowed" car now found its way home in the dark. And he knew the sound of his father's car, down to each gentle grind of tyre on gravel to escape garage visits.

Another rev of engine came, and Ash eased slowly off the bed.

Not bothering with slipping on a T-shirt, he made it out into the hall—the landing light always kept on—and cast a glance at his dad's door as he passed. No movement came from inside, but then he didn't really expect there to be, not with how his old gaffer stayed out with Miles until the early hours. Bare feet light on the stairs, he made it down into the kitchen.

Go back a few months, the darkened mass blocking out the natural moonlight through the door would have startled him, probably sent him running over to Chase to regroup and laugh the fear away at more scary-fucker sex, but now?

But now?

There'd always been a "but now" where this night walker was concerned.

Ash padded over and stood breath to breath with the man who had a butterfly sewn into the top pocket of his shirt, that sadness in dark eyes.

"You left the door unlocked, flittermouse." Raif watched him in the darkness.

Raif.

Ash's ghost in the machine, one who drifted in and out of his life. He'd thought Raif had almost faded for good until he'd seen him tonight at Mack's. Something was always pulling the mass of body away and seeing Ash lose him for weeks on end. He got Raif back at the weekends, and that security was always there as Ash's locked door saw Raif make a home out of their garden shed and greenhouse. Ash had pushed him away when Johnny died, but he hadn't been able to push him away enough to not see that food found its way into the shed for him on weekends. A hot drink… a bottle of whiskey… a duvet. All were replaced when Monday came, Raif seeming to know exactly when Ash's dad would use the greenhouse. What sane person kept to a shed during the night to watch over someone? Ash didn't care for the whys. That feel of safety when Raif was here had kept the pitch blackness to layers of grey that thinned as the weeks went by.

Ash looked behind Raif to the door now, how it stood unlocked. He'd unlocked it? Yeah. Guess he had.

Raif's look seemed to ask a thousand questions, each one chewed over so slowly, testing the whys… the whens. Fuck. Ash had missed that. So fucking much. Each detail slowed, processed, turned over so slowly in dark brown eyes where worlds and galaxies moved and turned faster. But by the time you tried to give him an answer, he'd already anticipated your thoughts, your actions. And like fuck had Raif turned and drawn out the details over that night when Peepshow took that photo, the details over Sandy, the one who had just been missing a Dom's touch, then Freddie. And all for Ash to only cry crocodile tears over a picture being taken, catching him in the act of hurting someone else, not giving a fuck….

Raif had taught Ash a lot about himself that night,

mostly how he just… lingered even when given the opportunity to run and shout for help. He hadn't and that seemed to have confused Raif in turn, kept him coming back… here, but it also saw Raif leave without any reason for weeks on end. Then Ash had lost Johnny and locked the door on him too, not wanting any ties back to normality, even the strangest one that saw him sleep with a man who only turned up in the early hours of the morning.

"Flittermouse still, huh? You know I'm no bat." The nickname still stood, and Ash snorted a smile.

But Raif looked around the kitchen, the darkness. "You lost your echo and the ability to move around as one in the night, though, mouse." Raif rested back on him. "You shut me out for weeks. Why did you leave the door unlocked tonight, Ash?"

Ash tilted his head slightly. "Why did you push it open to find out?"

Raif let out a hard breath, his hand coming up and brushing Ash's cheek. He wore no gloves and the roughness to the fingertips still startled. Scars touched each one, distorting tissues, breaking down any marks and the need for leather gloves that would hide his fingerprints. Ash had seen it in an old gangster film, how thugs tipped acid on fingers to remove traces of identity. This was more focused, more professional as it only took the pads. Raif lived up to his status: Wraith, the ghost shifting from home to home as the owners took a holiday, and only existing when he was here, flesh and blood. But ask why he walked and lived by the streets at night…?

Raif sighed. "Jury's still out on that one. But if you're this intense over giving me your trust, fool that I am, maybe it's because I still want to know what it would be like to see you fall in love."

The sadness there had Ash tracking each serious line to

Raif's face, then not happy, he reached up and followed the rough ridges from temple down to jaw, and yeah, it was still there. His body liked it… being here, with Raif. It just always took longer for his head to catch up.

"Because I'm a cunt, right? One, who among other things, only pisses on your BDSM lifestyle to get his kicks?" he said gently, letting his hands fall to his side.

Raif reached up and caught a strand of auburn hair between thumb and finger, but his look was on Ash's eyes. It was still damn disturbing how many people rested back on his eyes, not saying anything for a moment, like they held him intimately against his will in those few seconds, then saw something else just beneath the skin and quickly turned away. It's why Ash hated photos, especially ones that caught and held that look when he hadn't given his permission. But with Raif…?

"Never seen eyes like yours, mouse." It came so quietly, and the touch shifted from his hair to brush his cheekbone. "They don't look as though they play to hurt." A soft smile came now. "Just… just traffic-light green, left to burn through the night… but only bringing that deep sigh that comes with seeing the signals change from red, to amber, to… to being so fucking alive and given permission to move safely from home to home…." He frowned, his head now tilting slightly. "I'm not good with words. I don't know how to express what my head's going through other than… other than to say I'd always be here, testing the lock on that door to see if… when you'd be okay to let me back in, despite you being a bastard."

Christ. How Raif had proven he could break into any home, Ash's boss's for one. The fact he respected Ash's simple wooden door, how the bolt stayed locked, Ash felt it now, that harder beat of heart that said maybe, just maybe, this wasn't a game to be played. Not with Raif. Not from

Raif. Not with how Raif had watched over him the past few weeks from the garden shed, despite being locked out. But games were all Ash knew, all he trusted. And Raif still played his own. He still disappeared back into the night during the work week. But he was here, with Ash. Now.

"You stole a car I'd hijacked because I was being a bastard. Again." Ash said that so quietly.

"I was hoping to hijack you for being a bastard. Again," Raif answered, just as quietly.

Ash gripped the back of Raif's hair, forcing his gaze up, then ran a long lick from collarbone to jaw before he knew what he was doing. "Top. I like to do the hijacking." Ash eased his hold, now closing his eyes and gently running his nose along Raif's throat. "We still good with that?"

A touch dusted Ash's hips, not moving any farther than that, and it's what had Ash coming in closer.

"Still fighting that natural Dom side, mouse?" A kiss brushed his cheek. "Still think you only piss on the BDSM lifestyle, that it means nothing?"

"Want to ask me how you asked last time? You had me bound then."

"The bastard in you didn't like it."

"The night got more intense when you untied me."

Raif seemed to fight a smile. "Stranger... you made my life a little... stranger."

Ash lost all his confidence then. "You kept coming back. Why the fuck do you keep coming back?"

No answer came, so Ash eased his arms around Raif's neck, all that strength, all that hardness and hard climb of body. He let a touch brush under Raif's eye, held that deep-space look, then frowned into it.

Life was fucked up, locked deep in the Twilight Zone, where fuck-and-tell BDSM games were daytime normality, and the promise of a loving D/s hold belonged only to the darkness of a dreamer's landscape.

"I'm sorry," Raif said gently, pulling him in. "I'm so sorry about Johnny, Ash. I know how much you and Chase loved him."

This wasn't just him, right? Ash wasn't the only one holding on to past echoes, how they kept slip sliding into the night and making him want to stop, stand still, just cry into the night and hold on to the ghosts? Because he felt it now, all that grief, that loss. How Raif wrapped an arm around him and offered to soak it up, how he disappeared into it, all games forgotten. How Raif kept coming back even if he didn't know why himself....

And if Ash did run into this darkness, giving in wouldn't hurt, just this once? Right? He wasn't twisted for wanting to taste what this night visitor wanted? He wasn't a coward for breaking now and needing to hold on to Raif, all doors open...?

CHAPTER 7
DON'T... TASTE THE ECHOES

EAR TURNED SLIGHTLY towards the bedroom door, Jan Richards listened, not having moved for a while now. In the darkness of the bedroom, he sat in bed, numb to the Saturday night chill. Loose sheets pooled around his hips, leaving the sweat to mould the covers to his body from his ass down. But he didn't notice.

No bumps came in the dead hours, no shouts or muffled anger from down the corridor to the seclusion room. But then over the past few days, everything had been shifted to the ground floor, Craig and everyone else tucked away in downstairs corridors that stretched and warped into the distance.

Such a long fucking distance. Quiet. Dark.

Jan fisted into the sheets.

Still he kept his ear to the door. Still he listened.

Still that crushing weight from a fading dream he couldn't remember came at his chest as he sat there, waiting. The darkness hugged around, feeling too intimate, too knowing, almost offering the quietest sigh, the quiet

73

whisper and soft laughter at how it knew what came out of the darkness.

It had Jan scared for the first time in months now.

Because the night knew it hid the worse things out there. And this time there was no light at the end of the forgotten nightmare, no Gray, no Jack, those startling silver-grey eyes to crouch by the bed to say…

"Hurt you real bad, didn't he, Richards?"

Jan pulled his knees up to his chest, burying his head.

In the darkness of the bedroom, Jack's eyes had looked so bright as he knelt there by the side of this bed. Christ. Jan could still smell him. He rocked gently, because it hurt so much now, everything that came after. Even ghosts and memories did their best to fade away and leave him alone. He didn't want to be alone, he wanted…

Jack's head pressed in close. "Head fuck," he said so quickly, voice hushed, "so fucking bad, Jan." He screwed his eyes shut. "Love you both so much. But it hurts. Everything fucking hurts. You know. You're hiding in here from it too."

Jan gripped tighter around his knees.

"Stupid," Jack whispered heatedly. "I say stupid fucking things. Wasn't you back there, wasn't us, never fucking us except when I kissed you on the floor, when it hurt more being pulled away from you. Just… my head. It's everywhere and I can't ground it long enough to stay with you. I want to so fucking badly, baby. Just… just please hang on in there. Stay with me."

Jan rocked, just slightly as he clung onto the fading ghosts. Maybe it was because this was the first time he'd been left alone, really alone, and the ghosts knew it, because the ones he held all came out, shifting shape, changing colour… texture… taste… And he hated how it brought them all back together: him, Jack… Gray, where—

❧

"… Jack?" Gray was awake behind Jan, and Jack suddenly jerked back, away from kneeling by the bed and nearly falling onto his ass. Maybe it was the darkness that jolted him, maybe the threat of rape and a black gas mask easing up from behind Jan that scared the hell out of Jack. Didn't matter which; they lost him to wherever his head had kept him hostage. Gray was already up and out of bed, scrambling over Jan, then reaching to try and help pull Jack up as Gray hit the floor.

"Fucking don't," hissed Jack, scuttling back.

"Jack," said Gray again, this time easing back as Jan rushed to join them in the darkness of the bedroom. Jack had pushed up to his feet, back pressed firmly against the wall, trying to look for a way out, then Gray was up against him, body pressed in close.

"Easy, stunner," he said quietly. "Easy." He played his hands around Jack's face, just gentle swipes with thumbs against jaw, and Jack calmed for the first time in weeks after Vince's head fucks, after his rape, the psychological reconditioning.

❧

Christ. Gray and Jack, they'd stood just there, off to Jan's left, up against broken mirrors that had long been replaced and fixed since that night. Hands shifting over his head, Jan screwed his eyes shut. Part of him hated the memories, wished them away. But another part clung to them so desperately now because it's all he had. He knew why Jack hid in Martin, and he cried out at the unfairness, how Jack got to hide from… this… how everything came back to… this. Fading scents, fading tastes, fading memories…. How everything faded away and kept him frozen on the sheets and breathing like he drew arctic wind into his lungs because… hurt. Like hell did this hurt now. He even clung to the rape, didn't wish it away because… because he'd got to hold Jack then too. Jack held him, and that was them, even then it was them and….

≈

"… Move." It took Jan a moment to realise that had fallen from his lips as he lay on Jack's bedroom floor, eating dust. Only Jack was OCD extreme. He wouldn't allow dust like this to hide. Wrong. It felt all wrong. Jack's room, his house, everything. It felt so wrong. "Fucking move, Jan."

Another shuffle on the bed, this time followed by a soft groan filtered over.

"Jack?" The drugs in Jan's system sent his world spinning even though he stilled.

A mumble came in the darkness, just the slightest breath of name, and Jan suddenly crawled over to the bed, dragging himself up and pulling Jack onto his lap and kissing repeatedly at his head.

The last time he'd seen him, Jack had been raped by a studded whip, breath-play played out so cruelly as Vince tried to drown him. Now the drugs hung heavy in his system too, the mirror of Jack's bedroom offering no safety as Jan cuddled him on the bed. "'S okay, baby. 'S okay."

On his back, an arm over his face, Jack blindly found

Jan's arm, mumbling something, then tugged Jan down to him.

"C'mon, baby." Jan choked back tears. "Need to go. Need to... to move."

"Wrong..." Jack murmured, then he twisted onto his side, and Jan found he was taken down with him, a hand finding the back of his neck and holding on tight. "Something's wrong."

Jack added more pressure to his neck, forcing Jan to lie next to him when run... they needed to run now. But as Jan sank into the warmth of the covers, Jack was instantly coming in close, leg going over Jan's, an arm snaking around his chest as Jack hid in his shoulder. *Tough... this bastard wasn't so tough.*

"Wrong," breathed Jack. "Something's so wrong."

Jack felt it too despite the drugs. How this wasn't home no matter how it tried to look like home. Life spinning as Jan grabbed Jack's shoulder, Jan tried shaking some life into him. "Gray. Need... need to go get Gray. Find... just get Gray."

"Jan?" Jack gripped harder, almost trying to climb inside him. "Stay. Christ. Don't go again. Don't hide from me... please."

Jan choked a sob. The drugs played hell with their systems: here one moment, gone the next. Nothing but a bad dream to each other, allowed only to hold each other when the nightmares came and—

The bed shifted as someone lay down behind Jack. Black eyes peered over Jack's shoulder, huge round holes that reflected Jan's blank stare in alien orbs. Breathing was strange, filtered through a black gas mask that almost seemed welded to the thick skull it shaped.

Not real. This isn't fucking real. Just some dream. Part of one huge messed-up dream. Jan needed it to be a dream; to cry out how it was nothing but a twisted nightmare.

"Yeah, Jan's here," a voice whispered in Jack's ear. Vince. "He's always right fucking here for you, kid."

Jack fell deathly still.

"No." Jan cried that out, and an arm went around Jan's throat as someone climbed in behind him, sandwiching him and Jack together. *"Fucking no."*

Vince took a hold in Jack's hair, then made sure Jack looked at Jan. Pupils were dilated, greyness focused somewhere else, on something else, on the crawling inside his body. "'S okay, baby," Jan whispered, trying to shuffle closer, rest his head against Jack's, just try and give him something else to ground his head. "They fucked up, baby," he whispered. "Gray knows, he'll come, he'll find us. Time out. You never said time out," he mumbled. "He'll fucking know it wasn't you. You wait and see. He'll be here."

Something was whispered in Jack's ear, and the briefest flicker of a frown crept to his face.

The whisper came again, this time accompanied with a thump to the side that had Jack doubling into Jan's shoulder and crying out.

"Don't… kiss Jan."

The confusion tore through Jack, that need to fight the whispering in his head, to fight his disorders, but at the same time be forced to do exactly what Vince wanted. Saying Don't around Jack had always been so fucking dangerous. Vince knew it… he used it.

But something else also fought in those grey eyes: the need to hide with a lover, to find comfort with a lover, to take comfort and cry out as lovers, and...

And Jack came in, shivering, holding so tightly that he hurt Jan's neck and stopped breath. There was a gentle nudge at Jan's jaw to get his attention, Jack asking Jan to respond, needing a response, needing comfort, needing security, and tears ran down Jan's cheek knowing what the intimate code meant.

He wasn't asking for Jan, he wasn't after his attention, his comfort or strength. He asked for Gray; he needed Gray now.

Only Gray wasn't there.

"Christ, baby. Stay with me," Jan mumbled, kissing at his head, allowed to kiss at his head, his cheek, not caring where so long as he felt Jack against him, so long as he felt him. "Don't listen to what they say. Stay with me. Stay with—"

"Don't... fuck Jan for me, Jack."

~

Jan buried a silent cry, pushing off the bed and stumbling into the bathroom. Lights on, nearly blinding him as he blinked and touch-felt his way to the cabinet. The methadone vial came first, then a needle, then...

Jan gripped onto the unit until he cried the hurt out.

He didn't want to feel it, how Jack's body had jerked into his as Vince had raped Jack into him. How Henry had matched Vince's fucked-up brutality and raped him into Jack. Jack had fought the voices in his head, refused to touch Jan, and that had been their reward. Vince and Henry had taken everything right about touching Jack, about them touching each other, and made the innocence of bump and grind nothing but sickness as rape was forced to mingle, as——

The vial and needle smashed up against the wall, along with a line of expensive colognes and other items Jan couldn't see anymore as he cried out.

"*Hurt… fucking hurts too much, Jack.*" Jan slumped to the floor, covering his head, then in the next instant—he was up and crawling around the bathroom to pick up the broken pieces.

Jack's OCD… it had caused every twist of cock into them both. A mother to kidnap her kid and see him reconditioned in a sick and twisted version of rape to straight. She'd wanted his disorders straightened out, Jack's love of kink, of Gray, all buried, just to bring back the hard-nosed thug who gave a fuck about no one. Completely obliterate everything Jack was.

Only Jack, as he was, he was just that tough fucking loveable puppy with a kickass attitude who only shattered and crumbled when left without someone to hold. His mother had wanted to destroy *that?* Only…

Only somewhere in the cries, shouts, silences that seemed to cry out much more hurt and damage as Jack was erased, Jan had been forgotten in the hell.

He'd dealt with this. It hadn't been this bad for weeks. But it still felt like his cries went unheard despite the people who moved and shifted inches from him. And like hell did he envy Jack's fall into oblivion, into Martin, but he hated him for it too. He hated Martin more.

He picked up the pieces to the broken cologne and stood looking down. Glass cut into his fingers, leaving thick red dots to paint life. He didn't remember cutting himself, didn't feel it with the small comfort he found in the methadone, and he closed his eyes briefly.

Back in his Villa, alone, so many a night had been spent like this just after Jack had been sectioned. Chasing nightmares, denying everyone's existence, including his own, finding and living in heroin. For a while back there, he'd denied Jack too, not taking the calls from the psych unit when Jack had finally been sectioned. Not giving a shit about anyone outside his own locked doors, because, Christ, no one had given a shit about his hurt, just expected him to deal.

He hated how it had just been expected that he deal. Gray had gotten to walk away; Jack later had hidden in Martin to get at Kes, and deal... that's the only choice he'd been given, because he couldn't walk away and hide, right? Gray had sealed his fate when he'd said he'd trust no one else with Jack. And standing next to Gray when it came to caring for Jack? It was a huge mass of shadow to fill, when all Jan wanted to do was get lost in the darkness it provided, the obscurity and normalness of just... breaking, and being allowed to break along with everyone else. Yet in all of that, Jan had fallen into obscurity. Had needed to fall into obscurity and not be noticed in the crowd.

Only the heroin had allowed him to do that. No one had noticed, and that had been fine with him.

On his birthday he'd gone to the gallery to get his latest fix, and he knew Gray had been behind him at a distance, just watching but not seeing why Jan had really been there. Jan could have turned around, gone over to speak to him, because he knew now Gray wouldn't have denied his existence. But he hadn't wanted it: not the ties back to all the hurt. His own cowardliness and how he wanted to hide from it all himself had kept his back to Gray.

Had Gray touched his life back then because he knew Jan had been close to shutting all life out, and that had been his *hold on, Jan* quiet touch? He touched so bloody quietly like that. No communication, just… there. Always fucking there.

Jan started to shake.

He missed Gray not being… there now.

And Jack?

Jan wanted that moment back. Just that one touch, the feel of one shared breath as….

"I'm here, baby" came a whisper into Jan's ear. *"Takes me a while, but I get there in the end."*

Jan dipped his head, the broken glass left discarded in the sink, the line of blood running into the granite sink and mingling with the shards.

Gray, he was always just there, somewhere in the distance but still wrapping a hold around him. And Jack… Jack always got there in the end.

Jan just needed it to be the end now.

He needed Jack back.

He wanted Gray.

He loved them both so fucking much but missing them cut so much deeper.

Ignoring the shaking going on with his hand, Jan glanced back. Past the bed, over to the door, to the darkness that carried on behind it.

To a familiarity that had him taking the cover off the bed and walking into a darkness that Jack had traced so many times before Martin took him down and buried him away so deep. Jan needed to feel Jack, to haunt the ghost that still tried to walk the halls. But he needed to feel Gray too, to find him in whatever darkness took him away from home. Away from them.

CHAPTER 8
DON'T... WALK INTO THE DARKNESS

THE COOL OF the hall walls played under Jan's fingertips as he walked, body on automatic, his footfalls falling into the same mechanics too. The sheet he'd pulled off the bed slept happily enough over his shoulder, keeping away a bite to his bare chest that he barely noticed now. He'd gone back to wearing his pyjamas since Gray was gone, and it helped keep the chill away too.

He felt a little better now, life less dark, less threatening as he kept the hall in darkness. Yeah, he knew it was the methadone, that it wouldn't last, that it would never feel the same as heroin. But this....

He tilted his head as he padded bare feet on thick carpet, focused entirely on the bumps and grooves that ran under his fingertips.

Jack had walked these halls like this over the years, felt his way through the darkness as if the walls offered a bridge between reality and wherever Martin kept him locked safely away.

Was this how Jack felt? Here but not here? Seeing

Martin touch, but never feeling it himself? Was it what Gray felt when he was lost from home too?

Jan would never know, he knew that, but it was another link to hide and hold on to. Hide away from the hurt but hold on and to try and reach Jack and Gray, stop them from hiding and feeling alone.

This was a bad place to be, he knew that. So fucking bad. He'd come so far, not needing this. Not needing to live in a third dimension where colours and shapes shifted along with who hid just out of sight, always out of fucking sight and mind. Hiding in someone else. But it's all he had, and he wanted to touch it a while longer.

He'd made it down the long stately wind of stairs and into light before he knew it. For a moment he stood staring at the front door, missing something. Waiting for it to open, feeling hollow when it didn't, but then he turned away, tracing the walls and sometimes closing his eyes as he walked on.

The ridge of a disinfectant dispenser bumped against his touch, and he smiled at the gentle reminder of Jack. An idea played there, but it was the quiet at the end of the hall that took his attention.

No guards stood on duty outside of Jack's detainment cell, but then the early hours wouldn't see there would be. Baz and Craig would be in the staffroom, no doubt fighting tiredness as they observed Martin via the CCTV.

But even Martin's cell slept quiet now, and Jan made his way down the hall, not wincing as his hip caught the table outside of the little corridor that would take him into Jack's.

Not Jack's. This cell wasn't Jack's. He had a home, an apartment in the city now his house had been sold, and all the ties to Vince had gone with how he'd used a mock-up of parts of Jack's house to see them raped in the safety of Jack's own bed. All to mess with his head. To break him down.

Jan stopped by the door, fingers tracing it as he rested his head against the cool frame.

This, this was Martin's home. Locked up behind some fucked-up door, but still there. Martin was still here when there was little else left to hold on to.

He ran a touch over to the access panel that would allow him to enter. Craig had quick access via a remote he carried with him, so all Jan had was this without his phone. He had access via that too. His thumb stroked the button, not too hard to press, just one light touch and....

"Hey, Jan." Someone took a gentle hold of his arm and eased him around. Jan blinked against the light of the corridor as Craig gave the softest of smiles. "Everything okay?"

Jan blinked again, frowned, then looked back at the access pad. "Just... just..." What? What was he doing here? "Jack." He nodded, offered a gentle smile back. "Just here to see... to see Jack. Not tough... not such a tough bastard. Gray shouted at him and he walked home alone that night. He held onto me that night when we got back to his, and... and he just held on. He hid under the covers as though he was still hiding from Gray's coldness, but also looking like he was trying to find a way back to him at the same time. He was going to call Gray in the morning, '*Get my head out of my ass and just kiss the fuck out of the bastard,*' had been Jack's words." Jan shivered. "But when it was just us in his bed, he held on to me and said *thank you for coming after me*, as though doing that was everything. For someone to just find him when he... he...." Jan fell quiet.

"Not tough…" he mumbled quietly. "Not such a tough bastard at all…."

Craig came a little closer, holding two, maybe three fingers up, Jan couldn't focus enough to decide which. "Okay. How about a deal? You come into the staffroom for an hour or two, let your head clear of the methadone, then if you still want to see Jack, it's okay with me."

Again Jan frowned at the door, then rubbing at his head, he found Craig again. "Bad dream," he said so quietly. Craig nodded and gently stroked at his arm.

"I know. I can see that, bud." Craig tilted his head in a friendly way, one that only sent Jan's world spinning again. "That deal? Is it okay with you? Good company? Some friendly faces?"

Jan sniffed, then scratched at his arm, where the needle mark should have itched. "Yeah. Long enough to see sense too, huh?"

Craig tugged him down the corridor, off to the right, into the staffroom. "Long enough to let you hurt, away from the fog, and without that bastard in there feeding from it."

Baz, or was it Paul? Jan tried to focus. Whoever it was with Craig, they shifted from the monitors and put the kettle on as Jan found himself led over to a very comfy chair and eased down. The cover was tugged off his shoulder, then he found it resting on him.

"I'm gonna be right here, and we can talk until the cows come home, okay? Or you can sleep." Craig crouched down and took a coffee off Baz. Yeah, it was definitely Baz. The cologne had been changed. Had it unsettled Jan just as much as Martin? Craig offered the coffee over to Jan. "Drink a little of this first. Just a few sips."

The coolness of the mug startled him, so too did the taste. "That's…" Jan pulled a face. "That's not coffee."

"No," mumbled Craig, taking the mug back off him. "The coffee is for me. You get fluids to stop dehydration." He frowned. "Have you been sick at all?"

Jan knew the signs, and Craig had no doubt seen a few now, but Jan hadn't been sick.

"Good." And Craig nodded. "I'm going to ask you that every half hour, okay? Just to make sure you're still okay. So… talk or sleep?"

"Hm…." Jan tried to focus. "TV… TV, please. Movie?"

Craig smiled. "Movie it is. You like *2012*, right? A bit of a disaster movie guy at heart. I'll see if it's still on Netflix."

And Craig was gone. Images flickered on the flat screen, but Jan stared at the wall until the next offer of fluids came; then he remembered focusing a little more on the pictures hanging off kilter on the wall later on. As the third offer of fluids came his way, along with a fourth ask if he was okay, what was in one of the pictures took his attention more.

The wanted poster was split in two, the same image of Jack on either side. One side offered an *Award if Found*, with the following list printed close by:

1 Goes by the name of Jack, (Craig prefers 'Loki', 'bastard', and 'woo-hey—dances with dart sedatives in his ass')

2 Favourite phrase: "Fucking peachy, mate"

3 Pilfers newspapers and defaces crosswords (Note name change to 'fucking bastard' here)

4 Goes nuts over chocolate biscuits (for God's sake get him to keep his nuts in his boxers. P.S. throw chocolate biscuits away).

5 Gets horny when put in a straitjacket because it's BDSM not seclusion-room time to Jack (don't ask about the knives and knife-play—seriously! Gray will kill us under the secret kink act (we have pictures to look at instead!))

The other…

Jan snorted a smile, then found a laugh as the cool of the staffroom really started to kick in now.

The other side offered a shoot-on-sight policy, with several giant sedatives drawn warningly next to Martin's neck. As for Martin's list?

1 Goes by the name of… fuck it, just go with 'bastard'.

2 Likes nursery rhymes, twisted ones: like, *don't ever repeat them to your kids and scar them for life* nursery rhymes.

3 Will pilfer newspapers, start fire in cell, tie up staff, and roast them pig-in-a-blanket style over it. (Note to staff: no newspaper or flammable liquid)

4 Think ankle tag and sedative first.

5 We mentioned think ankle tag and sedative first, right? If in doubt, knock 'im out!

"Oh… just fucking peachy, mate," Jan murmured through a smile.

"I'd kill to hear Jack say that again." Someone crouched by him and smiled over their shoulder as they looked at the poster too. "But I've got a soft spot for Martin. And you've not seen that one, huh?" added Craig.

Still chuckling softly, Jan fought a headache as he shook his head and rubbed at his eyes. "Has Gray?"

"Fuck no." Craig grinned back at him. "CCTV's not for Martin, but to check to see when he's around. We've got a list for Gray too."

"Christ—no!" Jan couldn't stop the chuckles. "Don't get

it out please, I can't breathe as is." He tried to stretch out, then cursed as all joints were frozen or stiff. "Christ..." He found the floor but gave up for a moment with standing. He was more tired now, which was usually a side effect of the methadone during taking it, not when it was filtering out of his body. Yet when he caught the time on Craig's watch, he understood it a little more.

"Sorry," he said quietly, looking over at the door and avoiding Craig more than he liked to admit. "About tonight."

"Don't ever apologise, Jan." Craig sounded hard with that, and he eased Jan back to look at him with a touch to his jaw. A search came of his eyes, skin colour, dampness to the body... and Jan seemed to pass the quiet checklist as Craig nodded. "It's why I'm here when Gray isn't where you're concerned. He loves you." Craig eased back. "Do you need to call anyone?"

Did he need to call Gray? That's what that said, and Jan pushed up to his feet, taking the sheet with him. "No. I'm just... just so fucking tired now."

"I'll get Baz to escort you upstairs—"

"No." Jan waited for Craig to get to his feet, then headed on out. He stopped by Jack's cell. "We had a deal, remember?"

The pause was there, that quiet checklist coming in that said *fuck no*. "Why, Jan? Why now, at this hour?"

Jan frowned at the door, then let his head drop a touch. "Because I'd rather be locked in there, with him, than be out here with Vince."

Nothing came from Craig, then—"That's not Jack in there," he said so gently. "You know that. You know Martin, how he plays can be worse than Vince."

"Only Martin's no rapist. He's all up here." Jan tapped his head, knowing he mimicked Craig's own words.

"Meaning?"

Jan looked at him, and Craig raised a brow as he explained. A smile crossed his lips. "Okay, could work," Craig said gently. "It's time I did an obs check on him anyway. He's been too quiet tonight too." He pulled out his radio and spoke to Baz. Baz came out a moment later.

"He gets restrained whilst you're in there, okay?" Craig tugged something free: the remote to Martin's ankle tag that would see Martin hit the floor in 0.9 seconds if he kicked off. "You wait here until I give the all clear."

Jan nodded and stepped back, the sheet tugged from his shoulders now he felt more human. Then he waited as Craig went in....

CHAPTER 9
DON'T... ENTER

"CLEAR." CRAIG HELD the door open a little more and Jan entered, eyes adjusting to the semi-darkness. Baz had disappeared for a moment, but he came back, handing something over to Craig as Jan took to the big chair in the detainment room. It wasn't as comfy as the one in the office, this one all plastic, and it came screwed to the floor, with nothing left exposed for Martin to kick off with.

Martin himself sat up in bed, his back against the wall, breathing heavy, a little too deep, and maybe belaying a struggle with Craig that his cool gaze couldn't shake. The bed was screwed down, the mattress itself coming with a tamperproof covering in case Martin wanted to get at the springs inside. One wrist lay cuffed to the railing; his other arm rested comfortably enough across his raised knee. And still that heavier breathing and light sweat to his body kept the cell company.

Craig came over and crouched by Jan, his back not turned on Martin, but happy enough that the chair sat a good eight feet away from the bed. He handed Jan three things. The last Jan slipped into his PJ bottoms, the other two....

"Little late for a visit, Janice." Martin sat watching him. He hadn't moved, not even to lie down. "You look like shit too." A smile. "Made a visit to junkie land, have we? Bet Gray loves working over at MI5, dining with the likes of spies and foreign intelligence agencies, all to come home and see you... all sweaty and stoned to your eyeballs. Classy."

Craig tapped on the arm of the chair, making sure Jan stayed focused on him. "You know how to get out. And don't mind Peachless there. He's running a fever and just a little pissed he had no fight a moment ago."

Now Jan looked at the bed. A slight flush marked Martin's cheeks, the tip of his nose too. The heavy breathing and sweat wasn't easing, not like it would after a struggle. Was that why it had been quiet in here? Or had Martin heard Jan by the door earlier on and given no fight because he knew he'd come in eventually?

"I'm calling Halliday in a few hours." Craig's look was serious now. "This disruption has gone on since Baz's aftershave, and this fever is something new."

Something new since Gray had gone.... It wasn't said, but it was there, and Jan knew the significance behind that. He nodded, just the once. Enough for Martin to tilt his head and narrow those silver eyes at what was being said. Although, no. Not at what was being said, just a real curiosity over why Jan sat there.

"I'll also talk to Halliday about your meds too, okay?" Craig's look was softer. Jan knew he was being polite. Craig would have a responsibility to talk to Halliday as both he and Martin were under Halliday's care. "He'll no doubt want to see you too."

To see why he chose to sleep in here over his own bed. Yeah, Jan saw that now. He frowned a little, then gave another nod.

"Whispers."

Jan looked at Martin, hearing that. Martin had closed his eyes, and he turned his ear towards them.

"Always fucking whispering...." Silver eyes refocused on Jan. "I was born through whispers. You know that, Janice?" Such a cocky grin now. "Jack's old lady.... Loved cutting herself and wiping it on Jack's cheek."

Craig turned his ear now too.

"Wouldn't let the boy wipe it off. Used to hold his hands down, deny his OCD, and guess what she used to say?"

"Stop." That came from Craig.

"*Jack, get dirty*. Because, y'know, real men, they always get dirty."

Jan denied the twist in his gut that came. It hurt that Martin knew something about Jack that he didn't. It gutted him more hearing how Martin knew those memories of Jack's: did it hint that they really could lose Jack to Martin? Blend those personalities, with Martin being dominant? Jan eased back in the chair, made it look like he was getting comfortable, that he felt normal, but men.... He pulled the sheet over him. Yeah, real men got dirty. Like Vince and all his come on Jack, not allowing him to clean, to....

"Humpty... dumpty." Martin hummed a little of the rhyme, how he sat on that wall—"Watching shit fall." Craig eased to his feet as he carried on. "That you now, Jan? Watching all the shit fall like Jack did? Going a little crazy... needing to hide?" A smile. "But Jack hides in here with me. He'll always hide in here with me, because I'd never come all over Jack as Vince raped him. I mean, that is what you did, right, Janice? Come all over Jack? You watched Vince rape him, got hard, came over him, then never let him find peace and wipe it off. Instead you threw him headfirst back into being covered with blood, back to him needing me. Back to how he'll always turn back and hold me when it comes to burying the shit you help cause."

Jan stopped Craig from going over, a gentle tug on his arm and a nod making sure Craig stayed back.

Instead Jan eased his legs up, let the semi-darkness play out—then plugged the headphones into Craig's iPhone and turned up the volume as he put the earpieces in.

They were two of the three items he'd asked for. Martin was all head games, so Jan simply wouldn't allow him in his head long enough to play those games.

Jan gave Martin a smile, and the look coming back at him simmered enough to say Martin would do serious damage if his hands were free, but as Craig had seen to that….

He got a quirked brow off Craig, a small smile, then Craig headed on out. The door wasn't locked, not tonight, but Martin's steady gaze never shifted from Jan, even though he would have heard that change.

Cameras in place, Martin cuffed, lights going a little darker still, Jan eased his head back and settled into the deep pulse of the music. "State of My Head" by Shinedown gave him that little adrenaline kick to keep his eyes closed and trusting the people behind the cameras, which, coming from scenes where Jack's mother had sat and watched both of their rapes, that was a damn huge step. With the methadone clearing from his system and the nightmares a world away now, life settled. Calmed.

That deep trust in who Gray chose to be here crept up.

Trust in Craig. Trust in Gray. But mostly a trust in himself.

As the song finished and another drifted in, Jan briefly opened his eyes.

Martin still sat there. Still watched.

And that was okay. It was all he *could* do.

Jan completely settled. Breathing came deep, almost mirroring Martin's, but that was good too. They both carried their own illness tonight, the result of Jan's keeping him here as much as Martin's kept him quiet tonight. Or maybe Martin was just recalculating the situation, always looking for that way to exploit the edges of any madness. You could never tell with Martin. You could never trust.

As the second tune in the playlist ended, Jan making a mental note of the song and artist for his own iPhone, he opened his eyes again, just briefly.

Martin lay down now, his free arm covering his eyes, one knee up, but that breathing still deepening his chest. The black V-shirt he wore saw that same heavy perspiration dampening toned shoulders and sticking the shirt to his chest. Long black hair carried the same dampness, spreading on the pillow in strands, and loose jogging bottoms gave him all of Jack's ease, with looking good no matter how or where he rested his head: park bench… manor.

The third track kicked in, a slower, deeper beat, and almost dragged Jan into sleep with it. Part of him didn't want to drift off, not now, not with how calming it felt to be next to Jack, no matter how small an echo it was of Jack. So he denied sleep, just letting it carry him through how empty life had felt.

The slow piano piece that came on next caught Jan's calm more, especially the vocals that haunted it with how someone took a walk with a lover in a soft light. It was one of those songs that stopped the listener in their tracks and quietened the world for a moment as they turned their ear to the music; nothing but the music existing, and it was that mood Jan didn't want to end.

Again his look fell on Martin, but this time life quietened just as much with what Martin did.

With all the scrapes and grazes that came with handling cars, the back of hand that drifted lightly over Martin's hip, over the length of cock hidden in loose jogging pants, was so fucking gentle now, the same tone and tempo of a pianist drifting a touch over piano keys. Jack—and that was Jack's touch there now, Jack's look and slow burn of heat—he shifted just a touch, arching his back slightly, stomach muscles pulling in deeper as the back of hand was exchanged for the gentle drift of fingers over cock.

Jan closed his eyes, shutting the image out, but the music still played it out in his head.

Lost. He could get lost in Jack's gentler hold. All the roughness and D/s kink Gray took with Jack, that Jack took with Gray, there was always this pull back to a purer innocence with Jack too. To just hide, cuddle up, tentatively explore the body when so much damage had been done. A need to get back into experienced and well-trained heat, but still showing such damn shyness over testing a body out, of touching....

Christ. Jan looked, never more comfortable to look despite the cameras being there, despite knowing he hadn't even thought about the cameras in the past few moments.

Jack's natural place behind the camera played on display. All the years of being Gray's Master sub... of being a switch and teaching Doms... subs... of being beneath Gray and learning how to test and tease his body as Gray watched, knowing decadence…. This was Jack. The tail of shirt eased distractedly up his abs, but that touch traced beneath jogging pants now. The play on his shaft came as long, as slow as the play of piano, as gentle as the singer's voice as it filtered through, and Jan shifted for the first time as his own cock reacted naturally to Jack's touch. The swell and rush into full hardness against silk pyjamas took Jan's breath, the silk nothing but the brush of lips against his tip as it strained into the fabric.

Jack's breathing seemed to hitch in the same instant, the pull of stomach muscles showing it. His tip lay exposed to the night, and maybe the heat of his fever heightened the cooler touch of the air, because his pace quickened, the sweat lining his body and hands maybe helping, maybe hindering with how he tossed around a little, fighting something now.

Jan tugged out an earpiece, wanting to hear as well as see, needing to hear Jack now too. And it came then: Jack dug his heels into the mattress, head tilted back, and the softest escape of breath came, how nothing mattered in that moment as Jack lost himself to it… Jack always lost touch with them in the best kind of ways when he came.

Christ. A knot of pleasure twisted so hard in Jan's stomach, one that caught his own breath and forced him to close his thighs beneath the sheet to stop the hurt of not touching himself, of not sharing that moment with Jack.

The first stream of come touched Jack's lower abs, the second hitting a little higher. Same with the third. The fourth and fifth forced Jack to tense his body so much that the fine cords in his neck were as exposed and angry as his cock.

Heat would be running Jack's shoulders now, the blush that burned his cheeks as he came hitting his neck and upper body, never more on display than when he started to relax into the comedown. Cock still displayed, looking happier and sated as come stained his abs, Jack let his arm fall back over his eyes. Breathing started to calm, but the perspiration lining his body was heavier now.

Yeah. That was Jack's look there. One captured by Gray in his studio and framed in his private gallery on many occasion because Jack's disorders and turmoil were never more calm than when he'd been under Gray's touch.

"That's for you, Janice. You hard from watching? Or do you need Vince here to really get you fucking Jack up?"

That? That was Martin.

"Wanna get your tight ass in that maid's outfit and wash this off for me? Give me five minutes, you can toss off as you ride my cock for an hour or so too, hm? That *is* what you need now, right? A good fucking. Vince didn't rape you hard enough, did he?"

Closing his eyes and burying the hard bite that cooled his body, Jan eased back into the chair and put his headphones back in.

Martin's laughter filtered over as he did.

For half an hour he lost himself to the music, too wired to sleep, too irritated not to, needing the music to uncomplicate this whole fucked-up mess that heated and cooled him in the same breath. Yeah, sometimes he envied Jack for being able to shut everything out and hide.

Sometimes he hated him too.

"Everyday", a stunning hard and fast piano piece by Carly Comando finished playing, and the twist of body against mattress caught his attention now. Was Martin asleep?

A rough cough came, mirroring Gray's in many ways,

especially with how Gray always seemed to want to deny its existence, no matter how long Jan looked at him. The smell of sweat was pungent, as well as the run of shakes and shivers.

Yet the scratching at Jack's hip? Where Vince had branded his name into Jack (how Gray's tattoo now covered it, waiting for it to be shaded) scratching drew bloodied patches over it now.

Something irritated Jack, enough to burn through Martin in the sleep that took hold.

The headphones and iPad went onto the chair as Jan stood, the sheet going with him, and Jan headed on into the makeshift bathroom. The end of the sheet went under the tap and cold water soaked the edge. Taking something out of his pocket, he went back over to the chair, bypassing it and heading for the bed.

The door to the detainment cell came open in the next minute, a soft call of his name warning him off. But he was there, already by the bed.

Martin had been asleep, that hadn't been faked, but he jolted now, almost as if sensing someone close. His reaction was instant.

Jan's was quicker.

As Martin shifted to grab his arm, Jan hit the remote on the sedative. Martin's ankle tag kicked in, forcing out a cry, a shift of intent as Martin tried to grip his ankle and stop the sedative hitting his system, but he was out in the next breath. Almost. "Oh I see why Gray likes you now, sweetheart." And the softest smile touched Martin's lips. "Yeah, you've got a good wicked streak there too, huh? That's... that's something to watch out for. But Christ... fuck is it sexy. Do it again. Go on."

Jan waited for him to relax completely into the bed, then giving a glance back to Craig, he knelt down.

This. This was Jack. This was Jack's reaction to having come left on his stomach. Jack lived for sex, but his OCD saw that he just couldn't stand the come left on his skin once the heat of sex had faded.

He pushed up Jack's T-shirt and wiped his abs down, making sure everywhere was clean. Craig came over a moment later, handed Jan some antibacterial wipes too, and Jan nodded his thanks. "He'll need a clean shirt and sheets."

"Yeah," Craig said quietly. "We'll take care of those." And after watching for a moment, he headed on out.

Jan took care of Jack's hands, palms, crease of fingers; then he wiped Jack down from head to toe, taking his time across Jack's brow and wiping there a few more times than necessary.

Then he kissed at Jack's lips, just briefly, before feathering a kiss at his abs.

"For you, Jack. Always just for you, baby. Never for that fuck."

Something mumbled into the darkness, but the pull on the sedative already held both Jack and Martin captive now.

Craig came back into the cell with Baz, and Jan stepped back to give them room to change Jack and get the bed clean. It wasn't an easy task, and Jan frowned, wondering how the weight of doing this over the years took its toll on Gray. He never spoke about it, but then how he kept coming back always did speak worlds for him there.

"All done." Craig stepped back, and Baz left, heading out to "get the kettle going."

Jan didn't say anything, his look on Martin, on his abs.

"Jan."

Now he looked at Craig.

"When in doubt, knock 'im out.... You took it in and saw his game." Craig patted his arm. "You did good here tonight."

Jan scratched distractedly at the crease to his arm. "Jack's so close," he said gently. His mind was more on the come staining Martin's abs, how Martin reacted; how Martin itched enough to say he needed to clean himself down. And that, that was Jack, not Martin, not any blending of personality. Hopefully. He wanted to make damn sure, though. And Jan held his own when it came to head games. "I've got an idea."

"Oh?" Craig quirked a brow. "I'm listening."

Jan offered a small smile back. He'd had enough of walking in the shadow of psychopaths. Only the fool walked on, tasting it blindly.

CHAPTER 10
THE FOOL?

"YOU OKAY, ASH?"

The darkness of the kitchen came back into focus for Ash as Raif's quiet call of his name broke through.

"I lost you for a moment."

Lost? No, not lost. Maybe claimed him back a little. But the worst or best part of him? Did he have any good left?

Ash took Raif back to the table and stood there between his thighs as Raif sat down. He didn't trust what he touched not to walk out of his life again as easily as he walked back in a few moments ago. He traced over Raif's face, over that one side that never seemed to smile despite the look he caught in those eyes: black pools in a blacker night.

Yeah. Maybe Raif held a good part of him, because having missed Raif felt good. That had to be a good sign, right? Ash kissed him, gentle, just to taste, to feel those lips against his lips, to remember Raif as those hands rested on his hips.

Three decades separated them, yet this... how Ash

pulled off a little, one hand on Raif's hair, the other under his jaw and lifting his lips up to meet Ash's, it crossed ages, said fuck to difference, and blended it into one shadow. Theirs.

If this was him being lost, he needed to stay here a while.

Raif gave a smile, deepening his eyes, showing the emotion where most wouldn't see it in the hard ridges of his face. Most ran away. But Ash, he'd... lingered. Ash hadn't run from him; he hadn't had the life too. And maybe that had confused Raif more. People either fought or they ran away screaming from him. They didn't... linger. And it confused the bear, making him ease down and sniff around in the hope of figuring out why something smelled wrong.

Now a gentle push came at Ash's waist from Raif, a little distance put between them, then Raif traced his hands distractedly up Ash's hips. Still that easing down, still that quiet sense-tasting over why Ash hadn't run into fight or flight. Yeah, Raif was still questioning why he kept coming back here too.

Ash let out a breath at the gentle touches. Then as Raif bowed his head, Ash traced fingers through his hair. A soft sigh came, Raif's this time, then that touch on Ash's waist slid along the band of his jeans all for a hand, a breath, to tease the material covering Ash's cock.

Christ... Ash frowned at the gentle play, running with the sensations found in a touch that knew exactly how to fill a guy's cock through material.

A tug came at Ash's waistband, then Raif rolled him free, a deep sigh coming off Raif. The single, long stroke—the night-cool grip on the sleep-warmed heat filling his cock— it forced Ash to twist his look away slightly, his grip on Raif's hair tightening now.

Raif mumbled something, his breath playing wicked games along Ash's exposed head. When Raif finally looked up, it was to watch his own hand-play, that cocky smile touching his lips as he fisted Ash's length.

"That's... that's still a damn good cock size, Ash. Missed it."

Ash matched the stroke and play on his cock with a brush of thumb at the back of Raif's neck. Raif tilted into it, eyes now closed at the contact. Despite the shivers racing up Ash's back and across his shoulders, there was no rush here. It wasn't to mark remembered first-time touches, to deliberately keep the pace slow, just... them enjoying the night. Enjoying the quiet.

This was Raif's time, when he was most awake and alive, and Ash was content to rediscover just how that touch played.

"I'm a skinny shit." Ash smiled at how Raif tilted his head to watch his touch on Ash's cock. "Seems to come with its own magic mirror to make us look bigger."

Raif kissed at Ash's tip, and Ash let out a hiss. "Nope." A lick came, a bite on the foreskin. "That's... that's still a real damn good-size cock there, Ash. Damn bloody good."

Ash tugged Raif away from his cock, the grip tight in his hair and leaving Ash cursing at the loss of heat across his head. "So, you know I'm clean how?" It hadn't occurred to him when Raif had first fucked about with him. They'd played bareback then too.

Raif swiped a thumb over Ash's cock, forcing out another sharp pull of breath off Ash as Raif smirked. "Talent. You're clean, flitter. I know."

Ash didn't register anything beyond that as lips slipped over his tip, the hands on his ass pulling him in so every inch was buried deep in Raif's mouth. He was held there for a moment, Ash breathing hard, heavy—waiting there in the darkness with eyes fully open and again seeing every aspect of his surroundings: the sharp edges to the frosted window pane in the door, how it split the moonlight into a thousand pieces on the kitchen floor. Then Ash frowned, that grip on Raif's hair tightening as he realised what Raif offered with not moving, with staying there, waiting.

Ash pulled back, then groaned softly as he took Raif's mouth, pushing his cock back in between teeth and lip. Like the first time they'd done this, Raif could have still tossed him onto the table and forced control and Ash would have been too ass-thin to have stopped it. Yet he didn't. So as Ash feathered the back of Raif's neck, sometimes gripping hair, sometimes just playing through it, Ash kept his pace slow, gentle, watching each slip of cock into Raif's mouth, returning that gentle control.

If this was being a real Dom, having this trust, having this strength, this man here, allowing Ash to play and want nothing in return... it offered the sweetest offer of normality that Ash needed to hold on to.

But as a tug came at his jeans, this time to expose Ash's ass, to touch his ass—

Ash stilled, stopping any play.

Raif looked up, a frown there, then he moved his touch around Ash's hips, away from his ass.

Ash's cock thudded back against his abs, and a gentle kiss went to it. Nothing had been said, it hadn't the first time Raif had tried to expose his ass, but there didn't seem any need to as Ash took Raif up to his feet with a gentle grip on his hair. Ash was tall himself, but Raif... Raif was that beefed-up werewolf raising up on its haunches to really show you how small life could get. One that understood

Ash in ways that most never stayed around long enough to see.

Ash kicked the chair away a little, then backed Raif up against the counter. He wanted Raif up close and personal against him, to have those large hands roaming his hips, holding him so close that there was little else to do but fuck in the close confines and not stop until they were both wasted. He pushed into Raif now, feeling his cock rub against Raif's jeans, a thick thigh, as Raif split Ash's legs with his knee. Ash played that spiked hair, tugging Raif down, kissing his lips one moment, then biting into Raif's neck the next.

Fuck, he loved the cords in that neck. How his teeth grated against them and forced Raif to look up slightly with a groan. Hands again found Ash's ass, this time helping to grind his heat into Raif's groin, nothing more, not going past Ash's need to stay covered, and—Ash ground in hard, cock against thigh, lips, chasing long bites at Raif's neck, then—

"Fuck..." Raif caught up with his kiss for a moment. "So fucking fast, Red. You still burn up so fucking fast."

Ash mumbled something, didn't know, didn't really care what. He found Raif's cock, how the tight pull of jeans always framed it like body wrap, then Ash gripped around Raif's neck, now back to biting as he rode his cock along Raif's. "Not..." He groaned. "Too long waiting.... Not gonna last long, Raif. Don't want to—"

"Kind of the whole point tonight...." Raif grabbed both of their cocks, and Ash hissed, pushing away slightly and watching as he fucked Raif's hand, how Raif's cock matched his pace. "Take what you need," breathed Raif, and as he brought a hard stroke into play, it pushed the heat too far in Ash's body. He buried his cry as he came.

"Shit, shit-shit." Ash cupped Raif's neck, trying to ground himself, and screwed his eyes tight shut. It took a moment to realise Raif was teetering on the edge of coming, so Ash pulled back slightly, still shaking, his hand around their cocks now. Ash fucked his shaft along Raif's, despite the shocks crying through his body that said he'd had enough.

And there…. Legs parted, resting back on the unit, Raif came, eyes closed, mouth slightly open. Ash caught Raif's groan before he came, loving the repeat of first-time touches, of come on cocks, stomach, making the last few moments of any orgasm just so… really fucking filthy.

"Fuck, fuck," breathed Ash into Raif's kiss. "Fucking missed that. Missed us."

"Mm…." It's all he won off Raif for a moment, that sneer, most definitely a smile, trying to win attention on his lips too. "Something along those lines, yeah. Fucking fuck."

Breathing heavy, Ash pushed away, a hand on Raif's chest as he looked down at the party aftermath. Finding Raif's gaze again, Ash backed him over to the sink and started wiping him clean with a damp cloth, taking his time and watching the play of cloth over muscled stomach. He hadn't even known when he pulled Raif's shirt free. But he loved it now, how the cloth found the ridges and grooves to the muscles.

"It still comes so naturally to you, doesn't it?"

Ash looked up at Raif. "Hm?"

A hand brushed his cheek, and now that heat was gone, Ash felt like stepping back, just cooling back in his own personal space.

"Caring for someone?"

Ash cocked a brow. "That still surprises you?"

Raif fell quiet for a moment, and the draught from the kitchen door played around Ash's shoulders.

"It does when I see you pull the shit you did tonight."

Ash stopped what he was doing, his head tilting slightly, his turn to let the details sink in. "Oh, right. Back to Sandy and fucking over the BDSM lifestyle, is it? Or in this case, fucking over the man who took the photo? So you taking the car again from me was, what? To teach me *another* lesson? You showing up here was to teach me another fucking lesson in humility? After all the shit we've been through these past few weeks?"

Ash pulled away, tugging his arm free when Raif tried to catch hold of it. "Fuck off, Raif. I'm the cunt, when you're the fuck who still keeps walking out of a night and leaving for weeks on end?"

This time the rough grip made sure Ash turned back and didn't lose sight of Raif. "Phone."

"What?"

"Chase's phone." Raif held out his hand. "Give it."

"Fuck you."

A hand dug in his pocket, then sorted through the other before Ash could fight off anything else. "No."

Raif pulled Chase's phone away, already sorting through the recent files and pressing Play.

Rough grunts from a fucking harmonised with the raw sound of wind through trees, but Ash closed his eyes when the dick disappearing into Peepshow's ass lit up the kitchen.

Raif stilled for a moment. Ash didn't like the long look he got a moment later. "For what? Ruin a guy's life, no doubt a family, just for you to bury your hurt deeper than Chase could bury his cock in his ass? That what you're doing lately?"

"*Not.* Your. Concern. My fucking life. One you always walk out on."

"I didn't walk out on you; you shut the door on me. As for what's my concern—" Raif pressed something on the phone, then tossed it back at Ash. "—when you're being a cunt like that, you need pulling up."

Ash thumbed through the phone. The video file sat empty. "You—" He'd have deleted it anyway. He wouldn't have opened Chase up to be screwed over when Chase's head wasn't in the right place, but to have Raif do it? "*You fucking cunt.*"

The phone hit door, smashing to pieces right where Raif had walked back into his life. "Lesson fucking learnt." He caught Raif's hard stare and the *fuck* did he give one back. "Promise I'll be a good fucking boy now, Dad. Want to throw in a belt across my arse with that?"

"You would have deleted it purely because Chase was hurt, not because you'd both wanted to hurt a man who has a family. And here was me thinking you'd started to change. Although nice to see you're still daft enough to break phones in temper. Last time it was Johnny's you smashed. You do realise that's Chase's phone you've just killed now?" Raif stayed on him for a moment longer, then moved over to the counter, tugging out two pieces of bread and some ham. Ash stood there as he made up a sandwich, grabbed a Snickers from the fridge, a Coke, then headed for the door.

He glanced back at Ash before the night air had a chance to rush in. "You're still missing it, Ash. You're missing what your real problem is. And you'll still end up on your own and hugging the darkness because of it despite everything I do. So fuck you this time."

"What…" Ash held his hands out. "What the fuck is that supposed to mean? Everyone's got one hell of a mouth tonight when it comes to my life."

Raif snorted, shook his head, then pulled the door open. "Figure it out."

"So you're back to the streets, right? To whatever keeps you walking away every fucking time." Ash knocked the bread on the floor for good measure too, then went back over to the open door. "Well fuck back off then, now you've fucked with me."

Raif didn't seem to need telling twice, and Ash slammed the door behind him.

Yeah, why hold on to any echo of trust; it only fucking faded away into the night, right along with Coke, ham salad, and a fucking Snickers bar. Always to a Coke, ham salad, and a fucking Snickers bar.

Ash leaned back against the unit, briefly closing his eyes. What the fuck was so important about that damn Coke, ham sandwich, and a Snickers bar? He kicked the door, hands running his hair.

Johnny. He'd lost the best of friends to the night.

Ash looked at the mess around the kitchen, the back door, how the sound of his dad's car started up again.

"Fuck… no." *Not the car.*

He grabbed a hoodie from the washing basket and bolted out, oblivious to the bits of phone that dug into bare feet. Raif couldn't take the car again and leave him in the shit. He hadn't been that much of a bastard tonight, and he couldn't stomach any more burns on his body in with everything else.

CHAPTER 11
VOODOO MAGIC

THE QUIET OF the street unnerved Ash as he made it around to the drive and climbed in the car, beside Raif. Again that feeling was there to look over his shoulder, and this time he did, rubbing at his arms.

Raif had just enough time to pull the sandwich off the passenger seat as Ash sat down, and now he glared at Ash, one arm over the steering wheel.

"You can't be here, Ash. The streets... they're too fucking dangerous lately. What the fuck are you doing here?"

Ash broke his death stare with the night beyond the car and held Raif's gaze, sitting back and folding his arms. He was going nowhere.

"Gonna be like this again, is it? You not taking the hint to fuck off despite the door being unlocked for you to do just that?" Raif put the food in the glove box and shifted into first. "Fair enough."

Ash was forced forward a little at the jolt back down the drive, then his home disappeared around the corner the next moment. Black leather gloves covered Raif's hands, and Ash frowned. What kind of burglar put gloves on after he'd broken into someone's home?

The dashboard clock blinked one in the morning, and he hoped to God his father would be stopping over at Miles's tonight now. Car keys dangled in the ignition, only adding to more frustration over just when Raif had taken them, but then this was Raif.

"So." Ash gave a sniff, looking out the window at the speeding darkness. "Nice night for it, I guess. Where the fuck we going? Or do I just get that *shut up and put up* shit from you as you try and disappear?"

Raif jammed hard into another gear. Ten minutes later, they pulled up at the back of a common, and Raif got out and dropped some trainers in Ash's lap.

Ladies trainers? Ash scowled down at them. Why the fuck would Raif need ladies trainers on his night travels?

He didn't have much time to question it. Raif walked away from the car, leaving him there, and Ash was sick of seeing Raif's back.

He slipped the trainers on and followed. Occasionally the screech of a fox drifted over, giving the night a different life where the animals ruled after lights out. Ash rubbed his arms against the cold. The mist hung heavy here, the common itself dipped, the area in general and hills and homes living in a wide soup bowl, so everything lingered here: life, loss... the weather. Everything but Raif.

They made it over a bridge, but Raif ignored the main road, instead opting for a garden fence. Ash only stared as Raif eased so easily over it. Ash's breath came hard and fast already, the bottom of his jeans wet from the long grass, feet soaked and....

Fuck. He pulled himself up.

The drop down caught him unawares: it wasn't as long as he'd thought, the garden being more elevated above the common, and Ash landed on his ass, jarring his ankle. He grabbed at it, rubbing, and ground a few teeth away. Fuck's sake.

Someone crouched down in front of him, and Ash jerked his head up.

Raif watched him for a moment, eyes narrowing. "Go home. You don't want to be here."

Yeah, he wanted to be here now, his silence and how he got to his feet said that, and Raif shook his head as he got to his.

"Still like that, right?" Raif snorted, then headed away, over the back of the garden. They took three more like that, Ash fighting with a horde of garden gnomes that sat playing Game of Gnomes on Thrones. He didn't argue with them: they looked as mean as Raif. Then as they came to the fifth back garden, Ash found he was tugged down to a crouch.

Raif raised a finger to his lips.

Ash didn't understand the reaction. Thigh-high grass did a good job of hiding them away from life in general, and a broken old shed that had a door missing blocked the view of the house. On top of that, the rusted swing did a bloody good job of masking any noise they might have made.

But the night did seem to go a little quieter, as if listening too, and Ash turned his ear.

Raif gave a light whistle, a lovely run of soft high and low pitches that sounded like a bird waking up too early for the morning chorus. The beauty of it was haunting compared to Raif's rough outer shell. And from within the

117

dark hole that led into the shed, a reply came, just a softer shuffle of feet on wood, and Ash stiffened.

Raif kept low as he tugged Ash over with him, despite the fact Ash didn't want to go near the damn thing. It looked like a shed reject from *Saw*. He didn't want to see who or what was in there.

Just before the grass could escape into the blackness of the open doorway, a scratch came at the wood, and Raif reached down and repeated the same pattern. Five light touches.

Ash bit back pulling away as someone—a lady? He couldn't tell with the amount of layers of clothes and gloves and hat that did their best to mask humanity, let alone sex—came out into the mist and moonlight.

The contrast between Raif and the scrawny figure given more weight by the layers of clothing was immense, Raif in jeans, leather jacket, trainers, then shed lady in… rags. Yet the small smile she got should have sent the ragged lady back into the shadows, but didn't.

Raif shifted, tugging something out of his pocket, and Ash half expected the food to be handed over. The bunched-up notes surprised him. Cash was handed over, and from how gloved hands counted through the notes, there was enough to pay the electric bill for a month.

"Any issues?" That came so quietly and the man… woman… in the shed shook their head. "I had footwear too, but they've been hijacked for the night."

Ash grimaced as he got a look down his body, to his feet. A snort came.

"Yeah. My thoughts too." Raif nodded, then shifted away. Not wanting to stay looking into the blackness of the shed, just how cold and lonely life could get, Ash pushed away, grateful of the grass and how the length wanted to hide the shed at the bottom of the garden.

He wasn't happy as Raif stopped outside the house and stood looking at the back door. As he reached to the handle, Ash stopped him. "You're fucking breaking in?" he hissed on a breath.

Raif worked something into the lock, then eased the door open.

"Oh." That stopped Ash. Did he have keys for here? It looked like a key. "It's yours?"

Looking a little angered, Raif again raised his finger to his lips. Ash didn't understand the need for quiet if this was Raif's home: he'd had a key. In fact, Ash pushed through first, more than a little pissed himself. They'd met at Jim's when Ash had house-sat there, then Mack's, then a few nights later at Ash's home, but never Raif's home turf. Why the fuck would he need to stay quiet here?

A hand stopped him, this time gripping so roughly at his arm it hurt, and Raif kept hold of him when he again tried to tear it off. "From here, you say nothing. You do nothing. We clear?" That look wasn't playing anymore. "You don't frighten what's up those stairs."

Me frighten someone? It was there on the tip of his tongue, but he frowned at Raif's look. There was a request there, a quiet… *please, don't frighten what's up there,* and it made him pause. After a moment, he offered a nod.

The rough grip released his arm and Raif took the stairs, making no noise. Ash followed suit, not really sure why, but the smell of cat piss on the wood perhaps added to it. No carpet covered the wood, although a wood stain job had done its best to try and give the stairs some life and colour. The same went for the staircase: no paper, just a thin coat of paint and kid's drawings on canvas added at various places to help give it some colour. Three doors sat at the top, one leading into a bathroom where two toothbrushes sat: a kid's Buzz Lightyear and an adult's cuddling in close. The other door looked over the chaos of a woman's bedroom: bras and pants strewn over the floor, hairdryer on a unit with a basket of makeup close by. A few action figures kept the bed safe but didn't seem to mind their intrusion. The bedroom itself was empty, but it had that cheap perfume scent that said the room hadn't been empty long.

The second bedroom. It confused Ash. A lock sat on the outside, a chain that drew across to allow a little look inside. Raif seemed taken with it, too, before he reached up and quietly took the chain off.

Ash followed him, a little puzzled as Raif went and sat on a single Buzz Lightyear bed that, for the most part, looked empty. Again the floor was littered: clothes, crisp packets, toys, and Ash leaned against the doorframe, careful not to tread on anything. This home was lived in, if not in need of a little love. And Raif seemed to know his way around, yet nothing suggested that a man lived here.

Pulling the food from his pocket, Raif rested it on the bed, then leaned forward to take hold of the bottom of the duvet. A tug pulled it off the floor, then—

"Hey, missy."

A scuffling noise came, the sound of a sleepy reply, then Ash jerked slightly as a little girl came from under the bed. She couldn't have been more than five years old and... and...

Ash shot a look behind him, to the main bedroom, to the stairs.

Downstairs. The mom must be downstairs.

"How you doing, Voodoo Doll?" Raif asked that so gently, and Ash gave the girl her dues, she looked like a spell caster: long dark hair, wild, huge blue eyes, pale, but... but... holding on to Raif like she knew him, how the leather gloves hid his scarred hands, not from doing harm, but from... her, and—

"Jupiter."

Confused brown eyes met his, and Ash realised that was his own original name for Raif and that he'd spoken it. Again a finger came to lips, then a little hand tugged it away and wrapped it around a small waist. The girl cuddled in close, almost lost in Raif, but possessing him in every way in her sleepiness.

"Rowy. Mr Rowy tonight?"

Raif smiled, distractedly running a hand over tangled hair. "Yeah, you been good for your momma, shrimp?"

Voodoo Doll pulled away and nodded, very quickly. The smile there said she had. "'Course, stupid. Miss Shed tell you? She played Roblox with me last night." And she suddenly shifted like the wind onto the bed. Sitting cross-legged, she unpacked her food.

Raif turned to help. "Sandwiches, Coke, and a..."

"Snickering bar!"

Christ, Ash felt his heart slip. So this... this was who he lost Raif to.

The Snickers bar was lined up soldier-straight and a giggle drifted over. "Snickers... giggling bars."

Raif moved it away from her sandwiches. "Mum sez no treats till after dinner, if I remember right."

Voodoo nodded. "She did. Smart mommy. You can

come and meet her." The Coke popped open. "I told her you and Miss Shed could come and meet her."

"Hmmm, and she said what, Voodoo?"

A big bite went into the sandwich. "Good to have friends."

Raif nodded as Voodoo yawned. "I woke you up, huh?"

"Gettin' old," said the girl, and Raif choked a laugh. "Can't stay up so long anymore."

He ruffled her hair. "That's okay. You need your sleep."

She rubbed at her eyes, the midnight picnic forgotten. "Stay, though, right? Till just before Mummy is back?"

Raif moved the food and pulled back the covers so she could climb in. "Always, pumpkin."

"Good." She nodded, hair falling over eyes that were already half-closed. "And Miss Shed? She stay here too?"

Raif stroked over her cheek, a continuous brush of the back of his hand that had her breathing deep within a few moments. "Yeah, Miss Shed too. She likes to know you're asleep and safe...."

Ash's heart beat so hard against his chest. They shouldn't be here. They shouldn't be in this room, this house, and unease kicked in every instinct to run and get back into daylight. But he stayed there, leaning against the doorframe. He stayed because Raif pulled away from the girl and sat on the edge of the bed, reading a newspaper he slipped out from underneath his shirt. He stayed because there was a lock on the door that kept this little kid locked in her room at night, away from the world. Raif had opened the world up to her, but he hadn't let her out.

The only time Ash moved was when the clock started to touch 4:45 a.m., and he watched as Raif slid the chain back in place, keeping the sleeping girl locked inside.

Confused, angry, with guilt sneaking in too because he'd left a little girl locked there in the bedroom, still no fight or flight, he walked down the stairs before Raif had finished.

∾

Arms folded across his chest, Ash sat in the Ford again. Everything around him felt as dull and as black as the early morning mist that seemed to remember it was actually cloud and shouldn't be loitering with intent on the ground.

They were back driving through streets that Ash knew, Raif casting a glance back every now and again in the rear-view mirror.

"The mother…." Ash straightened and wiped a hand over his face. "She locks her daughter in there of a night?"

Raif didn't say anything for a moment, then eventually he reached over and switched the radio on. The clock touched 5:00 a.m.

"She does."

Ash looked at him. "And you… you *let* her? You walk about of a night knowing she's kept in that room."

"Yep."

Raif said nothing else, and Ash half shrugged, half raised a hand to try and physically catch whatever it was he was missing. "And?"

"And."

"Why?"

Raif switched on the heating as Ash blew hot air into his hands. Ash flicked him a look. "There are people that can help her."

"Yeah?" Raif shifted up a gear. "Did it look like she

needed help?"

"She was locked in her fucking room."

"By her mother."

"Yes—by her fucking mother. In what world is any of that okay with you?"

Raif shifted slightly and tugged out his phone. "Call it in," he said quietly, tossing it over. "Do the right thing in your world, Red. Or use your own phone you have on you that you haven't managed to break yet."

"The right thing in *my* world?" Ash couldn't have caught that right as he sat there. "In my fucking world?" He huffed. "There's another option here I'm missing?"

Raif stayed quiet for a moment. "Given the choice, not everyone calls for help, Ash. I thought you of all people knew that."

Ash sat back, more let life crumple for a moment as he looked down at the phone in his lap. Raif drove as though the road ahead was clearer than the streets, now the mist had lifted.

"Where are we going?" Ash asked numbly, putting the phone out of his mind for reasons he didn't understand, then handing it back to Raif. No. That was a lie. He did understand. He'd never called for help back when he'd met Raif, either, just flatlined, forcing Raif to sniff around in confusion as he played dead. Was that what this was? Another lesson in how he was a coward deep down, one that lingered, as lonely as a little girl locked in her room with Raif the only offer of humanity? Bastard.

"Home."

"Home?" Ash frowned.

"Aye, we're going back to yours."

"So this is what you do? You look after people of a night who you think need looking after? I'm a charity case?"

Raif didn't say anything

"Well fucking epic fail." Ash focused back on the window. "You missed saving the one who mattered. You missed saving Johnny."

CHAPTER 12
THE DOM

THE LOUNGE FELT odd, even with it being his home. Even though the shoes sitting in place of father's slippers marked that his father was home and in bed, Ash felt displaced as he sat on the settee, back rigid and straight. Maybe it was tiredness that gave it that spaced-out feel, but as he shifted awkwardly on the settee, it felt like something shifted with him. The angle of the painting above the mantelpiece of some ocean scene his dad liked cast longer shadows on the wall; smiles off the people walking the beach seemed brighter, too, as if they knew something was going on and they watched, a reversal through a TV screen where characters got to view the watchers for a change. A reversal of Jim's home, to here. Like at Jim's, how after he'd met Raif, the place seemed cleaner, or Ash felt dirtier... he didn't know. He couldn't put his finger on what it was. Life just felt... six-dimensional again, and he was still missing where this new night-time angle came from.

He'd wanted to know what Raif did, where he went, but the reality of it? No, not quite the reality of it. Raif always disappeared to Voodoo's of a weekend, just for a few hours. That didn't touch on where he disappeared to during the work week. What lost soul did he focus on there? Why did he focus on lost souls? Maybe he didn't intend to? Maybe the lost souls were more just a part of life he bumped into through what really kept him on the streets at night? So again it all came back to… what the hell was Raif? Who the hell was he?

Footsteps from the kitchen drew his ear, but he didn't look when someone came over and crouched down by him.

"What are you doing, Red?"

Raif's voice sounded wary, tired. That tiredness was there in his eyes when Ash looked up. He held a holdall, and when Ash said nothing, Raif paused a moment with a frown, then looked away, more turned his nose as if he chased a scent. The frown didn't shift as he refocused.

"Is there someone else here, Ash? Besides you and your dad?"

Ash frowned, looked around. Shook his head. Shrugged. "Just felt odd the past few days, a little crueller…. You been watching the place over the weekend? I mean, you must have, to have known I'd gone to the pub, right?"

Raif sniffed, then reached into the holdall and pulled out Coke, a Snickers bar, and two pieces of bread, and a few slices of ham. Never a loaf, always just what he'd used. "House rules," muttered Raif. "Always replace what you use." Had he been out and done just that: replaced what he'd used? The clock touched 6:00 a.m. now, so it was possible.

Ash laughed, really laughed, enough that he covered his nose when he snorted a little in the mix. "And you'd replace me, how?"

Raif rubbed at the ache in his kness. "I'm still not sure why, but you're the only part in my life that I'd never use or see replaced. No matter how much you piss me off." He eased to his feet and took his holdall into the kitchen.

Giving a frown, Ash took the food and followed the noises into the kitchen a moment later. He kept to the safety of the doorway, how he'd been around Raif when they'd first met, but also keeping one ear turned towards the stairs for his dad.

All fight in the kitchen had been cleaned away, the phone picked up, and Ash buried a groan. Whether his dad or Raif had tidied up was beside the point. He now owed Chase a new phone. Raif sorted through his bag as he sat at the table, and it amazed Ash how he worked as his dad slept. Yeah, it was still there, how they always said spiders were never more than a few feet away from someone, yet most people walked by not noticing. Raif was like that: there, in your home, but no one really ever noticing.

Ash folded his arms and rested his head against the doorframe. "How many waifs and strays do you visit?"

"How many have you heard about?"

Ash shrugged.

"There you go."

Ash snorted. Back to this again, how they'd met at Jim's. "You're just being an asshole again now."

"Aye. And you can leave and go to bed at any time you want, Red. There's nothing stopping you from crying help here with me. What does that still make you?"

Ash fell quiet, his look down at his feet followed by a look back into the lounge. Yeah, the coward who never ran, never cried for help, only kicked back with vicious games. "Tell me about the mother."

"Hm?" Raif was caught rubbing at his forehead.

"The mother." Ash rested his head back against the doorframe. "Tell me why you don't call for help."

That caught Raif's attention, more startled him a little with how his brown eyes hardened for a second, but then he eased back into his chair. "Her husband left her and Voodoo Doll about a year ago. Another woman and her family turned his eye, so he left one family for another." There was no judgement, more the *shit happens* account of facts. "Voodoo's mom had been working full-time up until then, both her and her husband working opposite shifts so Voodoo always had someone around. Normal struggles, normal life."

"Then the affair?"

Raif nodded. "She's a single mom on her own, working full-time during the day, and forced to take a few hours in the night at a garage to pay for school meals… school trips."

"She can't get Child Tax Credits? I thought they were there to help single families."

"Government takes a pretty hard line. Voodoo is full-time school age. Her mother has to work full-time. Full-time doesn't cover the cost of housing, Council Tax, gas, electric, school clothes, food…" Raif tapped lightly on the table, his mind somewhere else. "So she does the best she can with the little she's got."

"Even if it means locking her daughter in her bedroom of a night? Leaving her alone?"

"She's never alone, especially lately."

Ash scratched at his head. Still not understanding, he went over to the coffee maker and pulled two mugs free.

He made them both up, breathing in deep the rich roast. Two sugars went in Raif's, then he added a third without thinking.

Raif glanced up as he offered one down. "You're not gonna throw it over me?"

"I'd like to try and see even you delete a coffee."

Raif snorted a smile, then took it after he moved his holdall off the table.

Ash moved back over to the door, still listening out for his dad and when he'd have to start offering up reasons for the car. He'd no doubt been too drunk to notice last night, but Miles hadn't, and it was usually Miles who brought him home. Miles was good at shaking his head at Ash, though. He could smooth it over with Miles. "How did you know about her? About Voodoo?"

Raif took a long sip of his coffee, then another. "With Voodoo, a year ago I heard that Kerry had gone off the streets."

"Kerry?" Ash blew steam away from his drink. "Miss Shed?" It was a wild guess, but as she was the only other connection in this, it made sense.

Raif raised a brow at the name, then nodded. "Her tracks led me to Voodoo's, to the shed she'd taken to." He gave a hard sigh. "People live on the streets for multitudes of reasons. Kerry walked out on her family nearly twenty years ago after the death of her baby. He was a month old. She never looked back, not until she took a bottle of sterilised milk off Voodoo's doorstep and heard her crying in her room." Sadness crept up. "I don't think there's a good mother alive who can't answer the call of a crying child."

Ash watched him for a moment. "Or a good father?"

Raif kept coming back here. For a few days? Weeks? A month? Did he keep coming back for her? He had every look of a father, grieving. Was that what had caused the stroke and that haunting ability to only manage half a smile anymore? Had he lost a child? Ash felt such a bastard for pushing him tonight.

Raif said nothing, just gave a stretch, unfolding the full mass of his body, and Ash still felt like ducking away, even from this distance. "Was there a point where you wanted to call the police?"

Raif looked over. "No," he said quietly. "Voodoo's mom… she's working hard to look after her kid the best way she can with what life has given her. Mention her name to Voodoo, and it's there: her eyes light up."

"So where her mom can't give those few hours of safety during the night, there's this nightlife who do?"

"Nightlife?" Raif laughed softly, and it was the one element that didn't offer a bark or a bite. "They're just homeless, Ash, not different creatures walking a different world. But they've pulled ranks lately. There's a bad taste about."

"It's nightlife, so speak for yourself. It was bloody scary out there last night." Ash frowned. "And what do you mean about a bad taste?"

Raif's brow creased. "Not sure. Can't pin it down." There was a lie there, and it surprised Ash how he could read that in Raif. His look said he'd seen something that had disturbed him. "But when the homeless go quiet and start listening, you know something's wrong."

"And you've been with Voodoo more and more since we last met?"

Raif shook his head. "I've been away." And he left it at

that. "You were scared?" Raif frowned. "Tonight?"

"Shiteless."

"You didn't have to come."

"You were being a prick with my dad's car."

Raif took the last sip, then put the mug on the table. "You took it first. I brought it home."

Ash did a dance between them with his finger. "This you-me shit, been here before."

"Yeah, and again you didn't cry out for help, Ash, just… lingered. Why was that?"

Raif left that hanging there, and Ash dropped his head, catching on and maybe adding *cunt* to his own list now. Raif had a good heart, hands scarred but big enough to hold a little girl safely. Again Ash had pissed all over that.

He gave a heavy sigh. "So you give money to Kerry." He found Raif again. "Why don't you just give that money to Voodoo and her mother?"

"And then have her mother wonder where the money keeps coming from? People aren't stupid, Ash. Not if a lump sum of money suddenly turns up in the letterbox."

"So it goes where?"

"It goes to Voodoo's dad."

Ash scowled. "What the hell for?"

"Child Maintenance." And it was said as if it made perfect sense.

"But…" Ash shrugged. "If that bastard cheated on his wife, there's no guarantee in hell he'd pay child support."

"He pays."

Ash waited for the rest. "Why?"

Raif got to his feet and took his cup over to the sink.

"He just does."

"As simple as that?" Raif came back over, and Ash shifted to allow him to go into the lounge. "As easy as that?"

"He has a nice home, too."

Ah... oh. He bet Voodoo's dad hadn't been on holiday when Raif had stopped there, just like when Ash had been house-sitting at his boss's when Raif had "visited" there.

Raif eased down onto the sofa, looking ready to call it more than a night and sleep. Ash stayed by the door, but the coffee cup found a shelf nearby. "Have you ever been caught?"

Raif didn't lift his head up off the back of the sofa. "No."

"But you are homeless?"

"Nope. I just have many homes." That sneered smile, maybe more than a little cocky now. "I'm the best at what I do."

Giving a wipe at his nose, Ash glanced back at the bag. He didn't see it, though, only a black-haired Voodoo Doll who could charm beasts from the forest, who had seen the beast and never once chuckled and called out *scary fucker*.

Ash dipped his head, then went over to Raif and straddled his lap, coming down and framing his face with his hands as he went close to his lips.

"You scare me every moment I'm with you," mumbled Ash. "You know that?"

Raif nodded, his hands coming into play on Ash's hips, his back, but never touching his ass. "Likewise at times, Red. You scare me."

Ash frowned, his touch still mapping Raif's face, all the

roads he'd walked of a night right there for the reading. "Sorry."

"Sorry?"

Ash brushed a kiss at his lips. "For being an asshole and scaring you." He gave a sad smile. "You're a damn good man."

"You're not?"

Ash rested his head against Raif's and closed his eyes as he shook his head. "I linger, and I'm scared I'll be doing it for the rest of my life, alone."

Raif's touch pulled him in a little tighter. "Yeah. You lost your echo despite still shouting at the world, flitter.... Maybe that's why you keep me coming back." He said that so quietly. "I'm going to say it again, Ash. Do you know the symptoms? I mean really know the symptoms?"

Ash gripped a little tighter onto Raif. They'd tried to have this conversation before. Ash hadn't wanted to hear excuses for what he did back then either.

"With PTSD? Because I do." Raif stroked at his side. "Reckless behaviour, the revenge porn, following me tonight despite the danger? I saw you vomiting at Mack's at the thought of going to the police. Intense irritation, mood swings, trust issues.... Hyper-vigilance over thinking you're being watched... have you seen how you've been watching the night lately?" He fell quiet. "How long have you been scared, Ash?" he whispered in his ear. "And I mean really scared beyond just meeting me for that first time?"

Ash stroked at Raif's jaw, the hardness there. "Don't reason my shit with excuses, Raif. I don't think there are any."

"Yeah? That barman whose life you could have ruined last night," Raif said gently, teasing a bite at his ear. "He won't be the last you play like that until you get help, you can see that, right? You and Chase? And I damn well know he wasn't your first over the years. Sandy… do you know he ended up in hospital a few days later? He overdosed. Freddie… he lost his boyfriend and walked out on his job because of the shit you both pulled. Did you even know about that?"

Ash stiffened. He hadn't known. No.

"Hm," said Raif. "You don't think the barman's wife would have taken his playing around just as hard? You've been hitting out like that for years, not weeks, Ash, not just since Johnny's death. You need to admit there's a problem here."

Ash gripped Raif a little harder. Yeah he knew. He and Chase, they had a problem. It's why Raif had stuck around a few months back. But was that why he hadn't told Chase about Raif? That he'd kept Raif away, locked in the night as much as Raif lived by it, because he didn't want to risk exposing Raif to Chase… what they did when they got together? Johnny had been exposed to it and they'd lost him. Would he lose what little he had of Raif too, if Raif kept seeing them play together like that?

"I would have deleted that video," Ash said quietly.

"I know. But…." A sigh came. "But you need to stop."

"I had."

"You fell back into it, if only a little." A touch traced inside Ash's hoodie, up his sides. "All that ill intent…. What the fuck would it be like to see you fall in love body and soul, not just body, and see the good in you come out? Because it's there, Ash. So bloody much. Stop fucking about and poisoning it. You… you're such a unique find."

"I'm nothing special, Raif. But how you keep pushing

those locked doors to make me feel that way? Thank you...."

Ash shifted, taking Raif down to lie on the settee and coming down on top of him, keeping lip to lip and chasing his tongue. Raif's leg split his now, and he dipped his hips, once, twice, riding that thick thigh and the friction it drove into his cock. A nip caught Raif's neck, then Ash went in, biting and roughing up the skin as hard as he rode Raif's thigh.

"Fuck." Raif groaned, gripping Ash's hair and tugging him in closer, feeding the bite, the run of marks Ash left. Then his hand slipped between their bodies again and rubbed hard into Ash's cock.

Ash took him by the wrist and made sure it found the space above Raif's head. He did the same with the other, his body now flat on Raif's, lips held inches from neck.

"Can I fuck you?" Ash kissed at his cheek, his lips, then paused as he cuddled in close to the curve of his throat. Christ, he'd missed all this so fucking much. "Even though I've pissed you off tonight?"

"You feel you can't ask me something because I'm angry, we have problems, Ash." It came so gently. "You feel you can't touch me when I'm angry, we have bigger problems."

Ash took a long hard breath. "No. If I ever forget to ask to touch, especially when you're angry, then I have no right to any part of you. So I'll ask again, even though I've pissed you off, even though you've been angry with me... will you still let me touch you?"

"Christ." Raif shifted, flipping Ash and putting him on his back, underneath Raif, nearly crushing him, but the weight roughed his cock in all the right ways, leaving him lost for breath. "What you have inside, those fucking instincts, Ash…" A return vicious bite came at his throat, leaving him twisting his head and taking it, loving it—his cock hurting from it. "Come on. Fuck me."

Ash shifted with Raif, first onto his elbows, watching as Raif pulled off his jacket, his shirt, then easing up and over him as Raif eased down onto his back.

Raif gripped the tail of Ash's hoodie as he did, and Ash pulled his arms free as his chest and abs were exposed to the cool of the lounge.

"Come on." Raif met him for a kiss, roughing up his lips and almost stealing the pace, so Ash grabbed his hair, tugging his head back down to the settee and exposing his throat again.

Raif was all chest and chest hair, muscular thighs with the same thick black covering, and Ash nuzzled down, finding his way and bruising a nipple, biting long and hard enough to have Raif's hips up off the settee. Ash's hard grip into his jeans, a crush against balls, had Raif cooling in the next breath, then Ash shifted back, peeling jeans and boxers away. It left Raif naked and sprawled out, thick cock curved at the tip and dancing at being free. Balls were heavy in Ash's palm, full, and he tugged them down, away from Raif, forcing Raif to arch his back. As Ash released his grip and Raif instantly eased into the couch in relief, Ash went with him, his body back over Raif's.

He took Raif's hands above his head, pinning him down press-up style with one of his as he put a little distance between their chests. Then he freed his own cock, fisting the length, swiping a thumb over the tip to catch the precome as he played his cock against Raif's hole. It looked good down there, Raif left damp from him, damp with him, so he shifted, catching their cocks together and working more precome as he rutted into Raif.

"Christ yeah, come on, baby." A shiver ran Ash's shoulders at the huskiness to Raif's voice, as thick as the chest hair coating him, as warm, as welcoming. Ash played Raif's hole a little more, then grinned as he dipped his fingers in Raif's mouth, hunting more lube as he fucked along Raif's cock with his own. Their balls collided, stealing groans and grunts from both of them; then Ash had had enough of playing. He'd played too much tonight. He just needed Raif. To be inside Raif and knowing nothing else.

Raif seemed to pick up on the change too, knee lifting just slightly to allow more up-close and personal access.

Still holding him down, Ash teased his cock against Raif's ass, that shiver infecting his whole body as his cockhead touched home for a first time, then focusing him completely as he fisted himself against Raif for the second, the hood of his cock exposed on each swipe and meeting skin.

A dip of his hips, Ash pushed against him, testing, just stretching the muscles, then his head breached Raif, and Ash cried out a little with it, dropping his head a touch before he sought more: pulling back, pushing forward until he buried his first long fuck into him.

"Shit... shit. That's a fucking damn big cock, Ash." Raif brought his knees up more, knowing his own body, guiding Ash to peg the right spot inside—then Ash groaned and didn't stop fucking into him, barely losing pace with how the night had driven his body too much already. Sweat ran his back, dripped from his lips, and he licked it off Raif's as he stretched his body to the limit. At one point Raif had a hand free, raking Ash's back, forcing Ash to curve his body into it, then he blindly found Raif's hand again and tugged it back above his head.

It felt too good, knowing Raif took him, allowed Ash to take him, so he framed Raif's head, fingers now linked as his strokes became faster, shorter, leaving him panting, fighting his orgasm as Raif writhed and called out quietly beneath him.

Then when another bite went to his throat, even to bruise... bleed... Ash came, everything calming and exploding in the same moment. All the time Raif bit his neck through it, either threatening to draw the come out of him there to focus Ash, or cry out his own need and stem any noise.

"Fuck... fuck." Ash breathed hard, screwing his eyes shut and collapsing onto Raif. Hands roamed his ass, his side, thick thighs moving and rutting into him.

"Fuck." That came from Raif, his groan and shift of body rubbing his own come into Ash's. Ash loved the feel of being so close, still being cock-deep in Raif, come between them, shared heavy breaths, body heat, fast-paced hearts that only just started to cool to the aftermath. It had been fast, over quickly, but leaving him utterly exhausted because of the flash flood of heat.

"Yeah, how fucking good would it be to see how intensely you love away from sex, Ash...."

Ash kissed his lips, his jaw, his neck, then shifted slightly and sought out his hoodie. Raif cocked a smile as Ash eased up and started wiping at their lower abs, then between Raif's thighs.

"Yep, you know you've been with someone a while when they use a shirt to clean up the mess."

Ash flashed him a smile, then buried a yawn as he left the hoodie between them and came back down on Raif. "You gonna stay around long enough for me to fall to sleep? Just a few more minutes? It's getting on for seven, and you usually run off by now."

A long stroke came at his side. "Do you need me here for a few more minutes?"

Ash cuddled in, his arms wrapping Raif as Raif shifted to his side, tugging Ash with him so they faced each other.

"Yeah. I need you here for a few more minutes."

A kiss came at Ash's cheek, his jaw. "Then get your head down, flitter. I'm going nowhere for a while."

That was the lie, Ash knew that; Raif would be gone as soon as he fell asleep. But he settled and slept with it all the same.

"Just... Ash?"

"Hmm?" He was nearly gone.

"Don't go out in the dark on your own, not unless you're with Chase. Not until I can find out what's going on with Sasha... Johnny, okay?"

"Hm?" He caught that. Barely.... "Dark... Sashes... Johnny. Chase. Sure." Goblins. Chase had mentioned something about goblins and being gobbled in the night.... Ash gave a sleepy smile, a soft laugh. Better times... it had been better times back there, with Johnny....

CHAPTER 13
BURN

HUSHES AND THE sound of muffled laughter drifted up, and Ash fought the need to turn over and bury it all in his pillow and more sleep. But the thud that came next had him sighing and glancing at the clock.

11:30 a.m.

Ash got up on his elbows, then scratched his head as he looked around his bedroom.

Ohhhkay. The settee and being pretty damn comfortable came to mind, so did Raif. Raif ass-naked on his couch especially came to mind, but… but….

Always that fucking but with Raif.

Other images filtered through. Being nudged off the settee, forced to find his feet, then chuckles as he'd called the bastard responsible a sadist, one he was going to hook up to his dad's car battery and light up his balls like those on a Christmas tree, then his own shuffle of feet up the stairs.

His cheeks burned. Just after seven, had Raif put him to bed? How fucked up was that?

Another thud came from downstairs and... fuck. 11:30 a.m.

Carole.

Ash scooted out of bed and rushed to change his jeans and tug on a vest to get downstairs. It was Sunday, Carole the carer's day, and.... Fuck. He'd had sex on the settee this morning, with his hoodie nowhere in sight up here in his bedroom.

He made it downstairs, the stair lift sitting happily at the bottom, and showing his dad was already up and roaming the house. Ash groaned. Not only the car missing from the drive last night, but also sexed-up shirts on the lounge floor, showing he'd really had one hell of a party. Double shit....

He skipped the noise from the kitchen, dodging the doorway and scrambling into the lounge, but a quick look saw Ash relax. Raif lived up to his name: leave it as you find it. All cushions back in place and no sign of a come-stained hoodie. He let out a steady breath, gave a rub at his hair, then headed on into the kitchen.

Football results came through on the radio and Carole tutted her way through them.

"Hey." Ash did a quick check of the washing basket. His hoodie already sat safely through a hot wash. "Where's Dad this morning, Carole?"

Shutting the oven door with her knee, Carole glanced back and smiled. Her crisp beige shirt was crumpled in places, and powder marks on her hips suggested she'd been grappling some home-made Yorkshire puds, and losing, by the look of the batter splatter close to one breast. But Dad always insisted on having the Yorkshire puds for Sunday dinner, same too with mint sauce, except, of course, with beef. "You don't ever dress beef up in kink with mint sauce, lad. Not right... not natural," he always said.

"He's in the greenhouse." Carole turned the heat down on the spuds. "You eaten, love?"

He patted his stomach. He couldn't remember the last time he had. He got a look that said it didn't matter what he'd eaten, he obviously needed more of it. Spotted Dick sat ready to be baked in the oven, and Ash bit back every grin over getting free reign to say "dick" as a kid. Come nine... ten years old, every lad would jump on any reason to go for the groin. It was the one time most boys didn't suffer on the language side and suddenly found they had an affinity for using the proper terms. Dick, cock, balls, sac... they all came out at that age. "Got any custard for that pudding?"

"For you, maybe, and—" The latest Man U and Liverpool result came in, and Carole waved him away, turning her ear to the radio as she checked the sprouts. "Greenhouse. Miles is in there too."

Ash brightened. Miles was good. Miles meant backup, or some at least.

The greenhouse overtook the lawn on many counts. Ash had long since stopped needing to kick a ball about, so his dad dove into his veg and flowers like a madman over the last year or so. Yet as he made his way over, to the backdoor, something made him pause, just stalling something inside of him as the key in the lock held his attention.

You're not a good man, Ash?

He frowned at Raif's words.

He was good, right? At some point he hadn't twisted the game play to his advantage and danced in the fallout. He'd trusted the cops. Christ knows he'd loved one, still did. And he'd been loved back, right? Back then, before that… that key in the lock, how it swung like an old friend from a tree, a life pendulum that counted the minutes away, each swing matching the ticking of the kitchen clock, each swing counting down how life shunned the body, left it lingering….

PTSD. Do you know the symptoms, Ash? Because I do….

∾

Ash, age 9

"I can't talk to you or Chase." Johnny sounded really quiet on the phone as Ash sat on the stairs, cradling the receiver to his ear. "But Mom had a word with Dad about us getting suspended from school, and they said maybe we can hang out when your suspension is over." He perked up a little. "Said it would be good, pinching that hair from the salon and clogging up the drains by the sports hall. Got us out of PE, dain't it?"

Yeah, and one hell of a suspension for all three of them. The headmaster hadn't been happy. "You heard anything off Chase?" Ash asked eventually.

"His nanna's at home at the moment, so he's not had any comeback yet. But he's quiet."

Ash sighed into their silence. "Preston's a—"

"Assbat," said Johnny. "Don't let him get to you, Ashy. Ride the suspension. Preston's a…" He whispered the last word, and Ash could picture him covering the mouthpiece. "Dickhead."

Ash chuckled. Preston was. One of the biggest. He glanced into the lounge, then at the hall clock.

"You gonna be able to ride the grounding your old dad will give ya?" asked Johnny, his voice quiet again.

"Yeah. He's not back yet. I'm still sitting with Miles."

"Another ride in a police car? Not your first, though, little Ashy. It's your future."

Ash chuckled. "Not funny, Joshbone. So not funny. Miles stopped me when I walked home early. He's just worried."

Johnny was laughing now when a voice from his end drifted through, calling his name. "Ughh, gotta go," he said, going quiet again. "Just a week, though, bud, right? We can do that?"

"Yeah, we can do that. Try and get in touch with Chase for me. Make sure he's okay."

Johnny's name was called again, louder this time. "'Kay, 'kay, I'm getting off now." And back to Ash—"This time next week, I'll be at your door! Chase's too."

Ash glanced at the door, the image already there and making him wish the week away. "Good, good, mate."

Ash slipped the phone back on the unit and headed back into the lounge. Miles was on the settee, flicking through the channels now that Ash had set him up.

"You need a drink, kid?" said Miles, glancing over. He didn't look like he wanted to move, though, not now he looked comfortable.

It had done his street cred loads of good with having Miles pull up and pick him up as he'd headed out of the school gates. Certainly turned a few heads.

"No, I'm good. I have a Coke in the kitchen." He pointed behind him. "You want one?" He should offer to get him a drink, right? That's what his dad always asked him to do.

"No, I'm good." Miles smiled over, then he picked up the PlayStation remote. "Fancy a game?"

Ash grinned. Like hell did he.

The cut of headlight shifting shadows across the lounge had them both looking towards the window. The familiar crawl of tyre on concrete calmed Ash.

"Oh…" Miles put the remote down and Ash got a ruffle of hair as he stood. "Another time, chimp. Dad's home."

And the turn of a lock came…

The door pushed open, and Ash ambled behind Miles into the hall. Mumbled hellos and byes came before the front door shut behind Miles and keys were left to swing in the lock. His dad's coat went on the coat stand, then Ash sniffed as polished shoes made quiet footfalls on their cream-coloured carpet.

"Dad—"

A light tap to his jaw said it was time to face the music and he caught the concern there in his dad's eyes. "Yeah, I heard."

His uniform wasn't that different to Miles's, just carrying two pips to show an inspector, instead of the stripes belonging to a constable or sergeant. His dad had attached a few onto Ash's police uniform, back when Ash was four.

"I'm sorry." It came out fast, followed by a rush of why, when, and how, but his dad sighed and waved him into the kitchen. "You know the rules, Ash." His dad went over to the kettle and switched it on. He patted the unit. "C'mon, assume the position."

Ash went over, looked at the unit, then eased himself up.

"Right." His dad handed him a Coke before easing up onto the unit next to Ash. "Good before any… negative."

Ash smiled down as his dad's legs dangled lower than his. Scuffs marked the cupboard, showing how he was catching up fast. This shared sitting place had seen them grow over the years. Ash wasn't quite as tall, but he'd get there.

"Well, despite us pinching hair from the salon bins to stuff down the shower room, then flooding the hall because of it… Miles nearly hit Mr Preston's car on the way out too." Ash hid a smile against the Coke can. "Said he hadn't changed from when he used to be there." He bypassed the part about the head's office and him, Chase, and Johnny getting shouted at for flooding the PE hall.

His dad glanced down at him. "Only nearly hit it?"

Ash nodded.

"Shame." Now his dad fought a smile. "We get so many call-outs to that school because student support can't implement a decent anti-bullying programme. Even my sergeants are starting to feel like bullies for the amount of times they have to go in there and—"

"Bully?"

"—convince them to handle kids who are being bullied. They need more liaison with the likes of CAMHS."

Ash nodded, although he didn't really understand who CAMHS were and what they did. It fell quiet for a minute, and Ash played with the rim of his Coke. "I'm really sorry, Dad."

"I know, kid. But let's leave it for a while, okay? I've just got home from a… shit day, and I don't want to talk about it when all that…" He frowned. "All that anger could rub off on how we handle this, okay."

Ash let his hand find his dad's leg. "'Kay, Dad. Can… can I get you a sandwich?"

"Chips." His dad grinned at him. "I fancy chips, paperwork, then a few hours on Pacman before you get your bath."

"Pacman? Anyone tell you how old you are?"

A hand patted his. "But I still beat you at it, kid. That's not old. That's skill!"

Ash dried himself down, then slipped into his PJs, hating how his damp hair suckered the collar to his neck. Shivering slightly, he padded on through to his bedroom and slipped beneath his bedcovers. His PS2 was still on, and he retook up his fight on *Ape Escape 2*, loving the feel of clean sheets on clean skin.

He was lucky. Johnny's occupancy of his bedroom over his own or Chase's told him that, but so did the sound of footsteps on the stairs.

The smell of hot chocolate drifted over as his dad placed it on the bedstand. It mixed with the smell of smoke, and Ash frowned a little. His dad must have had a tough day. He only smoked when he was stressed.

"C'mon, chimp, budge over." Ash shifted over as his dad sat down, one hand aimed carefully away from the bed as he then lay down on his side. "You know this is the last night, then you're banned for a week on this?"

Ash nodded, fingers moving light over the remote. It was part of the punishment: no talking to Chase and

Johnny. No PS1 or 2 for the duration he was suspended. Bed by 7:00 p.m. No movies after seven either. All the money he was saving for a PS3 would go towards any costs Preston sent over, but other than that?

Ash cast a quick look over to his dad, then eased down under the covers a little more.

They were okay. They had been all right before his mother left. Now, they were more than okay.

"Right." His dad looked at his watch. "Seven it is." Ash got a tap on his PS2. "Lights out, kiddo."

Ash didn't even protest. He dropped the PS2 on the bedside table, took a sip of hot chocolate, killed the table lamp, then settled down to face his dad. For a moment, his dad blinked, just watching him, then a sad smile crept up.

"Christ, you have your mother's eyes…. Missing her?"

Ash shook his head. He hadn't thought about her in years. Sometimes it was easier not to think. She'd walked away; his dad hadn't. His dad was real, not some dream he woke crying from, chasing blurred images and distorted feelings down the school playground.

He got a stroke to his cheek. "I bet she misses you?"

"Don't think so," said Ash. "She wouldn't have left if she did."

He got a nod off his dad, then he was pulled into a hug. "Ash, you're a good kid. Don't change that. Okay?" A hand rubbed his back, distractedly tugging on the hem of his PJ top and catching skin. Ash shuffled slightly, cuddling up close and needing the contact.

"Like today, records stay with you, kid. Stay with you and—" His dad took a deep breath of smoke, exhaled, and—

Ash cried out, not recognising the cigarette touching

down on his ass cheek until his dad pulled him in close, rocking and cursing out loud.

"Fuck... sorry, so sorry, kid!"

Ash tried to push away and grab the hurt when the burn still seemed to sear into his skin, but his dad held him close, catching his hands and hugging him tight.

Ash lay there sobbing, long strokes at his hair doing nothing to calm his shaking.

"Accident. Stupid accident, kid. Sorry, so sorry." His dad cried too, and Ash stopped fighting, torn at the grief. His dad never cried. "Didn't mean to hurt you. Didn't mean it, but ugly. Like that record you earned today, scars stay with you, and ugly... they make you so fucking ugly, kid—"

"'S okay, Duh-Dad." Ash held on tightly, knowing his dad would get something for the hurt. He was just upset now, but Dad would get something for the stinging soon. He'd do that, right? Soon? Because the longer he didn't, the more it hurt. "Sorry, Dad. Don't... don't be sad, please."

The rocking calmed him a little, maybe even worked some magic, because he felt a hard drag into sleep despite the shaking going on with his small body.

"Don't change, Ash. Please. Stay good."

"Pro... promise, Dad. Good. I'll stay good."

"Love you, kid."

"Love... love you too, Dad."

CHAPTER 14
AFTERBURN

IGNORING THE HURT hidden under his pyjama bottoms, Ash... lingered in the doorway to the kitchen the next morning, watching his dad. Two breakfast bowls sat on the kitchen table, spoons lined up by their sides, and milk glistened in a cooled jug, playing ref in the centre. Juice made friends with his bowl, a steaming mug of tea with his dad's, and from the radio the football results came through, leaving his dad muttering behind his gardening magazine as he sat at the table.

Ash still stood there in the doorway, arms hugging his little stomach as he leaned into the doorframe. He'd been there for a few minutes, but an invisible field seemed to stop him from going any further, from making any noise.

Sunlight warmed the kitchen tiles, streaking across them and sleeping happily enough over his dad's slippers over by the door. He had his polished shoes on now, ready for work, and the tick of the clock, counting up to eight in the morning said Miles would be knocking on the door soon.

Ash would usually be in there now, getting another cup

for Miles and having his dad look over his magazine as he made Miles a drink. That was his latest level he'd unlocked: big enough now to handle the kettle, so long as his dad stayed close, making sure he didn't scald himself, because...

... ugly. Scars stay with you and make you so fucking ugly....

He didn't want to be ugly. Not in his dad's eyes. Never in his dad's eyes.

But no matter how lightly the sun danced around the kitchen with the music, he felt ugly, like he didn't belong. He'd gone to sleep in one game, then woke to a beta version where things were still the same *except* him because....

...ugly, kid. Scars make you so fucking ugly....

He started to shiver.

"C'mon, Ash. Battery's got to be fully charged now. Carole'll be here soon."

Ash jolted at the shout, despite how his head expected it, and his dad jerked in the same instant, turned back, smiled over.

"Ah, Christ, you scared the life out of me, Ash. Come on. Come and get your breakfast."

He paused, watching his dad, then his dad broadened his smile and waved him in. "C'mon. What you being a plank of wood for?"

Ash's heart skipped a little faster. That look didn't say he was ugly. He hadn't screwed up. He went over, the tug of pyjama—how it caught the bubble of liquid from the burn on his ass—hurt, sure. But his dad went back to reading his magazine the same way he did every day.

Ash pulled the chair out and slipped down, keeping to the edge, feet flat on the floor to keep any pressure away from his butt cheek. He hadn't looked, didn't want to see the ugly, just fingered around it as the covers kept him hidden in his room this morning.

Ash shivered as a knock came on the back door and his dad hollered a "come in." Ugly. He wasn't ugly, right?

"Morning, sir." Miles put his policeman's hat on the table, then Ash got a rub to his hair. "Mornin' to you too, chimp."

"Morning." He kept that quiet, ducking away from the hair roughing.

"Ash, tea."

He looked up and his dad shifted his jaw in the direction of the kettle. The smile still sat there. That was his dad still sitting there. And Ash... that look, the same smile, it said he didn't have any ugly on him. It was gone from last night.

"Go on, then, lad. Get Miles a brew."

Ash slipped to his feet, then made it over to the counter where the kettle sat. He pulled a mug off the rack and heaped two sugars in as he boiled the kettle. When he glanced back, Miles frowned over at him, and Ash quickly looked away. Concern said he still wore some ugly. Could Miles see the burn? Ash stilled. He didn't want anyone seeing the burn. He wouldn't let no one see the burn. He took the tea over and pushed it back to Miles, a little mad that Miles worried.

"Thanks, bud." The ruffle of hair he got off his dad set his insides hurting. They were good. They were still good. It hurt too much to think he could be anything but good and change that.

So Ash shoved the hurt away, put it in a box and shut the lid tight shut, as he sat back down. Miles tried to catch his eyes a few times, but Ash kept his eyes on his dad. Heat filled his cheeks if he let his thoughts stray to the hurt on his ass. What kid got hurt on his ass? Only babies. Babies or…

…kid. Scars make you so fucking ugly, kid, and….

∾

"Ash?" Standing by the kitchen door, watching the keys swing in the lock, Ash was brought back by the call of his name. "You okay? You look like you drank the wrong medicine."

Ash frowned back at Carole, not really seeing her for a moment. "Yeah… yeah." He wasn't, he felt like throwing up, but he wouldn't. Ugly… just keep it on the inside.

Ash tugged open the door, then pushed outside and headed over to the greenhouse. Careful to make sure the door shut behind him, keeping the heat in on an already body-melting day, he made his way through the lines of carrots, broccoli, and beetroot, always loving the scent of the peony and orchids growing a few feet away. How had Raif gotten on in here over the past few weeks? Had he carried this scent away with him when he'd left for the work week? Would some of his scent be here?

Ash smiled to himself as he tested that theory out, and yeah, there was… something in here that shouldn't be.

The creak of the wheelchair gave his dad away, and Ash headed over and kissed his head. "How you doing, Pops?" He didn't need the wheelchair often, just on bad days. Today must have been a bad day.

Miles stood close by, arms folded, and looking like he'd climb out the window if he could. He'd switched roles with his dad at one stage, Miles taking the rank to his uniform and his dad retiring, but sometimes, just sometimes, he got caught out with a look off Ash's dad that put him back to PC, waiting around. Not that Miles's smile said he minded. Miles just tried to mouth something to Ash that made Miles look uncomfortable.

Car...? Doesn't know...?

Oh! Ash caught on. His dad *hadn't* noticed the car had gone missing. He gave Miles a *fuck, thank-you* wink as his dad waved him closer, but made sure he covered up the echo of his last burn so Miles couldn't see that. Ash bent to look at the stream of tomato plants his dad had just watered, from how the watering can sat teetering close to the edge of the work station. Ash pushed it safely back into place.

"Damn greenfly again. Look," said his dad.

Ash focused back on the tomato plant, then shrugged at Miles. A single greenfly dirtied its way on the stem, and a tut came from his dad.

"I thought bug killer was supposed to work?" Ash picked the fly off with a tissue and made sure it wouldn't bug another plant. He offered it to Miles.

"You're on your own, there, mate," he got back and Ash chuckled, tossing it in the bin.

"She got the wrong one."

Ash frowned at his dad. "Who did?"

His dad waved back in the direction of the house. "Her. The bitch. Good job she makes a killer roast. I'd have sacked her ages ago."

"You'd have to pay her first, Pops."

His dad mimicked his speech with his hand, then tugged at Ash's sleeve, all to return the kiss Ash had given him. "Afternoon, son." He got a school-teacher look over the rim of glasses. "You didn't come home last night."

Ash looked down at his fingers. "Just got in late," he said quietly, then gave a sad smile up at him. "I said I might head out with Chase if he could drag his mood to the phone." Ash winced. His dead phone now. Christ, Chase was gonna kill him. "I told you, remember?"

"You did, huh?" A frown came.

"Left a note here too, Pops." Ash took the sticky note that had gotten lost under the mail, pinned on the board by Carole.

"Ah, yes, you did." His dad smiled again. "You eaten?"

"Yeah."

"Meh, liar. You never eat." A wry look gave blue eyes some old sparkle. "But you want pudding, right?"

Ash grinned. "Yep, pudding."

"Then go get a shower and have it with us after dinner. Miles, you with us?"

Miles shook his head madly at Ash.

"He's got to get back to Rhiannon, Dad." Ash buried a chuckle at the return *fuck, thank you* that came his way.

"Speaking of such. Look at the time." Miles didn't even check. "Catch you two later." *Much later* his eyes cried as Ash patted his abs on passing. He left them to it.

"Maybe you could invite Chase and Johnny too, Ash?" His dad shifted the glasses on his nose and leaned in to inspect the tomato plant again. "They always come around when there's a whiff of food."

The tug of hurt hit so hard. "Johnny..." Ash frowned as Miles paused and passed a sad look over. He left a moment later. With his dad's mini-strokes and reduced oxygen to the brain and memory, Johnny lived and died a hundred times over in this house, along with the burns and scalds Ash took. Each time forgotten, each time... "Johnny's busy, Dad. He says hello and sorry for not coming around to see you." He couldn't face the truth again at that moment. Sometimes the lie helped. There was always that room for Johnny to come back and do that in his dad's eyes. Always the innocence that Johnny wouldn't be the sort to get caught in some kinky sex act.

A huff was given. "Chase it is, then." Quiet. "But you two boys are too damn old to be sharing the same bed nowadays."

Ash choked. "Erm, yeah, sure. Just... just make sure you wash up, Dad, okay? Remember you're dealing with chemicals."

"Stop mothering me, kid." But his dad reached for the soap wash anyway, then did a double wave to show just how clean they were. Ash loved and hated him for it, for those hands and how playful they were one moment, then burning into him the next.

"We do good now, don't we, kid?" He got a sad smile back. "Us? You're a good lad."

Going over to the door, Ash reached for the handle. There seemed to be an apology in there somewhere, although the puzzlement on his dad's face said he couldn't for the life of him remember why he should apologise. Ash gave a nod back, burying old angers, ones that some guy would cry out for him later. Seemed there were some excuses after all. Not one of them made him proud. "Yeah, Pops. We do good now. See you later."

"Ash."

Ash looked back to see his dad holding up a paper.

"You forgot this."

Ash frowned. They didn't have one delivered, his dad preferring to keep away from all the shit that went on outside. He went over and took it before heading outside.

There was only one other person he knew who carried a newspaper around with him for late-night visits. And he never usually left behind any evidence.

Ash flipped to a page that had its corner folded, where it showed this week's crosswords.

None of it had been filled in, and only two words in the clues were circled:

Midnight. Saturday.

Ash quirked a smile, then wondered why. The bastard had been gone by morning, but that was good men for you. Always a kick in the guts somewhere along the line.

He looked around, then sighed.

Midnight Saturday next week it was, though, no doubt after Raif had visited Voodoo. A big part of him didn't mind being put second. He liked the image of the ogre sitting at the bottom of a girl's bed, reading her a story.

You aren't a good man, Ash?

No. Ash had grown up along the way too. Now he tore everyone else down away from here because he couldn't tear his dad to pieces. Nothing more, nothing less. He couldn't explain that to Raif and expect him to understand. Ash wasn't Voodoo. He was everything she should never grow up to be.

And badness only ever attracted badness.

CHAPTER 15
DON'T... FEED THE BADNESS

FROM ACROSS THE backyard at No 12, Gray took a sip of his coffee before readjusting the lens on his telescope as it focused on Ash and his dad. Ash trudged his way back to the house, shoulders dropped and gaze on the path he walked.

And what a stunning path he walked.

It hadn't cost much to rent out the property just at the back of the Thomas' residence. From what the estate agent had said to Andrews, the two-bedroom flat had been empty for a few months, like one or two others clustered together along the street. Furniture was a bare minimum: a three-piece suite in the lounge with a flat screen, the latter kept on just to keep up appearances with any neighbour nosy enough to listen in. The fridge in the kitchen kept the basic stock of milk and bread, with coffee and a stray packet of cigarettes keeping the cupboards company. He'd started smoking a little more lately, maybe missing Jack's old habit by taking to courting another. Either way, he didn't keep his usual brand here, just a cheap alternative, the same with his cologne. In the bedroom that gave him a good surveillance point for the Thomas residence, a single bed slept with some of his surveillance equipment: standard listening equipment that required no devices placed on scene, camera, various lenses for his telescope, and just under his bed, a choice of small firearms. He kept his silencer closer.

At his side on the bedside unit sat a laptop, the details he'd picked up kept stored on an external cloud system. For the time he'd been here, only one name was written down.

Raif.

All details surrounding Ash hadn't taken long to find, and Gray had everything from Ash's employment to place of address within the first few hours of arriving on scene. His history with Chase hadn't taken much longer: their game play with other men, video files, school, school records, medical history, how they'd been lovers for a while before realising friendship was worth more. That had led to wider circles of how Johnny had been friends with them at school, how they'd all gone to work at the same factory, with Johnny knuckling down most and moving up the internal inspection ladder, more so than Ash or Chase as they seemed content to fill in the manufacturing gaps wherever possible and play whatever games to get their kicks on the sidelines. As he'd listened in, Gray agreed with Raif's assessment: Ash had symptoms of PTSD, only he'd classify it more as Complex PTSD: established over years, not weeks.

Ash and Chase had found Johnny's body, and from conversations Gray had picked up, Ash and Chase still thought his death was a suicide. There was no lie there in their grief and anger. Nor in how they were factory boys working a factory week. Only their play with other men kept him watching them both.

Ash's abuse had taken a little longer. That intel had come from Ash's dad and confidential psychiatric evaluation reports that had helped see Ash's dad into unnatural early retirement. When Ash had been at home over the weekend, the signs of Complex PTSD hinted at childhood trauma to Gray. Yet when Ash had left to take a ride out on Saturday night with Raif, learning more about Raif had been Gray's priority. So while they'd taken a ride back into town, Gray had used the time to look around Ash's home and test Raif out. The aftershave had been left around to see if he was sharp enough to pick up on invasion of his territory. And Raif had, just briefly. He'd asked Ash if anyone else had stayed with him and his dad. With the tracking device on the car Raif drove, he'd also had time to track them to the Wright girl back in Jefferson Lane.

Gray took another sip of coffee.

Jan couldn't have grown up much different to Ash or Chase. Maybe more so with Johnny: a council home, the latchkey kid always sitting alone in the lounge, waiting for a parent to come home. Maybe—

Gray drew a sharp breath in, pushing Jan out of his line of thought. It hadn't been the first time since Wednesday that he'd crept into his thoughts. It hadn't been the first time over the past year. The distraction was good; it hurt in all the right ways, but it distracted him nonetheless from the name written on his laptop screen.

Raif.

It's all he had. Nothing more. Even the search of Ash's had brought up no fingerprints, and he knew Raif hadn't worn gloves. That hinted at acid burning to remove ID. And that was damn unusual.

With the strange relationship he'd made with Ash over the past few months since that photo in the pub, there had to be a play on words with Raif too. Pseudonym? Acronym?

Didn't matter. Raif niggled at every turn. That ability to be more comfortable on the streets in the dark, to move from car to car, home to home as homeowners were on holiday, and with a confidence that had that cocky *won't catch me* edge, because everything was left as though it hadn't been touched.... He left no indication he'd been there and replaced whatever he used.

Raif was no common burglar.

Most importantly, he was no killer with a fixation for butterflies, despite showing an instinct that said he knew something was wrong on the streets. Maybe one or two of the homeless had gone missing, or maybe it was just down to how quiet everything seemed to be? But being the Holly Blue killer, that would tie him down to a specific area with raising them. He didn't fit the MO, but he did set his own unique profile.

Something tasted wrong in so many directions here: with Raif, with whoever had killed Johnny. The latter stayed out of sight like Gray did. No one had gone back to the murder scene. Gray kept a camera there, up in the trees to see if the killer liked to stay close to his victims, but the tree where Johnny had danced against a rope stayed devoid of any life. Ash hadn't visited, neither had Chase, not in the past few days.

Yet that feeling was there: something was wrong here, and it kept Gray watching them all.

He leaned against the bedroom bay window, not disturbing the blinds. Three weeks had been too long a time to get a call out to cull a potential killer, which meant someone had been here before him from his team. Someone had seen something that went a little deeper than the culling of a potential serial killer. And he kept coming back to the same name as he suspected they had.

Raif.

Maybe not enough to have Raif pulled in to find out just who he was, but enough that he'd turned a few eyes in his direction and more digging was needed. This wasn't just about a potential serial killer anymore. Raif hid his tracks too professionally. Even Andrews and his skill on the dark web had drawn nothing on the man.

As of yet, Gray only had his gut instinct, that the man was too skilled for it to have been picked up on the street. He was trained. But trained to do what, when, and where remained the question.

Gray stifled a cough.

The "why here" seemed obvious enough. The man had ties to the Wright girl, enough to risk himself to not have Social Services alerted to how the mother abandoned Lucy at night. Which also meant he had ties to the woman who lived in the girl's garden shed, watching over her. It seemed an emotional tie on Raif's part, one Gray wasn't yet ready to disturb, like he wasn't ready to disturb how Ash had found that butterfly in his bed. Ties like that always came in useful at the worst times, for the cruellest of reasons sometimes, and Gray knew them all.

But the lack of history on the man: no driving licence in the rucksack he'd kept at Ash's, no passport, National Insurance Number, even ID photo fit…

He didn't exist in every way possible, even down to his fingerprints.

And that… that was… interesting.

Raif's flaw was Ash. Whatever connection they shared, however they'd met, it potentially left Raif open to screwing up because the ghost in the machine obviously kept coming back.

He wanted a talk with Raif.

Badly.

The sound off his mobile made Gray stiffen, his coffee cup stilling inches from his lips.

It came again a moment later. A second text, then quiet.

He was on communication blackout. Nobody should be contacting him via this number, not unless they wanted to risk blowing his cover, endangering the caller too, and thus pissing him off. Seriously.

He thumbed the first message of the ID-withheld number.

One favour. No more.

Gray frowned and thumbed the next message.

Leave.

A third text came through.

You're not there for a murder. You're there to gather intelligence on Raif.

Quiet, then another text.

Go home, Gray. Jan needs you more.

Nhad. d328

That jolted Gray. Jan needed him more? Had something gone down? How would his own father know that? The text came through in Welsh and with a code that Gray hadn't seen since he was a teen, one his father always sent him to make sure he got home from school okay. Didn't matter where in the world his father would be, he'd get this code when it was safe for him to talk. Gray had seen it as nothing more than a private game, just for the two of them back then, something for him and his dad, only for him and his dad. The impact of it didn't really hit home until he started to tour in the SAS, when codes and safe communication were a priority. Now he used it to talk about Raif? To talk privately over Jan? And he'd used the Welsh for father: *Nhad*.

No. Jan. He was damn smart. He'd call if there was a problem.

His thumb hovered over the Delete button, where no reply would mean he was working and refused to acknowledge orders outside of his directive, yet... yet....

Jan. He'd been a latchkey kid too, no better than Lucy and going home to an empty house as his mother worked to keep a roof over her kids' heads. It's why Jan had stolen his father's money. Why Jan had taken those drugs and tried to hide from everything. Why Jan hadn't been able to say there was a problem....

Martin. What had Martin done to threaten that?

Fuck. He hated this. That creep in of mistrust. How his father planted that. No communication came with no distraction, and he missed that, how he could usually step away from life, then step back in when he was ready. Yet now his father stepped across the line, blurring the line, and forcing Gray back a few paces.

He hadn't spoken face-to-face with his father since he was twelve, when he'd forced him to run after his mother died. No sub like his father should have allowed his other to fall, right? Or that's how it had been back there. He still wasn't allowed intel on how his mother had died, even after all these years.

And now his father was asking him to back away and

look after his own. Why? Why now?

He trusted Jan. He'd have called if there were any real issues. So that just left his father and the mention of Raif. *Why* his father would mention Raif now and expose a connection.

He glanced at the code his dad had used. There was that personal ask for something. To go look after Jan while he looked after his. He needed the time to look after his.

Gray tensed his jaw a few times as he looked out of the bedroom window.

There was too much going on here and instinct said he shouldn't walk away. A car passed by the house every few hours, suggesting friendly surveillance already from another department, and the texts from his father confirmed that surveillance on Raif did come from MI6 now. His father had gotten here first, making this case officially their territory, with Gray treading on their toes. Even cullers could call enough and let MI6 run through their legalities.

But he'd walk away knowing some ill tension remained here. That bite was still there at his insides.

It felt wrong to leave.

But at the cost of Jan? Of Jack? Of…

Who? Who had he wanted to tag on to the end of that?

Who else was he missing? Why the hell was his father twisting the knife and making him glance back over his shoulder, towards home, to question that?

Christ. He rubbed at his head. Life had turned into the dark web, bleeding through into every perverted vein. He wasn't a stranger to liking it, he was just a stranger to liking having it bleed through into his home life.

Another message came through.

Please.

Nothing more. Gray glanced briefly out the window, then, feeling that stronger pull back to how Jan would say please, to Martin and how he'd burn before letting that word pass his lips... to whatever illness had gone on between them....

He thumbed the return code without thinking, without having forgotten.

He'd be going home.

It was that simple. He felt as though he shouldn't be, and he was putting a lot of trust in his father's words that he needed to back away, but Gray felt that hard tug back that would see him home in the late hours after he'd shut this end down. That eased the muscles in his shoulders and body more than he wanted to admit, but he was going home.

Whatever happened here was in his father's hands now.

CHAPTER 16
DON'T... WORRY

BY THE TIME the car and clothes had been exchanged at the halfway house, it took Gray longer than he would have liked to head back into London, now touching Monday morning. There was no pause here on the motorways, no lingering on the roadside to see what crawled out of the darkness when his main gates came into view.

The worst thing out here on the road tonight was him, and he was home now.

As he went into the hall, he gave a look at the stairs, up to where he knew Jan slept, then bypassed them for a moment and headed down the hall, through the double doors. He'd catch up with Ray in the morning; his unease carried him more towards Craig. Giving a scratch at his head, Gray tugged out his mobile and thumbed through for a number.

"Andrews" came a voice on the other end. Didn't sound like he was sleeping either.

"Give me a report on your new case in Croyden. Did you need to upgrade?"

A shuffling of paper came through. "No device found. We've had the library under surveillance since." He sounded a little off, like he'd eaten something sour.

"What?"

"The number of people in the library, it matched the number given by our potential bomber: nineteen. The majority of them late teens."

Eighteen to twenty had been given. "So the library has been under surveillance at some point. And I take it this was for internet usage in the library." He didn't stereotype here. When it came to teenagers, most UK libraries and their IT sections were the only draw. Free internet for an hour. Great for low-income families, but also giving potentially free access to online radicalisation.

"Yes on both counts. I've ordered CCTV of the area, but with no devices found on scene, this should be downgraded now."

"But you don't want to?"

"No." Quiet drifted over as Gray walked. "Something feels wrong."

"Okay. I'm back in the office later, around twelve. We'll review, but look at retaining the PI(b) threat and possibly upgrading as needed, no matter what the director-general advises here." He trusted Andrews's instinct.

"Good. Thank you. Night, sir."

"Night."

It took a few corridors to get where he needed, and the line of disinfectant dispensers at frequent intervals that changed colour with each corridor caught his attention as he headed on into Craig's staffroom.

Internal cameras kept a watch on Martin's room, and Baz sat at one, sipping a coffee. He soon sat up seeing

Gray. Gray offered what he hoped was a *take it easy* half-smile, but it only seemed to make the man slide his chair into position a little more.

"Gray." Craig came over from back by the TV, two coffees in hand. He looked like he'd got a call that Gray was near home, as he offered a steaming mug over.

Gray took it and flicked a look at the wanted poster for Jack and Martin. He buried a smile in his thank you and took a long sip of his coffee. Craig tried not to look back as well. He saw what had caught Gray's attention. "There's been a problem?" Gray said eventually.

Craig frowned a little, that *how do you know* look. It confirmed his father's words over Jan needing looking after. Maybe. Who had leaked that information would be another debating point with Ray tomorrow. It meant there was a fucking spy here. "Why wasn't Rachel notified?"

Craig moved over to the internal cameras, his own coffee resting down. "It was handled. *Is* being handled." He glanced back. "There was no need to call you. I'd like to know who went over Jan's head and did that."

Gray kept his look off Baz and buried a cough in his hand.

Craig flicked a look over, then—"But as you *are* here now and looking ready to settle for a while, you might as well see this." He pressed play on a computer and CCTV footage from Saturday night kicked into life.

Even in the semi-darkness, the brush of hand against cock was as clear as Martin's hard intake of breath as he lay on the bed.

Jan sat in the chair, a sheet tugged up around him. An iPhone and earphones slept in his lap as he watched Martin play. Yeah. He watched and was never more comfortable to watch. That was beautiful to witness.

Martin fed Jan's heat, but Jan in turn fed Martin's. Breathing matched breathing, even as they lit up the night like different colours to the Northern Lights.

Yet as Martin threw his head back now, neck muscles stretched as he came, his look was on the camera: for the camera.

The wink that came from silver-grey eyes right then… that was for Gray.

That had been Saturday night, yet Martin had known Gray would watch. He could have meant it for Craig, but… no. That look was for Gray, to show just what he'd been missing. The offer of the finest and fastest ride came too: how the arch of body, play of abs, exposure of cock all gave the perfect slipstream design that Gray would hand over thousands to get inside and test drive, MI5 style.

Martin settled into the comedown, his quirk of a smile seeming to know that. Then what fell from his lips in the next moment, the—

"That's for you, Janice. You hard from watching? Or do you need Vince here to really get you fucking Jack up?"

Although the camera angle saw Jan let an earpiece slip out every now and again in the heat, Gray was thankful that those headphones shut out Martin's head games most of the time, although the hurt was there in Jan's eyes. Smart man to use the headphones, but then Jan always did have a clear head when it came to Martin.

As Craig took the video forward thirty minutes, Gray saw that clear head kick in again. Jan took Martin out without a moment's thought, then—

The kiss at Jack's lips… his abs, it tore hard at Gray.

"Jan took a heavy dose of methadone before he went

into that cell. He'd handled everything really well up to Saturday night, but it hit then," Craig said quietly, and Gray looked at him. "Just a few hours before this." He explained everything, although more CCTV footage on Jan walking the halls, running a touch on the walls with eyes closed... that spoke it more.

"This is him tonight." Craig switched on the live CCTV and Gray moved closer. Jan still slept in the plastic chair, headphones in, as Martin slept on, cuffed to the bed.

"Said he felt safer in there than out here."

Gray frowned seriously at Craig. Craig still watched the CCTV. Baz tried to blend into the shadows and give them all some privacy, although Gray caught how he still cocked an ear in their direction. "I called Halliday Sunday morning, and he came over and had a session with Jan at dinnertime, with more booked over the next few days. But Jan...." Craig gave a ghost of a smile to Gray. "He handled all of this despite that. He handled Martin. You didn't need to be here at ungodly hours on Monday morning. Although I know Jan will be more than glad that you're back now."

Martin too. Gray buried that and tapped at the screen, where Martin slept. He'd picked up on the perspiration. "Is he ill?"

Craig rested against the unit as Gray did too.

"Yes." Craig rubbed at his head. "The disruption over the cologne carried on after you left Wednesday, and we noticed the heavy fever Saturday night. First just a temperature, then shivers, then he started vomiting. But the illness comes on the back of the cologne issue, with a vicious twist."

Gray looked back. "Vicious twist?" And since the cologne... with Baz. Anger bit at his insides. Had that been a fucking deliberate play? On who's part? Baz's? Was Baz the spy? From his own father? Why? Because of Raif? To keep him *away* from Raif?

Craig took his coffee and stole a sip. "It's the same STD illness Jack had after Vince raped Jack: the peritonitis with the rape from the baseball bat. Martin's mimicking all of it."

What? "How the hell can he mimic an illness that Jack had over a year ago?"

"Martin's showing the same symptoms because—"

Such a sweet, sexy kid beneath all that roughness. But you know that, don't you, tough guy? It's why you keep him close.

Vince's words caught him off guard and paused the coffee inches from Gray's lips. Craig stopped talking too.

"You okay? You need a break now? You look like it's been a long drive home."

Gray rubbed at his eyes, forcing the memory back. "No. Just tired." More seriously fucked off. Then he frowned. "Jack's infection was bacterial and treated, so too was his peritonitis fever. The cologne somehow brought all that back up?"

Craig nodded, his gaze a little distant. "Baz triggered Martin with the aftershave. It triggered a few other things too, like the illness now and how Martin's struggling to process what's happened. He doesn't have most of the memories, just the emotions to go by, and it's the emotions that's taking him through his illness again."

Oh, wasn't that just fucking peachy. He refrained from dragging Baz outside, over into the woods. This *had* been done fucking deliberately. He just needed the proof. "But he's remembering some of the memories? You said he didn't have most, which suggests something has come through from Jack?"

"Martin mentioned how Jack's mother had been a self-harmer, cutting herself and wiping the blood on Jack, then refusing to let Jack wipe it off and ease his OCD."

Gray stilled.

"Oh." Craig eased off. "You didn't know about that?"

No, he didn't. Not the cruelty that had fashioned Martin. Jack forgot the details but got there eventually. Had that been something he'd remembered whilst in Halliday's care and it now filtered through to Martin? Or had Jack written it down so he wouldn't forget and Martin had caught it in note form? Martin was damn sharp. He'd seen some of the rape play out in the hall as Gray had broken Jack down to get at Martin, so Martin would have seen who Vince was. But Martin also played puzzle master: maybe not having all the pieces, so shooting in the dark with something just to see what stuck and what reaction it earned. Then he pieced life together. He could have found out about Jack's mom any number of ways, but if Jack's illness was bleeding through, then that meant the memories could as well; that Jack was giving up. Craig's look said that too. "So the illness is psychosomatic?"

"No." Craig took a sip of coffee. "Halliday saw Martin Sunday afternoon too. Halliday termed it conversion disorder." He looked at the screen as though his voice would disturb Martin's room. He was much quieter when he focused back on Gray. "It's a perfect and very real mirror of Jack's illness. Martin has symptoms affecting sensory functions, psychological factors aiding the emergence of the illness, not to mention unfeigned symptoms. He's sick in every physical and neurological way that Jack was, only he doesn't know why because he has no memory of what exactly Jack went through: he just pieces it together via what his body goes through. It's why we've kept him in this detainment room for the moment. Halliday recommended keeping him down here for another week or two, mostly because of the cool temperature and how the heat rising from below could be the cause of the scent disruption. It settled Martin a little, but he's still so bloody restless and sick with it."

This was Craig's natural compassion coming through, how his concern was there for Martin as much as Jack. "Isn't conversion disorder tied closely to fugue states? To Jack's fugue states?"

"Precisely." Craig came away from the unit, his coffee finding a home there too. "Martin's echoing Jack's scent-association, like with Jan's cologne, only with a stronger neurological signal."

"But if he mirrors Jack, is there a chance he could blackout like Jack? He could black out and go into an aggression that nearly saw one of his rapists killed?" The worry was there with how close Jan was.

Craig shook his head. "There's been no evidence of that. Martin was created to cope in ways that Jack can't and allow Jack the skills to live life when his collapses into the likes of the fugue states, OCD, and trauma."

"Only Martin is still Jack at heart, come all Jack's flaws."

"No one is built flawlessly. Some are filtering through."

"And if more filter through and we lose Jack completely?"

Craig fell quiet. Gray didn't like that. "We watch. It's all we can do at the moment."

Gray gave a deep sigh and put his coffee cup down. "And Jan?"

Craig frowned.

Gray nodded to the medkit over on the settee. "Did he need methadone tonight too?"

Craig's smile was sad. "No. He just had one bad night, that's all, but look at the pads to his fingers. He cut himself Saturday night and wrecked your en suite a little."

Having his home damaged, that was nothing new. Who was doing it now, that was. Gray watched the CCTV for long moments, then pointed distractedly behind him, to the first of the new disinfectant dispensers. "And those?"

Craig snorted a chuckle. "Jan's idea. It came on the back of Martin's little display for the camera and how not being able to clean the stain away showed more of Jack. Jan thinks the offer of routine might trigger Jack a little more."

"Has it worked?" Gray caught Craig's wince. He also knew Jan would be thinking of losing more of Jack to Martin. He wanted to talk to Jack on his level with the dispensers.

Craig reached over and forwarded time on the video again to yesterday morning.

Looking unsteady on his feet, Martin stumbled down the corridor, no doubt for some guarded time out in the gardens, and he punched at every one of the new dispensers. "Fucking move them, Janice. Or I swear I'll open your skull and piss on the candle I stuff inside it."

Gray winced. So, he guessed Martin didn't like the idea. "Am I okay to visit?"

Craig put his coffee down, then looked at Gray. He seemed ready to say no, and Gray wouldn't blame him, but—

Such a sweet, sexy kid beneath all that roughness. But you know that, don't you, tough guy? It's why you keep him close.

Craig fell quiet and frowned a little. "Yeah. You can."

That focused Gray. "I think it would be good for you."

Gray stiffened.

Yeah…. It had hurt not to be here with them both. Craig saw that. Is that what his father had played on, ensured? Not to help Jan, Jack, or Martin, just to fuck about with head games and protect Raif, just stir up memories and…

Such a sweet, sexy kid beneath all that roughness. But you know that, don't you, tough guy? It's why you keep him close.

It's what kept him coming home. Over the next few days, it's what would see Baz buried if Gray found any trace of evidence that linked him to being a fucking spy for his father. And as for his father, if he'd started all of this to target Martin… Jan, all to keep Gray coming back home…?

After a brief look at the CCTV, at Baz, Gray turned away.

∾

As he pushed on through to the detainment room, semi-darkness made sure Gray kept the noise down to a minimum before he closed the door behind him. The scent of sweat lightly held hands with the dark, running alongside the slow back and forth of a fan that Jan, no doubt, had added once Martin was asleep.

Jan sat curled in the oddly uncomfortable-looking chair that seemed big enough to swallow him whole. A blanket was pulled up to his neck, as if still protecting against whatever could come out of the darkness and bite him. But the lines on his face were soft, as much comfort in seeing as in being seen now, and Gray made Jan his first stop, ignoring how *2012* played noiselessly on the TV. Jan seemed naturally drawn to disaster. The irony there hurt.

Gray took the earphones and iPhone first, slipping them into his trouser pocket for safekeeping, then a gentle stroke against Jan's jaw had Jan easing an eye open and lifting his head. The kiss Gray gave to his lips had him stretching out from underneath the blanket.

"I'm back now. Go to bed. Get some decent sleep," he whispered quietly in Jan's ear, his look on the single bed and what lay bound there. "I'll be up in a minute."

Jan said nothing, just followed his gaze, and Gray felt a hand drift down his side as Jan eased him back so he could stand. A return breath brushed his ear, and that hand against his hip was so gentle now... "Glad you're back." Quiet. A rest of head on his shoulder. "Missed the hell out of you."

Gray shifted a look at Jan and life stayed quiet between them for so long. Then Gray tasted Jan's lips, the sleepy look he had going on there. Everything about Jan. Then he took Jan's hand, turned it over, and ran his fingertips over the few cuts there.

"It was dealt with," Jan said quietly.

Gray gave a distracted smile. "Not by me. Not yet." He looked at Jan. "Bed," he said eventually.

"Bourbon?" Jan whispered back, and Gray cocked a smile.

"Man after my own soul."

Jan eased into a long breath. "I'll settle for the man, because the bastard always did belong to someone else." Jan looked at the bed for a moment, then gave Gray a tired smile before he padded out of the detainment room. "Don't linger for too long," he said before he left.

The fan kept the air cool, and occasionally it swept over Gray's hand as he looked down on the bed. Restraints had been called in again, keeping Martin's hands bound at his sides even during sleep. A thin sheet covered him from the abs down, leaving his chest bare.

Perspiration covered brow and body, dampening his long hair around his face, with a stray strand caught on his lips. Long gone were the come stains that had no doubt fallen. But that heat to his cheeks and long pull of breath cried that heavy drag from a pool, like Jack was there and just dropping into that deep sleep after an absence or blackout.

Only it wouldn't be Jack here when he woke. The longer this went on, the more he wondered whether it ever would be.

Gray sat on the bed, feeling the weight of loss and grief, or how his body wanted to grieve but he was forever locked in this semi-dark limbo, waiting, wanting. But mostly always wanting.

As the fan drew a path down Martin's body, disturbing the sheet slightly and making it lap lightly at his abs, Gray wiped his thumb over the sweat lining Martin's temple. The heat there carried through to his touch, so Gray kept his handling light. Something was mumbled in the partly-lit night, a stray call of *old mukka*, and Martin shifted, a frown disturbing the dampness on his forehead. Yeah, sometimes Jack was so close to the surface.

"Still here, stunner. Still waiting." Gray swiped away the long black strand of hair touching Martin's lips, then replaced it with a stroke of his thumb, wiping away the fever there. "But I'm tired of talking to the shadows and hoping one is close enough to whisper in your ear and let you know just how old you've left us all." He looked away, preferring how much easier it was to bleed into the darkness. "Yeah, still here, stunner." He wiped across his own mouth, then leaned down and kissed Martin's lips, refusing to see Martin then, only Jack. "Never far from fucking here." He closed his eyes. "And fuck you for that, you cunt. For always pulling me back."

Taking an unsteady breath, a last taste of Jack, he got to his feet and headed for the door. Yeah. If his father had done one thing, it was to teach him how he lost sight of who mattered at times. He wouldn't allow that again. Not with Baz and spies walking his halls.

"Just me here."

Martin's words sounded so tired, drugged, as defeated as Gray felt. Silver eyes were closed, screwed tightly shut to the world for a moment as coughing rattled his body, then when they opened, it was to stare at the ceiling.

"Put you in a cage like this and keep feeding the sedative into your throat, would this… this bullshit heal you, Gray?" The smile couldn't have been more dejected; all play for Jan, for the camera, now lost in the lonely hours of the morning. "Because us, psychopaths and sinners, we're not broken, not deep down. We don't need fixing, Gray." He shivered, the fever taking hold a little stronger. "You'll kill me doing this, and I'll damn well make sure I take Jack down with me when you do."

Gray looked away, to the wall. To the door.

"All that emotional bollocks you're feeling…." Martin's voice trailed off a little. "Did it bring you home too soon?"

Saying nothing, Gray headed back for the door.

"Let's just hope that decision doesn't come and hunt you down, mukka—"

Gray stilled at the name.

"No, not mukka. Welsh…" Martin sounded so drowsy now as a soft laugh came through. "Yeah, you're Welsh… Welsh and from the valleys." Again Gray nearly lost him. "From chasing killers to kissing… Jan." Quiet and that sadness seemed to creep back in. "Your lips were so cold against mine. Be sure to warm them up before Jan gets a taste. He'll shiver against it, never understanding why we chase and shiver *for* it like we do. I mean, you didn't just come back here for Jan tonight, did you…? It wasn't just for Jack."

The hum off the fan came.

"And who did you leave behind, hm? Who's gonna pay the price for this… weakness of yours as you play here with us?"

CHAPTER 17
LUCY

LUCY TOOK A bite from her Snickering bar and shifted her little bum into the fleece blanket, loving how her mum always opted for the fur over the scratchy sheets she used on her big bed. A panda with huge black eyes coloured itself all over it, and she stroked distractedly at its ear, the fur as familiar to her as her closed door as she tapped away at her iPad.

Roblox kept her giggling as she unconsciously knocked the few remaining sandwich crumbs onto the floor. It wasn't a game for little kids, and something Mum told her she shouldn't play, but her mum had downloaded the game anyways, and she sat trying to avoid getting killed by a flood. Mr Rowley—only she called him that—had been here last night, but not with his strange friend with the Slender Man frame: all long arms, long legs, lovely gem-like eyes and fiery hair, but… something about him that made her want to stay right by Mr Rowley. She kind of liked Mr Rowley all to herself, and she'd let Mr Long Man know that when he next came around.

For now she frowned at the game. Most kids talked

about Pokémon at school, but that was stupid, and she was grateful to remind Ellie Barrow-Fieldman how stupid she was for liking it. And for having two surnames. That was just greedy. Nope, she wanted one surname and that giggle that came with trying to run away from tornadoes and acid rain… not that she'd ever seen acid rain or really knew what it was. In the game, it burned through metal and stupid people who stood outside.

There were a lot of stupid people who stood around outside, especially in school, in year two, one year above her in particular. They even ran around pretending to be stupid Pokémon while she rode the waves from a tsunami. The slide always made a good escape chute.

The low battery sign flicked on the screen and she frowned. It was the second time it had come on, and she let it rest on Panda's nose as she climbed off her bed, bored now.

Sun from her bedroom forced her to blink, and she found tiredness tugging her eyes down as though she was drowning, caught in that flood on Roblox where bodies broke then reset themselves. She should have been asleep hours ago, after Mr Rowley left; she always promised to sleep. Mr Rowley wasn't stupid, though. He'd just looked at her as if to say "Liar, liar. Pants caught in a forest fire."

Maybe she'd have gone to sleep if he'd stayed, but he never did. Not until her mum came in anyway.

Lucy grinned and climbed onto the ottoman by her window and peered out under the blinds. She ignored the Tuesday-morning chill frosting the windows, although she liked how her breath made patterns on the glass. She drew a heart, then rubbed it away when it blocked her view.

Shed Lady always waved, and it surprised her how Mum never saw it or her. Shed Lady was really good at hide-and-seek, always offering a wave from the shed window, or sticking her foot out the door and wiggling her toes. With how long that grass was just a little way from the bald path that led into the shed, Mum never went outside in the backyard anyway. Even the washing hung from radiators in the house or tumbled in the dryer. Lucy didn't mind. She liked it out there: she got to be like a worm on Slither.io, wriggling and writhing, then bumping into Shed Lady and eating her mass, or more the burger bun from McDonald's the old lady sometimes had.

Lucy gave a sleepy smile, a wave. Shed Lady was still there now, her foot sticking out of the door, no shoes on her feet. She must have been cold this morning. Frost crept on the windows, giving green grass white highlights like Jack Frost. Only no wriggle of bare toes came this morning. No wave hello. Her foot looked a funny colour too.

Lucy waved again to make sure Shed Lady wasn't going to wave back.

The downstairs door came open, one turn of Mum's key, the push down on the handle, but no wave from Shed Lady. It usually came about now as Mum came home.

She managed to climb down and get back in bed as the stairs creaked lightly. She hid under the cover, burying a chuckle behind her hand.

Mum always played like this.

The door eased open, a creak with it, then—quiet. Lucy matched it with a big grin and all her quiet, body so still now.

A brush came at the blanket, forcing a little giggle, then a gentle tug as—

"Boo."

Lucy squealed as light assaulted her, along with a run of tickles under her arms.

"Morning, sweetie." Lucy was pulled up onto her mum's lap. "You had a good sleep?"

"Sure. Mr Rowley came again and gave me a Snickering bar and read me a story, but Mrs Shed didn't wave this morning. Can I go give her some toast?"

Long black hair was tucked around ears that looked more elf than those in the fairy books, and her mum had prettier green eyes, too, although she always seemed to be looking at the bedroom door a lot. Now she had a funny smile on her lips as Lucy got a kiss. "Rowley came again, did he, munchkin?"

"And Mrs Shed didn't wriggle her toes."

"From under the shed?"

"Not like the witch from *Wizard of Oz*, stupid."

She got a raised brow.

"Not stupid nasty, stupid nice." She kissed her mum's cheek. "Can I get some toast?"

"Sure." Lucy found herself on her feet as her mum got up and ruffled her hair. "You need some worms too, to help her wriggle her toes again?"

She giggled. "She doesn't eat worms, stupid. People don't eat worms." She frowned. "'Cept that Bear guy on the TV. I think he eats worms."

Her mum chuckled as she headed for the door. Her walk looked tired, sleepy, and her look into her own bedroom was long, like she'd seen some Snickering bars in there and was hungry enough to attack with not caring how the wrapper kept it free from bugs.

"Clean those wrappers up off the floor, honey. You

shouldn't be sneaking them in there during the day—"

"But Mr Rowley—"

"Charger's in my room for the iPad too. If you can get it charged before school, you can have ten minutes on Roblox. Go get yourself charged up for being a good girl for Mummy."

Her mum didn't mention she hadn't been here last night, so she didn't either. It was their secret. She was good with it. She had Mrs Shed... Mr Rowley and his new strange friend.

Wrappers were hastily stuffed into the pink basket in the corner of the room, then she scrambled to get her iPad as her mum made it downstairs. She was big enough to switch the charger on now, so she bounced on her mum's bed and crawled over to the other side and slipped down the small gap.

Among the flick of the switch and clicking the charger into place, a soft thud came from downstairs. Lucy looked back, but the little zap of power pulled her iPad back into life and, a little rush of excitement, she clicked on Slither.io.

Footsteps on bare stair half caught her attention as she sat between the wall and bed. She didn't look up until they passed her mum's room.

"Here, Mummy. Just chargin' it."

Big work boots stopped by the end of the bed, and she looked up as someone crouched down.

"Hello." She smiled over. "Are you a friend of Mr Rowley's?"

The man smiled, now reaching into his pocket for something. "I am, Voodoo."

Only Rowley called her that, and she offered her iPad over. "Want to play?"

He nodded. "In a minute. We'll play in a minute. Can you hold something for me until we can play?"

She put the iPad down and nodded.

The man opened his hand and a fluttering of blue wings trapped in a plastic tube played in his hold.

"I'll come get you when we're ready to play, okay. But I want to talk to your mummy first."

She frowned at how the butterfly tried to get free, then took it from him anyway.

A ruffle came at her knotty hair. "You get to spend some extra time on her iPad, okay?"

She beamed at him. Happy. "Thank you. Can you tell Mummy?"

"Sure, baby. Sure." Hands went on knees as the man pushed away.

"And you'll get toast for Mrs Shed lady?"

Quiet.

"Sure. I'll get her some toast."

~

Her tummy grumbled before she realised it was getting time for school. Her mum usually came in a few hours before they drove to school, and she should be having breakfast by now. Or that's what her tummy said should be happening. "Mummy." Lucy had given up on Slither.io, a round of Roblox disaster, and was into a round of popping balls on Dodo Pop, and not winning. "Mummy, can I come down now?"

Footsteps came on the stairs. As they stopped by the bed and the man crouched down, Lucy frowned at the red hairy paint kissing the steel in the toecaps.

"Did you keep it for me? Butterflies get lonely, you know."

Lucy had almost forgotten about the butterfly. "Sure." She took it from her side and handed it over.

"You keep a hold of it, okay?" He pushed it back to her.

Lucy frowned down at it. "Not moving so much now. It looks sleepy."

"That's okay. They get sleepy too." The man held out his hand. "C'mon, baby. Let's go play."

"With Mummy?"

The man nodded, and she slipped a hand into his as she stood, her iPad left charging on the floor.

～

"Did Mummy hit her head?" That was the first thing she noticed. How long black curls had a sleek shine to them, like her mum had washed her hair, leaving it wet, black, only closer to her head, red touched the skin. She lay on the settee, curled up as though sleeping. Under the thin sheet, her breathing said she was sleeping, but it sounded funny. A bubbling rattling sound came, almost like drowning, but from the inside out. Clothes also made a scatter box of the floor, but some looked more like rags a dog had chewed at. Lucy tugged at the man's hand, not looking up. "Is she sleeping?"

The man knelt by the settee. He stroked at her mum's hair and something twisted in her tummy. She didn't like how he touched her mummy.

"She's sleeping, baby. She gets really tired, doesn't she?"

He smiled at her. "But she's happy now."

Lucy found a smile hearing that; her mummy hadn't seemed happy in such a long time. "She's happy?"

"Yeah." He held out his hand. She looked down at the butterfly, then handed it to him. "You know when you're happy and you get butterflies in your tummy?"

She rubbed at hers. It didn't feel happy now but fluttered with something else.

"Well, your mummy has those now, seeing us."

The sheet inched up at her mum's side, and as the man exposed a deep long gash close to her bellybutton, a gash that dripped with white sticky stuff, the man then started to unscrew the lid to the tube that held the butterfly.

Her mind refused to show her anything else, making sure she hummed her favourite Roblox tune to block it out. And maybe she said Mr Rowley, but that was silly. He didn't come to the house in the daytime. She wished he'd come to the house in the daytime, take her to school, just leave with Mummy. Yeah, she wanted to leave with Mummy now, or just hold on to her and stop that strange breathing noise that made red bubbles from her lips.

CHAPTER 18
WAITING GAMES

"C'MON, RED, COME out and paint the town in rainbows with me tonight! It's Saturday night, for God's sake. And you owe me for a new fucking phone, you jackass. How the fuck did you manage to break that again?"

The sound of water hitting toilet pan came over the line, and Ash rolled his eyes as he got comfortable on his own bed. A little disgruntled he'd heard nothing off Raif all week, he'd made it back by six after the rugby match they'd watched. Both of them still weren't able to watch the footie on the telly and wanted to get some sleep before midnight tonight. But something made him pause.

"Chase, you're taking a slash as you talk to me?"

"Nope." That sounded strained. "Just finished." The shaking of a dick came, closely followed by the pulling up of a zip.

Ash gave a deep sigh. "And you want me to come and hold your hand?"

The toilet flushed. "Promise I'll wash 'em first. And be grateful I didn't need anything else."

"Christ, Chase. I'm eating." He wasn't, but he felt like chucking up what he had eaten that afternoon. They hadn't long got back, and Chase was already on about going out and riding the rainbow, although Chase didn't sound in the right mind to play fairly.

"Aww, c'mon. You know if it comes from our supple asses, even our farts are sexy."

"Annnnnnd I'm hanging up now, Chase."

"What's that?" Tapping came at the phone. "You want to blow me again? You *dirty* boy. I've not washed my dick yet. You fancy a golden shower instead?"

Ash chuckled and eased back onto his bed. "I'm catching a few hours' sleep—"

"At seven on a Saturday night? You fucking freak. You're dead to me, Red. Dead."

"Because I've got company."

Quiet.

"*Company*, company?" More quiet, concern. Ash still hadn't told him about Raif yet. It felt odd somehow, especially as Raif liked to keep his touch in darkness, away from life. "This stalking business, you're lousy at it, you know that? You're supposed to worship me. No one else." Ash caught the sadness. "And when the fuck were you last out on a date without me? I love you, bud, you know that."

"Fucking liar. You're on a date tonight without me."

"Oh yeah!" That sounded genuine, as if he had forgotten, which he hadn't. Bastard. "Well, we're comparing fuck pics later and posting them 'round town, then, yeah?"

"Chase—"

"Just joking. This kid seems really sweet. Check in

halfway through, let me know where you're going, and, oh, Red—don't fuck anyone I wouldn't. Ever, okay?"

Ash frowned. Was this grief talking? The check-in was new, so too was the "don't fuck anyone I wouldn't."

"Likewise, bud. You know that. Give me a call if you get lonely," Ash said quietly, then he said his goodbyes and hung up. A moment later the mobile phone in his pocket let him know he had a text, and he thumbed through it without thinking.

"Fuck, Chase." He was getting a head-start with the pictures, and the one of Chase doing a moonie with *Wish You Were Here* written on it had Ash holding the phone away and crying no.

Although picturing him writing that on his ass brought up a few chuckles. Yeah, Chase was worried and the *keep in touch, no matter how* was there in the undertones. Everyone seemed worried lately.

He deleted the picture and settled in to catch a few hours' sleep.

∾

He woke at half eleven, thirty minutes before Raif was due, and was up, showering, then downing a coffee in order to miss his dad and Miles coming back later. On the table a note explained that he was at Chase's for the night.

Ash's guts twisted as the darkness outside the door kicked in. What the fuck was he doing? He'd not thought twice about the darkness when he'd staggered out of the pub with Chase that night, or when he'd changed hours and worked the six-till-six nightshift, and that same blackness had been on his back in later winter months. It

took on a different face now, not familiar, not scary, just…
there.

Ash let out an unsteady breath, then closed his eyes and inhaled deeply on the coffee. Yeah, what the fuck was this shit? Johnny's death had him rattled.

Giving a scowl, he took his work backpack and packed some beef sandwiches. Crisps went in, along with a few chocolate bars and a carton of orange juice.

A look over at the clock saw it blink eleven-fifty, and Ash grabbed his coat and started to shut down the house, turning off lights as he went. He paused at the back door and let his touch hover over the handle as a buzz in his pocket had him quickly shifting to shut it up, but he caught the image that flashed up.

Chase was already home by the look of it, and he was there, with his date, grinning as Chase took a selfie of him drawing on his date's ass.

Wish you were here too.

"Fuck." Ash laughed. He'd already had a text on where Chase had gone that night, and another came through a moment later.

His name's Jess, and he's got a wicked sense of humour. And just happens to be two's company, three's a riot too. He's not one I'm willing to show off in public, either. Really sweet kid.

Ash doubted Jess was three's a riot. He looked pretty focused on Chase. Ash flicked a look at the clock.

12:20 a.m.

He frowned.

Red…? Either come over or let me know if you're still at home.

Ash's smile faded just about the time a sweep of car light swept in from back down the hallway and arcing over feet.

I'm still at home. Dad's back too.

Ash. Sorry, bro. Give me the name of the dude who stood you up, and I'll go break a few legs, then post the blood and guts on the internet.

Hey, don't sweat it, bud. It wasn't that kind of date. Easy come, easy go. Have some fun. I gotta go. Another reply came in, but Ash was already tucking the phone into his pocket. He kicked his backpack under the table, threw the note in the bin, and headed back through to the hall, knowing the sound of the car that pulled up.

The key went in the latch from the outside, and Ash paused for the briefest of moments before shivering, more shaking it off. He beat Miles to it and opened up to slip an arm under his dad's shoulder.

"Ah, shit." Miles jumped back a bit. "Christ, Ash, you scared the life out of me."

"Sorry." He flicked a look at him, but his dad was caught mid-grumble, and Ash got a push to his shoulder.

"Can manage. Don't fucking mother me, boy."

Miles winced at the shove he got too, but Miles came back in, looking over at Ash, then helped tug his dad through to the stair lift. "How about you make me a coffee and I'll get him into bed?"

Ash hated how easily he wanted to run into that and not have to go upstairs. "You sure?"

Miles nodded. "Usual, please."

Ash waited for Miles to get his dad into the stair lift, then satisfied they were both okay, his dad already into apologies that Miles smiled away, he went back into the kitchen. His dad apologised so easily to Miles and a little anger crept in.

The door still stayed closed, the kitchen keeping its

emptiness until Ash switched on the kettle and started making Miles a nightcap.

Maybe Raif was just late. Or maybe Raif had known Miles was due back and was holding off until he'd gone? Fuck. Ash frowned as he stirred the coffee. Raif wasn't all-knowing. He wouldn't know Miles was due back. But he might have been outside and seen it.

Maybe?

He glanced at the clock.

12:25 a.m.

Christ. Dammit. Raif had been the one to say here, now. Why the fuck should he give a damn if Raif didn't stick to his own plans and couldn't find the way to his door in the night?

Ash wiped tiredly at his eyes. Good men... The fuck-over always came. So why the fuck did he keep leaving the door unlocked to let Raif back in?

Shit. He'd give him until one, then lock down for the night and say fuck it. He was worth waiting another half hour for at least.

"All done." Miles came padding through, and Ash glanced back as he pulled out a chair and slumped down. He looked exhausted and didn't reek of beer the same way his dad had. Ash took his coffee over and sat down with a fresh one for himself.

"I'm sorry, Miles. This isn't fair on you. And I bet your Rhiannon is about ready to string us up." Miles had married over five years ago, and whenever Ash went around, the atmosphere got colder and colder.

"It's doing nowt to give my own old gaffer a grandkid, let's put it that way." But his tired smile was easy over his coffee cup.

Ash winced. "Do I need to say sorry again?"

Miles waved it off. "There's fun in scrambled practise sex."

Ash choked a laugh, albeit an embarrassed one. He didn't think he could do embarrassed. Listening to Miles talk about sex was too close to listening to his dad talk about sex. And he didn't stay around for that. Ever.

"How's Chase?" Miles gave a heavy sigh as his cup went on the table. He looked around. "I miss seeing Johnny here. How are you holding up? Shit as usual?"

Ash lost his smile and dropped his head a touch, watching the milk bits bob on the surface of his drink. He really made lousy coffee.

"You remember having to walk into town to go to that fancy dress party? You wore Batman, Chase, Batgirl, and Johnny—"

"Johnny went as Daffyd, the sole gay in the village from *Little Britain*?" Ash laughed his way through the memory. "Oh Christ yes, I remember that!"

Miles's body shook, his shoulders taking the weight of laughter. "That was one of the strangest call-outs I got."

"Hey, it wasn't our fault how Johnny stopped to help that woman with a flat tyre and another passer-by thought she was being carjacked—"

"By Batman, Batgirl, and the one gay in the village." Miles half-covered his face to hide the chuckles. "Christ, you three…"

"Johnny knew how to party despite being the one to stand in the corner and hide from the crowd."

Miles eased down and smiled softly. "It's good to see you laugh, Ash. I know how rough it's been. I can't believe that shit they spread in the newspapers." He went to say something else, looking a little angry, but seemed to force himself not to say anything. "Just hold on in there, okay? It'll get better. It always does."

Ash rubbed at his head, elbow now on the table. "Yeah, bullshit." He sighed. "Changed us all that night."

He got a pat to his shoulder, then a rub. "You shape your future, Ash, even when it feels as though it's working against you. It doesn't have to be dark all of the time." Miles gave a stretch, then stood. "I better get back, kid, before the hounds of hell are sent to pick me up."

Ash looked up as he sat back. "Shape your own future, huh?"

"Hey." Ash got a soft cuff up his ear. "Some things are worth lying on your back and getting a tickle for."

"No, just…" Ash screwed his face. "Don't go there."

He got a wink. "Get yourself to bed. It's getting on." Miles looked at the clock.

12:50 a.m.

Fuck. Ash had needed to see it too.

"I'll see myself out."

As Miles sorted for his car keys, Ash collected the mugs up. "Thanks for getting him home, Miles."

He got a look over. "Anytime. You know where I am if you need me. You tell Chase the same, okay?"

Ash nodded and took the cups over to the sink and washed them up as the front door closed. Seemed he spent a lifetime making coffee and clearing up afterwards, only he missed a working dishwasher that helped do just that. He'd be glad when the new one came.

12:55 a.m.

Shit. Ash looked up, out the window, how the light from

the hall didn't make a blind bit of difference to the darkness outside and what it could hide, or didn't, in this case.

It shouldn't have bit at his ass. Having Raif not show up should have shown how downright suicidal this had all got.

Ash made his way back over to the table and set the chairs back into the same position that he had over countless years.

1:05 a.m.

He stared long and hard at the clock; stared long and hard as the silence of the kitchen played around him.

Okay. Like that, is it? He'd lock up, keep everything locked up from here on in, and walk away. Life was too odd, too damn well out of sync with everything he knew.

Even Raif wasn't worth that.

1:09 a.m.

Ash looked back over his shoulder, to the blackness beyond, then down to the rucksack at his feet.

PTSD and irrational behaviour, huh? He picked up the rucksack and headed on out. This was all such fucked-up bullshit, but he might as well own the tag Raif wanted to give him, right?"

CHAPTER 19
IRRATIONAL BEHAVIOUR

HE DIDN'T KNOW where to go, let alone where to start looking, and the first half-an-hour outside of the safety of his lit home, Ash turned his collar up to the wind and light rain as feet pounded concrete. The scream of a fox drew his attention back the way he came, or more to the park and common beyond.

Ash tilted his head slightly as the fox came out, carrying a mouse.

A green pipe. A common. There'd been a common on the way to Voodoo's, as well as a fox. He doubted very much that it was the same fox; he'd lived around here long enough to know the sheds and rubbish bins offered living space and fast food outlets to keep at least twenty-six foxes and their vixens living the highlife in the country. But foxes... there'd been a fox on the way to Voodoo's. A common. A shed.

The soft shift of car on road crept up and light raced over the hill. Ash glanced over, then made his way back down the park, this time cutting over the lonely cry of the swing and sending the fox scattering. The common beyond would come at Voodoo's from a different angle, but he remembered which garden to cut across that would lead him on through all the others…. Maybe….

∾

He wasn't as lithe or stealthy as Raif, and Ash felt tenser now that he was alone. He dropped onto the grass next to Voodoo's and stayed down for a while as the cold cut into his lungs, making it hard to breathe. The rain hadn't stopped, and it offered that constant light patter that would have soaked through if he didn't have his long coat on. Ash ran a hand through his hair, then crept over to the fence and blindly found the grip and footing to help him over the last fence.

Again he dropped down into long grass, and he downright ignored what spiders and general eight-legged creeps crouched and listened there with him. No voices drifted over from the shed, but the door stood open, hanging off one hinge and shifting slightly in the night, almost as if it were in some Morse code with the swings back at the park.

No light touched the house windows, but the shed door hid most of it from view. Keeping low in the long grass, he made his way over. As much as the night took on a pitch blackness that didn't want to make him look into the mouth of the shed, he inched in anyway, making sure his tread of trainer on grass was very, very light.

There was no way he could mimic Raif's bird call; he'd sound stupid trying, but he did keep his crouch low and tapped lightly on the rotten woodwork to let someone know he was there without calling out. Five scratches.

Nothing came from the shadows. A musky damp wrinkled his nose, but it had nothing to do with the rain and rotten wood. This was sickly sweet, where armpits hadn't been washed, or underwear left on for longer than should ever grace the human body. Something else too...

Cologne. Something familiar and expensive, maybe Ck One.

Ash gave a sniff. Yeah. Ck One.

A rustle came from outside, just maybe the lift of tarpaulin to see what lay beneath, but Ash couldn't remember any covers being left around before. He hadn't exactly been looking, though. The creak of the door had him shifting away from its mouth, with the flat of his back pressed up against the side panel.

One-one thousand, two-two thousand....

Ash closed his eyes. Nothing else came but the sound of rain on roof, and he let out a very uneven breath.

It was the weekend now. For all he knew, Voodoo and her mother could have gone away. Hell, he wouldn't want to stay in that house, so this was perhaps the stupidest idea he'd ever had, coming here.

Giving a rub at his head to ease the building pressure, and needing to be out of here now, Ash made sure he kept low and found a safe way outside, back into the knee-length grass.

As he did, a hand slipped over his mouth, and a moment later he cried pain into the gag when his arm was forced behind his back. Breathing came hard, heavy, and he was forced face-first into the rotten wood, mere inches from a spider weaving her web.

Fuck. Fuck. Ash tried to struggle, but the hand shifted

from his mouth and the elbow digging into his neck as his feet were forced apart had him stilling very fucking quickly.

"Raif." He kept his breathing even. A moment later he was spun around with a hand roughing up his long coat. "Stop. It's Ash—"

A noise from back by the house had Raif shifting his hard look, and a finger went to his lips.

"What?"

"That means stay fucking quiet." All friendliness seemed gone at the heated snarl. Then a whistle came, one that sounded pretty much like the one Raif had used, and Ash was left reeling a little as he was shoved away as Raif answered it. A moment later, someone else came around the back of the shed.

Ash eyed the new man up, and he caught that hard dig of anger at how Raif and this man shared that bird-like call. He wore a duffel coat and glasses, pretty much putting him sorting happily through any old bookstore, looking for that one novel he wrote years ago. Raif dwarfed him, yet the other man held his own with how he eyed Ash like gutter trash. Ash got the once-over, then he was dismissed with a look that put him as garden furniture: easily moveable if in the way.

"She's gone. Been taken into care." The man looked at Raif as he took off black leather gloves. "A few hours ago from surveillance."

Raif wiped a hand over his mouth. "And Voodoo's mother?"

The man was quiet for a moment. "Same as Sasha, only this time the body has been removed by the locals. Reports say the girl stayed by her since Tuesday before someone anonymously called it in how she was on her own. School hadn't gotten off their asses and sent someone around to check on why she hadn't been at school for a few days."

Raif groaned, nearly pulling away before Ash stopped him. If Raif was asking for details, he hadn't been in town for a week, so where had he... Ash jolted. *Wait—What?* He looked sharply towards the house, even though the shed dwarfed it. "You..." Ash stepped up to Raif. "Voodoo's gone? And her mother... her mother's dead?"

The man flicked him a look as he lit up a cigarette, but he said nothing. Raif's fists were clenched, the bag of food he'd brought with him with the Snickers bar inside more than a little lost in his big hand.

Hurt was there, and Ash instinctively reached to touch his hand.

Raif pulled away and fixed a look on him. For a while he said nothing, so much going through his mind that Ash could almost hear it ticking away inside.

"Who have you spoken to, Ash? What fucking vicious game are you playing now?"

For a moment he thought he'd misheard, not so much the words, but everything that each syllable suggested. "You?" He frowned. "You think I was the caller? That I've something to do with this?" He shifted slightly. "You think...." It stung, mostly because he could see how hurt Raif was. "Her fucking mother's dead?"

"And Voodoo had a visit from the authorities: that's who discovered her."

Ash frowned. "So you're saying what?" He took it in. "You think I'd see Social Services take her from her mother? Are you for fucking real?"

"Someone gave them a tip-off."

"*It wasn't fucking me.* But you know something? She was

fucking lucky someone did, otherwise she'd have been around her mother's body for fuck knows how long before someone found her." Ash almost wanted to stuff that back in as soon as he'd said it because Raif's eyes hardened. He'd just given Raif a reason why someone might have called. "Fucking me, Raif?"

"Keep it fucking down." The man let smoke curl into the night as he watched Ash. "I never mentioned Social Services." The cigarette was stubbed out a moment later, only half-smoked. But it was stubbed out on the man's leather gloves and the burn holes there said it was a habit. He put the half-smoked cigarette back in the packet, no ash left around his feet. "The only way you'd know is—"

"What?" Ash went in, but a hand on his chest off Raif kept him away from the man. "As it's Social Services who usually deal with shit like this when a kid misses school and a parent dies—"

"Is murdered."

"*What?*" Ash looked at Raif. "Murdered?"

Raif wasn't even looking at him.

"Goddamn it, you fuck, you look at me. How the fuck could I have anything to do with this?"

"Strange how the only time you come here, she's taken a few days later. I know the vicious games you fucking play." Raif tensed his jaw a few times. "Just how much have I pissed you off? You want to return a lesson now? You've obviously spoken to someone."

"What I did back then is a far fucking cry from wanting a mother dead and a kid fucking hurt, you bastard." Ash started to shake. "How the *fuck* could you think this?"

"Easy, Raif," the man mumbled. "Too many variables at work here. You know that. It's not the first time someone's tipped someone off prior to a body being found. Remember Sasha?"

"MO was different," Raif snapped at him. "You were contacted then, source still unknown. Ash—"

"Ash what?" That focused Ash so much now. "Fucking say my name again like that, you cunt."

The man flicked his hood on as he nodded. "Whoever's involved in this with getting Voodoo taken into custody, we've got a serial killer here now." Raif got a look. "Any tie found to the I-dosing case?"

Raif briefly shook his head as Ash's fight fell. "Serial killer?"

Raif still wouldn't look at him. "Kerry, Voodoo's mother... Sasha."

"Who the fuck is Sasha?" More to the point—"How the hell do you know?"

"Not your concern." That couldn't have been colder. "All murdered, mutilated... raped. And you mention nothing, to no one, now."

Ash pulled back a touch. The emptiness and smell of the shed took on a whole new meaning now, but also the order of what Raif had just said. "Murdered, then raped?" Ash closed his mouth, not understanding what the hell had gone on. "But... but...."

The other man's face couldn't be seen. "It's done." He spoke to Raif now. "There's nothing you can do here. You have your cases to focus on. This is mine. You shouldn't have been involved in the fucking first place. Focus back on the job you were called here to do."

"I want Voodoo." Raif levelled a look. "I want her with me. No one else."

"Not your decision."

He went close. "More than my fucking decision. I know her better than her father. He doesn't deserve her."

The man stopped Raif with a hand on his arm as Raif went to walk away. "It's done. Move on." Ash felt a shift of hood in his direction. "Some candy just leaves a real bad taste in the mouth. But I won't let go until it bleeds."

"What the fuck is that supposed to mean? What the hell do you think I've done?"

But the man was gone, pulling himself up over the fence and leaving Ash staring at Raif.

"You talk to Chase about her?" Raif still wouldn't look at him.

"No."

"You talk to Chase about me?"

"No." That came out harder.

"You're best friends. You like your games. You always talk."

"Not about *this*."

Raif finally looked at him. "Nobody else knew, Ash. Even her father didn't know she was left alone. Social Services had a report come in that mentioned she was being left alone."

"So your only alternative is me? That I spoke to Chase and advertised on Murderers Unite for a girl to lose her fucking *mother*? To what? Keep you all to myself? Or just fuck with your head like I fuck up everyone else's?" Ash looked away, then wiped rain from his nose. "You know what, Raif?" He glanced back. "Fuck you. School, neighbours… any one of those could have caught on to what was happening here, and you still can't take the time to figure it out that if they hadn't come, she would have spent more time with her mother in there? Around her body? Instead you—" He cut himself off and tried to bite down the anger. "Fuck you, Raif. Just fuck you." He pushed past. "I've got enough fucking guilt over Johnny to be drowning in this too."

Yeah. Didn't matter when or where. Good guys. The burn always came. He left Raif there and hauled himself over the fence. Something dug into his leg, tearing his jeans at his thigh, but he ignored it now, just needing to get away from how pissed off and ugly he felt. He hadn't spoken to Chase, but he was doubting even himself now as he went through every conversation over the past few months. Raif hadn't been mentioned; he hadn't mentioned one damn thing about him to Chase. He hadn't mentioned Voodoo. The only time they'd spoken about Voodoo was at home last weekend. No one else had been around other than his dad.

He hadn't spoken to Chase. But would Chase be vicious enough to disrupt the waters between him and Raif if he did know they were together? He didn't know. He didn't know fucking anything anymore.

CHAPTER 20
WOUNDED

KNOWING HIS FATHER was asleep, that it touched four in the morning and darkness still felt thick and heavy, Ash swore into the night and found himself easing the door shut. Rubbing at his forehead, he didn't bother with any lights after he locked up, just shrugged out of his backpack, toed his trainers off, and headed upstairs. His jacket came off in his bedroom, and he slung it over his computer chair before a grip at the back of his T-shirt saw him tug it over his head. It landed on the floor as he slumped on the bed, an arm back over his eyes.

"Cunt." He didn't know whether he directed that at Raif or himself for getting caught in all of this bullshit. Whatever the fuck this bullshit was.

The sting in his leg ached a little more, and he rubbed at his jeans. The tear there was about two inches long and blood dried the edges of the material together. "Just fucking great."

Shivering at just how close he'd stood to death and dreading knowing the details to what Voodoo had been traumatised by, Ash pushed off the bed, cursing when the darkness saw him tangle himself in his T-shirt and nearly floor himself. He made it into the en suite and pushed his jeans off his hips before making sure they found a home in the wash basket. The light came on next, and he tore his gaze away from it for a moment as it stung his eyes. Then he fastened his hair back out of his face, hating the length, the colour, the curls, but mostly how good it had felt to have Raif play thumb and finger through the wilder strands.

The basics were always kept close: lube, condoms, but also some painkillers and antiseptic lotion. Work in a factory, handling car parts, meant sharp edges easily tore through skin, and the small cuts around his wrists had earned him a few curious glances in the past. Protective gloves only protected so far.

One foot on the toilet seat, he grabbed a towel, for the first time stopping to stare at the shaking going on with his hands, then eventually ran the towel under some warm water before cleaning the gash. It wasn't too bad, barely even match-wound worthy to what Johnny went through… Voodoo's mother, Kerry—Voodoo. Whoever the hell this Sasha had been.

He couldn't stop the shivering this time, nor how long he stood there, caught.

Voodoo. How old was she? Just what had she seen…? He'd cut Johnny's body down and kissed at cold lips to try and breathe life into him, even though his training at the factory said he didn't need to do that with CPR nowadays. But he'd been an adult. Voodoo… Christ. She was nothing but a kid, and she'd stayed by her mom for days. Had she even noticed the smell as she'd clung to her mom?

Shit.

He cleaned the blood, then winced feeling the sting as he

covered the small patch on his inside leg with Savlon. All the Savlon in the world wouldn't take away Voodoo's hurt. It wouldn't take Raif's either. His own. And he was always left licking his own wounds as—

"You do that outside, with me?"

The quiet to Raif's voice startled him, but nothing unnerved Ash more than finding the big man leaning against the bathroom door.

"The door was locked downstairs. You aren't invited. Piss off." Ash eased around, more than suddenly conscious of how he only had his boxers on, then headed towards his bedroom.

Raif caught his arm as he passed. "Ash—"

"*Let me get some fucking clothes on.*" It came so heated that Raif instantly raised his hands and backed away with a frown. Forcing his breathing to stay calm, Ash headed over to his drawers and pulled out some jogging bottoms.

Hands easing into his pockets, Raif stayed quiet until Ash finished tugging the bottoms over his hips, then he frowned and looked away. "You ever see the look you get in your eyes, Ash? Like you're taking a breath, but you don't care that you can't feel what you breathe in?"

Ash headed back towards the bedroom door and held it open. "The majority that comes my way is fucking poison, anyway. And noting such, fuck off, Raif."

Raif came over. Again he reached for Ash's arm, and again Ash made sure he didn't make contact. "Fuck. Off."

"I'm trying to say sorry," Raif said so quietly, his eyes as dark as the bedroom around them, despite that bathroom light. Again his hands found his pockets and he shrugged. "Seems I'm fucking that up too."

"No, you fucked it up by coming back here. Don't you

have a little girl to save, someone else's world to straighten out?"

"Ash—"

"Piss off."

"Ash, please. I—"

"I've never had sex without my clothes on."

Raif frowned at him.

"All the games I play, you'd think the end goal was to get naked. But even Chase, when he'd touch my ass, I'd back off." Ash kept his voice level. "See, I stand still waiting for the fuck-over because it always comes, no matter how long it takes. Mostly from good men. Damn good men."

Ash hooked a thumb over the waistband of his jogging pants and inched one side down enough to show the curve of his ass, the first run of scars and grooves that could have given the moon a run for its money when it came to marking out the hits it had taken throughout history.

"This one here..." He ran his thumb over a long line that scarred its way over four cigarette burns. "Bonfire Night. Ten years ago. After I'd set off some fireworks in the park with Chase and the cops had gotten the call... instead of putting the sparkler in the water bucket to cool it down, my father burned it into my ass to remind me how they scar people's lives. I was told to never touch one again. So you know what I did instead? I set fire to the neighbour's shed when my neighbour was inside, just to watch Miles run in and pull him out." Ash looked down at it. "See, the night I took that to my ass, that was the night I kissed Chase for the first time too. It's why we'd set off the fireworks, just so scared and excited at how it changed us a little. Who knows, maybe my dad got the call about that too and saw to it I'd never let anyone kiss me again either." He looked up, still flatlining everything inside. "I'd ask him, but he's fucking forgotten, and apologise… he always looks like he wants to say sorry, but he can't remember why. And part of me loves him so much for it, but I fucking hate every inch of his bastard soul for it too. So I'm here, still fucking here, locked in and not moving forward because the past always holds me still, because I can't get my head around why I fuck up other men's lives when all I want to do is ram my dad's head through a fucking glass window for it. But good. I'm meant to be such a good fucking boy, right, only he's sometimes in a wheelchair now when the pain hits really bad. So I can't fucking hurt him even if I tried, because he needs looking after."

Raif looked down at his feet, arms folded, face hard. "The burn on your arm…. He did that. He's… still doing that."

Ash ignored him. "Me and Chase. Yeah, we're best of friends, we talk. Fuck, we talk and play games to try and bleed out our hurt because we've both seen enough. But Johnny…" Ash tried to stop from hurting Raif the way he wanted to. "Johnny…" He gave a snort. "Christ, Johnny hated that we had secrets between us two, that we played games. You could see it in his eyes. But the truth was, me and Chase, he'd tried to speak up once before for me, to Miles, and Miles, bless his soul, he'd done what he always did: tried to look out for the family and have a word with my dad. I got a lighter on my ass for that one. So me and Chase, it wasn't secrets we kept from Johnny after that, it wasn't to do with trust, we just learnt never to speak up. Chase was simply there in the aftermath to stop it hurting." Ash forced a smile. "That's what killed Johnny; that he saw how close we are. That we never told him, we never trusted him when we damn well knew he'd always been the one to pull us back from the shit when we got too vicious with it."

Raif was close, so close, and Ash didn't back away, didn't stand down now. "So why the fuck would I talk about *you* when I can't expose my body, let alone my fucked-up mind to anyone? Not even Chase?"

"Ash—"

Ash backed away from the touch that tried to dust his bare shoulder. "I mean it. Piss off, Raif. I know you're hurting, but I've only ever pissed about when it comes to love, and Johnny was the price of all that pissing about, because me and Chase, we were never that serious even when I knew Johnny loved Chase. I don't piss about with trust anymore: mine or anyone else's, certainly not a fucking girl's and—"

"Kerry was my wife."

Ash's anger stalled as Raif's hand found his pocket.

"Christ..." Raif snorted bitterly. "I shouldn't have carried on doing this surveillance job I've had for the past few months... this past lifetime. I should have been there. But I...." He shrugged. "I lost her.... I lost the little girl who gave her everything we'd already lost as a father and mother all those years ago." Thoughts paused and that slow process with evaluating every detail now had its flaws, almost locking Raif in the languid reveal of detail. The smile he gave came with such a cold beauty that it silenced Ash.

"Toast. Voodoo won her over with toast. Kerry never had time for anything, not as a new mom. So I used to take it to her in bed, used to bring it to her when she was too busy breastfeeding, or running late to the shops because she had milk on her blouse. Then when our son died, she stopped eating properly for such a long time. Until she met Voodoo."

Ash frowned.

"Kerry came alive on the streets, as though all ties and grief in her life were wiped clean. It does that to you: the streets. Then when Voodoo saw her keep coming back to look after her, she made Kerry toast."

The grief there was so raw. Raif had already lost a son. Now his wife... Voodoo.

"Any other time, I wouldn't have hurt you like that, but..." Raif dug his hands in his pockets. "I lost them all over again. A little girl who didn't see monsters in her garden shed, a woman who grieved for her own kid. Neither of them looked at me like I was typecast as the anti-hero who lived under the bridge." Raif eased back against the doorframe. "The hard thing is, that...." He paused, maybe confused, maybe just angry. "Voodoo seemed to know; she seemed to know the arrangement wouldn't last and she'd lose. And she lost so badly this week, Ash. She knew that once she was taken away for whatever reason, the lady in the shed would crumble to dust."

Again that cold beauty of his smile, like a lake that kept its waters chilled, knowing the winter moon made better company than the blistering heat of the day.

"I'm not perfect, Ash," he said gently. "I have flaws, I get pissed off, but—" He frowned at Ash. "—but when I love, I'm there for the duration, no matter how tough it gets. And Voodoo, she just about stole all that I have to see any sense tonight. I shouldn't have taken it out on you. You came when I found out, and I was just so pissed off with myself that I'd let another man's son consume me for weeks so that they were lost in ways I swore I'd never lose again."

He looked down at his hands. "Dark matter," he mumbled, so quietly. "It's what I feel like sometimes with what I do. Able to slip through anything unnoticed but hold on to nothing at the same time."

The need was there to find out just where Raif had disappeared to for the week, but that wasn't what made Ash close the door in that moment. Saying nothing, he took Raif by the wrist and pulled him behind him, towards the bed. He twisted Raif around at the last moment, then made sure Raif sat down on the bed as he came in and split Raif's thighs with his own. It mimicked how they'd stood in the kitchen last week, in that darkness.

Ash tugged off Raif's jacket, then his shoes, then eased Raif down onto the bed, going down next to him. After easing to his side, he pulled the covers up over them both. "Get some sleep, Raif."

At first there was quiet, just the sound of the clock from the hall downstairs, then Raif shifted slightly, coming on top of Ash. Again that crushing weight, again the feeling of being wrapped in a wall of muscle, but it was such a good feeling.

Arms framed Ash's face, then thumbs swiped gently at Ash's temple. Dark brown eyes watched him, and he watched Raif right back.

"Would you allow me to take you," Raif said quietly, "even though I know I hurt you tonight?"

Ash frowned at the soft words, and Raif's look softened as his brush of thumb across Ash's brow smoothed it away.

"Please," he said gently. A kiss came at Ash's jaw, his neck. "I need to hold on and feel something. Feel you."

People dealt with grief in different ways. Anger was

mostly Ash's reaction, but Raif...? This was his.

Tenseness raced Ash's body, and Raif mumbled into it, tracing his side, his rough grip-release-grip already working to massage it away before small shockwaves of worry rippled under Ash's skin. "Could you take me, Red? Would you?"

Ash gently nudged against Raif's head to get him to look down at him. Raif did, and Ash dusted fingers over Raif's side as he shared a gaze, that same question: Could he? There wasn't really any question there. Raif needed to move in sync with life and in turn have life move in sync with him for a change.

Ash arched, gently moving his hips up into the wall of muscle above. Raif felt like dark matter: he thought he'd fade away and no one was left to reach in and pull him back. But Raif had been there for Ash through his grief, even if it had been at a distance, keeping to the shed when Ash had needed to try and deal his own way. So Ash gave him this, arching up into him, then tugging Raif back down.

Sex terrified him. It wasn't that he hadn't done it; he just couldn't handle being seen naked through it, being touched with all his scars on display. It brought that tenseness to his body that always made sex awkward... stiff... painful, or fears on it ending in pain. But he'd meet Raif halfway. The darkness was Raif's turf. Ash could keep to the shadows without being pushed naked into the light. Right?

A bite came to his neck and he groaned, in the same moment catching Raif's hand and guiding him down to the waistline of his jogging pants.

Now on one elbow, Raif stilled, his weight eased off Ash's. "You sure, baby? We can take it slower. We—"

Ash kissed his jaw, his neck, then paused by his lips.

"Just don't..." He frowned. "Don't touch my ass. Please. Don't look."

A long gaze, then a kiss stole his breath, then instantly shifted to his neck, his pec, biting a nipple and causing Ash to jolt and groan at the sudden shifts. A tug exposed his cock, a lick met it, a kiss at the head, then Ash gripped onto the headboard as Raif swallowed him to the root, massaging his balls. Whatever fear his body had, whatever fears his half-half cock had, the mouth on his cock stripped them all away, sending his body headfirst into crying youth and lack of control in just a few strokes, grips, and licks of a rough tongue.

"Fuck... fuck..." He forced himself to come back down, growling at being taken to the edge so quickly, then denying his own release. Raif was back up close and personal with lips, his body again swamping Ash's, hard cock on cock and being crushed between them.

His jogging pants had gone, his boxers too, but Ash hadn't got a clue when.

Sadness shone in Raif's eyes, a little devilry too as Ash realised.

"Talent," Raif mouthed quietly.

Ash roughed a kiss to his lips for that talent. Then a thick thigh split Ash's, and Raif made sure he spread wider as Raif nestled fully between Ash's thighs.

"Fuck." Ash arched up, head back, eyes closed, that rush to get in and walk that forest of chest hair.

"Yeah, yeah..." Raif gripped at Ash's hip, released, gripped again as he crushed his cock hard into Ash's, wetness making life messy, heated... dirty but so fucking good with it.

Ash gripped Raif's hair, then instantly let go, regretting

it. Instead he dropped a lazy arm around Raif's neck and used a leg to pull him in close, to get that full pressure between his thighs. He didn't top from the bottom. But bare, naked beneath Raif, scars on display but respected... hidden, he wanted fucking. The *fuck* he needed fucking by... by all of this. Raif.

"C'mon." Ash rested his head against Raif's. "Make it hard, make it hurt. Fucking feel me, Raif."

Breathing hard, deep, Raif played his cock and the sounds were adulterous: slicked-up, long, slow... the tip thick as it touched Ash's hole once, twice.... Fuck. When had Raif taken some lube? The sounds, the slicked up feel between his thighs was unmistakable, but any thought on voicing any of that was carjacked from him as Raif gave one hard push of thick head into him.

"Christ, Christ," panted Ash. It had caught him off guard, but there was no apology from Raif, maybe some anger, a lot of grief, but so much more heated need to obliterate memories in the darkness, and Ash was fucked if he needed any apology for it. He rode what his body took, that heavy-weighted head breaching, fucking, filling him. Raif hit root-deep, then those thick thighs pushed hard against bone, keeping it there.

"Fuck, fuck." Ash hissed. "Just..." *Fuck.* Yeah. That was *talent.* "Move." Ash couldn't breathe, and he knew he'd hurt, taking what came next but—"Move. Fucking move, Raif. Please."

And it came. Raif fucked hard and fast, grunting... groaning, taking Ash with him each time he slammed in, jolting Ash's body.

Ash rode it, eyes screwed shut, sweat dampening his own lips as his loose hook of arm around Raif's neck turned into holding on for dear life now his body was pushed further, deeper... the tug of Ash's leg up onto Raif's shoulder stretching him wider, harder, and—

Ash writhed, fighting what his body cried out.

"Come on," Raif snarled, taking him root-deep, grinding it into Ash. "Fucking come on, baby. Cry it for me."

His ass ached, hurt. Hips too from the roughness, but in every right way. The burn, the stretch, the fucked-in fullness that left him panting and scrambling to grab his own cock. He bit at Raif's shoulder to try and control some of the building, but Raif stopped grinding, back now to putting every ounce of strength into the fucking he gave, so Ash let go. Not with his bite, not to bury his noise, but because he forgot he bit anything as he came.

"Yeah, baby. Yeah, baby." Raif pulled away, now up on one elbow, rubbing a path along the line of come before it even stopped falling, crushing all Ash's wetness back along Ash's cock, slicking him up into one heated mass and finishing him off with a hard and fast grip on Ash's cock. "Fuck... fuck... beautiful. Bloody beautiful."

"Christ." Heart and head pounding fast, Ash collapsed into the bed and didn't protest one bit when Raif groaned, coming back down on him and fucking back into him, taking what he needed to get off. There was no pain, not anymore, just his writhing under Raif, a dig of nail all the way down Raif's back to drive him home and take anything the fuck that he wanted.

"Yeah, come on." Ash pulled him with a tug on his ass. "Fucking own it."

Raif buried a cry in the curve of Ash's throat, and Ash groaned as his cock stretched him wide, the ground of hips threatening to fuck ball-deep in there for the release of come, then uncontrolled fucks into Ash took the rest from him.

Ash let a soft smile creep in, his breathing matching Raif's. "Fuck… yeah, you got it."

Raif caught his breath for a moment, then frowned down at Ash.

Ash ran a hand through his own hair, the sweat making it stick to his face. "Fucking talent, Raif." When had he lost the band that held it all up?

Raif choked a laugh, then came back down on Ash. Ash didn't try and move, not with how quiet Raif fell. He slipped an arm around his big shoulders, pulling him in close. Keeping him close.

There were no tears, just the quiet, a slight shivering as sleep crept in with Raif, but enough to show he fought something in his dreams.

At one point Ash managed to break free, just to clean up, get his jogging pants back on, but he got back in, spooning up close behind Raif. The few cries that came out during the next hours brought some names Ash knew, a few he didn't, then a tenseness in body and twist into the covers. So he held on again. Ash held on again because Raif felt like dark matter, because he thought he'd fade away and no one was left to reach in and pull him back.

CHAPTER 21
DON'T... DARKEN THE MATTER

CATCHING THE SUNDAY morning chill, Gray stood outside the manor, looking down at his mobile. The last time he'd stood here, two pheasants had been wandering the green, looking for something. Jack had been at his side then, and they'd shared a cigarette, shared the smoke as Gray had gone in to steal a kiss from him. Nerves. They had been so bad back then.

Now the pheasants were gone, lost somewhere in the woods, and Gray hated the irony. He leaned against the wall and dug his hand in his suit pocket as he read the text message again.

White female: aged 45, yet to be identified. Beaten to death, with rape occurring after death (necrophilia). Unusual bruising forms with the rape of a cold (dead) victim, different to that of a live victim as cells start to break down. Bruising also lasts longer on a cold victim, giving clear signs of penetration weeks after death.

Chrissy Wright: single mother, aged 28. Beaten, raped, mutilated. Holly Blue butterfly and semen inserted into the stomach. Semen matched with that found on white female and Shipman; DNA found on scene. No matches found.

Lucy White: Aged 5. Witness. Left on scene with deceased mother. Now with Social Services, under psychiatric evaluation.

Gray closed his eyes.

Four rings on his mobile came next, and he set his jaw tensing.

"*Shw mae*" came the male voice on the other end as he answered.

"*Sut mae.*"

"You got the new details."

"Just."

Quiet. "Why did you pull out?"

Gray kept it short, far from sweet. "I wasn't assigned there to cull a serial killer. I was assigned there to find out why there's MI6 interest over Raif. You knew MI6 were already there on scene."

More quiet. "Yes. I knew. But if MI6 had been given the intel that you'd been assigned there to gather intel on Raif and not the killer, they would have shut doors with no chance to observe."

"So that means you know he's either working for them, or with them on something." Gray went quiet. "There was no need for blackout on information like that."

"You're in personal communication with the head of MI6. Yes, there was."

Ahh. His father. And there still would be a need to watch communication if his father insisted on more contact. And with Baz being here, he was pushing for full control. Gray didn't blame this caller for his mistrust: they'd both been pushed into a corner. "Understood. What intel did you have on him prior to me going in? Why the interest from you?"

"Unclear at the moment. Sources are silent on any intelligence on this man." There was honesty there. Maybe. "I'm curious why MI6 are being stubborn over information on him when there's such heavy activity there now from them. I'd like to know what they're all doing there."

Yeah. That irked Gray. To deny this man information wasn't a healthy decision, not with what they were called in to do. Old codes, old courtesies. Not talking always ignited attention. MI6 knew those risks.

"I'd like you back on scene now. MI6 will be warned formally not to interfere. Your priority is now your original cull, Holly Blue. Leave any cleanup to housekeeping. After that, D & I Raif."

Detain and interrogate. "*Nos da.*" That was just fucking peachy in his book.

Gray headed back on in, ignoring his grandfather's glance up from his morning paper as he sat at the table. Jack's father, Greg, had taken a seat with him. They'd taken to playing cards more lately, most times inviting Jan's mother over too. The cards became an alternative to seeing Martin on Greg's part, and Gray didn't blame him.

"Morning," said Greg, giving him a nod and a friendly offer of a smile as he worked his crossword. Gray smiled back, but nothing was said from Ed. He seemed to recognise Gray's call, and his grandfather turned his gaze away as much as Jack. Strange considering how he and Jack bit and nibbled at each other's throats as a rule yet shared this quiet.

He headed through the reception, bypassing the lounge. He knew where Jan would be this morning. Gray had mentioned privately that Jan not deal in secrets around Baz, and even though Jan hadn't pushed for a reason over why, and Gray couldn't offer any without any proof, Jan started to shut Baz down with close and isolated contact with Jack. That was just damn fine by Gray. Phone slipped into his pocket, Gray glanced at the line of disinfectant dispensers as he made his way down the hall, to the seclusion room. Craig came out of the staffroom as he passed, and Gray nodded in his direction before reaching the door and thumbing in the code on his phone.

"Two minutes," he said as Craig came over, frowning. Gray didn't wait for a reply as he pushed on in.

Jan turned his way, already reaching for his headphones and tugging them free. "Hey," whispered Jan, glancing back as he came over. Gray took the headphones off him and slipped them in his pocket as Jan looked set to forget they were loitering with intent around his neck. "He's still pretty quiet," added Jan. The soft rise and fall of Martin's ribs said he slept through the remains of his illness. He'd barely picked up despite the medication. He lay on his side, facing the wall, arms wrapped around himself as though he knew he only had himself to fall back on.

Something jolted inside Gray, maybe a snap of resentment that Martin hugged himself as if Jack were there, hiding in a return hold with Martin that only ever allowed Martin in on all their secrets and hurt. Or maybe... maybe it was a snap of something else, how Martin would always hold himself as though he knew he only had himself to fall back on, and, fuck... how all that confidence came alive with how he was perfectly fucking peachy within the beautiful isolation and freedom of it all. He needed nobody, not like Jack. Or at least he thought he needed nobody. Baz was proving him wrong on that front. And if he found out Jan was the one there keeping Baz at a safe distance, just how much would that play with Martin's head?

Jan's touch to his arm and the concern there in his eyes called out Gray's confusion. "I'm... I'm losing you to business again, hm?"

Gray kissed at his lips. "A few days. No more." He rested his head against Jan's, loving the soft flutter of Jan's longer hair into his eyes, but not liking how Jan needed Martin sometimes too; that there'd be a chance Jan would lock himself in here with Martin and rather face everything Martin had to give than face an empty bed, life... heart. But they were all tied together for the duration now, so closely intertwined.

"Hey. Always right here, stunner," whispered Jan, brushing a kiss against his lips, and Gray pulled back, running a discreet touch along Jan's lips.

"Too fucking right," he mumbled back. It kept hurting too much every time he had to walk away. "Two days, no more." He ended that with a cough, this time wincing at the ache in his gut.

Jan nodded, frowned. "I'll have a bourbon ready."

"Some fluffy pink slippers and silk knickers ready for him to wear too, Janice?"

They both stilled and looked at the bed. Martin didn't face them; his shivers were barely hidden beneath the covers as he spoke to the wall.

"Gray would look stunning, huh? Just his holster wrapping that tight body, gun in hand... stocking, suspenders.... Or is that something you're saving for Jack?" No bitterness played in his voice, the tone set to normal, everyday. "You ever thought that's why he's over here, holding on to me for so long? I mean, Jack. He's a tough cunt in his own right, and you, you looked at Jess in that tight dress as Jack was forced to watch from the sidelines, and if you could have made him wear it, you would, right? You got any idea what that does to a man like Jack? The humiliation?" Quiet. "Yeah, you know how Jack looks humiliated, right? You lived for it back then at that dinner table."

Jan's frown played out a few hard and fast emotions: how that was Jack's memories there, how his own kink was a guy in a skirt, or more Jack in a skirt. How he knew Jack, how all of Jack's blushes and "manly fucking chuckles" would see him burn a skirt right along with the latest artwork that didn't line up to perfection in his OCD world.

Jan went to speak, to come back with something, maybe bite back on how Martin had his demons and Baz played them to the full now, without Martin picking up that one vital hazard, but Martin had hit hard there, and Jan was forever the lover who knew Baz watched everything that went on now. It had him searching Gray's pockets and taking out the headphones. He needed to shut it out, even as he walked away from the cell.

"I'll… I'll get Ray to bring the Merc up. I had it taken to the carwash because of the marks it picked up."

Gray went to stop him, but Jan shook his head, his gaze briefly on Martin. He'd had enough and needed out. Gray watched him go before heading for the door himself.

"Came back to bite you in the ass, didn't it? You wouldn't be staying away for a few days and leaving Jan alone here otherwise."

Gray didn't look back this time.

"Well you just leave Jan right here with me, Welsh. He's developing a tough streak that's damn sexy. Seems it's

Jack's flaw: picking those with a tendency to shift and dance with devils. Who knows, maybe Jack can make a visit when you're gone, be all loving and soppy-like. Imagine the guilt afterwards with that one! Enough to get Jan dangling from a noose if nothing else, eh? Him fucking a damaged psychiatric patient in a straitjacket. Christ knows you ran back home to Wales for months after fucking me, right?"

Gray headed over to the bed and tugged at Martin's arm until he lay on his back. Then he kept his grip on his arm as he sat down.

"You don't fuck with him while I'm gone."

"Ooooh. That a threat there, Welsh?" Martin grinned, then winced and frowned as Gray applied pressure. He didn't stop until Martin arched his body, cuff rattling on the bed as he fought showing just how much it hurt. "Getting to you, am I?" Martin coughed, heavy, hard. "Fucking peachy that, huh?"

Gray wiped at Martin's forehead with his free touch, along with the fever playing with Martin. Cameras were in here. He needed discreet threat. "Stay good, pet."

Martin chuckled. "You need to learn how to ask me, Welsh, and—" Martin hissed, head thrown back, leaving Gray dusting a thumb over his cheek. He'd gripped his arm hard enough to leave bone creaking.

"Stay good, pet. Don't fucking push him anymore."

Another run of coughing came, rattling the bed, a smile, the force of a tear, then—

"Mukka, please… don't."

An arm suddenly slipped around him, then a nose brushed Gray's neck, a turn into Gray that asked to hide, to—

"Tuh-tuh-tell him I'm sorry, okay…?" Dampness

touched Gray's throat. "Don't... don't know what I've done, but... but just tell him I'm sorry, okay?"

Gray knew the conversation. Another time, another cell, Steve had stood in the corner as Gray had broken Jack and taken him down to the floor. Jack had faced Cutter, how Cutter had raped Steve, how he'd raped a little girl, how Cutter earned his name by cutting Jack and exploiting Jack's disorders, all for Jack to call it the fuck on and run headlong into control by Cutter's blade. Jack had faced all of his disorders in its destructive beauty, and seeing all of that, facing jail, facing Gray, Jack had turned into Gray, hid, and whispered softly—

"Sorry." The mumble came so quiet now too. "Means nothing, I know, but... but.... So sorry, mukka. So fucking sorry."

Was it where Jack was? Stuck in one moment where he was always holding on to Gray, hiding from the horrors done... apologising for every horror done... never free from that cycle because Martin was always there, always fucking life up?

Christ. Gray jolted, just slightly. "Juh—" He couldn't finish his name. It felt so long since he'd called it, that Jack had turned in his direction, hearing it. Frowning seriously, he slipped his arm around Jack and just held on as Craig came through into the cell. Gray shook his head at him, keeping Craig back as his own grief caught up and threatened to break. Every time, every fucking time. He'd forgotten just how hard his heart could beat, whether it was hurt, grief... everything else that Jack forced him to feel.

"Jan. You keep him safe, stunner." He whispered it heatedly in his ear, gripping a little tighter. "Do that for me, please. Because I can't at the moment. And he needs looking after, so badly, stunner. You remember that? You keep him safe...."

He kissed at Jack's cheek, tasting the fever as it raked shivers through Jack, and it came then, just a gentle nudge, a shift of nose along Gray's jaw. That quiet talk between switch and Dom when both knew how deep words could cut into bone.

"'S okay, mukka. I'm here."

"Fuck." *Please, please, please.* It kept repeating over and over again, and Gray screwed his eyes shut and ran his touch up Jack's back to his hair. He gripped just as tightly as he'd needed to break through Martin's arm a moment before, but for whole new reasons now. "Stay here, please. I need you here, because I'm never far from fucking here and you keep running away, you bastard. Stop running away, Jack. Please. For Christ's sake.... Please."

Jack jolted, grunted like he'd touched a car battery and forgot which leads went where, then Gray got a shove, a vicious push away. "*The fuck?* Get off me, cunt."

No play was in Martin's eyes. That had caught him out as much as it did Gray, and Gray eased back, dropping his head, maybe losing his heart.

"Gray."

He looked over at Craig.

"Time out, now, please. For both of you?"

Gray didn't argue, but he didn't look at Martin again as he left. He needed that taste of Jack that he'd been given to last just a few moments longer, mostly because he was tired of losing no matter how long he stayed here for Jack.

≈

By the time Gray made it to the courtyard, the Merc slept on the concrete, purring softly against the morning. Jan was nowhere in sight, and the keys in the ignition said Ray had started his rounds.

Frowning, Gray pulled out his mobile as he headed over to his Merc. More travel details were needed, more arrangements made with Andrews to cover Monday morning meetings tomorrow and ops debriefings with Gray's staff.

But a text came through as he reached his Merc.

No, dammit. This is MI6 business. Stay out of this. Stay there, Gray. Stay with yours. I'll handle this.

Nhad.

Gray stilled, the glare of the early morning sun catching the screen of the phone. He looked away for a moment. His father had used MI6 on a text message as well as his name, so this was hitting close to home for that kind of fuck-up to come up. *Fuck you.* He wasn't playing now, or as eloquent. *Target-only business,* he thumbed back, letting him know Holly Blue was his concern. Anything else, it was nothing to do with anyone else but him and his targets.

Bullshit. You would have been ordered to D & I beyond the target. I'm asking you to leave him alone.

Gray didn't reply. Not this time. He would detain Raif. He would interrogate him, mostly because of just how dirty his father had played with Baz. His father knew his moves too well, too personally, and Gray had observed Baz enough over the past week to find out he sourced that information back to MI6. So either there was someone else in MI6 involved, or his father walked Gray's halls without permission. He'd push this with Raif to see if and when his father screwed up over admitting he planted Baz.

Another text came through which read his silence well enough.

Give me twenty-four hours at least. If your Holly Blue isn't identified by then, I'll hand over all surveillance my team has and you can go in. But I need the time to move your D & I target out.

Why? What's the target to you? Gray waited for a reply, and he waited a long time. *Why is he there?*

Eventually one came through.

Stay with Jan, son. With Jack. Let me look after mine; you take care of yours. One favour for another now: in return for Jack's mother.

Jack's mother. For killing Jack's mother. Gray tensed. And... *Mine...* That put Raif on a personal level with his dad.

Noise from behind saw Jan leaning against the lamppost. His smile said he'd be okay. But the fact Jan stayed away, allowing the distance to grow, had Gray distractedly running a thumb over his mobile phone screen. Those headphones were visible around Jan's neck, the wire leading down to the iPhone in his right pocket.

Gray went to him and slipped his hands to Jan's waist, then closed his eyes, now resting cheek to cheek with Jan.

Martin wasn't the only threat here; Baz was too, which put Jan at risk, from both of them. As tough as Jan was, he couldn't handle both now. And if Gray's father was focused on Raif, maybe, just maybe, that left Baz here. Isolated.

"Christ. Tell me to say fuck to life, fuck to everything, just for twenty-four hours if nothing else. Tell me you need me to stay, Jan." He needed to stay now. He'd had a taste of Jack and didn't want to lose that either.

Jan pulled back and watched him for long moments. That independence was there, the look that said he'd be okay eventually. "What's happened? What's gone on?" He wasn't talking about the phone call. "This to do with Baz, or Martin?"

Gray rested a gaze on where Jack's new cell slept. "Both, but more so Baz." Why was there a pull towards Martin on that front? Why did Martin creep into Gray's thoughts too?

When Jan slipped an arm around Gray's neck, this time pulling Gray in, it was for Gray, how Gray needed to stay. "Say fuck to life." A harder exhale came from Jan. "Christ. Say fuck to everything outside of those gates, if only for twenty-four hours, Gray."

A collar slept around Gray's throat, one that would always tug him home, one Jack always owned, Jan, but for the moment, his father too. So Gray would take down the spy in his home first, then he'd deal with his father. And if that meant going through Raif....

He just hoped Raif had the sense to get out when he was given the chance, because once he was done with Baz....

CHAPTER 22
GETTING OUT

DAYLIGHT CUT ACROSS the bedcovers, forcing out a grunt as Ash covered his eyes. The cold feel of bed forced him to shift his arm off his face, and he eased up onto an elbow now Raif's space lay empty. Jacket was gone off the bed, shoes and socks off the floor and...

Giving a hard sigh, Ash eased back down and ran a hand over his face.

Somebody needed to nail Raif's cock to the fucking floor. Although Ash didn't blame him for not facing the morning after a breakdown.

After throwing back the covers, he padded on into the bathroom and washed up. With a fresh change of boxers and a more comfortable fit of jeans barely hanging onto his hips, he tugged on a vest and tied his hair back as he went downstairs.

The sound of hissing hit the pan first, then the scent of bacon drifted over. With a look at the clock to see it barely touch six, he doubted his dad was up. His dad liked to hug the covers almost as much as he did.

"Morning." In the kitchen, Raif flicked a look over, then slipped the bacon onto a sandwich. He put it on the table as Ash took a seat, wincing at how raw his ass felt. Yep. Talent. A coffee found its way over next. "You sleep okay?" added Raif, his lopsided smile more cautious and slower in coming this morning. His grief was still raw.

Ash eyed the bacon up and gave a small smile. "You didn't know I was gonna get up. Again. This is yours, isn't it?"

Raif glanced over and offered a shy shrug. "Still a big man here: needs food. Always."

Oh yep. Raif always seemed to live in a kitchen. Ash rubbed at his head, even shivered a touch. "Before you leave, right?" He hadn't intended that to be moody, but he wasn't used to mornings after, especially with Raif. He'd usually disappear by now.

Raif's smile faltered as he came over and crouched by him. Ash got a tap at his arm that asked that he look at Raif. "I'd like to think I could come back again." That small smile crept back up. "Even if you take the chair, and I take the bed."

Ash snorted as that broke the tension a little. "Been here before, Raif. It ended up in you blushing and being called a virgin."

Raif looked pleased. "Good to know how you remember every word I say to you."

"Hm, what was it you said… 'imagine what I could do in a bed, because, like, I'm a big bloke here—'" Ash loved how madly Raif blushed now. "I mean, don't get me wrong, now I know you're a big bloke… here… I'm inclined to leave my front… and back door open a little more. It's just I had you down pat as a gent. Yet there you were when we first met. You going on about your size."

"Fitting in your chair and not breaking it." Raif pointed a finger at him. "I was talking about fitting in your chair."

"Suuure you were." Ash gave him a long and very deliberate wink.

"Asshole."

"But goddamn sexy with it," said Ash, only to have Raif blush some more.

Then Raif went over to grab his sandwich, and he glanced down at his pocket as though he'd got a call. He fished his phone out a moment later.

Ash straightened in his chair, uncomfortable with how poker-faced Raif fell. As though what he was reading was never meant to be shared. Again. Same as always. "Problem?"

For a moment he didn't respond, then flicked a look up. His phone went back in his pocket a moment later, then he took a sandwich bag out of one of the drawers and, from the spare slice he'd left for himself, tucked a bacon bap away for later.

Ash got to his feet, his food left untouched on the table. "You're leaving."

Raif glanced over as he finished tucking the bap into the bag. "I've…." The frown there puzzled Ash. "I've got to."

"What? Wait? As in got to go and not, what? Come back?" Ash pulled the bag away, tossing it on the counter, away from Raif. "Because that sounds like a hard and fast goodbye to me." Anger bit at his insides. "Why the fuck did you come back last night or at all just to fuck off this morning?"

He didn't answer, only continued to mess with the sandwich bags.

Ash grabbed it away and made sure it found the wall. Raif glanced at it, then Ash, then... nothing, just the countertop.

"So you're leaving Voodoo too."

"*No.*" That came out so harshly. "I'll... I'll be there as best as I can for her."

Ash folded his arms. "So it's just me you're saying goodbye to? Why? What's suddenly changed?" He took a step back. "You know that fuck-over? There it is."

Raif let out a rough sigh. "I'm trying to keep you safe, Ash."

"From what?" Ash held out his arms. "Big bloke here. You don't get a say in what keeps me fucking safe."

Raif slammed down a knife he'd picked up. "This isn't a fucking game now, Ash. I didn't get a say in what kept Voodoo and Kerry safe. *I damn well do with you. You got that?*"

Ash denied the jolt that came on the back of Raif's anger, and he looked away, mostly to calm his own. "Is Raif even your name? Is Kerry even your wife's?" He chewed his cheek for a moment. "Would you even tell me if it wasn't?"

"Why? Would you trust what I tell you anyway?"

That sounded just as bitter and Ash glared at him. "It's been a few months, Raif. Just a few fucking months that we've known each other. What the fuck do you expect from me? For us?"

Before he knew it, Raif was there in front of him, body pressed in tight, cupping Ash's face.

"I don't know what I fucking want, and that's what's fucking with my head. You do, Ash, every fucking time. I never know whether to stay... to go...." He rested his head down on Ash's. "I need... Ash, it's such a bad place to be now." He closed his eyes. "It's getting more dangerous to be around here from tomorrow. So now, if you want me to stay—" Raif adjusted his stance, coming in a little closer. "—ask me to stay, Ash. Make me understand that you need me here."

Ash didn't understand the intensity or the way Raif held on as though the ship was sinking fast. "You need to stay for Voodoo."

"No."

He was being pushed into a corner here, and he stood blindfolded and struggling to get out. But he also kept looking at the door, how he'd hate to see it close behind Raif again. "I barely know you. I don't fucking trust you."

Raif nodded. "I know. I keep thinking I know you, that I trust you to calm. But—"

"But?" Always that fucking *but*. "But I... look, if you want it, you..." Ash frowned so seriously. "You can have my chair tonight. I'll take the bed."

Raif suddenly softened his features, laughed. "Demoted to the chair now, huh?"

Ash shrugged. "Fuck off. It's my gaming chair... cost more than the bed. Means a little more to me than my bed at the moment. It's meant to be a compliment, but I'm really fucking shit at those too, as shit as this morning-after bollocks as you are."

Raif let out a laugh and it travelled into his mass of body, jolting Ash and forcing up one from him. Then Ash was pulled into a hug. "In that case, it's worth staying around for a while to take your... chair."

Ash watched Raif, how his eyes closed against the daylight. "Why are you scared now, Raif? Who are you scared of?"

That hard sigh came again. "The past. The present." A shrug. "Mostly the future and passing through it with no one left to notice anymore."

As Raif pulled back, Ash searched the look in brown eyes as they found his.

In the next moment, he backed Raif up, his kiss hard enough for teeth to clash against lip and leave Raif wincing. In the second Raif's back connected with the counter, Ash brushed his nipple between finger and thumb, catching Raif's breath as he played it roughly through the material of his T-shirt. The smell of leather jacket hit Ash's sense, then he was lost to how his own body came alive and fought against Raif's.

"Fuck..." Raif gripped Ash's hair, pulling his gaze up. "Ice and heat.... I keep forgetting how fast you come alive."

Forget? Ash grunted, the friction against his cock as he rutted into Raif's thigh paused for a moment. The "forgot" comment refocused him so fast. He tugged at Raif's belt and had the clasp to his jeans flicked open and his cock out faster than it took Raif to blink in surprise.

Ash made his strokes fast, rough, enough to leave Raif grabbing on harder to his hair and burying a cry in the softness as he came. So quick, so hard. Fast.

"Fucking forgot?" he said to Raif, feeling the deep breaths against him, the increase in hold as come lined hard abs and the hem of his shirt.

Raif laughed against him. "Maybe that was the wrong choice of words, hm? Or the right ones... depending on viewpoint."

"Fucker." Ash gave him a gentle kiss on the cheek, then smacked the tip of Raif's cock, forcing out a hiss off Raif before Ash grabbed a cloth off the sink.

Raif fell quiet, watching Ash as he wiped up the stains and did the best he could with his T-shirt. "You didn't get anything out of that."

"Because sex is all about me, right?"

"I was hoping for 'to be continued'?"

Ash raised a brow but loved how Raif was able to draw these little things out into the open. He found Raif's pockets and hooked his thumbs in them just as a vibration from Raif's pocket did call out he had another text this time.

Ash gave him the space to take the message, moving away and starting to clean up.

"Okay. Fuck...." Raif didn't sound happy as he pocketed his phone, his message now replied to. "Today I'm going to talk to a few people about getting to see Voodoo. Then I'm finding somewhere out of sight to dig down for a few days after tonight."

"Why after tonight?" Ash looked back.

Raif came over and picked up the sandwich. "Because I was given twelve hours to get out, which usually means twenty-four at a push. Part of me wants it, though. Somebody is going to be hurting soon."

A push for what? From who? Who the hell would be hurting? The killer? "And after that?"

Raif kissed him on the lips. "Would you come away with me for a few days?"

Ash faltered, his look going to the stair lift as he heard it kick into gear.

"Make arrangements to get him looked after but don't let him know where you're going, nor Chase," whispered

Raif. "But if I stay, I need to keep my head down. Yours too."

Ash frowned. "What the hell are you involved with, Raif? Who are you involved with?"

A touch went to his ass, pulling him closer. "Yeah, *what* might be the best term here." He didn't sound happy. "I know who his target is, and I don't want to be around when he comes here, finds them, then gets bored and starts looking for someone else to play with. Those bastards, the dark web would be better company."

Dark web? What the fuck was the dark web? Ash narrowed his eyes. Was this something to do with Kerry's murder, Voodoo's mom? This Sasha? That whatever he'd been here to do originally was now twisted in with that? It had to be. Raif's look was enough to tell Ash he needed to get out for a few days too, though. "Okay. I'll arrange something."

It took a while, but Raif let all the doubt there ease away. "You sure? I'll be back tonight. Leave the door open. We'll stay the night, then we're gone." He got a very rough kiss, then Raif headed for the door. "By the way, I prefer your hair down, Ash. Damn sexier, wilder, less likely to say you're pissed at me and want to do bad things to my cock."

Ash gave him the finger, and Raif left, smiling.

As his dad came into the kitchen, Ash shifted into gear and picked up the sandwich bags and started stacking the plates and mugs in the sink. He'd be glad when the new dishwasher came later today. He'd be good enough to stay around and help install that so his dad didn't have to struggle, though.

"I heard voices." His dad yawned and rubbed at his stomach. "Better still, is that bacon that's been cooking?"

"Yeah." Ash wiped his hands and tossed the cloth on the sink. "Chase popped around and dragged me out of bed. You want a sandwich?"

"God yes." His dad sat down. "Coffee too?"

"Sure." Ash set to work.

"You gonna be here later to see the dishwasher's installed? They're coming about…"

"Hmm?" Ash glanced at the door again as he tossed the bacon in the frying pan.

"Ash, the delivery men. They're coming at four o'clock. Will you be around? I'm over with Miles and Rhiannon today."

"Yeah." He glanced back. "Sure, Pops. I'll get Chase over to help. Then we need to talk about me having a break and going away for a few days."

His dad looked over, his face darkening. "Oh?"

JACK L. PYKE

CHAPTER 23
DEVIL'S ON YOUR SHOULDER

"YOU WANT ME to do fucking *what?*" Chase didn't sound happy, and Ash didn't blame him. Putting the Hoover away and hating how long it had taken him to gut the house and skip Sunday lunch, let alone pack, he balanced his mobile phone between shoulder and ear, ignoring the fresh pain from the lighter burn to his side.

"Dishwasher..." Ash closed the cupboard door. "The delivery guys will be here in half-an-hour and I need to get the old one outside so they can install the new one. Get your ass over here."

"Ash, they usually do that for you, don't they?"

"Dad didn't want to pay the extra. It's gotta go outside for scrap."

"The tatters don't take dishwashers. You need to stick it in the garage until we can get a work van or something."

Shit. Ash hadn't thought of that, and Chase's chuckle came over.

"Where's your head lately, Red?" Chase sounded distracted almost as if—

Ash straightened. "You eating? Mash… meat… gravy?"

"Yep. All of the above."

"And your mam still does enough for three… thousand?"

Chase gave a hard sigh. "So not only do the boring shit with hard graft over a dishwasher, but also bring you food?"

Ash finally found a grin. "Big lad. Needs food… lots of it."

"'Kay, 'kay. Give me ten, you asshole."

Ash grabbed a fork from the drawer and stuffed a mouthful of mash in as Chase fumbled with un-plumbing the dishwasher.

"Jeez, thanks for all your help, Red." Chase grunted as he switched off the water supply.

"Shush." Ash grinned around his food. "Eatin' here."

He got a grin back, then Chase pulled out the water pipe and rested it in a bucket to catch any excess water. "You told Jim over at the factory about how you've got a sudden need to piss off for a few days?"

Ash winced. He hadn't been able to tell Chase too much, and frustration had set in Chase's eyes at the lack of explanation of needing time away. Ash had never taken time away on his own. "Yeah, he's okay with it, but I don't get longer than three days."

Chase mumbled something, causing a grin from Ash as the grumble mentioned Chase having to work on his own at the factory. Chase really didn't like playing alone with anything.

"Fuck." Taps came at the water pipe as a look of disgust went into the bucket. "That's... fuckin' gross, mate. Your old gaffer been getting gruesome with those bugs pissing him off, and now he's feeding them to the family?"

Burying a wince as he moved, Ash leaned a little closer as Chase got to his feet and wiped his hands on his thighs.

Five blue wings lapped against the side of the bucket, a few stray legs too. The bodies were missing, and Ash frowned, then looked down at his fork. "Ughh." The dishwasher hadn't been used for a while, but... fuck. The fork Ash used had been in there, maybe tumbling around with a few dead butterflies, and he'd... he'd... his mouth... digesting.... "Gross... that's... that's...." He bit back sickness only to hear Chase laugh. "Not funny."

"You going *alien, fuck-me* green like that? Damn funny."

Ash left his food on the table, very quickly. "Had one of those in my bedroom the other night."

Chase kicked the bucket a little. "Could be the same one."

"Yeah, him and his aunts and uncles." Two wings looked smaller than others. "Not to mention little Dickie there too."

Chase rolled his eyes. "Always back to dick sizes with you."

Ash looked at him. "How?" he mouthed as he opened his arms. "How can you get from butterfly wings to dick sizes?"

Chase shrugged. Grinned. "It's a lot less kinky than washing your utensils with butterfly bodies." Then he tapped the dishwasher. "Garage, then?"

Ash nodded. "I'll just let my old gaffer know." He sent

over a quick text, his hand resting lightly just above the burn when the material grated against it; then he slipped his phone back in his pocket. "I owe you a pint for this."

Chase danced the dishwasher out of its spot more. "Just a pint?" He looked over, more lowered it to a schoolteacher look. "You *only* owe me a *pint?*" He grinned a little, showing it would cost Ash so much more than that, then he lifted his end of the dishwasher.

Ash didn't lift his, only groaned as he looked over at the rusty garage door, visible through the kitchen window. All of his dad's work things were stored in there and usually kept locked away from everyone. No, not everyone. That wasn't fair. It was just kept locked away from his dad nowadays. It hurt him too much to look at a life he could barely remember at times.

"C'mon, then, Daisy. I've not got all day," said Chase, looking a little red in the face.

"After you, fucked-up buttercup."

Chase was left mumbling as they worked the dishwasher back through the kitchen and into the small hall where they could gain access to the garage. Ash took the key from the hook and bit back a wince at the smell of years-old paper and the dust that came out. Even flicking the light on saw dust particle waltz with dust particle in the subdued light.

"Over here?" Chase wiped at his brow, then thumbed at a free space over by the big garage door.

"Looks good to me."

They fought their way over, walking the dishwasher and leaving behind some scrapes on the floor as they went.

"Christ… I'm fucked." Chase flopped on top of the machine, arms going out either side.

"Y'know, it's not actually that heavy."

Chase didn't move, just lay there across the top. "Six beers, three shots, a curry, and a few hours of being fucked raw… trust me—it's fucking heavy."

Ash followed the curve of Chase's ass. "Jess again? He's a top and you're keeping him, huh?"

"Stop looking. I'm not showing you."

Ash chuckled. "Get said hurt ass into the lounge with a beer. I'll lock up here."

Chase cracked an eye open. "Fine." He pushed up, then backed his ass towards the door, literally dancing his ass backwards and brushing it against Ash. "Enjoy your domestic-goddess lifestyle. I'm gonna go grab a beer, watch some footie, and scratch my bollocks on your settee. When you're done, you can come over and clean mine."

"Your bollocks?"

"Huh?" Chase scratched his head. "No, clean my apartment." He laughed. "But if you insist, get down on those knees, boy, down—"

Ash pushed him out and caught hold of the nearest rag to wipe at the sweat on his own face. Taking it with him, Ash locked up, then headed for the kitchen, needing that other beer now.

Voices filtered through, and Ash jolted slightly seeing his dad and Miles push into the kitchen.

"Oh." Ash caught himself, conscious of how he'd stalled. "I thought you were out all day?" He really hoped they'd be out all day. He'd hoped to be able to smuggle Raif in without an audience.

His dad's glance shifted to Ash's arm, then back up to Ash.

"We were out all day," said Miles, coming up behind his dad and nearly bumping into him as his dad went still.

"Hm, oh. Jeff here wanted me to come back and help move the dishwasher. But it looks like you managed."

Ash frowned at his dad, not understanding why he wasn't coming any closer. "Yeah," he said to Miles. "Chase helped. He's crashed on the settee."

Miles eased Ash's dad aside. "Kids..." he mumbled, smiling over, then he paused too, looking a little confused as to why Ash's dad hadn't gone over to the table and taken the weight off. "You need a hand, Jeff?"

Ash fidgeted under his dad's scrutiny, then he glanced down at what held his dad's attention.

The rag.

It didn't register, not at first, not the grease stain on the denim jacket: how it looked like someone had been under a car and forgotten to take the coat off before it was ruined. Not how he knew it belonged to the only person who'd gone out, buying denim because he'd finally won the fight against his weight. Only Ash and Chase had bought Johnny this.

Ash frowned, the denim jacket now turning this way, that, in his hands. "This... this is Johnny's."

He ran a touch over the long grease stain, even brought it close, not to smell the grease, but to catch a fading scent of a friendship. "He... I saw him in the morning on Chase's phone. We'd just bought this and he was wearing it. Yet he wasn't wearing it when... when..." Ash could still feel the burn of sun on his cheeks from that day, how despite being hot, they'd bought Johnny this, then how damn cool Johnny's body had felt in the woods because...

"He died." That came from Chase, and Ash glanced behind him briefly as Chase came up close and took the jacket from him. So much grief swam in Chase's eyes.

"He'd looked so fucking fit in this that day. We were going to meet at the pub and celebrate how long it had taken for him to get down and slip into this. He'd set his heart on this jacket for so long."

"How..." Ash looked from the jacket to his dad. "Why is this here? Did... did he come around that day after I went to meet Chase at the pub? Did... did you see him, Dad?"

"He." His dad faltered, as if chasing the memory. "He fixed my car so I could use it. Remember? I said I'd get him over to look at it."

Ash frowned. "Dad, you took the car to the garage to get it fixed a week before Johnny died. There was nothing wrong with it."

"Then..." His frown was serious. "Then he must have done some last-minute checks for me."

"But you..." Ash stepped a little closer. "You saw him that afternoon, before he died? How... how was he, Dad?"

"Johnny died?" It seemed to crash his world, nearly crumple his form, as it did every time he told his dad.

"How was he?" Chase went over, pushing past Ash. "Did he say anything? Did it look as though someone had had a go at him? Would—"

"Hey, hey." Miles came between them, gently easing Chase back. "Slow it down for him, take it easy, okay."

Ash was looking at the coat in Chase's hands. "Why didn't you tell me about his jacket, Dad? Why didn't you say it was here?"

"I... I just didn't remember" came the quiet answer.

Ash flicked a look up. "Yet... yet you knew it when you came in. You..." Ash felt his heart beat a little harder. "You came back early after I sent a text letting you know I was moving the dishwasher into the garage."

Chase looked back, hurt, confused, just as downright out of place as Ash felt.

Trying to control the shaking that started from the inside out, Ash went a little closer. "Dad, did you say anything to Johnny that day? Did you argue? Did you…. You'd sometimes shout at Johnny and Chase too, remember?"

"When they kept you out late, yes. When they got you into trouble too. But with Johnny… we just talked."

"*About what?*"

"*I can't remember.*" His dad covered his ears, more gripped at them. "Shouting, so much fucking shouting back then too. It hurt. He was drunk. Speech so slurred."

"You…" Chase took a step back, more by Ash now. "You shouted at Johnny?"

"No, just…" His dad glanced around the kitchen, maybe chasing past echoes. "Just so much shouting." He gripped onto the counter, even though Miles had taken a step closer and seemed to hold him up.

"There was shouting at Johnny?" said Miles calmly. "Can you remember what was said, Jeff?" He looked as startled as them now. "I need you to remember."

Why?

Why would Miles need him to remember? Was there something about Johnny's death that didn't sit right with the policeman in him too? Did Miles know something about Johnny's death they didn't?

"Just… just he was taking you and Ash away. And hurt, he was…."

Chase seemed to jolt, and he went from calm to kill in the escape of a breath. "*You fucking hurt Johnny?*"

"What?" Ash's dad jolted.

"Did you hurt him like *Ash?* Did you fucking burn your way onto Johnny, you fuck?"

"No, I... I, I was mad at you—" He pointed back at Chase. "—you slept with Johnny *too.* You slept in Ash's bed, but you slept with Johnny too."

Ash sighed hard. "We're friends, Dad, we—"

"*No.* Chase was *Johnny's* boyfriend. I heard them in *your* bed."

Ash stiffened. Chase and Johnny had slept together? Where.... What?

When? *Why?*

Chase looked back at him in that moment too, and it was there in his eyes as Ash stared at him, head tilted slightly and—

That day at the factory, when Ash had found Chase in the restroom.... Chase had been so heated, so....

"Who you been fucking?" mumbled Ash.

Chase groaned. "No one, and it's frustrating the fuck out of me, Red."

"Yeah? Whoever it is, teach him to fuck you before you come to work, okay?"

Christ. Johnny. Johnny had held that same look of heat on his cheeks just before Ash had found Chase that day. Because Johnny had been there in the restroom with Ash first... they'd....

They'd been good friends, the best of friends, but Chase's hurt, his look said so much more now, how—

You didn't put Johnny there, Ash... Christ, Chase had taken that barman up against a tree as if he was trying to love the life out of something just outside of his grasp. He'd...

Yeah. There it was. The fuck-over always came. Not one of them had been able to tell Ash they'd both fallen in love. Why? What made any of them feel as though they couldn't tell him?

Chase moved to come over. "Don't, Ash. Don't fucking look like that. It's why we agreed not to say anything, why we didn't want to hurt you, to see you hurt again. You've been fucking hurt enough over the years by this fucker."

Ash went still as ants raced his skin. "You forced him to love you on the side? Forced him to watch how we touched all the time, into sharing someone he'd waited a lifetime to love, only to then take his own life because you said I couldn't be hurt? Big fucking bloke here, Chase. You don't ever fucking decide anything for me, not at the cost of Johnny."

"*What?* No." Chase's anger hit hard. "We didn't put Johnny there, you fuck. We played our games in front of him, remember? He knew, and he was always the first to use his voice and ask us to stop when it got too much for him."

Fuck. That photo Peepshow took. Johnny had stepped in when Chase had hidden in Ash, caught out and made to feel uncomfortable in the game. He'd done it for Chase. Because a lover was in trouble and didn't want a picture taken. Ash stepped up close. "All because he fucking loved *you*. You didn't think *that* would kill him inside, watching us fuck about? I mean, what are we talking here? Weeks, months? Years that he's been watching as your boyfriend?"

Chase pushed him back. "Don't. You know it would have killed him more for you to have found out like this and be hurt. Don't turn Johnny into something he's not. That I'm not. We loved you. We just didn't want you to feel like you were alone. And look at you now." He stepped back a touch. "This fucking look you always get."

"Big bloke." Ash flatlined, killing all feeling. It came so easy lately, like denying all the burns to his ass, all the ugliness gathered over the years. "You don't—"

Chase was up in his face. "*I fucking do.* You know why, huh?" The tug came roughly at his shirt, exposing the latest burn. "Because I know how you fucking hide, Ash. How you hurt. How your dad burns into you still, but we are the ones who help keep you under his lighter burns by not speaking up. It fucking twisted us all in the process, enough that we were all just too scared to talk in case we caused more hurt. So always better to hurt someone else first, right? For every cry we heard off you when we stopped over and your dad took you out of the bedroom, we made damn sure someone else cried just as loud, for just as long. Because that's us: twisted friends, twisted fucking lovers, burying all the screams and cries."

Anger finally kicked in with Ash and he shoved Chase back. "Johnny—"

"I hurt you?" That came so quietly that Chase and Ash stalled. "I didn't hurt you too, did I, Ash?" his dad asked. "I didn't hurt—"

"*Oh, you're fucking kidding me, right?*" Chase tried to shove Ash off, but Ash stopped him. "What was that latest one for, you fuck?" shouted Chase. "Did he tell you he was leaving for a few days, eh? And you didn't like it? You thought he was hiding something? That he'd done something?"

"I..." His dad frowned. "I wouldn't hurt you, Ash. You... you're a good—"

"*Don't... Ah.*" Ash tried to cover his head, but shirt material grated on the new burn, and Ash thumped into the door instead, crying out. *"Don't fucking say good, Dad!"*

"You see this, you cunt?" Chase grabbed an arm around Ash, pulling him in and roughly kissing his head. "You see what you've done? *What you're still fucking doing?* How—"

Ash snarled, pushing Chase off, then pushing him towards the back door. "Out."

"What?" Stalling, Chase looked stunned as he stumbled to a stop.

Ash grabbed his own coat off the back of a chair. "I'm out. So are you."

Chase's eyes widened slightly. "Out of here?" He suddenly came in close, hugging him hard. "Fuck yes. Fuck yes, baby. C'mon. It's about fucking time."

A call was being made from Miles, something about getting someone over, then he was over by them, guiding them out the door. "Time out, lads. Let's get you calmed down."

"Leave us the fuck alone." Chase pushed at Miles. "You knew what that cunt did to Ash. You stayed quiet too. Did you know about Johnny as well and said nothing there—"

"What?" Miles gripped tighter and tugged them both towards his car as Ash shoved out of the hold.

"Get the fuck off me."

"Easy, easy, Ash. You're both coming with me, because there's something you need to know about Johnny's death before this tears you all up any more."

"Like fuck, you cunt." Chase managed to pull away this time. "I'm going back in there and gutting that fucker for hurting Johnny."

"Hey!" Miles pulled him in by the scruff of his neck, quieting him down. "I didn't hear that. Get in my car before I lock you up in a cell to calm you down instead."

No. Out of here. Ash wanted out of here with Raif now. He got in the car but didn't look at Chase. Ash had taken Johnny's jacket off him, wrapping the damage to his own knuckles, and he sat staring down at it before fumbling for his phone. He thumbed through for Raif's number, then bit back a snarl.

Right. Raif hadn't trusted him with a phone number.

"Okay." Chase slumped down next to Ash, hands shaking now as he shut the door. "Christ... Jesus fucking Christ, Red...."

An arm hooked around his neck and Chase tugged him in close because of it. Ash pushed him away in the next moment, leaving Chase frowning hurt at him.

Yeah, the fuck-over always came, from the best of people.

Chase was wrong.

They'd both killed Johnny.

Only where Chase had known why, Ash hadn't.

JACK L. PYKE

CHAPTER 24
DON'T... DANCE WITH THE DEVIL

MARTIN'S ELECTRONIC ANKLE bracelet stayed waterproof as well as Peachless-proof. He fucking hated the commonality over that noun. With how the fever had kept him confined to bed for a while, the hot tub that bubbled around him offered enough confined space for him to burn out some of his Sunday afternoon illness, although not enough space or time to "drag a fucking staff member in here and drown him," or so Craig had threatened he'd do if given the chance.

And they locked *him* up for paranoia.

Strange how Craig's aggression never quite touched the look in his eyes. There was care there, which was always damn stupid. It could be exploited. Craig could be exploited.

Martin buried a grin. As for Gray?

Gray stayed so close today. He kept an eye on just how close as Gray sat there on the lounger, body relaxed and not looking like he gave a damn. Craig stayed at a safe distance in the pool area, the door closed, but CCTV always giving him that edge.

He'd love to wrap that wiring around Craig's throat and tie it to the back of Gray's Merc. That would make the bastard dance for a while.

Nah… Martin eased back into the water, giving a sniff. He really couldn't care less about Craig. He'd gotten what he wanted. Jan stayed away, sulking in some corner of the manor with his headphones on to avoid the noise; Jack's father didn't bother him anymore, and Gray…

Martin quirked a brow.

Gray was right fucking here. So fucking close. Had Jack done that, hm? Had crossing the line and nearly going for breaking bone changed things a little, set Gray re-evaluating, taking stock, reorganising how things danced from here?

Now they played this watching game, neither speaking. Martin didn't whore himself out with his body like he had with Jan. Gray was a different delicacy. One where the anticipation needed to be shaded into life, colour by differing colour.

So when Gray picked up his mobile and let it ring four times, then did the same again before someone answered, Martin pretended to ignore it; as Gray pretended to ignore how he listened. Something had definitely changed, but the why remained to be seen.

Gray's voice stayed flat enough. "I need some details leaked to one of my staff members. A carer named Baz…."

Oh… Was this *business*, business? Now why would he stir the staff? Who had pissed him off? More to the point, why say it here, now?

"Mention how I don't want news channels hearing about

MI6's interest in the West Midlands' butterfly killer. Connect Johnny Shipman's murder to the others, and be sure to mention butterflies as a connection, but don't mention what classification. I want to clip the wings of four birds with this information."

Four? The first seemed clear enough: Gray had a spy in his home, or he suspected as much: Baz, and it made sense Gray mentioning it now as Baz was on his break. So if this intel made it to the news channels, that would confirm it, but...

Now just who were the other three? Who else was he after in the West Midlands?

The phone was put away a moment later, and Martin eased up in the water. Gray sat up now on one of the loungers, a stroke going distractedly at his lip.

Yeah. He was giving a player's push in order to get the ball rolling on something. But mentioning it here, in front of Martin? Was this another dig in to break bone and see how the reactions triggered Jack? Or was it something else entirely?

"Butterflies, hm?" Martin pushed out of the hot tub and stripped down to his boxers. Okay, so he'd whore his body out just a little here. He faced side-on to Gray, the corner of a towel pulled up to his abs, the other wiping all too coyly at the curve of his tanned ass. And damn, he knew he made it look good, even let the fever add a shiver along his body, adding Jack's vulnerability into the mix.

Gray's gaze never faltered. Jan really needed to start opening his eyes to this, to what he missed when Jan left them alone. The fucking would come, like fuck would it come, and damn, would he see Gray live in hell for it afterwards. He'd knifed Gray the last time Gray thought he'd taken Jack down to the bed for his first time with Jack.

Martin would always have that: how Gray had fucked him thinking it was Jack taking everything he had to give. Their first touch was his; all the blood that came after when Gray found it wasn't Jack he'd fucked. So if Gray wanted to go for blood and bone to get to Jack now, he'd fuck that blade into Gray's stomach again, his returned *try it, baby.* If that was Gray's game. But he looked a little different today. A little... darker.

"Tell me more about these butterflies, Welsh." Martin glanced over through soaking black hair that shaped the nape of his neck, covering his eyes. "They getting you hard? You into insects during sex now? Or is it what the handler does when he handles them?" He was shooting in the dark, not really understanding what went on here. He just knew Gray. His quiet. How quiet he'd gone since he'd stood in that courtyard with Jan, looking torn over leaving. Yeah, he'd seen them there. And as you couldn't kill with butterflies, someone had to be doing something twisted with them to earn Gray's shift of head in their direction.

Gray pushed to his feet, and Martin stood his ground as he came over, all polished black shoes and shirt and trousers. Jogging pants were tossed at him, along with some dry Calvin Klein boxers. Those he'd had on were soaked.

"Get dressed."

Martin slipped on the tight boxers but tossed the jogging pants over his shoulder. He wanted to fuck about with Gray just a little more. One good thing about Jack, he took damn good care of his body. Although this fuck-up of a fever played more havoc now.

"Not talking beyond two-syllable words?" Martin went up close, then eased to the side in the next minute to reach for a fresh towel off the bench as Gray glanced away.

Those suit trousers felt good against Martin's skin. "Now why did you mention a possible leak, hmm? Baz? Come on, come play with me fully."

As Martin towelled his hair dry, Gray looked at him, looked down at his body.

Jekyll and Hyde had nothing on Gray. All calm and control with Jan around, then feeding these little vicious titbits when they were on their own. Just to goad reactions. To stir reaction. To get at Jack. For Martin to return the bore into bone and get at Gray. They both knew each other's attack, the devastation of the outcome, but were drawn to play it out all the same.

"Oh...." Martin cocked a smile. This wasn't to do with Jack. Not at all. It was an invitation to play along to another game. Why? What had Baz done? Martin really wanted pointers if the hired help had dug deeper into Gray than he had. Gray hated spies, Kes being the last. Kes being six-foot fucking under now with his ears bleeding out along with blood in his brain for arranging for Jack and Jan's rape. So just what had Baz done?

Is that why Gray kept coming home? He kept getting told things were going down... here. Which meant Baz reported to someone who had access to Gray in the field. Someone who... Oh. He narrowed his eyes. Somebody beyond Baz didn't want Gray in the West Midlands, so Baz was here to, what?

Lately, Jan was always in the cell with Baz when Baz came in, when that cologne, that... cheap cedar-wood now drifted across his sense, only it wasn't really there, not fully, but it still twisted his stomach, as it had been doing since he'd first met Baz.

Oh.... Had that been Baz's secret game play on orders from an unknown source? Disrupt psychosis. Play head games with scent-play and get at Jack and Jan, twist this sickness, burn through enough to make sure Gray had to stay here and control the fallout? Or at least attempt to? And it had knocked Martin off his feet? Baz had knocked him off his feet?

That… oh that stupid fucker. Yeah, he wanted to play now too.

Martin sniffed again, then got a little closer. "A favour for a favour, for catching Baz and having a whisper in that fucker's ear to get that information to whoever planted him here." Blue eyes found his. "Just the answer to a question, Welsh. Nothing more. Calm that look down." He gave the sweetest smile. "No harm ever came from listening to one of my questions, right?"

A hard look filtered into Gray.

"Tell me." Martin leaned a little closer to his throat, just catching his cologne and holding it in his senses. Gray's scent was so much damn better. "With you being a Dom, Jack your switch…." He closed his eyes, wishing to God he had Jack's memories then. "Do you have a code between you and Jack? One that goes beyond the D/s safety lines? One that dives deep into this… culler?" Yeah, Martin knew about that from their time together over the years.

Gray breathed, nothing more.

"No safe word?" whispered Martin. "No rape-fantasy? Just pure cruel burnout, where you lock Jack in and don't open the door again until the culler's been fucked out of *your* system, fuck what Jack needs?"

Gray's eyes narrowed, just slightly.

"Oh, yeah." He loved that. "You do. And Jack, he takes it, hm? Sometimes feeding from all the hurt, other times just taking it so you can burn all your heat out and lie wasted next to him."

Martin went to stroke his cheek, but Gray grabbed his wrist. In the same instant, he added a rougher grip to the back of Martin's scalp. Breaths were so close now, hard, heated.

Christ, yeah. A nerve had been hit.

The culler... he fucked so differently to the Dom.

Martin grinned. "Has Jack ever really tasted the full culler in you? Do you still hide some... perversions from him, ones you know you'd have to turn away from as the caring Dom?"

He rubbed a palm into Gray's cock.

"I like your collar, Gray. All those rules, the BDSM lifestyle—how they regulate and cool the culler?" The hardness there beneath his touch must have fucking hurt Gray. "Knowing Jack takes pleasure from the hurt... it's never quite good enough for you, is it? You'll never be able to fuck him how you really need to, not as a sadist, not as a culler." Martin let the hurt from the grip creep up into his eyes, and he made it look damn good. "It's why you're holding on so close to me now and not letting go. You know you could take me down to the floor as the culler, obliterating the Dom, really hurt-fuck me until those tears fell. Because they'd be honest. I wouldn't get a kick out of the brutality. I'd cry no and fucking knife you for hurting me, this time making sure you couldn't run back home to Welsh shores... and, Christ, how all that would make you want to fuck me more...."

Gray pushed him away, not hard enough to make him stumble, but enough to warn. He walked past, watching Martin all the way. "Focus all that intelligence on Baz. Don't fuck about with Jan again, pet. I'll drag you down farther than you could ever possibly understand."

Martin gave him a wink. "Promise?" He watched Gray head over to Craig. Something was spoken, then Gray left as Craig came over.

"Seems you need some outside time."

Martin raised a brow. "*Piss up a bush* outside time?" He flicked a look to where Gray had left as he tugged his jogging pants on. "Yeah, guess I do. Kill or cure, right? All that rain outside will no doubt get me back in bed again. Fuck me, Craig, you sure you ain't gay, for all the times you jump at taking me down to a mattress?"

"What's the alternative that gets you so scared, Martin?" Craig messed around with a radio. "Fearing that people help you because they actually care?"

Yeah. Martin stopped what he was doing, just briefly. Jan had fucking known about Baz. And he'd what? Still cared enough to stick around despite the head games? Kind of riled him... more so with Baz, how Baz had tried to touch his... soft toy. He glanced at Craig, softened his look. "Awwww, no biscuits with all that sweetness? Because, hold me back, mate. I go nuts over biscuits, me."

Craig frowned a quick look up. It asked how close Jack was, and...

Easy, this was far too fucking easy. He'd seen the list in the staffroom. Craig's problem? He cared too fucking much about everyone.

Martin started for the door, rubbing at his head.

"Wait." Craig caught up and pulled him to a stop. "We don't go out without two staff members present. We wait until Paul gets here and—"

Baz was on his break, but Paul could work too. Martin jerked away, out of the hold, and still rubbed at his head.

"Fine. You… you just really need to back off, mate. Just for a while, okay? Or at least fifty paces away from me. Paul's not wearing Baz's aftershave and at least he plays as dumb as he fucking looks when he's close by. I'm too fucking sick for any shit today."

Craig pulled back, looking him over. "Okay, Paul's in the lead. I'll give you some space. You know you only have to ask, right, bud?"

Christ. No, he only wanted to use Paul to pass on some details to Baz. When the doors closed and the lights lowered, those two talked. And strangely enough, Gray had given him permission to stir some shit up.

He'd taken him along to kill Kes too, but Gray had kept all firm control then to force some closure into everyone's life, to force Jack back. This… this was something new. Something different. He'd given Martin the control. Or some at least. So yeah… he'd play. He'd fucking burn this fever and its cause out.

He just wished he knew who Gray's other three targets were. He'd love to fuck about with those too, if they weren't being fucked with already. If one was the man who had planted Baz here, he would be Gray's focus. He was Gray's focus, and it tugged at Martin with how he wouldn't get to see Gray's game play. But…

But… Darkness held Gray more lately… back to nearly breaking bone in the cell, pack hunting with Baz. Christ. Had anyone even noticed Gray's cough had eased since he'd been in here… playing?

Martin bit back his grin. He'd missed the old Gray. Seemed Gray had missed him too, or at least the old Gray had….

JACK L. PYKE

CHAPTER 25
BUTTERFLY KILLER

RAIF SAT IN the car outside Ash's, arm resting on the sill, fingers distractedly massaging his eyebrow. Blackness kissed the streets, even threatening to gang up on the streetlights and mug their light. Raif wouldn't have minded either way. The quiet of the early hours almost lulled him into sleep that he felt like it had been years since he'd tasted fully. For the moment his home was No. 14 East Way, three streets down. The young couple were due back in two days, and for the past week and a half, he'd moved from home to home, usually just marking the next house up for… borrowing. Most people would have family who checked up on the place, but the notes on the counters usually told when they'd come around and what times were to be avoided. He couldn't remember a time when he'd lived any different. It was there sometimes, at the back of the boxes in his mind, memories on how he'd stood there changing his son, or holding him while his wife got dressed. They were still married; divorce seemed too cruel for everything they'd already lost, but it had been in name only for many years now. He'd always been bi. Ash wasn't the first, although he kind of hoped Ash would see that Raif stayed around long enough for Ash to maybe be his last. It was just so soon, with so little trust, and Raif didn't blame Ash one bit for not trusting what seemed to stop and stall between them. Raif didn't trust it either.

It still troubled Raif to the core that anything *had* started and shifted between them. Three months back, when Raif had met Ash at the pub when that barman had taken Ash and Chase's picture as they'd played cruel games with Sandy and Freddie, Ash had packaged him into a down-and-out on first meeting him. Not unusual in itself as most did on meeting him, but when he'd gotten Ash on his own at his boss's home later that night, there'd been that bare honesty there in sea-green eyes: the fear of the unknown, of being caught exposed, but not being able to run away, much like it had when he'd bumped into him again last Saturday night, and all the other times he'd come back to see Ash. He'd loved that. The grown-up kid who just looked so bloody tired and alone, despite being neck-deep in a crowd. Then when the grief hit... all the hurt that had swamped Ash's eyes....

But with that last meeting, in the car park with the barman? Filming him? The colour to those eyes changed, along with Ash: cruel, spiteful, with Ash looking to film some sex and post it God only knew where. But then that colour had shifted again, just a few hours later, because... because?

Because Ash had followed him into the night like a sapper, walking on to see where the bomb would take him down, this time over to Voodoo's... and there seemed such a sadness to it. Ash still took hits off his dad, still lingered, and.... Maybe Ash didn't need help: he'd just learned to live with his hurt the best way he could, but the way he lived, it was as much a lonely and dangerous existence as Raif walking the night and leaving them both just as blind, just as numb to life.

Maybe time away from here would do them both good, let them see each other fully in a softer climate, where the past didn't drag anyone into sapper life. Raif loved how the most basic of interrogation techniques could trip Ash up and draw out little bits of information about him. Ash played vicious head games, yeah, but there was blind youthfulness about it, nothing like the game play Raif was used to handling. Or should have been handling these past few months. Time away could see how they both relaxed more into each other.

Tomorrow should have taken him back over to Light's, his surveillance point for the work week and Light's university stay, especially with the new murder cases. Ferryman's orders were still clear: locate evidence of missing military equipment, see if Light had a tie to the dark web and where that equipment went, but now it needed to be done away from this area, away from Light. They still had two killers loose in the West Midlands: one with a tendency for necrophilia and mutilation of bodies and insects; another who was more subtle: using I-dosing and the Internet to cause cellular cavitation, a vaporisation of liquid within organ cells via headphones. But the latter had gone quiet over the past month, whereas the former....

Raif's grip on the steering wheel tightened. He needed to know Lucy was okay first, and just what the fuck had been going on since Johnny's death. Frank had had it in for Ash back at Lucy's, and his word choice and body language said Frank had been watching Ash long before Kerry and Voodoo's mum had been killed. Frank wouldn't say why; Raif knew better than to ask. Raif was too close to Ash.

Too personally involved. But learning what he had over the past twenty-four hours, about Johnny, Raif understood Frank's concern. His silence. Ash had emerging territory for... something, and Frank needed to see if it took him into butterfly territory.

With two killers here, it wasn't surprising how he'd gotten the text about culler intervention. One headcase always attracted another, and it was usual to be called off scene to allow the culler room to play. What had been concerning was how the text said his position had been compromised. That meant the culler had been on scene at one point already, doing recon, and attention had shifted in Raif's direction. Had they been there back at Ash's house, the culler as... focused as Frank on seeing if Ash had darker emerging tendencies too? He'd caught a different cologne shifting round the lounge, although nothing had been out of place. But it wouldn't have been out of place, would it? Raif worked the same way. It had just been a fading scent back there, a moment's pause at something new. And if it had been the culler and he'd left something around like that, it would have been purely to test out Raif in the process. Ash hadn't been paranoid; he'd picked up on something as well. But why would the culler need to test Raif out?

Raif had also been given a time period to be gone by, which meant someone had a leash on the culler for that time, but that time alone. Why? Why the reprieve? Why the interest in the first place? What had he done to draw a culler's eye? His work the past few months that had taken him out of town handled a darker side to life: gathering intel on the dark web and the faintest echo of an I-dosing website, or more a few cases of teenagers getting high off infrasound beat therapy via the dark web. Nothing new there: the military had been experimenting on low-infrasound and crowd control for years. It's no wonder kids were using the same technique to get high. Yeah, the girl he'd found murdered doing just that could bring in MI5 and get their attention, but he doubted that would have shifted a culler here. So the culler would be coming for Kerry's killer, Sasha's.... But that still shouldn't mean he came for Raif as well. They worked for the same side.

And when he'd sent a text back to Ferryman, asking about the reprieve, he'd gotten no reply.

So today, with work interrupted on tracing codes and addresses, he'd spent this time digging into Social Service files, tracking down Voodoo to Birmingham Children's Hospital and their care team. He'd find a way in to see her once he picked Ash up. She'd witnessed the killing, the killer, and he'd make damn sure she got all the protection she needed, even if it meant pulling strings to sit outside her ward. But he'd respect the culler: he'd be away for a few days to allow them the free space to catch the butterfly killer.

He'd caught the newsfeed a few hours ago, the detail that had been given about Voodoo's mother and Kerry, although Kerry's name hadn't been mentioned due to no formal ID. Kerry had liked her privacy as much as Raif did. Sasha hadn't been mentioned. Which suggested that his murder and body hadn't been discovered. Strange considering Frank had gotten the call that had made sure he found Sasha's body in that alley. Someone knew about it, but they weren't talking.

The surprise had come with the mention of Johnny's suicide now being upgraded to murder and connected to the other murders via the butterfly.

That he hadn't known. When the death hit and Ash had

pushed him away, Raif had buried himself in work out of town. And on the weekend, Ash had been his concern.

The breaking news spoke how the culler had already started to play his hand, giving out details to the public to upset and ruffle calm waters, and it was time to go. Or it would have been if he hadn't heard about Johnny's murder too.

Had Ash heard yet? How much had it torn him down?

The lack of movement in Ash's house lengthened like the stroke along his brow, and kept Raif on the outside, watching, waiting.

Something felt seriously wrong.

The clock on the dashboard touched 1:00 a.m. Monday morning, and the mist coming down gave Raif a little more comfort. Not many would bother with a new car sitting on the streets at this hour, in this, and for once this car wasn't *borrowed*, but the documents to it were falsified.

The picture Raif looked at on his phone wasn't.

The butterfly was a Holly Blue, one of the smallest around the UK, and very delicate with how pale blue and fine black dots along the top of the wings made up its colours. He hadn't been given that detail via the newsfeed; the local police had helped with that, although they didn't and wouldn't know it.

Two wings had been stuffed into Johnny's body. Same with Kerry, then Voodoo's mother after the killer had raped them. Also Sasha. Raif had pulled the wings from his body too. Had the killer also assaulted Johnny? He must have done for semen to be coating the butterfly in the wound and for the semen samples to match up. Is that what had happened to those two other kids who'd gone missing from the streets? Would they ever know? And had the police kept the detail from Ash and Chase because they knew their games, how vicious they could be, and they'd suspected them along the way too?

Just what had Voodoo witnessed that day? Had the killer made her hold the butterfly? Watch? Raif gripped the phone, nearly breaking it, then tossed it back into the glove box.

Always into the stomach, always via mutilation.... He was no psychologist; he rarely even worked on UK shores, but he couldn't see this meaning anything to do with growth and change. The butterfly was fully grown, past pupae stage: it had reached its full potential as far as beauty went. So... why? Why Kerry? Why Voodoo's mother? Why force a little girl to watch and let her live with that for the rest of her life? Why Johnny? Why Sasha? Sasha's murder had been violent, beating, strangulation, yet further down the line with Johnny, it had been more subtle: the external damage light enough to get away with classifying it as a suicide to try and draw out the killer. Yet with Voodoo's mother, Kerry... more violent again. It showed growth, perfecting a skill, then falling into chaos again. And why hadn't the culler released details of the type of butterfly or—

"Oh." Raif frowned, now stiffening slightly.

The bastard. The culler played both him and the killer, trying to draw them both out, disrupt one, provoke the other to go and get evidence, test out Raif's skills at getting evidence. Only Raif hadn't taken any evidence from the police, only a record of it.... Whoever the culler was, he wouldn't know that he'd had access to the evidence, but if Raif used it, passed it through channels, then it could be traced back to him, drawing out and testing his skill in other ways. Was it because his own identity was untraceable that earned him the wrong attention now? Raif's lack of identity pissed the best off, it always had. But it was never meant to test a culler's patience. They chewed to the bone and didn't let go. A heavy pit hit his stomach as he eased out of the car. He was too old for these bullshit games.

He kept close to the hedges lining Ash's garden, then eased over the back gate. He'd have to have a word with Ash about the bins left there, because they made it easy for any lout to invite himself over. They helped Raif down now, practically held his hand for him, then Raif made it around the side of the house, ignoring the greenhouse, shed, and scary-face gnomes that kept watch. The door didn't offer too much protest, but then he could get into most homes, blindfolded. He did make sure he closed the door behind him and kept the lights off. Eyes were adjusted better to the night anyway, it just made life easier for him.

The sound of the clock ticked its way through life as he stood there, listening, but no sounds of snoring came, no creak of floorboard as someone turned over in their sleep. Ash tossed and turned a lot in his sleep. He doubted Ash knew that.

One newspaper and a magazine sat at the table. Not something he'd consider unusual, but they didn't have Ash's forethought over keeping the place tidy that Raif had seen. The two lay together, where one lay open with a page crumpled up and tossed a little way away.

After easing down into one of the chairs, Raif pulled the crumpled page closer and started to smooth it out.

It covered Johnny's suicide, the sex crossed out in a raging red, and Raif wiped a thumb over the name.

Had Ash done this? The dig of pen in paper spoke of anger, hate... frustration. He could almost feel Ash's grief pour through his touch, or whoever had sat here. The picture of Johnny was striking: collar-length hair, playful eyes that didn't seem to carry a hint of the mistrust that Ash's did, but people hid themselves very well, Raif knew that. He'd lost himself in the darkness enough times. But like with Chase, Raif had stayed away from Johnny, just watching how all three of them played. Johnny had the best of all of them: decent, hardworking....

Frowning, Raif picked up the gardening magazine.

The upturned page showed nothing but an article on greenfly, but as he turned it over, the Holly Blue butterfly contrasted lovely with the darkness of the kitchen. The article itself went on to cover lifespan, how the Holly Blue emerged early spring, well before most other Blue butterflies, and it was the hardest to photograph with its wings open.

Like Johnny, the Holly Blue was also circled in angry red pen. Alongside—"Love is like a butterfly...."

Raif pulled back a touch.

Someone had sat here in Ash's kitchen, circling exactly *which* type.

And... Is that what this was about, that fluttering...? That fluttering in your stomach when you first meet someone?

Raif slowly got to his feet. Or when you've known someone for a long time and can't express what you're feeling anymore?

"Oh Christ," he breathed. Raif headed through to the hall and up the stairs. He stood in Ash's bedroom, just looking around, listening, hands clenched at his sides. Then he caught sight of the landline phone next to Ash's bed. He checked around it first, then prised open the mouthpiece.

The device was small, small enough to look at home with everything else going on in the mouthpiece of the phone, only Raif had seen enough makes and models of listening devices to spot one at fifty paces. He plucked it out and turned it over in his hands.

Ash hadn't told anyone anything, he already knew that, but this… it showed someone had been listening in. Not the culler; he wouldn't leave something like this behind. And where there was a listening device in one phone, Raif knew there was a good chance there'd be others too. Raif had been in the lounge and kitchen when they'd spoken about Voodoo; Ash hadn't told anyone anything: Raif had. And where Ash had broken Chase's phone, he'd taken his own to Voodoo's, with Raif, which suggested not only listening, but tracking surveillance too. So the type of butterfly never fucking mattered…. Only the players did, those who had inadvertently come into contact with Ash.

Ash knew the killer, and the killer reacted to Ash.

Raif glanced around the bedroom again, trying to level out his breathing. Listening? For how fucking long?

Raif made his way back downstairs, keeping his footfalls light. He checked the kitchen and found a few devices there. Pocketing them, he let himself out, keeping the flick of the lock as quiet as possible.

He eased back into his car, then pulled out a torch and some reading glasses out of the glove box. Long gone were the days that he could do this without needing his glasses.

Whoever had planted them hadn't expected to get caught, and why not? Raif turned one of the devices over, and in the light of the torch, saw it was pretty old, about two years.

Two years?

It had been in there that long?

Raif glanced back at the bedroom.

Just when had Ash and Chase started messing around? When they were kids? When those butterflies first kicked in? When or if they messed, like most kids, with bugs on wooded tracks? Ash had called it off between him and Chase, had that pissed Chase off? Johnny had somehow gotten in the way and that had really twisted Chase's head, enough to want to kill Johnny for it? Why? Why would Johnny be upset? They'd all been going on a backpacking trip together. None of them had seemed pissed off beyond the normal. None of them....

Raif got the strangest sinking feeling.

Johnny had arranged the backpacking trip. Raif was back on the scene with Ash. He was back on the scene and threatening to take Ash away again.

And Ash would have been heard saying he'd agreed to leave too.

Fuck.

Did someone need Ash to stay around?

Heart beating faster, Raif focused on the small run of numbers. Nowadays these were doctored, leading back to a false source, but the numbers didn't look scratched or tampered with. Keeping the numbers in mind, he flicked open the laptop placed under the passenger seat.

He brought up a surface web list of local security firms. From there, he knew the proxies to gain access into their computers, but no trace was found on the serial number. Giving a frown, he wiped at his eyebrow, then gained access to the local police station via going below the surface web into the deep web, where government files were passed and stored. They should've been doing their job and keeping a tabs on what came into the area when it came to surveillance equipment like this, but again, a search of their data base on monitoring security shops drew a blank. It wasn't unusual. Tracing something like this would usually be difficult if the people behind it knew what they were doing, but the fact the serial number hadn't been masked said amateur at best.

Or young… foolish. Lost in love and not knowing how to handle it when they were rejected? Lost in love and used to going vicious when the game didn't play out his way?

Raif went still.

Was there a double twist here? Was this Ash? Had Frank been right to watch him?

Was this all down to a confused young man who didn't know where to draw a line in the dust, mostly because it shifted and moved around him, distorting his reason and blocking him out to the daylight and all the damage he did? Maybe Ash never really wanted to leave, and this was his kickback.

Where had Ash been when Johnny was killed?

Who'd been with him when Voodoo last held her mom and emerging feelings had threatened to steal Ash away?

Was this Ash's unconscious kickback over being forced to leave?

Was this his real level of control?

Christ.

Just how well did he really know Ash?

No. Raif shook it off. He'd deny gut instinct there. Yeah, Ash's personality type suggested an MO for something dark, but he knew Ash. He was a rare find because he stood in the midst of an accident, never running, never fighting his way out, just looking so damn confused at the carnage.

Would Chase really be all that different?

They were both just kids. There was something else here. *Someone* else.

Raif changed direction and instead looked into surveillance equipment that the police used. Ash's dad was an ex-cop. Equipment could have been taken numerous ways when you're off guard at home and not quite sharp enough to have remembered to have taken it back to the station.

One slip-up, one location where items had been lost and who was around. One place where someone could have gotten access to it, it's all he needed.

Because he had a bad feeling now, one that would see him track down a killer for the culler to slaughter if they even got close to dancing a Holly Blue butterfly over Ash's skin. And if the bastard got him naked during any of that, if they forced Ash to expose his scars when Ash kept shyness even in a lover's hold, Raif would damn well slaughter the world and its monsters when it came to covering him back up.

CHAPTER 26
FRIENDS

"HEY." ASH DIDN'T hear Miles at first, his gaze on the TV, how the recorded newsfeed had played out twice now and pushed the time to three in the morning. He sat on the settee, legs drawn up, eyes fixed on flickering images he couldn't piece together.

Johnny…. He hadn't committed suicide. He'd—

"Ash."

A mug of coffee was pushed into his hands as Miles crouched down. "You okay, kid?"

Ash looked at him, blinked, let out a cold laugh that saw him spill some of his coffee. Miles took it off him for a moment and scowled at the damage.

"Yeah, I know you're not," he said gently, offering the coffee back when Ash finally controlled himself and wiped his hands on his T-shirt. "I just need to keep checking, okay?"

"My fucking dad." Ash gave a long hard look into his coffee. "Will you arrest him?"

Miles slumped into a chair, his own coffee almost

spilling. "What for? He's no killer, Ash. Sure, he's messed you up, and Chase... but... no. He's no killer."

"You know that? Of course you do. You've known about this all along and just watched us fall apart around each other."

Miles rubbed at his head. "Calm it down, Ash. Ease off on the bite. I'm doing my job to help try and catch a killer. Silence this time was justified, even if I screwed up things in the past with you. And you know that because you were with your dad the night when the other murders took place."

Ash frowned.

"On the Tuesday morning with the young girl... around eight." Miles sighed. "You were both at home. Unless you weren't on lates that day?"

Ash scrambled to think back, then felt sick. It had happened Tuesday? Voodoo had been with her mother *that* long? "But he was the last one to see Johnny alive. Maybe he forced Johnny to drink, maybe..."

"Your dad played head fucks like you do?" Miles's look was hard. "You think he'd remember how to do that, Ash? And besides it wasn't alcohol in Johnny's system. Heavy traces of a date-rape drug had been found. Johnny had been sexually assaulted."

"And you fucking knew." Ash groaned. They'd found come on Johnny's stomach. Someone had messed with him, had... "Christ, just... Jesus fucking Christ." He felt so sick. How had they missed that? But then, pulling your best friend down from a tree, loosening that noose... everything else faded to the distance. "Why the fuck weren't we told? Why the fuck didn't *you* tell me?"

"Because...." He let that fade, and Ash groaned.

"Because of me and Chase... what we've done in the past. You thought...."

"Easy, Ash. Not just that... those are details specific to the case, and any Tom, Dick, and Sally could have claimed it. The case is ongoing. I *couldn't* tell you."

Ash looked up sharply. "What about Johnny's parents? About...."

"They know." It came out so softly. "They had every right to know."

"*And we didn't?* As his friends? Chase as his fucking lover?"

Miles gave a hard sigh. "No one knew Johnny and Chase were lovers. He would have been told otherwise." He frowned. "How's he taken the news this morning?"

"How do you fucking think?" He didn't regret the coldness in that, but he went back to looking down at his mug. He was still so pissed off with Chase, with the cheating, being cheated on by his best friends, but Chase had watched the news play out and had crumpled with each release of detail. Then he'd broken down, just sobbed his heart out, and how Chase had been forced to find out... that pissed Ash off more.

Miles gave a sad smile, then seemed happy enough to let the darkness of the lounge hold them for a moment. Ash kept his gaze on the light fall of rain outside now, not really feeling in tune with the sound or the familiar look of the darkness beyond the windows. If he'd felt displaced with Raif, this... this pushed him into the surreal, where he'd not slept for days and every noise, every movement seemed louder, each stare out of the window more willing to stare that little bit longer.

"He finally asleep?"

Ash looked back at Miles. He nodded, then shrugged. "Grief. It does fucked-up things to you. The pillow's over his head, which means he needs his space, so fuck off to everyone." Miles had given them the spare room to this cottage, and Ash had curled up onto the bed and tried to block life out for a while. He'd placed some distance between them on the bed, and Chase stayed quiet, as if knowing it wasn't so much the betrayal of him sleeping with Johnny when he'd still been seeing Ash, but more that he hadn't told Ash, period. Neither had Johnny. It locked him out in a cold, but one he knew Johnny had felt most of his life. But, Christ, he'd have loved to have been able to see both of them happy and making a go of it. They'd have looked so good together. And that's what hurt the most: how they hadn't trusted him enough to experience that.

Chase hadn't slept, he hadn't spoken, and Ash had mirrored it, eventually being the first to pull away and head downstairs.

Miles had been in the lounge, the light from the TV flickering but making no sound as the news had played out for a second time. He'd been asleep when Ash had looked in to the lounge, looking just as tired, as drawn as all of them, but he'd woken on hearing Ash close the door. Coffee had been the answer. Ash wished it was the answer to everything, especially to this silence.

Giving a sniff, he glanced around the lounge, then back outside. "What is this place?" He hadn't noticed at first, how they hadn't drove to Miles's house the next street over from his own home. They'd gone an hour into the woods, onto an out of season campsite that looked like it would do great business when it opened. A small stream ran outside, along the cottage, and the hint of rose bush came through the window every now and again from the climbing bunch he'd seen outside. The home was perfect, all oak beams and wooden floor, with a log fire losing its last embers over in the hearth.

"It belongs to the missus." Miles rubbed at one eye, denying a yawn by the look of things. "Her father left her a little fund after he died, and she bought this place." He smiled as he looked around. "Thought it best not to take this home to her. I come here fishing when I get time off and need to vent. Me and your dah—"

He stopped there as Ash looked away. Yeah. He remembered the fishing trips into the woods his dad had taken with Miles over the years. All the usual shit that family and friends did. But mostly after his dad had burned his way into Ash's memory and ass.

Christ. Raif. Ash grunted. He missed Raif now, that quiet offer of a hold. He didn't think he'd ever need it. But now…? He scrunched his face slightly, then buried his fear, his confusion, his ability to focus, in his mug of coffee.

"That's mine, you cold bastard." His coffee slipped from his hands and he jerked slightly as someone slumped down next to him. "Still pissed with me, Red? Because, Christ, this shit hurts."

Chase sounded so dejected as he took a long swig of the coffee, not looking at Ash. "And since when did you leave me out with coffee?"

Ash looked down at his own hands, how he understood how Raif passed through life like dark matter: he couldn't seem to hold on to anything for love nor money himself now. Not even Chase. Chase had never been fully his. An arm eased over his shoulder a moment later, and again neither spoke, not until Chase dropped his head against Ash's, and Ash closed his eyes.

"Still love you, bud," whispered Chase.

"But you loved Johnny more, right?" There was no bitterness there. For however long they'd been seeing each other, Johnny hadn't been on his own when he died. He'd had Chase's heart.

"Yeah." Chase pulled him a little tighter. "I love him more. You okay with that? You okay with me?"

Ash looked at him, stared at him for a long while. "Yeah," he said gently. "I'm good with that. I'm more than okay with you. I just... just wished I'd got to see you both in love together instead...." He frowned. "Instead of a lover in mourning."

A tear rolled down Chase's cheek, but he sniffed it away, his eyes so wide now. "Hurts like fuck to know how someone fucked with him like we'd fuck with someone. That they'd touched him. You think it's payback for everything we've done, Red?"

Ash pulled him into a hard hug and kissed his head. "Fuck no, Chase. The bastard who did this, he's sick. Us..." Ash closed his eyes. "We know when to stop."

The ringing of the phone drew them apart, but Miles waved them into quiet as he got up and took his coffee with him. Voices drifted on through a moment later, and Ash looked at Chase.

"You gonna be okay?" Ash took the coffee back and stole a mouthful.

"Are you?" Chase stared down at his hands and gave such a hard sigh. "Christ, butterflies." He glanced at Ash. "That sick fucker buried a butterfly in him after they'd touched him."

Ash felt sickness rush into his throat. Voodoo's mom too. Raif's wife. And little Lucy.... Jesus. He looked at

Chase. "Oh fuck. That butterfly in my room."

Chase frowned.

"And those with the wings pulled off in my dishwasher...."

"Your...?" Eyes narrowed, then widened. "Fuck." Chase started to get to his feet. "You need to tell Miles. You need—"

Ash caught him by the sleeve as he turned away. "It could be coincidence. It could be—"

"Fuck coincidence. Johnny, those two women, Christ knows who else...." Chase crouched down. "I'm not losing you, Red."

Ash finally let him go, and Chase stood. "I'll go and tell Miles, get us another coffee too." A tear still roamed Chase's cheek as he held his hand out for the mug. "I'm glad we're good, Ash. I couldn't do this without you."

Ash glanced down. He'd had a coffee, but he hadn't tasted it and...

You ever see the look you get in your eyes, Ash? Like you're taking a breath but you don't care that you can't feel what you breathe in?

Raif. Christ. He needed him because, yeah, it scared the life out of him how he tasted life but didn't feel it now. He handed the mug over, hating how it wasn't Raif there taking it from him, then feeling guilty, so fucking guilty he wished Chase away like that. With a small smile, Chase headed over for the door.

Ash wished to God he knew how to get in touch with Raif. Did he know about Johnny now? Had he seen the news?

"Who's getting you to look like that, Red?" Chase paused and glanced back. "Talk to me. Is it something to do with what happened back at Jim's? When you stole Jim's car?" He came back over. "You've been walking in some twisted dreamland since then."

Ash held that softness for a moment, the hurt buried beneath it, and realised he'd kept his own secrets too. Hypocrite came to mind. "Yeah," he said quietly. Then he managed to snort a smile. "At Jim's, I got taught a vicious lesson by... by a good man. Although you wouldn't have thought he was a good man the way he did it with rope."

Chase narrowed his eyes. "Rope? A few months back? Not long before Johnny's murder? Before those other people?"

Ash stilled as Chase brought his concern really close.

"Red, have you listened to what you've just said? Fucking rope? Just how well do you know this other guy? And it is a guy, right?"

Ash tugged away, stayed quiet for a moment. "He's a good man."

Chase didn't seem to recognise him; hell, he looked ready to go and sign the sectioning notice that would lock him safely away from himself. Given everything tonight, how Ash had met Raif, Ash... didn't really blame him. It hit with just how dangerous it all sounded. The timing, Johnny... everything.

He tugged Chase back by the sleeve. "He's a damn good man, Chase."

A frown came up, a shrug of shoulder. "That's all you've got? He's a good man? Any evidence to support that? And I'm only taking photo, driving licence, and character witness by the fucking Pope at this stage, as it's all I'd fucking believe. *Have you listened to a fucking word you've just said, Ash?* This bastard tracked you to Jim's. He *tied* you up, just like Johnny was *tied* and made to swing from a fucking tree...."

Ash went to say something else, but he shut down just as quickly, even took a step back. "He's a good man."

"Ohhhkay." Chase nodded. "We get this sorted through the police. Now. Then we sort that fucking Stockholm Syndrome head of yours."

Anger hit Ash as Miles came back in, and Chase moved for him, glancing warily back at Ash.

"Miles, Ash met someone a few months back. Then remembered that there was a butterfly in his bedroom...." Chase scratched at his head as he reached Miles. "When I moved the dishwasher at his too, there were more in there. Damn weird how that all starts with this new man on the scene, with—"

Miles hit Chase hard, smacking into his jaw and snapping Chase's head to the side. His body followed a moment later, and Chase's head caught the doorframe just before his body hit the floor.

"What the fuck—" Ash bolted for Miles. But Miles moved faster, breaking away and snaking an arm around Ash's throat, almost turning him half a circle, back to the window as he shaped Ash from behind.

"Shush, shush-shush, Ashy. The call I just got. It let me know that Chase has surveillance equipment at your home."

"What?" Ash tried to shake free as a hand smothered his mouth.

"Easy, easy, Ash. I know this is hard, but this comes from someone called Raif. He's the one who just called. He wanted you to know and for me to get you away from Chase. Is that the man Chase spoke about? The one you met a few months back?"

"Raif?" Ash stilled, fell completely silent, and Miles eased his hold a little in the next moment.

"I'm sorry, Ash, so bloody sorry. I didn't want to hit him, but Johnny—"

"Bullshit." Ash didn't move. "Raif wouldn't ever give you any detail about himself over the phone. He'd never use his name." Ash's heart fell. "And I know Chase. I know him so bloody well to know he'd never hurt Johnny, not with how he looked at me just now."

Ash flatlined his feelings and frowned as he sorted around for some details. Rhiannon... his wife. How they met. Miles had thrown up over just asking her out. He'd asked Ash to do it for him in the end. The butterflies... Christ. The butterflies. "They were a sign you loved someone else, and you just couldn't tell them, could you?"

"Hm?"

Something else came back now. When Rhiannon had said no to Ash, that she wasn't interested in Miles, she'd walked so funny the day after Miles had gone to see her. Ash's dad took her aside, then he'd taken Miles out to the woods a few hours after. Miles had come back with a black eye, a few broken ribs.

Miles hadn't been able to ask anyone out before that, but after his dad had finished with him? Now?

Butterflies. He said it all with butterflies now, only— only—"Chase is the only one who hasn't had any."

Chase. Jesus. He lay so still. "You were trying to say you loved him, only going through everyone else to do it— through me again." Anger kicked through fear. "Tell me, did... did my dad keep you on track with being a good lad too all these years, Miles? Only when he wasn't there to rough you up for you raping Rhiannon, you got vicious, you raped her more. You murdered Johnny, raped Voodoo's mother, Kerry. You made Voodoo watch, you sick cunt. You—"

A kiss came at his head. "Products of our time. Ah... you got me, Ashy. But you almost believed me, right?"

Ash writhed, but whatever he went to say was cut off with a hand over his mouth—his nose.

"Easy, easy. I wouldn't hurt you in this, Ash; it's not just about Chase here. You two make each other. You need to understand it's never been about hurting either of you, just... just, fuck. Chase, his viciousness when he plays with you: we're all so fucking alike. He just needs training a little more. You do too. You're not there yet. Not fully. You've gone soft lately."

Ash jerked wildly, struggling for breath now, raking at the hand smothering his breathing. It hurt, all the fucking head games over who: Chase making him question Raif, Raif making him question reality, Miles twisting it to point bloody hands at Chase, and... and....

"Ash..." A head rested against his and a heated breath played down his neck. "You and Chase. How you are together... there's a danger to it, all fire in the blood when you both get going, and... and..." He gave a groan. "I need to play with you two now. Take it higher, darker, let you both taste life in ways most never will, because there's so much badness out there that needs fucking into our heads."

The hand shifted, freeing his oxygen intake via his nose, and Ash inhaled, rough and hard.

"Flutter by those butterflies.... You get it too, Ashy? When you're in the middle of doing something you shouldn't? Like when you filmed that barman getting fucked?"

Ash frowned. Hard.

"I saw it in real time. Not hard to hack a phone like that. And you and Chase—"

Ash choked out his fear, his confusion as he tried to shift his body and elbow Miles in the ribs. The hand shifted back over his nose and mouth, and Ash cried into the touch, not wanting that fight for breath again.

"Then Johnny turned Chase's head, and he curbed who you two are, who we are." He sounded like he wanted to throw up. "The fucker made me feel so dirty. So I took what I learnt off you two, how I'd loved raping Rhiannon, and played my own game with him. So fucking free without Jeff breathing down my neck, fucking breaking a few ribs to stop me hurting her again, but, Christ, as your old man lost his strength, his memory over keeping me... good...."

Christ. All those times Ash had gone around to Rhiannon's and Rhiannon had looked in anger back at him, it forced a cry out of Ash now. It was Ash's own anger staring back at him: caught in the abuse and dying within it too. How many times had Miles raped Rhiannon since his own dad hadn't had the mind to keep Miles in check? Just what had he forced her through as he'd progressed from rape to breath-play, to... killing someone and dancing bugs over—in—their bodies? Was that why they'd never had kids? She'd seen the way Miles had looked at Chase as Chase had grown, and that was her way of denying putting a child through what happened when she was left alone with him? Because it had been Miles who had told Ash's dad about Ash when things went wrong. It was Miles who sparked getting Ash burned most of the time as Ash had grown too. And Chase... Chase had been the one to talk to

Miles, to let Miles know they'd kissed, Ash remembered that... Miles had told Chase it was okay. He'd more than gone out of his way to encourage that they spend time together at Ash's. And then Miles had started to take his dad out when he and Chase got together at Ash's. Why? Had he been watching what they did all the way back then? In with fucking the dead, raping the living, getting his kicks seeing kids burned, and stuffing live bugs in abused bodies... he'd gotten off watching kids test out their sexuality too? Or had Rhiannon seen he wanted something else entirely? What had his dad seen over the years in Miles to beat him down the way he had? How it wasn't just watching kids he had the potential for...

Miles snapped his head back, now breathing heavy against Ash's cheek as Ash shouted out.

"Flutter by those butterflies...." Miles sang it so softly in his ear. "Come dance with me, Ashy... come dance with me..."

Blackness started to take away the fears on how Chase hadn't moved from by the door, on how it didn't seem to matter so much now that Ash fought against taking a breath.... Fight. It was just too much to fucking fight, because good men... the fuck-over always came.

And there. Miles. Miles had been the best of men for so bloody long that the fuck-over came so hard now that Ash could already feel his world shutting down around him. He didn't want this anymore....

JACK L. PYKE

CHAPTER 27
WALKING IN JOHNNY'S FOOTSTEPS

THE BREAK OF bracken and twig under bare foot should have left Ash limping from the dig of wood and rubble into his feet as he walked naked through the wood. Hell, his own nakedness should have had him running and crawling under a bush, shivering despite the oncoming spring air. Scars were on full display, moonlight sweeping over his ass with a silver-gloved touch. And he'd never let anyone touch, never let anyone see. Having that taken away from him should have sent him crying into the undergrowth. But laughter played around the tree trunks, just a soft catch of a few hollow-sounding breaths that ended in a quiet sob.

Run.

It was there, at the back of his mind. Go play, hide and go—

Fucking run.

The shaking in his hands cried it out. Something was wrong, but the reason hid among the trees, sometimes sneaking a look from behind a tree, a bush, and smiling slyly, then skittering back into the trees with a *come find me skip.*

On his hands, dirt streaked the tips and blackened his nails, as if he'd been dragged for a while before he stumbled to his feet. The same fight patterns of dirt on his fingertips marked his toes, the pads of his feet, snaking around his ankles and leaving splatter marks up to his thighs. Someone somewhere had struggled.

Fight. See, there's some fight left here, Raif…. Christ… I just need you here to see this fight.

Ash fought a sob.

Someone came in close, rubbing at his arms before pulling him into a hug. The body swamped his with warmth and heat mostly—okay *naked from the waist up* heat, but enough to leave him burying his head into the curve of a throat and mumbling out Raif. It felt so much like Raif, and he wanted the safety in big bear arms now; not BDSM bear arms, just a mass of muscle, hair, and aggression when triggered….

"Yeah, if you need me to be, baby. I'll be Raif."

Light rain started to fall, and that just made Ash hide his shivers a little more in the body against his.

A stroke came to his head and… so strange. That need to throw up. To… *run.* It bit harder than the heavier fall of rain.

Ash pulled back and rubbed at his eyes, hating how heavy his hands felt and how it left him seeing stars when he rubbed too hard.

"Just a little something to keep that head of yours good until we got here, Ash. Not a heavy enough dose to kill you like it did with Johnny." The whisper seemed too far away, and it forced Ash to blink and try to focus. "You go from static to being all ill intent when you remember you can fight."

Blood leaked down a face he couldn't really focus on. There was a broken nose there?

"Yeah. And you hit as hard as your old gaffer."

Ash staggered a little, and a hand shot out to steady him. He jolted slightly, glancing down at the blood smeared on the back of a hand, one that had hit something... someone it hurt to remember. Now a nose had been wiped. But there wasn't any anger from... Miles? In fact he seemed a damn sight more contented than who struggled off to their right.

Ash went still.

Hands bound above him by metal cuffs, Chase and all his nakedness was forced headfirst up against a tree. A clear polythene bag covered his face, all to bunch at the base of his neck. He kicked, writhed—fought for breath—but the effort seemed as drunk as Ash's.

"*Chase.*" Ash tried to bolt for him.

"No." Hands gripped his shoulders, digging into the skin... bone, if he carried on. "Just student-teacher time, Ash." A brush came against his cheek. "He's got to learn what it feels like before he can enjoy doing it to someone else. It's how your dad taught me: a plastic bag over my head, although I doubt he felt like we do when we play like this. And you, you get to feel what it's like to see Chase's breath fucked out of him. You get to fuck it from him too."

Ash looked at Miles. No, there was no anger there, just... something else. Something that heated Miles's cheeks, sent his breathing a little deeper, and forced Miles's cock to top his jeans.

Ash frowned. When the fuck had he undone his jeans…? Chase's slurred and muffled cries were trapped by the bag covering his face, and a rougher stroke came at Ash's jaw as Ash snarled and again tried to bolt past.

"Hey, easy…. Easy. Okay, I know you'd fight to protect him, and that's good. That's what I want between you two. We'll look after each other because of that instinct. He just needs to learn first. You both do, okay?" That calmness in his smile, that honesty, could calm a riot.

"S not… this isn't… isn't us." Ash started to shake, felt a tear fall. "This isn't me and Chase. Johnny started to prove that. Please… let Chase go."

A lick came at Ash's cheek, as if willing another tear. "You forget, kid. I've watched you two grow up. I know exactly who you and Chase are."

"No—"

A backhand split his lip and Ash tasted blood when his world stopped spinning again. "And I know what keeps you in check." A grip to his hair pulled his gaze up to Miles. "I'll fucking burn into you until you play with me properly. Being a copper's son, you get a time out card, but nothing else. I'll rape you fucking raw if you test my teaching skills too much."

Behind Miles, Chase struggled less and less, his body jolting slightly as though electrical shocks kept him on his feet too.

Ash had never felt more fear. "Chase…" He refused to look away from him. "He's the son of a butcher man. His mother works at Hayes, the car manufacturer. When he grew up, he'd sleep with a Batman stuffed toy he won out of a grabber machine on holiday. Do you know that about him, Miles? Because that's the kid he still is when the lights go down and he tries to hold on to you. He still has that Batman toy hidden in a box under his bed. And I rib him about it so fucking much, but he loves it too hard to let it go. His guilty pleasure, he calls it. Do you know that, Miles?"

"Yeah...." That breath against Ash's ear. "Of course I do. I have cameras at his too." A smile. "Those butterflies you say I never gave him...? He's had one every birthday over the years. Each one stuffed inside that Batman toy... Ash, he's hugged me a lot longer than he's tried to hold on to you."

Ash threw up until it hurt, then he hit the floor in the next breath, taken down to the floor the same way his own dad tried to teach him if things started to go wrong. Focused solely on Chase, Ash instantly tried to shuffle to his feet, snarling anger and hate as he tried to get to Chase and get Chase to fight.

A belt hit Ash's back, first between his shoulder blades, making him curl into himself, then across his back, ass, shoulder—never stopping until Ash found that strange, quiet numbness. He'd always flatline within when that burn came against his skin. Detachment came so easily now.

"That's not you learning, boy."

Something wrapped around Ash's neck. A thick collar of some sort that had him fighting against the choke hold. Then something clicked into place as his hands were pinned behind his back and he was dragged up the opposite side of the tree to Chase. A rough tug of rope came, and Ash was forced to his tiptoes to stop the threat of breaking his neck. All face-first into a tree now.

A touch drifted down Ash's ass, over the scars. "Oh fuck, don't disappear like this, Ash."

305

A bite came at his neck, just a tease.

"It's what I've fucking loved about you. This... this dead coldness... it would be like raping a corpse." A long, hard sigh. "You're my living corpse, Ash. You know that? And, fuck. I've thought about raping you so many fucking times like this...."

Ash stilled as the flick of a lighter came.

The burn to his left ass cheek came hard, fast, the lighter held against his skin. But Ash didn't cry out, he took it. He took it because he'd been taught to take it as a kid, to play dead until the hurt stopped.

"Fuck, Ash... yeah... that's it, that's fucking you, that's what I fucking need.... Play dead for me."

Bump and grind, a dick digging into his asscheek came rough as this time his shoulder blade took the burn. He wanted to run with how his mind wanted to shut down, hide, and move away from the pain as he'd been schooled to over the years, but...

You ever see the look you get in your eyes, Ash. How you take a breath but never really feel it?

Ash cried all the hurt now. He fought, kicked, writhed, making sure Miles heard every ounce of pain—heard that need to breathe and feel every breath he took back into his body. He *wasn't* dead inside. He wanted Miles to hear that, because if Miles did, then Chase would too. That he fucking cared the world for Chase. That Raif would hear; he'd fucking know he went down fighting, he went down wanting Raif to hear he was alive and still needed life.

Four vicious thumps smashed into his ribs, forcing Ash to dance away and cry out some more.

"That's not you playing fucking dead for me, Ash."

Miles was gone, now tugging the bag off Chase's face a

little. "This…." Miles gripped Chase's hair, pulling his head back for Ash. Chase's eyes were closed, his lips a lighter shade of pale… blue. "This is how you play dead. I rape him now, it's your fault because you didn't learn that you're the student. On the rare occasion, you open your legs for your teacher."

Chase's hips jerked forward and Ash's world fell. Miles grunted out and kept his rape slow… languid.

"Fuck… cold… so fucking cold to fuck." Miles shivered. "Tight too, so fucking tight." He sighed, then pulled something from his own jeans pocket.

Two blue butterflies danced in a tube, scrambling over each other to get free. With practised movements, he gripped the stopper between his teeth while the tube was slid up into the bag and held there as one of the butterflies made its way out, fluttering over and around Chase's lips. The second butterfly was imprisoned once more by the stopper, and Miles gave Ash a satisfied grin as he made sure the bag went back over Chase's jaw.

Ash cried out, long, deep… enough that it hurt his chest and threatened to break his ribs. "You bastard. You sick fucking bastard. I'll kill you! I swear I'll fucking kill you, you cunt. You want vicious game play? I'll sound your cock, leave a tube for fire ants to crawl up inside, tape it shut, then let them eat your dick from the inside fucking out."

Miles closed his eyes, gently fisting the ends of the bag so the butterfly constantly fluttered against Chase's skin. He chuckled as he started his rape again. Gentle rocking that jerked Chase's body. "Sounds good, Ash. Hm… so fucking good…. I'd like to see you do that to someone…."

Miles jerked out of Chase, enough for Miles to grip the tip of his cock, as if to stop coming. "Christ, losing it too quick here. Fucking butterflies…" He dipped his head against Chase's, then fucked back in, his pace brutal and filled with grunts and groans that Ash shut out.

He buried his head in his arm and cried out. But the betrayal was there, how he cried Chase's name, but his body cried Raif now. This wasn't who they were, and they were being swept away, buried in who Miles was. Lives twisted, lovers… lost. And he needed to feel Raif, to get lost in all his warmth. *"Fucking, Raif…"*

A grunt came, but it was different from the rest. More like a gurgled sound, strangled out by force, and Ash looked up. An arm snaked around Miles's throat, cutting his cry short, and Miles was spun away in the next moment, more tossed face-first into the dirt, away from them and the tree. A moment later a kick went to Miles's head from a heavy work boot that saw Miles black out for a second.

"You and me, we'll fuck about in a moment, you cunt." Raif came over and pulled the bag off Chase just as Miles cried hate, got back to his feet, and rushed back over.

Someone shifted from the bushes behind Miles, Taser in hand, and jammed it repeatedly into Miles's throat until he hit the floor and didn't get up again. Ash recognised the smoking man from Voodoo's. He came with someone else who stumbled forward and started kicking Miles's head.

"Not my fucking *boy*." Miles got another kick to the head off Ash's dad. "Not Chase. Not Johnny. Not a fucking little girl who'd hurt no one in this life. *Not. My. Boy.*"

Ash yanked on the cuffs as smoking man pushed his dad back and bound Miles's arms behind his back. His head spun and he tried to stop the sickness hitting his throat. All of it focused on Chase. "Get these… get these fucking cuffs off me. Raif, get these fucking cuffs off me."

Raif ignored Ash, an apology—something else—there in his eyes as he cut Chase down first. He went down with him and started CPR as smoking man took out a firearm and kept it levelled on Miles.

"Off." Ash fought, tears falling, but he was as pissed as hell as language fell from his lips. "Get them fucking—"

Someone took the tension off Ash, pulling on the rope and taking a lot longer to unclip the hook to his collar. The cuffs came off next, and Ash cried out as he pushed his dad away and went to crash down next to Chase. Only he threw up first, choking bile after bile and crying hurt with it.

"Easy. Easy," his dad whispered in his ear, trying to get him to straighten. But Ash shook him off and tried to scramble over to Chase. "No. Let him work, son."

"Get the fuck off me." Son? He spun around, pushing him off. His dad had caused all of this bollocks: his twisted take on hurt to heal. "Fuck you. *Fuck you.* You did this. You fucking made him. You made us all."

A rough grip on his arm tugged him to a stop and Ash cried hate for it. "He's not fucking moving, you bastard. Chase... he's not breathing because of you and... and... just get... get the fuck off me. Get—"

His hair was grabbed. Hard at first to get attention, then loosening as a head rested to his. "Did... did that bastard... did he touch you, did he—" A rough sigh came, then eyes were screwed shut. "I don't forget Johnny, Ash, just that he died. And I..." Anger fought grief in his dad's eyes. "I kept trying to remember why Johnny made me so mad. When Miles asked Johnny to come over, it seemed the perfect time to try and remember, to ask him. But... but I remembered how Miles had looked at Johnny. It hadn't been long since Johnny had slept in your bed with Chase, and Miles, he looked so... wrong that day. Like how he looked after Rhiannon had told him no. Then I remembered the rape. I remembered the date-rape stock going down at work when he raped Rhiannon. How Johnny stood there looking at Miles with that same drugged-up gaze, and how scared he sounded when he heard how I shouted at Miles. He'd been laughing, but only because he was so scared. I didn't shout at Johnny. I shouted at Miles. Then they both disappeared, and I didn't know why. I forgot." He frowned at Ash. "Rhiannon... Johnny... their eyes were just like yours now." A wipe came at the side of Ash's cheek. "Ash, I thought Miles had helped, stopped me getting at you by getting me away when the stress hit hard, when I came at you. So I wanted to save him too. But I didn't know, I swear I didn't know he'd installed cameras to watch you and Chase. To listen in to you. To miss how Johnny and Chase didn't sleep together at Chase's because you were there with them most of the time. And I didn't know he'd started raping Rhiannon again, that it had all escalated to him locking her under the bed and leaving her to scream away the night as spiders crawled over her. And fault... all this is my fault. I shouldn't have hurt any of you...."

Ash frowned, at the same time stumbling back, away. He couldn't stand hearing his dad, being touched, knowing more details on Rhiannon and... locked under a bed? Spiders? Too much. This was too fucking much now. He dropped next to Chase, sending his own world spinning as he did, and looked up at Raif, just briefly. "You... you came."

"There's *nothing* in this life I can't fucking track at night, Ash. The streets are mine." Raif shook, so badly as he worked on Chase. "Get that into your fucking head. I'm here for the duration and I'll always come for you."

Ash fought down sickness, and smoking man was there a moment later. He'd gotten a case from somewhere and a needle was pulled out. Something went into Ash's arm.

"Just something to counter the Midazolam, Ash. Nothing more." Smoker rubbed at Ash's arm as his dad now had the gun levelled on Miles, maybe giving up now too as he sat on the ground.

"How…?" He tried again. "How the hell do you know what drug it is?"

"Because Johnny willingly walked into those woods," said Smoker, "like you two now, then put a noose around his neck. It's a drug that's used to influence actions, mostly in preparation for surgery, not like this, *for* this. Not unless you intend to rape. I'm giving you Flumazenil. It's the antidote that's usually kept on hand when Midazolam is used during surgery."

Most of that still went over Ash's head, and he refocused on Raif. "You knew we were here… how… the hell did you know?" He repeated the same question but couldn't help it. He needed the focus.

But it was Smoker who spoke. "Miles's name came up on the checks for the missing surveillance equipment." He watched Raif work hard on Chase's chest. "It was just a matter of following the trail from there, over to Chase's and how surveillance equipment had been installed there. It took Chase off the suspect list. That brought up Miles. His home. Rhiannon, and the box he had under their bed for her."

Ash glanced at him sharply. Raif had suspected Chase at some point too. And Miles kept Rhiannon in a box under their bed? What the *fuck*? That kept coming back and started Ash shaking so badly.

"Frank, can you stay here and carry on the CPR whilst I run back to the car for the oxygen, mask, and ambu bag?"

Smoker nodded as Ash tried to get his head around why Raif would come with all that oxygen equipment. Then he lost his stomach contents again, this time choking up liquid and a bitter taste.

"Hey...." Raif stood, and a moment later a long coat wrapped around Ash's shoulders. "Hold on in there, Ash. Just hold on for a few moments." Raif was moving away again. "Keep an eye on that fuck there." He wasn't talking to Ash, but almost as if in answer, Ash took the case Frank had been messing with and pulled out a fresh needle.

"Wait, kid, what are you doing?" Frank grabbed his hand.

"Chase has been drugged too. He needs it out of his system."

"Ash—Ash, stop. Think." Frank, Ash doubted it was his real name, pulled the case away, and set the needle up. "You think you can handle a needle with what's coming out of your system?" Frank made sure Chase got a dose. "He'll need another two more injections in the next fifteen minutes, then another one, maybe two in the next hour. Inject him, but if you can't, dribble it on his tongue, just make sure the mask that Raif brings stays neat over his air passages, okay? Can you remember that, Ash? Can you tell Raif?"

Two more in the next fifteen minutes... one to two more in the next hour... dribble on the tongue or inject. Ash managed a nod. He'd remember, although why he needed to wasn't as clear. Frank went back to CPR.

Ash ran shaking hands through Chase's hair. "C'mon, bud. Breathe. Just fucking breathe for me now, baby. Don't be Johnny... don't be Johnny." It came flooding back, how Ash had fought so long with CPR on Johnny but gotten nowhere.

Raif seemed to come from nowhere, then he took over the CPR as Frank set the oxygen up.

A blue butterfly wing touched Chase's lips, and Ash snarled, wiping it off. "Fucking cunt...." He briefly closed his eyes. "C'mon, baby. Don't let that bastard beat us."

Raif suddenly stilled and Ash stalled, knocked sideways at the implications. You only stopped when—

Raif held a finger up, silencing Ash, before resting it on Chase's chest.

One slight rise of his chest came. A shaky dip.

The next longer breath had Raif grabbing the oxygen machine and slipping the mask into place over Chase's air passages. For a moment there was a little fight, a groan, maybe an echo of masks and not being able to breathe, but any fight ebbed away after only a moment. But breathe...

"Yes, baby. Fucking yes," mumbled Ash as Frank monitored the breathing apparatus.

"You need to move. Now," said Frank to Raif. "Get him and Ash out of here. Go." Frank glanced back, then handed Ash the antidote case. "I'll handle the rest. Chase needs specialist care. You can't fuck about here with this now."

He still spoke to Raif, and Ash couldn't understand the urgency. Chase had come around; he was breathing.

Raif nodded as Frank's jacket went over Chase, then he shuffled Chase into his arms as he stood. "Ash. You're with me. Frank's got this." He looked at Miles the same time Ash did. "We're more than fucking done here."

"What the fuck?" Ash got to his feet too. "What about

this fucker here?"

Raif didn't shift his gaze off Frank now. "Frank will get him into custody. After that? He's a dead man fucking walking. You understand what I'm saying, Frank?"

Ash didn't. Then that twenty-four-hour period to get out of town came through the fog. "You...." He shifted from Raif to Frank. "You're handing him over to whoever's coming?"

His dad frowned between Frank and Raif too, but there was something else there. A knowledge.

"We're handing him over." The coldness there was hard in Raif. "Make it a fun kill for our other bastard." That was directed at Frank. "You send me the pictures of his body for playing cards after he's been culled."

Frank hit Raif's arm. "Got it. You go. I'll find you."

Raif started to turn away, but Ash didn't follow. He knew Chase was in the best of care. But Miles... he didn't know Frank. He wanted... needed to make sure Miles would see the inside of a cell.

"Ash."

Ash looked back at his dad, but his dad looked so ill.

"Go, get out of town with him, son." Did he know what was going on here too? "And if you find it hard to run with trust, run with what scares you most." He came over and pulled Ash into a hug. "Over the past few months, with him? You've never looked more scared. But it's been the best kind, the sort that injects life into you, not sends a boy into quiet or twisted games when he should be crying out as life burns him." A harder hug.

His dad pushed him away and looked at Raif. "I'm sorry. I scared him in all the wrong ways, so that by the time it came to meeting you, he couldn't feel the change in heartbeat between mine and yours." He frowned. "Promise you'll scare him a little each day? The kind that gets him to look at you again as he did when he saw it was you who'd come for him here?"

"Always," said Raif quietly. "Whether he leaves the door locked or not." Raif shifted Chase's weight, turned away, leaving Ash there with his dad.

Giving one last look at Miles, at where Raif had disappeared, Ash tugged his coat around him but still couldn't quite find it in him to hug his dad back. "We'll be back in a few days."

"No you won't, son. Not now." A kiss went to his head. "Don't let me know where you are, not for a while. Stay safe, don't look back. Ever. It's poisoned here. And you're right, I've helped cause it. I'm toxic, so is this place, these people. Go and have a life, kid."

CHAPTER 28
SAFE HOUSE

THE STRAY STREAK of car light passed by the window as they drove. The longer it went on, the more Ash tried to focus and ask why they'd long since driven past his local A&E. Raif had made a brief stop at Miles's cottage to get Ash and Chase's things: keys, wallets, phone… then to Ash's, picking up a duvet, pillows… clothes, passport. Sat in the back with Chase laid out on the seat, his head in Ash's lap, Ash made sure Chase took the Flumazenil on the tongue; he couldn't trust himself with a needle. Frank had already set up the dosage. Then Ash had struggled his way into some jogging pants, then given up to the shakes and wrapped him and Chase in the duvet. The oxygen mask kept a steady pace with the turn of the wheels, and Ash kept failing to deny the pull into a sleep that Chase already played with.

With how Raif handled the car, Ash dozed, jolted awake, then settled, with his arm wrapped around Chase as he felt the drag back into sleep.

At some point Raif was talking to himself, then Ash realised a light flashed on the steering wheel, indicating the hands-free device was in use. Some of the conversation seeped through his sleep-addled head, some didn't. A big part of him didn't care, only that he was moving away from home. That Chase was there.

And Raif.

Raif was there too.

It felt like they travelled for days, but the darkness outside never changed, except when he noticed they were on the motorway and the rush of cat's eyes and light forced him to wipe a hand over his face and try and sit up.

"Chase." Ash had been trying his name every now and again, but each time that deep sleep kept hold of Chase. Ash checked him over, the dampness to his body, the coolness to his skin. "Raif…" He tried that again when his voice cracked. "Raif, why the fuck aren't we at a hospital?"

Quiet, then—"It's nearly five in the morning and he needs specialist care, Ash. Not the kind found in an NHS hospital. Trust me, and just hold on another ten minutes."

"*Where the fuck are we going?*" It hurt to shout at Raif, but so did holding on to Chase and trying to drive that deep-rooted fear away. Yeah, Raif needed to get out, but never at Chase's expense, never—

"I'm not tempting fate, Ash. Leave Chase there and he could attract culler attention as much as you if you stayed. You could both be D & I targets because of knowing me. I was given twenty-four hours to get out, but beyond that, anyone is fair game. Chase also needs direct specialist care, but he needs away from here more."

"Wait? What?" Ash wiped a hand over his face. "He's fucking hurt. What sick fuck would make him a target seeing that… this?"

The soft beep of the hands-free stopped Ash.

"Here," said Raif to the caller. "Do you have an address?"

A London postcode was given by a voice Ash didn't recognise. A long pause came, then—"You'll know when to call me." He sounded older than Raif. Much older, with a very smooth and clear London accent. "How far away are you?"

Raif reset the satnav. "Twenty minutes."

"I'll have Cohan and her team meet you there."

Ash leaned forward. "Where the fuck are we going?"

As Raif glanced back, trying not to look a little angry, the caller went quiet. "Somewhere safe, Ash," Raif said under his breath. "And for God's sake, get your head down. With everything else messing you up, your pupils are dilated: you're in shock. Keep warm until I can get you there."

Raif looked as pale as Ash felt, and his grip on the wheel was tight. Ash wanted to stop shouting, just say thank you for being there, for being… Raif, maybe just say thank you by holding on to him for a minute. But the adrenaline was fading fast, the comedown of the drug hitting hard enough that he wanted to inject again just to escape the reality of all this shit.

"This place will keep us hidden from unfriendlies for a few days?" Raif was back with the caller.

Quiet.

"Yes."

"Good." Raif seemed to pause. "Check on Ash Thomas's dad. He has Holly Blue. Pass that intel on with every full fucking blessing of mine going to our friend. He's one sick fuck."

Ash eased back into his seat, saying nothing now.

"Get to the house and worry about yours. Cohan's team will let me know what they advise."

Raif cut the call as Ash leaned forward, head resting on the back of Raif's headrest. The motion and displacement toyed with his insides, and he bit down nausea.

"You still with me, Ash? You still feeling that sickness?" Raif glanced back. "Do you need to stop?"

Ash shook his head, then remembered Raif wouldn't see it. "No… I'm fine. Just…." He briefly closed his eyes. "Thank you." He fell quiet. "For coming. For… Talent. Being the best at what you do."

Raif messed with something and cold air hit Ash's face. "You make it damn easy to be someone who I'd come after, Ash. You know that, right?"

The air conditioning kicked in, dropping the temperature to settle his insides, but not contradict the warmth of his body as he hid in the quilt.

"How did you know where… where to find us?" Ash rested back, resettling Chase in his lap. "Back at the cottage?"

"Via the surveillance equipment codes at your home. Or more who had handled them during a Met op in your area a few years back. The magazines on your dad's table, it said your dad was trying to remember something about Miles too. About Rhiannon, her rape, the drugs, but also the butterflies. I thought you'd read the articles first, but your dad said otherwise."

Magazine? Butterflies. He was missing details and Raif didn't seem to want to overburden with answers.

"I… I need to know, Raif. I need to sort it in my head."

"Okay." He tapped at the steering wheel. "I found your dad up at Voodoo's, checking out the scene after he'd caught their names on TV and the information about the sexual use of the butterflies." An indicator came on and Raif pulled the car off the motorway. "Something clicked about what he grows in the greenhouse. *Myosotis* and *Hedera helix*."

"Forget-me-nots and ivy."

"Yeah. The ivy is eaten by a number of butterflies, including the Holly Blue, but only the Holly Blues eat the forget-me-nots. Miles had asked for cuttings of both for his wife."

"But she hates plants. Bugs. Bouquets. Rhiannon loves bouquets, but the kind that come bug-free and wrapped in pretty paper. Interflora paper at that." It made sense now why Rhiannon had a deep-rooted fear of bugs.

"That's what your dad remembered: Rhiannon wasn't a plant person. There'd be no reason for Miles to want those plants. Then he remembered how Miles had scared Rhiannon over the years with things like bugs in her coffee."

And bugs. Growing up, Chase had loved bugs. Had Miles seen that as another sign of kindred spirits between them? Was it why he'd stuffed Chase's Batman toy with dead butterflies over the years, imagining he was feeding it?

"The rest is down to Miles, Ash. Don't go there, okay. There's nothing you did as kids to drive this." Raif glanced back briefly. "A call up to the cottage confirmed where you all were."

"So that *was* you? You gave Miles your name?" Ash frowned, his head a little screwed with why Raif would reveal his name like that over the phone.

"On the phone? That was your dad." Raif wasn't happy. "He called before I reached you. Miles knew my name already via the surveillance."

Ash dug his fingertips into his forehead. "He…. he tried to blame it on Chase." He fought down sickness. "I nearly believed him." That hurt the most. He couldn't mention Chase had blamed Raif. Not yet.

"Yeah… I know. I thought of Chase too. Most evidence pointed that way, especially with Chase and Johnny's history. Rejection and grief can take a heart down a dangerous path."

Ash stroked through Chase's hair. Had Raif thought he'd done all this at some point too? Christ… Trust. "No. Not Chase. We've seen too much together." He fell quiet a moment. "Did you suspect me at one point, then?"

Again that grip on the steering wheel that appeared painful to Ash. "I should have trusted you with my phone number."

Ash gave a hard sigh. "Not easy, is it. This trust bullshit? Chase made me think it was you as well." It hit hard then, and Ash dropped his gaze and a soft sob jerked his body. Just how much had they asked for this? How much was their own fault?

"Hey, hey." Raif glanced back. "Not you. Not your fault, Ash. You need to get that into your head. And it's not going to be easy believing it."

∾

It took them roughly fifteen minutes to pull up outside the safe home. It sat in the expensive side of London, through to Park Village West, just east of Regents Park. And expensive…. It looked very expensive. Who the hell could afford a safe house like this?

Dawn just cracked over the top of the home, almost blinding Ash, and he looked away, but not before noting how empty the place looked: no fancy blinds at the windows, no car, no lights left on to warn the callous-minded night burglar. But then this was London. Electricity was damn expensive along with everything else.

"Who owns this?" He needed to see how much Raif was prepared to share. Ash gently shifted Chase's head and hoped to God that Raif knew who owned this place, considering what they were running from.

"No one yet." And that's all Raif said as he lifted Chase from the car. Ash took hold of the oxygen machine and made sure things were locked up behind them, then he went ahead of Raif, over to the door. The oxygen machine was lightweight, looking like it had a minimum of ten hour's battery life. Ash had handled enough parts over the years to make an informed guess, and it bothered the life out of him. If Chase didn't get the right help soon, would it last?

"It should be open." Raif shifted Chase slightly, frowning as Chase's head dropped lightly into the curve of his neck. "Get it open, Ash."

The door opened before Ash tried to, and out came a man and a young-looking woman, the woman wearing a white medical coat over smart trousers; the man a blue tunic and, strange enough, tight cycling shorts.

"This way." The man held the door open wider, waving Raif through. "There's a bed in the lounge, straight ahead."

Ash didn't catch any tags to their clothes and no one introduced themselves as Raif eased through. The oxygen machine was taken from Ash with a smile off the male nurse, then Ash was last in to close the door.

For a moment he rested his head against it, shivering against the chill, how no shirt and shoes took its toll on the rest of his body. The belt marks stung more, already into thick welts across his arms and shoulders, and his hands shook as he tried to not focus on the burns on his body. He stayed like that for a few seconds until the rush of activity coming from the lounge kicked him into gear.

Chase was already resting on the comfort of the hospital bed, side rails pulled up. The woman hovered closest, checking vitals, as the male nurse took blood pressure.

"How long was he without oxygen?" The woman looked at Raif, who stood at the end of the bed, one arm folded across his chest, the other hand stroking at his cheek as he kept his gaze on Chase.

"Sporadic asphyxiation was over..." Raif looked over and nodded at Ash.

What? How many times Miles took the bag off his head? Ash shrugged dejectedly. "Over thirty minutes at least. But I was drugged and out of it before I woke in the woods. There's no saying what was done to Chase before that."

Raif nodded. "We also had to resuscitate on the last."

"How long before he came around?" asked the woman.

"Seven minutes. It's how long it took me to get to the car and back." Raif took a step closer to Ash. "His body was stiff during that time, toes pointing, arms straight, hands curled."

Why was that important? Ash frowned, feeling lightheaded and dizzy, and Raif was there, backing him out of the lounge. "C'mon."

"No." Ash shrugged him off. "I need to be here."

"I know," Raif said gently, but still he pulled Ash away. "But you've got to let them work. I need to check you over."

"I'm okay." He tried to get Raif's hold off his arm. "I'm guh-good."

"No. You need warmth for shock, pain meds for those whip marks, and something for burns."

Raif had seen them? Ash stiffened a little. "He…" Ash glanced at the woman. "Chase, he was raped."

The woman smiled gently. "I know. We'll check everything over, but he needs some privacy now."

"You too." Raif was already drawing him away and Ash went with the motion.

He led Ash over to the open-plan kitchen, where the startling whiteness of the tiles and the granite surfaces looked too clinical, too perfect. There was no dining table, but two odd-looking stools had been placed at the square island bar. Being a startling red, they looked strange, out of place, maybe placed in the scene under duress. Grunting out hurt as he eased up and sat down, Ash caught the bits of dried mud that fell off onto the floor. His skin cracked in places with the mud-pack he'd been forced to wear, and he jolted slightly as Raif's fingers caught in his mud-caked hair.

Ash dropped his head, then looked up at Raif. "Why are you here, Raif? Why do you keep coming back?"

Raif gave the saddest smile. "I still don't know, Ash. I just know it screws with my head when I'm not around you." A cold morning draught played his shoulders, and Raif disappeared a moment to then come back, carrying a HypaGuard Compact Foil Blanket. It went around him, and Raif pulled it closed before tugging Ash in.

Ash stayed there a moment, unwilling to move, needing Raif's warmth more than the blanket's. "I couldn't think of

Chase."

"Hm?" Raif kept stroking at the back of Ash's neck.

Ash closed his eyes. "Tell me I'm not a bastard, please. When Chase was being raped... fighting to breathe... I just wanted this." He shifted slightly in Raif's hold. "Please tell me that's something good? Christ... tell me I didn't let Chase down, that I'm not ugly for shutting him out and needing this."

Quiet. "This doesn't make you ugly, Ash. It makes you human. If for a few moments you wanted to hide in something good other than feeling the hurt and feeling nothing, I'm... I'm damn glad it was us that you wanted to hide in." Another stroke. "Chase... he wouldn't have minded that. He'd have been in his own place, holding Johnny."

Ash jerked slightly as that hit. He took Raif's hand, letting it fall into his lap as he rested his head on Raif's shoulder. Yeah. Chase would have been with Johnny, safe in Johnny's hold. Miles wouldn't have taken that from him. And Johnny would have been there, holding him....

"You're shaking like hell. Scared?" A stroke came at his neck again.

Ash shook his head. "Wishing I'd seen them together as lovers. That I could see them as lovers. That they had... this."

"Yeah," Raif said quietly. "So maybe we both know why we're here, Ash. Why we love through locked and unlocked doors. Life throws too many of its own at us, so we unconsciously try to hold on to what we can, when we can. There's nothing wrong with this. It's us. Our way of loving. Chase and Johnny... they were happy just being able to see each other. They found their way of loving. Don't regret that for them. Let them have their way too."

Ash went in a little closer, whole body this time, not just head to shoulder. He wanted to say a lot more, so much more, but too much grief threatened to spill.

"You said Chase's body was stiff," he said eventually, pulling away and wiping at his eyes. "Why does it matter that his toes were pointed and his wrists curled?"

"Decerebrate rigidity."

Ash looked over Raif's shoulder as Biker nurse came in carrying a med kit. He started sorting through for a strip of pain meds after it went on the table.

The Biker flicked a glance up at Ash. "The body posture after asphyxiation is usually a precursor to brain injury."

Hearing it said out loud made Ash crumple in on himself a little. "And the length of time before he took a breath? Why is that important to know?"

"Take these." Biker handed over some tablets and a small bottle of water.

"Don't you need to know if I'm allergic to anything?"

Biker cast a look at Raif. "It's okay. We have your medical records."

Ash glanced at Raif.

"Talent," he mouthed.

Ash frowned. "What is it with Chase not breathing for nearly ten minutes?" He nearly snapped that out, then rubbed his head, pain meds screwed tight in his hand as his headache threatened to bleed into his skull.

"Usually after three minutes of no oxygen, brain cells start to die," said Biker.

Christ. That couldn't have been blunter. Ash took the meds. They stuck in his throat, giving that chalky taste that made him want to hurl, but he forced it down.

Biker came closer and Raif moved out of his way after they shared another look. "Can I check you over?"

Ash stilled. "I took a beating to my ribs, a belting to my back, ass, and shoulders, also lighter burns. Nothing more."

"Okay, but do you mind if I look anyway? Just to see for myself? You said you were unconscious, right?"

That hit Ash hard. What had Miles done to both of them when they'd both been out? No. Miles's focus had been Chase, at getting at Chase. Ash didn't reply, just watched Biker.

"Not below the waist," Raif said quietly. "Please leave any meds, and he'll handle them himself for anything else."

"Okay, not a problem. Not at all. I'll just check the whip marks and the burn on the shoulder."

Ash winced as he shifted the blanket and Biker started prodding at his back.

"Will Chase be okay?" He kept his gaze levelled on Raif.

"Ash, isn't it?" The new voice was female and small-heeled shoes called that out as she came over. She helped pull the foil blanket back over his shoulders now Biker had finished. "I'm Doctor Karen Cohan. I'm a neuroscientist with a speciality in anoxic brain injury. Which covers what's happened here to Chase."

Name. She'd given him a name, and part of him wanted her to take it back with how names were suddenly coming so easily now.

She seemed to sense his emotions and softened her eyes. "Positives," she said quietly. The black colour to her nails suggested she hadn't been on duty or on call. It also suggested a throwback into goth days with the lace necklace at her throat. What kind of party went on to all hours in London?

"There *are* positives?"

"Certainly. There have been cases with autoerotic asphyxiation where after twenty minutes of showing decerebrate rigidity, men have been able to recover with no neurological damage, despite the signs being there."

"This wasn't autoerotic asphyxiation." He needed that made so clear now. "Chase didn't do this to himself."

I know," she said gently. "But it has similarities. Chase started breathing, but he has been unconscious for a while now. So it's saying there's other underlying concerns here. He's in cardiogenic shock—"

"Heart?" That got Ash's attention. "His heart?" Fuck.

"The cardiac arrhythmia is recent, the past ten minutes," said Cohan, "and you've done the best possible thing by getting him here and keeping that oxygen flowing. Oxygen deficiency and hypothermia caused the condition, so getting that oxygen is vital. My team is already on their way and we'll take him to…" She gave a soft smile. "Well, to the best facility I know, where we'll start a biochemical profile and get brain natriuretic peptide and look at the stretching of the heart muscles."

"Will… will he be okay?"

"It's like with everything, Ash. We won't know the full extent until he regains consciousness. He's still got narcotics in his blood, he's sedated, and already ventilated by the sound of things. He'll be kept like that for at least seven days, then the sedation will be reduced, then it's down to whether he wakes or not."

"But he's in good hands," said Biker.

"The best." Raif rubbed at his shoulder as the doctor looked past him, to the cream Biker had put on Ash's burned shoulder blade.

"We need to get him moving. There's an ambulance already on its way," said Cohan.

"Here." Cohan wasn't the only one to catch the blue flash of light: Biker suddenly wasn't there anymore.

"Ash."

He looked back at Raif.

"I know where they're going, and I'll get you there. But you need to let them get Chase there safely."

"What? I can't go? I'm all he has here."

"You can," said the doctor, rubbing his shoulder, "but I'd prefer if you didn't. Chase will be going to intensive care. You need time to regroup, just take time to get cleaned up so no infections are passed along to where he'll be."

She ran a gaze over him, over the mud. "Do you understand?"

He looked at Raif, down at his own body. Christ. "You know where they're taking him, though?" he said back up to Raif.

"Yeah, I know."

"Okay." Ash wiped a hand over his face. He understood why there'd been an arranged meeting point now: emergency assessment, with instructions then given, depending on injury, on where to take Chase. "Just…" He felt his world slip. "He's got a good heart. The best. Look after him, please."

He got a smile. "I promise." And she was suddenly gone too as the house filled with paramedics.

The Villa fell very quiet, very quickly, and Ash was left looking down at his hands as Raif closed the front door behind Chase, locking it. It took a moment for Ash to realise Raif had been gone long enough to get the duvet from the car. He came over and spent a few moments with some wipes he'd also brought, just getting the mud away from the cuts.

"Too tired tuh-to shower, Raif... I... I...." He needed to sleep now.

"Yeah, I know. I can see that, Ash. So just a few more minutes to make sure the wounds are cleaned at least, then you can shower after you wake. I think they'd have left some towels here."

Ash nodded, hating how it sent his head spinning. He didn't know how long he stayed there, but eventually Raif took his hand and tugged him off the stool.

"C'mon, you need sleep."

"Chase's parents... I need to call them too."

"The call will be made as soon as Cohan and her team get to the medical centre. They have his details." He led him back into the lounge, where the empty hospital bed still sat.

After tugging the mattress off and setting it on the floor, Raif pulled Ash down onto it, threw the covers over them both, and pulled Ash into him.

They shared the pillow, the same ragged breath, the same heavy tiredness, and Ash felt sleep grip so hard... so fast.

CHAPTER 29
DON'T… JUST DON'T

THE MIDMORNING SUN irritated Raif to breaking point as it streamed across his eyes. Ash still slept on, body occasionally shifting under the covers as he cuddled into Raif. It felt good. Ash let life go when he was asleep. He liked to hold as well as be held.

Raif wiped a hand over his own face, mainly to try and wipe away the heat of the sun, then leaned into the back of Ash's neck to get away from the glare, just to catch Ash's own scent. But his cheek rubbed against something that had him easing back a touch.

He'd missed it when he'd cleaned Ash up: his focus had been the cuts, the burns, and keeping those areas clean, but covered in a mix of mud and speckles of blood, the red leather collar slept quiet enough around Ash's throat, almost matching that fired auburn to his wild curls. BDSM collars were sought after and given in Raif's world, although he'd never had one offered to him. This here? This was about rape, murder, sickness… an abuser's dominance. It spoke nothing of Ash, of representing the privilege of getting to hold someone like this, of having

333

that hold returned.

Raif gently pulled his arm free, calming a little as Ash shifted with him, then grabbed onto the pillow after Raif had moved his arm. Usually getting out after waking up in someone's bed was a skill, one he'd perfected before they saw just who they'd slept with, but it felt wrong trying to get away from Ash. Making sure he stayed covered, Raif went over to his jacket and took out a small pocket knife and his leather gloves. It came in useful for a multitude of reasons, some good, some not so. But now?

He knelt back down by Ash and gently slid a finger between collar and the back of his neck, now checking the fastening. This one came with a buckle and small padlock. Raif flicked a careful look at Ash to make sure he was still asleep, then he set to work on the lock, keeping his work light despite the size of his hands. Where his mind worked slowly with details, his hands took up the slack. The lock came free after a few moments, and with a hand under Ash's head, Raif slipped the collar free, then eased to his feet.

Ash mumbled something and a few stray dried bits of mud in his hair dusted the pillow as he moved again to get comfortable.

Raif nodded, and collar in one hand, knife in the other, he headed into the kitchen, hoping to use the wrapping for the foil blanket to keep the collar safe. He doubted the culler would show enough mercy to allow Miles to go to court, but just in case, the collar should have been removed before Raif slept because he'd been close enough to contaminate the evidence. With Chase and everything else, he'd slipped up and not removed it. Ash had been too exhausted or just too damn locked in the horrors to feel it.

The wrapping to the foil blanket still sat on the island

bar, and Raif put the knife down and started to wrap the collar, then—

The cold barrel of a gun pressed quietly into the back of his skull.

Raif hadn't heard anyone approach, but then he hadn't been listening either. The all clear had been given that this was a safe house, and his first thought was Miles, but Miles hadn't exactly been one for keeping his noise down in the woods. So that left who? Someone with enough skill to get in through a locked door. Raif started to raise his hands, but a harder press of the gun into his skull told him not to chance it.

Raif kept his gaze fixed ahead even though he was suddenly conscious of every sound that could come from Ash. "I'm invited."

Quiet, almost as though someone else was listening for noise from the lounge too. "Not by me."

The accent was hard to pin down. Male, yes, but with zero accent: well-trained and offering the Richard Burton reserved pronunciation he'd heard from many BBC radios. Only this one wasn't one for public service announcements, not with how he'd come up behind Raif, all quiet. The "not by me" gave a little away, though, because it came with a homeowner's protectiveness, and if a gun wasn't bad enough, a pissed-off homeowner always was.

"I can see this is yours." Raif widened his stance, mostly to balance how the gun pressed harder into his head, almost forcing him to lean forward. "And it's worrying the hell out of me that you have a gun when guns aren't considered as self-defence in UK law courts." Raif swallowed as he quickly glanced at the lounge. "You have my word, for what it's worth—I was invited here. I was told this was a safe house." He needed to see how the owner would react to that. If he wasn't Miles, he should react to that because the med team had been here on arrival to meet him, so there'd been no mistake that this was the agreed safe house. But no reply came. "If you allow me, I can show you."

A shuffling noise came from the lounge, feet on wooden floor, and—fuck.

"Ash." Not bloody foolish enough to try and move, Raif shouted as Ash came in. "Stay the fuck still! Stay—"

"What?" Ash's eyes widened slightly as he faltered. And in the same instant, an arm around Raif's neck pulled Raif away from the bar, spinning him back, off to the left. Where mud made a half-mask of Ash's face that any Phantom of the Opera would have been proud to wear, the gun that instantly levelled on him had Ash crouching, hands raised. "Stop, Christ. Please…" He sounded so damn scared that Raif cried out.

The gun stayed on Ash, not as a warning to Ash, but to Raif, with a *Him first, you next if you piss me off* move. It had Raif backing off a touch, hands still raised.

Now that he could see him, the man came with a suit, tailored so damn well to fit that slender form. Black leather gloves matched Raif's, and clear crystal blue eyes never left his, even though that gun stayed levelled on a head shot with Ash. Around his neck sat a black rope necklace with a small black cross sitting atop of a larger silver one, which seemed such an odd contrast to everything else about this man. Suit… shoes… all cried London's finest, yet a necklace that could have been bought anywhere on an Italian street market claimed a home around his throat.

The Glock 19 with fitted silencer was another matter. That wasn't any trinket you bought on a London street.

Ash went to stand, but Raif quickly shook his head, keeping him still. No shot had been fired yet, so there was enough control and inquisitiveness behind the gun to keep it cold. Hopefully enough to reason with. Hopefully.

He tried to keep his breathing calm. "Glock 19. That's not exactly a standard firearm, and something I'd tie to a close protection officer, but the price of this Villa says you're paid too much for that." Raif didn't look away from the firearm. "That silencer, that says something different too. MI5 don't carry weapons, despite all the movie bollocks that portrays that as the case. And as you're pissed off that I'm here, it means you're not MI6 either. Otherwise you would have had the same call I did about this being a safe house. If there's been a mix-up, it's a genuine mix-up, and I apologise. But please...." He looked at Ash. "Just let us go and walk away and let us forget about this place. We mean you no ill will."

Raif looked for the slightest flicker, the briefest look of... anything that would show the man's thoughts, but nothing came. And that scared him. He could usually read and anticipate, but with him? There was nothing.

"Please," Raif said flatly. "Take a look at Ash over there." He made sure the man knew his name, that Ash had an identity. "He's hurt. He's scared. We just need a place to hide out and stay safe. Then I can contact his father, his—"

Everything took its toll on Ash. He started to choke, maybe on the stress of having a gun levelled on him, maybe over the journey and travel sickness, maybe just grief and worry over Chase, or all of the above with PTSD hitting hard, but he looked so sick. The moment he tried to stagger to his feet, Raif shifted, knowing the sudden movement was going to get Ash killed, even though he was only throwing up. True enough, it gained a look off the man in the suit, but it was Raif's movement that caught the brunt of his attention more.

Raif didn't even know how it happened, but he ended up on one knee, his hand on the floor stopping him from falling completely. A little panicked, he went to get back up as Ash staggered to the sink and finally threw up, but a foot at the back of Raif's neck forced both hands and knees down to the floor before his forehead smashed into it.

"Stop. For—" Ash choked as he doubled at the sink. "For fuck's sake, stop this shit—stop it!"

"Ash!" Again Raif tried to shift hearing Ash's anger, and again a foot hitting his neck made sure he stayed on one knee, with enough force to almost make Raif lose his stomach and see stars.

Fuck, this bastard had martial arts training; the man had taken down someone three times his size and forced him into the *please, sir, forgive me* position without losing aim on Ash. "Please… please." Raif fastened his hands behind his head as he looked up at Ash. "I was given this address by MI6. If you let me make one call, I can get you clarification. You wouldn't be carrying that weapon in a house under your name if you weren't tied to either the Met or government business in general. I'm going to trust you and tell you that I work for MI6." He gave out his codename. Sometimes honesty was the best policy, especially with the likes of Ash in the firing line.

After a moment, the pressure eased on his neck, and the man took a step back; then Raif bit back every frustrated cry as Ash was manhandled and forced to sit at the island.

"Up." It came next, and the pull on Raif's arm didn't take no for an answer either. He was forced down next to Ash.

Raif instantly grabbed his hand. "You okay? You still with me?"

He got a nod. Angry, confused, with a look from a gaze that didn't stay on Raif, but more on the lounge now.

The man had moved into there and came back carrying Raif's jacket. He sorted through it, then narrowed his eyes as his search through his pockets brought up nothing but car keys and phone. The look questioned what MI6 op walked around with no ID. Which was odd, because that was more a policeman's look.

The man sat down opposite, and his gun went between them on the island. The look in the man's eyes was confusing. Did that coldness say warning—or *dare you*?

Raif caught the phone a few seconds later as it was tossed over.

"Make a call to Ferryman. Get him here."

Ferryman. Raif tried not to react, but he'd just called Raif's contact by his pseudonym within MI6. "If... if you know Ferryman, you'll know he won't break cover."

The man scratched at his jaw, at the sculpted stubble he had going on there. "No. He would have told you that you'd know when to make a call. Now's the time to make that call."

Raif frowned and thought back, to how they'd made this journey up to London. A postcode had been given then: *You'll know when to call me.*

Ferryman had known this would happen, that someone would come. Raif looked at the phone. "And I tell him what?"

"Pick a debating point. But try to start with why you're here, sitting across from me, when I gave you twenty-four hours to avoid... me."

Raif started to stand, to back away, for a split second forgetting about Ash, then reaching to pull him away in the next breath.

Culler.

Fucking culler.

All three of them came with military backgrounds: SAS at officer level, and a first-class Oxford University mind at masters. The three of them weren't just animals with a gun, but Raif felt safer with animals: they made mistakes. This kind, they were the Crown's dog soldiers, called in for culls on politicians, behind the scenes with regional instability, and arms and drug dealers who used the court systems to avoid courts. But give them a serial killer… they prolonged it. They loved it. Christ, they'd set the template for serial killers back in the Victorian era, when they'd been called in on the Crown's business. Back then, the public had called one Jack the Ripper, but those in the know called culler behind palace doors. Of course they'd work purely for the Crown… it gave them anonymity to dominate their own kind: all the psychopaths… the sinners. Because that's what *they* were.

As Raif backed away a little, the man shook his head, his light tap on the phone more a silent order to sit back down and focus.

"Let… just let Ash go. Please."

The culler didn't seem to hear him: made a good point of not hearing him as he distractedly tapped the phone again. "Your MI6 emergency code. Four two five, right?"

Raif sat Ash back down, more than a little numb as he took his seat again too. They'd been thrown into the snake's pit. The only safety barrier being: the snake seemed to still and pause as it wondered at the stupidity behind the sacrifice too.

Ash frowned over at him and Raif gently brushed a hand against his, then picked up the phone and made a call. "Four two five," he said into it as it was picked up at the other end. It said things had been fucked up by outside intervention. Badly.

Quiet came from the other end of the phone. "Put him on."

Him? So Ferryman *had* been expecting this man. As he offered the phone over, the culler shook his head.

Fair enough. "Face to face or nothing," Raif said into the phone, and he squeezed Ash's hand under the table. Instant relief came through when he got a strong squeeze back. Ash was a damn tough soul, used to games, and he picked up that one hell of a game was being played out here.

"Okay." A hard sigh was given over the phone. "I'll be there in twenty minutes."

CHAPTER 30
TWENTY

SAT AT THE table, across from the culler, Raif's heart started pumping hard and fast. Ferryman never broke cover. Why was he breaking cover now? Here? Raif cut the call and pushed the phone back over the table. "He'll be here in twenty minutes."

The culler never picked it up, but he did look at Raif, then back at Ash. "Holly Blue. Why would I get a call and be told he would be here, not you?"

Raif went to speak, then stopped. "You were told what? By who? We—"

"No." The culler looked at him. "You're MI6 and trained in bullshit. He isn't." He flicked a look at Ash. "You speak. He doesn't. As for who told me, that will be cleared up soon enough."

"Me?" The words came quiet, and Ash stared at the culler. "Okay. Listen. I really don't give a fuck what's going on here, you just... Raif. Leave him alone, please."

Raif guessed the culler would know his name by now, but he saw why the culler spoke to Ash. There was no subterfuge in his replies.

Ash coughed, choked a little more, then the culler surprised Raif by pushing over a bottle of water, left over from the nurse. "You're in my home. Tell me why you are and Holly Blue isn't."

"Yours? This is yours?" Ash saw the problem now and his hand started to shake as he took the water bottle. "We... we didn't know."

"I can see that."

Raif took the bottle off him when Ash kept trying to get the lid off.

"We... we just ran. Hoping..." Ash wiped a hand over his mouth after he took a drink, looking like he'd still hurl. "After what he did to Chase, we... we just wanted out, and for you.... You to stop Miles."

"What did he do to Chase?" That frankness spoke worlds to Raif. He'd asked for no details on who Chase was, so this was the culler who had been on scene, although the cologne he now wore was of a better class, no doubt more him, so he had been caught out with them being here. Ash went over the details, his tone more and more detached, an outsider looking in. PTSD and the act of breathing but not feeling anything now more evident more than ever.

"And Chase. He's over with Cohan at the MC?" Nothing changed with the culler, but Raif tilted his head slightly and let that process.

He's over with Cohan... the MC.

"You're Masters' Circle too?" Now that was curious. Dom or sub, he'd be guided by BDSM care and compassion. It also said that the culler knew what the MC stood for when it came to serving personnel, and that relaxed him slightly. So this bastard potentially had a balance: a conscience. Maybe.

"And you have access to the MC," said the culler, watching just as closely. "You've served in the army. You wouldn't qualify for their help otherwise."

"The MC look after the Secret Service too, as well as the Met."

The man cocked a brow and Raif caught his own slip-up again. He had confirmed he knew about the MC by naming the other departments they dealt with, but he'd also confirmed he'd been in the army. He was too old for this cloak-and-dagger bullshit. Games he'd played lightly with Ash.

It also seemed to relax the man too, as if the flaws were more acceptable than practised perfection.

So the culler respected truth more, and perhaps being open over working for MI6 had been his best move. Raif let the tension drain from his body. "I've never used them until now, until Ash." He kept his gaze on the man. He'd heard about the MC all right, and the idea itself to help ex-army, police, and Secret Service personnel back into civilian life seemed honourable enough. But a lot of it came through dealing with BDSM, either as Dom, sub, security behind the scene, or security away from UK shores. And that left a lot of scope of talk between the sheets. Although he trusted the BDSM lifestyle itself in a tightly closed community, there was just so much scope within the MC to fuck up. "I'm ex-military, yes, but I don't trust the MC and the potential pillow talk it can offer."

It was there, barely, but the culler smiled. "I doubt you're the first to think that. You certainly won't be the last."

"Wait. What? You're ex-army?" Ash stiffened and looked at Raif. "And what's this MC?"

The culler lost any humour and held Raif's gaze. Raif understood the communication now. Sometimes silence was the best option. "Ash, they're…" He gave a hard sigh. "They're just the people who have stepped forward to help Chase. Nothing more."

"And they help ex-army, like you? MI6? That's not nothing. Were you doing MI6 work around my home, when we met?"

That pricked the culler's ears too. And now Raif was torn. Ash was looking for trust, some detail to hold on to; the culler balancing his own bastard reactions on truths and deception. So Raif nodded at Ash and ran with truths. "Yeah, like me. And besides breaking the law by telling you who I work for, on *learning* who I work for, how far would you have distanced yourself from me, Ash? We've known each other just over a few months."

"Compared to being held hostage and tied up as you did a break and enter to my boss's home to play happy families for a few days, it might have been a damn better footing to gain someone's trust, don't you think?" There was anger there, rightly so.

"Yeah," Raif said quietly. "The door was left open, cuffs unlocked…. You were free to leave at any point, Ash." He stroked at his hand. "I'm damn glad you… lingered."

"But that doesn't answer his question," said the culler as Ash looked away, that blush touching his cheeks for the first time. He'd been caught out with how glad he was that he didn't walk away too.

But it didn't answer the question, no. And the culler seemed to appreciate honesty more. "Okay. I've been tracking a series of codes and people via the dark web. I found one young woman dead in her flat with cellular cavitation, a vaporisation of liquid within organ cells. It looked like damage caused by bi-neutral beat therapy and the drug effect of the two different frequencies played into stereo headphones; how the brain produces a third frequency and gives that LSD stimuli."

"I-dosing." The culler didn't seem to find any interest in this; in fact it just seemed to leave him with more unease.

"I-dosing? Dark web?" Ash's look was more confused. "What the fuck are those?"

"Okay." Raif levelled out his hand. "This level here, this is the web that most users use. It's called the surface web. You use search engines like Google, Yahoo, Bing, et cetera. to get to the websites you want to look up and visit." He levelled out his other hand just below the first. "This is the deep web. It's a protected level below the surface web that the likes of the police and MI5 used to pass on classified information, but it's become too compromised today to allow that. Hackers are just too damned good nowadays." He shifted his top hand, taking it to a lower level. "This is the dark web. It's a third level used by terrorists, paedophile rings, people who pay to watch torture and executions— basically all the bad stuff you can imagine, they have a website for it on the dark web." Raif let his hands fall. "You can't get to these websites via the normal search engines, and it's never a one-click search and you're there at the site. Codes are given in everyday places, whether it's on other websites, via phone calls, hidden pictograms around the city, and to gain access, you have to piece those codes together and know the shifting proxies in order to gain access. Those codes can be spread over months, different cities even, and you have to find each one. Because if you get onto the site, if you don't bury your IP address, and you're not supposed to be there, drawing attention to the MI5/MI6 ops that monitor the dark web for screw-ups, like Konami, then the men and women who run the dark web sites, they'll hunt you down and kill you for giving them the wrong exposure."

Ash's eyes widened a touch. "Fuck. And I-dosing?"

"The web-users' drug," said the culler. "Similar to how a lion will use infrasound to paralyse his prey via the tone in his warning call, web users use low sound waves to stimulate a drugged sensation in the brain, similar to LSD. It's usually debatable whether it achieves its goal without you taking harder drugs."

"Yes, but there's something more to the West Midlands investigation. The equipment needed for these injuries would need to be military infrasound equipment, not available on the surface web."

Okay, so that shifted the culler a little more. He'd seen why his muzzle would have been pointed in Raif's direction if military equipment was to blame, or perhaps more *who* from the military chain had allowed it onto the dark web, as this type of weapon was potentially a culler's toy. "*Just* that led you to the West Midlands? Standard intel gathering?" He didn't seem convinced that it would be enough to warrant *his* particular culler intervention, though.

"And Lucy, the girl I know. Also my wife, Kerry. Sasha." Details the culler probably knew by now, Raif could see that.

"Sasha?"

Oh... *interesting.* "Sasha was the first body to be discovered with a Holly Blue butterfly inserted into a wound. He was one of our informants." Raif frowned. "I found the body." He left out Frank here. "I took the call from an anonymous caller, found his body, then when I went to call it in, his body had been removed from the alley."

The culler frowned. "Anything else?"

"And Ash," Raif said quietly. "Ash kept me in the West Midlands."

Ash went to say something, maybe add a point, but stopped himself as the sound of the front door opening had the culler turning his ear back towards it.

The culler took the gun, but instead of heading back into the hall, he shouldered his firearm and stepped away from the island. Maybe it was to give more room to fight, maybe it was to force the newcomer deeper into the kitchen before he saw him, Raif couldn't really tell. The man's body language had changed, back now to homeowner pissed off at having his home invaded, maybe something else entirely.

Ferryman came in, carrying a box and also pushing numbers into his mobile with his free hand, not really paying attention, or pretending not to at least. Raif had always only known him as the Ferryman, nothing more, but they'd known each other for over thirty years. Ferryman's look was weathered and tanned, deep lines that spoke of many a different journey, but he had the clearest blue eyes that still called out youth and energy. Hair was white, yet ruffled to say he was far enough into the day to not want messing around anymore. His body set was larger than the culler's too: more muscled instead of supple. His position in MI6 was as hard to guess as the culler's outside of his… night job, but Raif trusted him, body and soul. Yet he only gave a slight nod of head, seeing Raif.

Strangely enough, the culler hadn't moved, just watched like that snake again, more prolonging the moment because of who now walked into his pit. Ferryman came over and put the box on the island. Fresh water came out and was handed over to Raif and Ash, then Ferryman sighed angrily and glanced back, just briefly.

"You got enough patience left to hear me out?" He tossed his keys over his shoulder. "I had a spare set cut a few days ago. You can thank me later for the text that got you here this morning."

Ferryman had told him Holly Blue would be here? What *the hell* was going on?

The culler caught the keys, then came close to Ferryman. Uncomfortably close. He took his phone off him and flicked through something. Whatever he found in the messages seemed to give him answers to a question he'd not voiced. "Baz. My fucking home?"

Ferryman set his jaw tensing and took the phone back, still not looking the culler in the eye. "My MI6 fucking family that you were turned loose on because of your military department's fuck-up over the frequency equipment. You bastards get really touchy when you're under investigation for potentially screwing up." He pulled out a mug and offered it over. The moment he did, the culler slammed it against the wall.

"My fucking home?" Broken bits of mug settled on the floor. "You plant Baz, you fuck about with mine, all to keep me there—with everything mine have already been through?"

Ferryman took out another mug, this time turning it over and over in his hand. "Yeah, to unsettle yours, with everything they've been through." He glanced at the culler. "Because you never could prioritise in the right directions, could you?"

"Bullshit." That couldn't have been colder. "You've not done this for me. You did this to look after you and yours, to stop my colleagues coming after you. When it comes to knowing about who to prioritise beyond that, you've got no fucking clue."

Ferryman nodded. "Aye. Certainly seems like that, doesn't it?" His eyes hardened. "And Baz. I take it he's not clocking in with MI6 in the morning."

The culler snorted a little.

"Right." Ferryman looked far from happy. "I find his body and get your prints off him, I'll see you go down for it, you fucking animal."

"Hm. And all that fire just for some I-dosing equipment?" The smile there was so cold. "Bringing them here, to my home, just for you to… look after yours? It keeps bringing this all back to why."

Ferryman stumbled, when to say something, but looked away, then offered a couple of mugs over. "Considering you're being such a bastard over yours and this being your home, you think you can handle making one of these like any normal homeowner? Or is that beneath you and your inability to shut the fuck up and listen?"

Ferryman knew him, that was obvious enough, and confirming that the culler lived here left it open for Raif to trace a name and make life uncomfortable for any culler. Ferryman had been damn smart about that. It forced the culler to move and shift with the game plan. The culler took the mugs after a moment as Ferryman pulled out a coffee maker.

He let it rest on the countertop, then Ferryman moved over to a unit and rested back at the same time the culler moved in the opposite direction and plugged the coffeemaker in. There was arrogance there, how the culler turned his back on Ferryman; the look from the older man called that out too.

"This your cuckold." The culler turned back to lean against his unit. "You think going cuckoo's nest with them here will, what? Force protection I otherwise wouldn't give? After the bullshit you pulled with Baz?"

"Maybe." Ferryman had taken his phone out and tapped something into it. Usually it would be a code to say that the situation was being handled, but it looked too long for that. "Is that still an option in your world anymore?" He slipped the phone back in his pocket. "Mercy? I mean, you've even turned your back on the MC lately."

The muscles in the culler's jaw tightened on the personal detail being given out. "I gave you twenty-four hours' worth of mercy. You gave me a fucking spy not only here but in my home."

"Baz knew the hazard. He knew you'd try and draw him out. His fuck-up was not getting out when I ordered him to yesterday."

Raif frowned. Was that the message the culler had seen on the phone. Confirmation of a plant somewhere on a personal level with the culler? This Baz must have been damn stupid. Stupid or out to prove something to Ferryman, maybe climb up the chain of command a little faster. Taking out a culler or getting in close would have been... really something on your MI6 record, especially with the tension between MI6 and the cullers.

Yeah, Raif doubted this Baz would be turning up for work come tomorrow too. Pretty much the same as Ferryman if he'd put Baz there. Although Ferryman would be slightly harder to make disappear.

Ferryman didn't seem too concerned on that score. He just eyed the culler, the coffee. "Does that conscience of yours only extend to twenty-four hours where I'm concerned?"

The culler smacked the mugs into the wall. Then he returned Ferryman's stance, but his free hand stroked his lip as if trying to stop his words falling.

"Okay. I'm going to ask that you listen and that you cool off for a minute." Ferryman gave a hard sigh. "Some facts for you. Raif's head of a sleeper cell for MI6. The two attempted bombings leading up to the 7/7 attack on London that you stopped? That intel came from his sleeper cell, who'd been active in Germany at the time. They also helped track down intelligence on the 7/7 bombings that you didn't stop. The past few months he's been working on leads within the dark web, I-dosing, and whoever fucked up your end enough to let that equipment loose on the dark web."

"No," said the culler, quietly.

"No?" Ferryman raised a brow.

"You wouldn't do all this—" The culler gestured around the kitchen with a flick of head. "—for an MI6 sleeper. There's more."

There was? Raif didn't understand what was going on here. His speciality was tech, or more the web and knowing the levels and undercurrents to how terrorist cells moved in those sub-levels. That's what he'd been doing for a few months with Ferryman: seeing if there was a link to any terrorism, especially with a possibility of someone— Light—getting their hands on military infrasound in the West Mids. Nothing else.

Ferryman didn't look calm now, though. Was there

something else? "Perhaps within MI5 you just don't look after your own as well as you should do."

"So you are MI5?" That was more than just interesting to Raif. He had a home address, a job outside of culling, so… why? Why the titbits of information? To shoot a warning shot across the culler's bow?

The culler never looked at him, although something dangerous seemed to settle in. He didn't seem to like the personal intelligence either. "We doing this all day? Pissing about over personal digs? Okay, I'll play too now. The last time we stood together discussing who did and didn't look after theirs, you lasted fifteen minutes before you walked out and never looked back. How many decades ago was that?" He went over, again getting close. "So, you tell me. Just who haven't I looked after?"

Ferryman looked away, tensing his jaw and… Oh… fuck. Raif eased back.

Now they stood close, he saw it. The same blue eyes that the culler carried, and….

Oh, Christ…. The warning shot across the bow had been for him. All the little details Ferryman had tried to feed through to Raif—that was Ferryman's son there.

That was *Bethan*'s son there, and—*fuck*.

Now he saw the problem. Now he saw who Ferryman was frantically trying to protect.

Light.

He was Ferryman's grandson. But the culler… *this* culler, that made him Light's father.

Shit.

Ferryman went in close to the culler. "I'm asking you now, even with you thinking you know who didn't protect yours, would you still protect mine now if I ask you to?

Would you look after Raif?"

Quiet.

Ferryman seemed to let the tension drain from his body. "Would you, please? Just for once would you let go on all that attitude and look after someone for me, without asking or needing any questions answered, despite how I've gone about this? I need you to not ask any questions just for fucking once. Please. Yes there's more, but I can't... won't tell you. Would—"

The culler turned away. "This is finished back at mine. This place doesn't have the security to discuss work any further. Anyone could be listening, especially with how everyone seems to have fucking keys to here. Discussion on Chase's care and long-term funding will need to be looked at too."

Raif guessed that first part was aimed at Ferryman, because if Ferryman had planted someone in the culler's home and now had keys to here, he could have surveillance equipment here too. No doubt the culler would order housecleaning by the time he got back to his.

"Yours? I thought...?" That came from Ash. "Look... listen. I don't give a fuck what's going on here, I just need to see—"

Ferryman came over, and Raif nearly pulled Ash behind him as he leaned close to Ash.

"This place isn't set up for safe talking," he said quietly, glancing behind him to the culler. "It doesn't have the security. So for now, the safest place for you is at his, where there's full security. You can shower and get cleaned up, then he'll have security drive you over to the MC."

"Will I now?" That came out so hard.

Ash frowned. "See? Why? Why the fuck would he help

355

us? You?"

Ferryman glanced over his shoulder before straightening. "Because he's a bastard, but one I'd trust not to hurt you if he says he won't."

"Yeah?" Ash looked up. "But he hasn't said that, has he? So he gives me his name, because I don't fucking trust him not knowing that."

Raif was grateful of that for the first time. Raif didn't have any trust for this man either. Not now. Not knowing who he was. Why he was....

The culler took out his phone. "Gray." He looked over. "Don't ever ask beyond that."

Ash eased to his feet, looking unsteady as Raif went with him. "Yeah, well, *Gray*. I'm Ash. And this, here, this is Raif."

Gray didn't smile as he put his phone away. "I know."

"Good." Ash shivered. "Because if anything happens to us at your hands, you damn well remember who we are, and that I'll fucking haunt you for it."

Gray gave a smile. "You're free to go at any point, Ash, the door's unlocked. Both of you are free to go." That detached playfulness was there. Because Gray would follow, this time without a muzzle.

Ash went over to him. "We'll stick around, thanks. Seems it's a bad habit of mine. And speaking of bad habits..." Ash fell quiet for a moment. "Shouldn't you be off now? Isn't there someone left out there to kill?"

"Ash." Raif went over and pulled him away. Tried to at least.

"You'd see a man killed?" Gray wasn't looking at Ash, but he turned his ear to evaluate everything that came out of Ash's mouth now.

"A man, no." Ash kept his tone level. "But what we left behind in those woods, it wasn't the look of a man, was it? And it's your job to kill that fucker. Go and do it."

Now Gray looked at Ash. "The decision to leave a man standing will always be harder than making one that takes him down." Gray went in close. "Because you look at Johnny now. You look at Chase. You look at a mother, a father, a wife. You look at a five-year-old girl and how she could grow up to think that she was responsible for a killer's death, and instead of starting to talk, she stays quiet, thinking someone dies if she shows her hurt. Or you look at the angry young man whose life has been riddled with trauma, how he could wake up a few months down the line and take his life, because for a few moments, just for a few moments, he was angry enough to wish someone dead, and that wish was granted."

Gray turned his ear again. "So, looking beyond yourself for a moment, at everyone who has been hurt in this, not just your own self-centred and blinded fucking need, do you really think you have the mental capacity to verbalise an order that would take another man's life, Ash?"

Ash stepped back, saying nothing.

Giving a nod, Gray glanced at Raif. "You?"

Raif stayed quiet, instead pushing Ash out towards the hall. Raif started to follow but paused as Gray stopped Ferryman from leaving.

"I said we finish this at mine. That means you too." Gray indicated to the door.

Ferryman looked him over. "Why? You got a speech for me too on not telling you your job?"

"My fucking home, my fucking lovers you tried to fuck over. This isn't about any fucking job when it comes to you. Ever."

"Yeah." Ferryman pulled out of the grip. "We're not good company for one another, you psychopathic bastard. You've long since proven that."

The conversation came out in Welsh from both men. Ferryman would have known the languages Raif was fluent within. Would Gray too? He hoped not.

"I'm not asking you to think. I'm telling you this is finished back at mine."

"With all you have on your plate, it's Raif who's getting you riled?" Ferryman looked Gray over. "*What the fuck's wrong with you, boy*? You have lovers at home who need you more. What other nightmares do they have to go through for you to fucking see that?"

Gray jolted a little, and Ferryman stumbled back a pace or two as Gray shoved him away.

"*First and final fucking warning. Don't* ever *come for mine again and add to what they've been through*."

Raif shifted, but Ferryman shook his head, warning him off, then he frowned at Gray. "You *really* think we should be in the same room together, son? Now especially?"

Gray turned away, and Ferryman gave a hard sigh. "Back to yours, it is, then," he mumbled after him. "I can see this going well, can't you?"

CHAPTER 31
JAN

STILL WEARING NO shirt, Ash felt suddenly very out of place as the car pulled up to the stately home. Gray had been right about the sodding security: even getting onto the long drive up to the courtyard had seen checks at the security checkpoint, then they were allowed past the thick run of wall that surrounded acres of land that could confuse the best of any pissed-up thug if they tried to get over the walls. Now the sleek Mercedes-Benz that Gray drove cuddled in close to a fountain, the water dancing and singing in different colours to a soft rave tune Ash couldn't hear. Off in the distance a tennis court and two summer houses could be seen, and Ash swore that if he listened hard enough, there'd be some stables in the mix too. The thick run of trees off to his left reminded him of home, of being in the middle of a forest he'd loved as a kid, how even that now tasted dirty. It took Raif opening his passenger door to get Ash's attention.

"Shoes," mumbled Raif, crouching down by him. "How the fuck did I manage to grab your dad's and not yours, huh?"

Ash looked at the stones, how sharp they seemed, how bare his feet were. Since when was he stupid enough to go anywhere without any fucking shoes?

Raif took off his work boots and put the first on Ash. "I've got thick socks." He offered a small smile up when Ash questioned the reasoning. "And some pretty rough-soled feet."

"Years in the spy business and walking away every few months do that to you?" He hated the bitter bite, how it sounded, and how Raif lost the light in his eyes a touch every time he bit back like this. But people like Raif who had been trained to walk, they very rarely sat idly by. He'd get the itch to walk eventually. The fuck-over would still come, right?

Raif fell quiet, then eased to his feet now Ash had both his boots, taking Ash with him. "I didn't leave Kerry, Ash. Even after I lost my son and saw Kerry die each day, I stayed with her when I could. It's who I am." His smile was soft. "*You* have the flight look about you now, not me."

He did? Ash felt his world swim a moment and gripped on to Raif's arm. "Fuck." He briefly closed his eyes. "Only towards a decent bed." He gave a hard sigh. "I'm an asshole at times, Raif. Fucking ignore me, okay? I'm... thank you. For... talent. Being the best at what you do."

A small chuckle. "You already said thank you."

"Yeah." Ash frowned and looked at Raif. "It's more than worth repeating, especially when I'm being an asshole."

Raif helped steady him. "You can be something other than an asshole? I've seen eighty-year-olds less ball-busting than you."

Ash scowled over as a new Rand Rover pulled up behind

them, drawing them apart.

Ferryman eased out and Gray glanced at him, just briefly as he made it to the door and the *Lion, the Witch and the Wardrobe* lamppost that stood watch outside. Gray held a mobile and he thumbed at it now. It looked like he'd really been caught out with Ferryman's text.

They all headed over and followed Gray into a reception hall that bested the British Art Museum for class and content. The Welsh connection to Gray was cemented with an oil-on-canvas painting of Owen Glendower just left of the winding staircase, although he didn't say anything or mention the English version of the Glendower name, knowing full well how most Welshmen hated the English variant. A few Japanese Samurai swords sat in glass cases here and there across the floor, along with a few other pieces he couldn't name for the life of him.

Ash felt dirty, very, very dirty and… lower class.

"This way." Gray closed the door behind them, then slipping his phone in his pocket after he got a message, he led them off to the right of the huge staircase. The size big-foot work boots Ash wore gave him a walk that put him in some mental hospital somewhere, and he winced at Raif, who looked back over his shoulder at Ash as he dragged his feet. The smile shouldn't have been there from the big bear due to everything that had happened, but Ash returned it, in many ways wanting the familiarity.

They stayed quiet down a long hall, then they pushed through into a kitchen that looked more like home than he cared to admit. No fancy dining table, just a lovely oak set that matched the working kitchen.

Ash put this as the servants' area, only the young man in there didn't look like any servant he'd seen. Although his brown hair was slightly ruffled, long on the collar, and looking more content with the idea of lying next to someone, the man modelled a suit that moulded a swimmer's frame.

He stood, the coffee left on the table as Gray went over. Gray stopped at his side, close to his ear, and something whispered its way into the young man's ear.

The younger man turned slightly, just listening, and a soft smile came to his lips as he did. The closeness was too personal, way too intimate to be friends, especially when a brush of lips went briefly to the younger man's cheek, confirming it.

It relaxed Ash a little. The culler was gay, or bi at the very least, with a gay lover. There'd be no prejudice towards sexuality here. But, fuck, that dude lay down with a killer? How fucked up was that?

Gray moved away as the man turned from him with a smile and came over to them.

"Hi, I'm Jan." He offered a hand over to Ash. No second name. Had that warning come from Gray? "I'm Gray's partner. You must be Ash?" Ash took his hand, conscious of the mud Raif hadn't managed to clean away, but Jan didn't seem to mind. Maybe he'd been forewarned, because something behind his eyes offered an understanding Ash didn't want to see right then. "And Raif?" Jan shook Raif's too. "Does a hot bath big enough for both of you sound okay? Along with some fresh clothes? Well, that's if you'd like a bath big enough for both of you."

"Sounds…" Ash rubbed at his head. "Sounds really fucking good, thank you."

"Language." That came from Gray. "Mind it around here."

Okay… that was him warned, put in his place.

Raif shifted slightly, more to move back the way they'd come, and that scared Ash more than he wanted to admit at the possibility of losing him again.

"We've got spare clothes in the car," started Raif. "I'll—"

"No." Jan's voice came so quietly as he watched Ash. "I'll sort the clothes out whilst you two get settled. I'll order some food too."

"We really need to get to the MC." Ash looked back down the corridor, the ghosts that seemed to walk there.

"Yeah, I know." Jan glanced back at Gray. "When you've had something to eat and you've cleaned up. Those guys know what they're doing."

Gray came over and handed Jan his bank card, and Jan nodded his thanks before tucking it in his back pocket.

"Jan?" That came from Ferryman, and Ash moved aside slightly as he came through. But the moment Ferryman offered his hand over, Gray pushed his way between them. He'd reached for something on a counter, but it was obvious just why he'd pushed his way through them both.

Jan frowned at Gray as Ferryman took a step back; then he shook his head slightly but didn't offer his hand to Ferryman. He seemed to pick up off Gray that Ferryman wasn't here on friendly terms.

"It's…" Ferryman smiled, and there was something there that didn't look unkind as he looked Jan over. "It's really good to finally meet you."

Jan didn't say anything for a moment, his look seeming to take everything in about the white-haired man, sort out a trust issue of his own. But where Gray wanted to cut Ferryman into tiny pieces to feed him through the cracks in the floor, Jan's look was angered, but maybe he held on to the good in people a little longer. He offered a hand over eventually, and Ferryman took it. Whatever was going on here flew completely over Ash's head, and to be honest, he didn't care.

"You too." Jan let go first. "What you did with putting Baz here, I won't forgive you for. You need to understand that."

A hard sigh came, but Jan got a nod. "I know, son. I appreciate your honesty. And on that note: I'm Ferryman to most, Caleb, or Cal, to you." Jan got a rub to his shoulder. "If it's caused you grief, I'm really sorry. How are you?"

"Since Baz was fired? Better." There was something there in Jan's look. It wasn't as innocent as the words said. He knew this Baz hadn't been fired. Ferryman had already said Baz wouldn't be turning up for work at MI6; Jan's gaze said that too, and in the brief look he gave Gray, it spoke worlds on where his head and heart lay when it came to protecting home once the doors were shut.

Yeah, fuck this. Ash took Raif's hand, more grabbed the cuff of his leather jacket and started to tug him back the way he came.

"Fresh start perhaps, then?" Ferryman said, stopping them. "Trust earned?"

Ash paused as he got a look off Ferryman, off Jan.

"They've had it pretty rough. Would you look after them for me? I'd like to talk to Gray."

Jan nodded. "You staying for lunch?"

"Is that a kind offer to stay for lunch?"

Jan gave a soft smile. "It's an offer."

"Then yes. Please." Caleb looked over at Gray. "But

start small, I think." He smiled at Jan. "Just coffee for now."

Jan seemed content enough with that too as he glanced back at Gray. "Coffee it is." Then he focused back on Ash and Raif. "C'mon, let's get you sorted and into that hot bath."

Something told Ash the offer of a bath was half in kindness, half to get them out of the way of Caleb and Gray. That was fine by him. As Ash headed down the hall with Raif, Jan passed him by at one stage, offering a smile as he eased Ash aside gently. Then giving a scratch at his head, Jan made it back into the reception, and they followed close by.

The static from a radio seemed to jolt Jan out of his thoughts as they reached the staircase, and he stalled, then instantly relaxed as another man came out from the lounge.

"Ray."

A smile came Jan's way from the man in the suit. Suits, everyone wore goddamn suits here. "Hey, Jan." He stopped by them, and Ash felt a little dirtier with the look that seemed to strip him bare and check anal areas for weapons. "I take it these are Gray's guests." Ash got offered a hand. "Name's Ray. I'm head of security. If you need anything, Ash, you use any of the intercoms along the halls and let me know. Zero-one-one automatically patches you through to me."

Ash. Christ. These fucks were quick with getting names and details. Ray already knew his. Ash took his hand, then eased out of the way when Raif was offered the same.

"Raif."

Ray got a nod back.

"Same for you," added Ray. "But if you need it, Raif,

there's a room just back from the lounge known as the Oval. It's wired against external surveillance equipment if you need to make contact with *home*."

Home? What the fuck was that code for? Then it hit Ash. MI6… Thames House. Home *home*. Jesus.

"Is it wired against internal surveillance too?" said Raif, but Ray only smiled.

"If you need anything, just let me know." Ray shifted attention to Jan. "Anything you need now, sir?"

Jan shifted in irritation. "Only for you to stop with the sirs, Ray. I don't pay your wages."

Ray smiled down at his feet, then shifted to get his radio as a message came through. "Aye, but Gray does." He tapped lightly at Jan's arm. "And I like my balls between my legs, thanks." He cocked a smile at Jan, then headed off towards the front door.

"Bath, right." Jan thumbed towards the stairs, his look a lot softer now. "This way."

"It doesn't do your head in?" Ash said before he had the thought to stop it, and Jan frowned back at him as Raif gave him a slight shake of head. Yeah, he got it how this place wasn't meant for questions. But… "The likes of Ray knowing every detail about you before you've even met?"

Despite not looking like he was bothered by the intrusion, Jan blushed. "Rather the known than the Unknown here." He glanced over his shoulder. "Things get… intense if Gray sees you in his home, touching his life, and he doesn't know you."

Ash gave Raif a quiet smile as Jan turned away. "So you were the Unknown at one point, huh?" Ash winced as he got another glance back off Jan. "I bet that was… *intense*."

That softness was back in Jan's eyes. "Wouldn't have it

any other way, Ash. Never where Gray's concerned. It's when he stops asking questions that you know you have a real problem with him."

CHAPTER 32
DON'T... SAY SOMETHING

CAL SAT AT the kitchen table, his fingers tracing over the ridges of the old oak wood. The table came with a history, but then most elements to this manor did. A coffee mug came in close to his hand, and he found it in him to offer a small smile up.

"This is from home. Wales." He meant the table. He'd recognised the ridges and family scrapes and wear from over the years. "You transferred a lot of the furniture and furnishings from there." He glanced around him. "Mostly." The Milton Painted classic design hid just how much the kitchen had cost, but it still kept that touch and taste of Welsh roots with everything else here.

"Mostly" came Gray's subdued reply as he took a seat opposite.

Cal found it strange. At one time Gray had always stayed as close as possible, pieces from one airplane model or another ordered in little groups on the table, next to them.

Silence back then had always been natural, that comfort just in closeness between father and son, but now Gray sat opposite, neither to the left, nor to the right, just in direct opposition.

And Gray twisted his mug of coffee in his hands, focused on whatever images the hot liquid offered him a door to, the silence dark… more awkward, but then they hadn't sat at a table together like this since Gray was twelve.

"A mother."

Cal frowned at Gray. "Sorry?"

"You asked me to walk away, and a young mother lost her life." Gray looked up. "That shouldn't have happened."

"You can't try and poison the whole world because of the loss of one, son."

A vicious kick came at the table leg, and Cal grunted as the rim smacked into his stomach, coffee spilling over his fingertips.

"*Don't.*" Just one word, but as violent as the kick to the table. "You're the one who's fucked about with mine and cost the life of another mother, you sick fucker."

A piece of Gray's broken coffee mug twisted and writhed on the floor, trying to escape the assault on the usual quiet.

Now here was the ugly teen, the one Gray had tried to rein in back with Raif and Ash; the one Cal had walked away so easily from. The argument, the flash-flood of fight… how "sick fuckers" and Cal were always mentioned on the same breath. He'd walked away feeling infected, sick, subconsciously carrying a disease because his wife had died and he hadn't been able to stop it. And, Christ, show Gray weakness and he'd feed from the edges of the poisoned wound, eating, gnawing on the badness until he got to where it really hurt, where it was red and raw. Cal had wanted to grieve back then, be there for an angry young boy because he was hurting too. But Gray couldn't let go. Even after all these years of distance, he still ran headlong into leeching off the poison, enough to make Cal want to get up and walk away and—

Gray beat him to it, already up and heading for the door.

"Hey, whoa. Wait." Cal shifted and stood, stopping him from leaving with a grip to his arm.

Gray argued, Cal walked. That's how it usually went between them. And for Gray to walk now, so quickly…. "What the fuck's wrong with you?" It was the second time today he'd asked that, and each time it left him just as puzzled. Backing down was something new. Walking away was something else entirely. "This is who we are: we're Secret Service. We play covert games to protect what and who we can. We can't protect everyone. You know that. You've played it long enough: you've taught others to play it. It's nothing personal. But now *you* walk away in disgust and call enough, after everything you've done as a culler? What the fuck *is* wrong with you?"

"Mine. You target fucking mine. I'd fuck with you in hell, but Jack? Jan? Mart—"

He stopped that so quickly, and… Shit. It was there, that kick of a young man standing too near a cliff edge and being caught with a *Fuck, just let me feel the fall into hell* look in his eyes.

With Jan? With Jack, or Mart—

Ohhh. Fuck. Cal slipped a strong grip on the back of Gray's neck. He'd only meant to trigger Martin. He really couldn't afford to have Gray in the West Midlands. *Gray* couldn't afford to be in the West Midlands. And with who Gray had here with the MC, Cal had only meant to offer a small distraction, because Gray was a tough enough bastard to cope. The MC could cope.

But Gray… something had been triggered in Gray too. Just how had he taken Baz down? Who had he gotten to help him? Jan knew, Cal knew that from their conversation, but had Gray fallen enough to whisper in Martin's ear? Like he had with Kes, only he'd… he'd gotten a kick out of pack hunting Baz, and it had… what? Excited in all the wrong ways? It was *exciting* in all the wrong ways? "Sit. The Fuck. Down."

Gray looked away, that jaw constantly tensing. Too much history played here, in this home, and Gray had never left it behind, just stood teetering on the tip of it, not knowing which way to turn, who to trust. Cal knew he'd added to the weight of that with Baz. He hadn't lied: this was what they did for a living, but his mistake had been treating Gray like Gray had treated him, because going soft with Gray would have—or should have—disgusted Gray more. Yet here, now, Gray seemed forever the young teen aggressive with love, but never more aggressive than with grief, and, yes, he'd pushed him too far. He saw that.

"Okay," he said gently. "Compromise. I'll make a coffee. I think I remember how to. You…." Cal swiped at Gray's jaw. "You tell me whether you brought her Erard piano?"

It seemed to shake Gray out of whatever cloud he hid under, because he looked confused now as Cal went over and picked up Gray's coffee mug.

"Piano?"

"Your mother's. Where is it?"

"I wouldn't see it left behind, if that's what you're hinting at."

"No." Caleb smiled bitterly to himself. So fucking

defensive at every turn. "I wasn't implying that." The sound of a cupboard opening came from behind, and by the time Caleb came back over with fresh coffees, Gray had cleaned up the floor and the table.

"It's in the east wing," said Gray as Cal sat down. He took the opposition again, looking more tired, so much older now. "Ed has it tuned every so often, but lets no one touch it."

"Not even you? Does Jan know you play?" Gray didn't answer and Cal nodded. Bethan could put her hands to any classical piece of music: Vivaldi, Mozart... all self-taught and bold as brass when compared to anyone who had been trained traditionally. Some talent came naturally, and Ed had ensured his daughter had the best possible instrument to temper that talent. Although the Erard never had compared to Bethan's soft chuckle when the old home had settled and she'd lain in bed with him.

"You still wear her ring."

Cal looked up, then felt the weight of the chain around his throat that held the white-gold wedding rings. "Aye. Like you still wear Jack's necklace, despite all the grief."

Blue eyes found his the moment he'd mentioned Jack's name. "And just how would you know about that?" It almost looked like he'd get up and start checking for listening devices, or do something much worse. Just what had happened to Baz? He doubted he'd ever find out, and Gray wouldn't ever divulge details.

"Easy...." That look hadn't changed over the years, just grown older, more perfected, and it still wore a man down. "I know your love for art and antiquities. But you forgot you're my son along the way." He took a sip of coffee. "Jack's half Italian; the necklace is Italian design and not the most expensive. You wear it because it keeps you close to Jack and your history, not because it's some artefact that's moved through history and gained value by withstanding time."

Gray snorted, now shifting slightly and distractedly slipping a hand into his suit pocket. "You don't know me as a son, then. I don't acquire art and antiquities purely for aesthetics value."

"No, you preserve the delicate art of someone else's history because you constantly fail to handle your own and those who you allow in close." Cal gave half a smile as Gray set the muscles in his jaw tensing. "And you've collected a lot of art over the years, Gray, yet few people close enough for you to call friends… lovers… sons."

Gray eased up in his chair, looking ready to drag him over the table for the fun of it and fuck interrogation, he'd cull him; that or call this quits. He looked like he couldn't decide which. It was getting deep and dark very quickly. But Cal knew talk over fathers and sons would do that.

Cal sighed and wiped a hand over his face. "Okay. Let's try this again." He eased back into his chair, relaxed, hoping to maybe relax Gray. "So, you're gay?"

Gray choked on his coffee, coughed, then laughed as he covered his mouth. It was damn good to see and seemed to burn through the tension. He hadn't caught Gray off-guard like that in—just too long.

"I'm forty and not about to sit here discussing my sexuality with my dad." But he'd relaxed a touch, at least enough to take his hand out of his pocket and not look as though he was hiding something he shouldn't have touched, but had damn well gone ahead and touched anyway. And most definitely relaxed enough to have called him dad. Now that… that was surprising. So, too, was all of this. There'd been no talk of Raif nor the MC, not yet.

So what was this? Why had Gray ordered him back here? Was he questioning that himself?

"And you?" Gray was back to looking at the rings around Cal's neck. It hurt in a way, mostly because Gray hadn't cared enough to check over the years. Cal had checked, knew every detail about his son: the MC, being a Master Dom, even down to Jan's fraud, Jack's....

Cal frowned.

"What would you like me to say, Gray? That I've spent these years with nothing but your mother in mind?"

"*Yeah.*" That came out hard, rushed, then Gray wiped a hand over his face and slumped back in his chair a touch, hand back in his pocket. He was fighting old feelings and slipping a lot, but the effort was there to stop it hurting and take Cal with it in the process.

Cal understood it. Most of the grooves in this table had been from Bethan and her attempts to teach Gray the basics on how to survive. And no matter how many times he couldn't figure out meat took longer to cook than a root vegetable, he stayed by her side, listening, waiting to be asked to pass something, and by hell, even at the age of five, would Gray get her anything she asked for.

They'd both made sure she had everything she'd asked for, but then she'd been their world.

"I mean no," Gray added quietly, giving a hard sigh. "She wouldn't have wanted you to be alone all these years." Quiet. "Neither would I."

Cal nodded but hated the lie that came out. Sometimes there really was only one person that you were designed for, but he didn't want to see any more hurt in Gray either. "I haven't been alone; life's taken me away most of the time, but it's been good."

"Any more kids? Grandkids?"

Caleb bit back a smile. Oh the possessive look going on there. Gray had never been one to play nice with others. Was that why there was such aggression over Raif? Cal said he'd look after his, but his MI6 family had never replaced... what sat opposite. Only Gray would never see that. He'd never want to.

"No." Cal cocked an eyebrow. "I'd have loved a daughter, but if she'd turned out following in her brother's footsteps...."

Gray looked over, went to say something, then started coughing. Cal leaned forward with how congested it sounded.

"How long have you been like that?"

Gray glanced over. "Just a cold from France."

That had been over six weeks ago. He lied. Cal could read it where Gray had schooled himself to fool most. "Get it looked at. Don't mess about with your health."

Gray shook his head slightly as he took a long drink of coffee, despite the heat. Quiet fell again, and that uncomfortable tone darkened the warm and subtle touches to the kitchen.

"How's Edward?" Cal asked out of courtesy, out of respect for how Gray felt about his grandfather, nothing more. Some waters couldn't be bridged. Cal had lost a wife in the line of fire; he'd lost his son with the aid of an old Welsh grandfather.

Gray cocked a smile over his coffee mug. "He's giving you... space. He's off playing poker with Jack's dad; Greg, and Mrs Booth, our maid."

"How very *decent* of him." He didn't keep the anger from that and regretted it when Gray frowned down at the table as he put his coffee down.

"He's a good man. He stayed close despite the grief off a kid who didn't know better."

That hurt, more than Gray would ever know. "And Jack... Jan... they share that same assessment of... antiques like Edward?"

Gray snorted a laugh. "Jan, yes. Jack... not in a month of *fuck him with a Taser* Sundays."

Cal grinned. "I like Jack."

"Yeah." Gray tapped the table with his finger. "I think you two would get on somehow."

It hadn't surprised him that Gray had been drawn to Jack all these years. Not with how their unique mean streaks played head games and fuelled the best and worst in the both of them. Jan was the surprise, and he hadn't meant for it to sound that way when he'd first met Jan in person, but... but.... Jan just seemed so... Jan. Not Gray. Not Jack. Just... Jan. As much out of his depth as the young man Raif had fallen for. Yet the way Gray had touched Jan in the kitchen, it had been honest, without hidden doors or secrets to how they felt.

Gray had changed. *Something* had changed Gray. Maybe it was for the better, but he knew Gray better than most. Getting close came with an aggressiveness that could eat the strongest, the closest. And it forced the next question.

"How does being a father fit into all that?" He thought that would be the dealbreaker, that he'd lose Gray there. It was certainly dangerous territory on Cal's part, considering Raif's surveillance point in the West Midlands. The look about Gray cooled enough for him to call enough, but instead Gray twisted his coffee mug a few times in his hands, then looked over.

"I'd make a lousy father. You know that."

"I'd have thought the same if you took a lover. Yet you now have two."

There was a blush, the first in years, but one that said having two lovers had caught him out too. But it faded quickly enough. "Yeah." That came out so bitter, and the grief behind blue eyes that almost came to the surface pulled at Cal. "In body if not mind, right? Mine to have but not quite hold. All I deserve, and all that bullshit." Gray toasted him, then as he got up and went to leave, Cal caught Gray by the cuff of his jacket and made sure he sat down next to him.

"The tragedy comes when you're left holding on to nothing. You have something, even if it's just a private reminder between you and Jack that says he'd never lie, he'd never cheat, that he'd rather see himself hurt over hurting you or Jan, if he could just hold on to a control that most take for granted."

Something was there in Gray's eyes. Whatever memory it was, there was such a sadness with it: regret, grief.... But a burn to taste it. Get lost in it. To hold on and walk away from life with it.

"Yeah." Cal nodded. "As for what you deserve.... When you love obsessively, intensely, you deserve to be loved just as obsessively, just as intensely back. Just remember, though, that who you love should only make you a better person, not make you lose who you are."

Again there was another jolt of grief, then noise from somewhere back down by the hall turned Gray's ear and that mask he'd been trained to wear came back down, but it took a moment. "I'll give Raif protection, but Holly Blue—he's still under contract."

Yeah, he knew why Gray had pushed Ash and Raif into a corner over a decision like this always being Gray's. It had to rest on his shoulders in order to give everyone concerned a clean break, a clearer conscience. Because Gray could so easily remove any of his conscience when it came to the final decision, and taking the cull in the first place would have seen him agree to it a long time ago after he'd reviewed the evidence. He could be ordered to kill, but the final decision to make the kill was always a culler's.

Cal took his wallet out and pushed something over. The silver coin sat on the table close to his coffee mug and the look about Gray shifted into something else entirely. And yes, it was there, that natural affair with life running headlong into hurt and pain. It's something Jan and Jack would always lose Gray to.

"Payment from the Ferryman. Make sure it hurts for Holly Blue. He took a mother."

Gray took the coin.

Next came Cal's phone and he brought up some details. "This is Officer Miles's history."

Gray thumbed through the screen. "I know he has a wife."

Family could make a contract awkward, and that had to be taken into consideration, but with what Rhiannon, Miles's wife, had been through, he wondered if Miles's death would be more a relief. But Gray still wouldn't want this death on her conscience either.

"Call in housecleaning for a good cover story when you're done, one that takes the blame off everyone's shoulder. Just make sure this bastard doesn't see a court and legal assistance."

Gray gave a small smile. "You don't want Raif dragged

through court proceedings. That's… that's a lot of protection for one man."

Someone had put Gray onto this cull in particular. They knew what Raif was doing, maybe why the West Midlands in particular, and Cal wanted to know who would see Gray pushed into a darkness he wouldn't come back from if he knew MI6 were sniffing around his son. Cal worked hard for that not to happen, even if Gray couldn't be allowed to see that. But the person who called Gray out was a well-kept secret nobody seemed prepared to divulge. And they played with fire on this cull. Gray had shifted into questioning now, which Cal couldn't allow. He stood to leave.

"Stay for dinner. For more than coffee." Gray caught his sleeve this time as he looked away. "I'm… I'm getting really too old for this fucking bullshit between us."

"You asking as a culler and MI5 director wanting to know intel about Raif, or are you asking as my son?"

"We both know each other well enough to know I can ask, but you won't tell me, where Raif's concerned."

"You're asking me as my son, then." He let a smile ease in. "That must have been so damn hard."

Gray gave a long sigh. "Seriously? You fucking think?"

"And you'll keep Raif and Ash safe, no questions asked?" Cal smirked. "Which I know is asking the world of you."

Gray sniffed, wiped at his nose. "Hm. Scout's honour and all that bullshit."

"You left the scouts after only two hours. You poured petrol over the food supply because the Scout Master told you no over having an early morning snack. You didn't stay long enough to learn honour."

Gray stood and started to collect the mugs. "Must have gotten that act of honour off my father. He just didn't stay around long enough to see it."

Cal looked down at his feet. "I was always here, Gray. You were just too much of a bastard to see it."

"Yeah," Gray said quietly. "Maybe." He looked around. "Being a bastard, I don't like Ash's instability," he added. "Not around Jan."

"Get them settled and fed, then if need be, I'll stay around when you leave later for the West Midlands. Raif's my staff and I'll do my turn with security."

Gray nodded over. "That mean you're staying for dinner and facing Jan across the table? You know he's mastered bringing bastards to their knees with just losing the softness in his smile?"

More noise came from back down the corridor, and this time Cal looked in its direction.

"Yeah. I'll apologise to Jan again." He really hadn't meant to take down him too. "But I think it's been a long time coming with meeting this Jack of yours anyway." He made a point of focusing on Gray now. "I'd certainly love to meet this Martin."

CHAPTER 33
DON'T... MEET MARTIN

KNEES SHAPING TOILET, hair streaking his face, Martin threw up for the second time in five minutes. Maybe it was the disinfectant, the run of fucking disinfectant dispensers suckered to the walls around the manor, or just the goddamn feel of the porcelain goddess under his touch when he'd rather be fucking someone up, or over. He was fucked if he knew what caused it all lately. But it had eased. Having Gray here, this goddamn fever had eased.

He slumped between toilet and wall, then kicked out at the wall because it was all he was offered. A room, toilet, seclusion, the occasional *walk the bitch* around the ground....

He played better with company, so take that away, leave him locked in a cell...?

Martin sniffed, wiping a hand across his forehead, then ran it through his hair, hating how grimy he felt.

So he'd fucked up his privileges by upsetting Craig and exposing Baz as the fucked-up grass, or more how he'd taken it a little further and kicked the shit out of Baz once Ray had pinned him to the floor. Baz had made a text to someone to pass on the details about the butterflies, and that's all it had taken to catch him. He'd helped kick Baz's head in, just the once, but enough to say Craig had been caught out in the background. But...

Fun times. Damn fun times. And Baz hadn't been seen since. So just what had happened when Gray had come onto the green and offered to take Baz home?

That same look had been in Craig's eyes too over the past few hours.

But Craig had locked him back up just after that, and that was him now: locked up. Away.

He hit his head once, twice against the wall, wincing at how it added more fog to a headache that still had him closing his eyes. He didn't understand where the sickness came from. Was it payback from Craig? Spike the meds? Nah.... That was far too creative for the old fuck. Maybe Gray? Jan? Yeah, he could picture Jan being a little sly. But enough to risk Jack? Nah, maybe just enough to keep him kissing the bowl, though.

It didn't help when the door creaked open, grating on his nerves enough to force him to screw his eyes shut that little bit tighter. Poked and prodded; someone always wanted to poke and prod, and he was really fucking sick with sitting still and taking it.

"You need something to calm your stomach, Peachless?"

Craig.

Martin eased his eyes open and rested his head back against the wall. "You still a little pissed over Baz and being back to the drawing board with staff? Over knowing you helped hire a spy that helped fuck with the people you're paid to protect?"

"No." He came over and crouched down, the remote to the ankle sedative there in his hand. "I'm worried how you're struggling to process this illness." And the concern was there in the softness of his voice. Maybe it had always been there, and the anger towards Martin had only been anger towards Baz, towards himself for hiring Baz. "I'll say it again, okay. All the rape Jack went through, the sickness... your body is bringing it back to the surface because you don't know the details over how Jack got sick. It's throwing your head and system out of sync, nothing more. It will all catch up eventually: memories and physical hurt. It will go away."

Martin licked at his lips, the sweat there. "You know, one day you'll open that door without the trigger to this sedative here, and I'll be right there waiting for you."

Craig sighed and eased back up. He went and rested against the doorframe, a towel slung over his shoulder. Martin didn't need to see it to know. "The mind is an amazing piece of machinery, Mart, and you add to it with how fucking smart you can be with this intuition you have over how people are wired, how to pick at their weaknesses. You see the deception or choose to ignore it. The genius personality in many ways over Dissociative Identity Disorder. But you're just like them. With faults, with flaws, deceptions, and also that lack of the genius personality to control the switch between you and Jack, throwing you back into being DID. And going on full steam like this will bring you down. Now, I take it that is a no from you, then, for you needing to calm your stomach?" Still that calmness, that never-ending fucking care. Christ, put him and Jan together and they'd end world drought with the sobs they could get from their puppy-dog eyes.

"Let me know if you change your mind, but you look like shit."

"If you're not gay, then what?" Martin levelled a gaze. "I'm taking a wild guess at you being married because, fuck, I've not seen you with a wedding ring." He shrugged. "Could be that you leave it at home so as to not cause any added damage when you take someone down in a padded cell. That would be you, right? Always thinking ahead, planning the safest route. Yet there's no tan around your wedding finger to say you've been married at all. No personal talk with staff on just who you're fucking." Martin let a smile creep up. "Oh…. All that care in you and there's no one loving enough to take care of you in return. You're looking, though, right?" Martin narrowed his eyes. "And you've been looking for such a long fucking time, you've either forgotten what a woman feels like, or you've never tasted one in the first place." He snorted at the irony. "And here you are, stuck looking after not one, not two, but three men in love with each other. Who's seen enough fucking to last three lifetimes over. Do you take your frustrations out on your dog when you get back, huh? You master the beast by fucking the beast?"

Craig gave a small smile, more pity than anything and that… that really got under his skin. "So sez the guy locked in a cell who can't fuck any beast to master it." He tugged the towel free and tossed it at him. "Heads-up. You've got visitors. You sure you don't want to clean up?" He tilted his head slightly. "You *really* look like shit, bud."

Martin flipped him the bird.

Craig turned away with, "You're welcome, Mart." So Martin introduced him to new ways to work the word *fuck* into a sentence, then nursed his head by burying it in his arms across his knees.

Muffled voices drifted over, then two pairs of polished shoes found their way into his room, and Martin sighed heavily, lifting his head and half expecting Halliday and his Looney Tunes Crew, but—

"Oh..." Now this... this was something different. Something new. Martin eased up the wall, then out into the bedroom, head tilting slightly as he caught sight of Gray, more the man next to him, and now he suddenly didn't feel so sick anymore.

"Well, well. Not one of Halliday's, are you? There's none of that forced practised sickly-sweetness going on in that look as they try to study *the evil that men do* in cell five." Martin smiled over at Gray. "You pimping me out again, Welsh? Like you did with taking Baz down? You want to see if Jack'll come out and cry *baby* for you? And you're staying around to watch it too? You kinky fucker, you. He knows I like top, right? Some protection... lube—snuff?" He batted his eyelids. "You told him about the snuff, right? I mean, if I'm whoring myself out on this fucker, I really need to get to choke a few people considering I'll be dancing around on *One Foot in the Fucking Grave* here...?"

"Ferryman meet Martin, Martin meet—"

"Now see what you did there?" said Martin to Gray, ignoring the newcomer. "You giving me his pseudonym over proper noun?" Gray stayed back in his cell, more resting against the wall, by his bed. The other man didn't come close either, but looked around the cell, finally coming to rest on Martin. Martin gave a sigh to Gray. "Of course you did. You're getting in the mood to piss about lately. So here it goes: I'll pretend not to notice you're playing enticement games, and you pretend not to notice you're setting up a game of Guess Who." He took another couple of steps forward, but Gray's hand on his abs stopped Martin in the next instant.

Martin grinned, loving the rush Gray's touch brought to his cock. He could put that down to Jack, but, well, why the fuck bother lying? "Hm," he sighed. "We dance fucking really well together, Welsh." He brushed a touch over Gray's hand, then grabbed it and spun Gray around in a gentle circle, coming in close to his throat and licking there just before Gray eased a finger between them and more than asked he step back. Martin did, even took a bow and ended it with a wink, a really long look down Gray's body that licked neck to penis tip. "One day, sweetheart, one fucking day... fuck and die. You and me...."

No answer came but there was something, just something there in that returned culler's stare that never wavered. Oh... the dark beauty of it. Martin would take every ounce of that stunning brutality just to have Gray shake it off and try and live with how by brutalizing him he'd brutalise Jack too. Fuck and die. Him and Gray. To have him lose all that control to get at Jack, only to lose Jack permanently because of it. That was just *fucking peachy* in Mart's book. They were born to dance like this forever anyway; he might as well take up permanent residence.

Or maybe he misread it. Maybe, because it was gone as the other man coughed.

Martin focused on him, but it was damn hard. "So, back to it." He scratched at his head, loving how Gray watched his every move. For now, Martin eyed the older man up and down. "Mr Ferryman... seems you're my in-house entertainment for the night."

The cell stayed quiet, and no signals passed between Gray and the newcomer.

So Martin went and sat cross-legged on his bed, just to prolong the moment. *"Guess Who,* right?" He rested his head back against the wall. "Really runs in the family, doesn't it? You Raouls really do only know how to turn up and cry 'what the fuck' after the shit hits the fan. And they call Jack crazy for allowing me to do that." He shook his head. "You don't think Gray could have done with a father as he was crying Jack's safe word as life hurt too damn much for him to take? But that's what Ed's for, right?" He killed just about all feeling in him. When it came to people hurting his toys, he didn't tolerate it well either, and this bastard had taken Gray away this morning, that was obvious. Considering it happened just after Baz had taken the long walk with Gray, that Gray had worked his talents to find out who Baz reported to, it wasn't hard to make a jump to how his father was the man behind the plant. And how did he know that? Because if it had been anyone else, they wouldn't be standing in this cell. They'd be in a shallow grave, next to Baz. So Old White here, he had *a get out of culler* hold with some kind of emotional tie, and that tie had fucking upset Gray enough to show Baz really wasn't the issue here. This bastard was. And this bastard, if he'd lost his contact in the house, would of course come here himself to bridge the gap. And so the vicious cycle started again. "Tell me, you leave fucking your wife to her old man too, considering you can't seem to manage the simple basics of family life and raising a young boy?"

No emotion stirred, but then he'd have been disappointed if it had. "Okay, so you're not after the beta version on Guess Who. You want some more." He looked him up and down, but he kept coming back to the pseudonym. "Gray didn't lie about that, did he? Your name?" He narrowed his eyes. "From the coin Gray received for killing Kes, you cross the palms of those who provide transport for those moving those on to the other side. Either MI5...6, or whatever pie Gray fucks his bastard dick into when he wants to feed that psychotic frenzy of his." He pointed a finger at Ferryman. "That a warning to me, though, hm? Fuck your princess over and you'll take me for a ride? Well…." He scratched his head. "You're about thirteen years too late, Dad. I've been fucking him over for years."

As he finished, Ferryman looked over at Gray. "Fifty seconds. That's impressive profiling."

Gray shrugged. "He likes to show off."

"The ring around my throat gave the family connection away, perhaps? I hid it."

"More your silence, I think. You had to be hiding your accent."

"There's too much regional blending on my part when it comes to idiosyncrasy. He wouldn't pick up the Spanish-Welsh from that, surely?"

"Skin tone too, perhaps."

"Actually," Martin said quietly. "it's because he's allowing you to stand in here. And that you took up the invitation. You lose Baz, so you use what little emotional connection you have left to fill that dark space." He didn't look away from him now. "And you don't think Gray knows that, Pops? That you're still only here to keep tabs." He narrowed his eyes slightly. "Now why is that, hm? What secrets are you hiding from him that make you desperate enough to stand in here?" He let a smile creep up. "Gray will let you stay, but it will only be to bide time and wait for your fuck-up, you know that, right? And, not being funny, mate, I hope those secrets you're keeping, they'll be worth what we'll both do when we do find them out. And we will. Trust me."

"Well goddamn." Gray's dad smiled, and yeah, Martin

could see all the family beauty there. "He does realise I'd have told him if he'd asked, right? I'm not in the mood for games."

Martin gave him all his attention now. "You're not, *Dad?*" He wasn't either.

Martin shifted from the bed, and Gray moved in the same instant. Part of him cried hate and hurt at how he knew he'd be stopped, that Gray would stop him. But he'd scare the shit out of the old bastard if nothing else. Jack.... One flaw, one fucking flaw in his own makeup, one fucking fighting spark that Jack had denied him and—

Fuck. Martin stilled.

Gray hit the floor, and for the life of him, Martin couldn't figure out how he'd spun and floored Gray with one move. But like hell did a grin start to fester as he looked down at his hands, his feet.... "Well, look at that, Welsh."

As Martin danced a little, doing a typical *C'mere, Princess* come-on with his hand, Gray wiped blood from a split lip.

"Oh... Jack's just passed on a few home-grown martial art skills now. Maybe he's pissed at seeing your old man turn up after all the shit too, hm?" Martin waggled his eyebrows as he did his fight-night dance. "So just what do you think that means, Welsh? That he's happy for me to stay here and say fuck to you on his behalf?"

As Gray shifted up, Martin focused on Ferryman in that split second. His dad had skill, but it wasn't anything like Gray's, and Martin hit home, crying fuck yes as he split his eyebrow and sent him staggering backwards. In the next moment, Martin had the wind punched from his lungs with a blow to the ribs, and his legs were taken from underneath him. He laughed as he came up close and personal with the floor, Gray now with a knee digging into his ribs, a grip around his throat.

"Jack's damn good." A breath brushed his lips and Martin licked across his own. "But he could never beat me, Mart. You're fucking here and he isn't because of me."

Breathing heavy, Martin cupped Gray's neck and pulled him down for a rough kiss. "Yeah? Fucking show me, Welsh. C'mon. Make it permanent. Fucking drop your halo and really fuck me over."

Gray pushed him away and Martin hit the floor as Craig came in. He opened his arms to show no ill will with Craig, but mostly not to be knocked out and forced to miss that look in Gray's eyes. He'd felt how that scuffle played hard with Gray. He'd felt how hard Gray had gotten.

He smirked as he was pulled to his feet and restrained.

"I've got this." Craig slipped his elbow to the back of his neck, making Martin wince but not let his gaze fall from Gray. "Calm it down, okay, Mart. You know how this goes. You—"

"Oh, I'm calm." He said it so quietly. "I really don't think it's me you have to worry about, is it, Welsh?"

Gray left the cell, but he got a longer look off Ferryman. Yeah. His old man could see it too.

∿

"There you have it…" Gray winced as he looked Cal's cut over outside the cell. "Martin."

Cal pulled away from him, not really liking the probing going on with the smack he'd taken.

"Look," he said quietly, "back there in the cell. I know

what I saw. You—"

"Leave it." Gray's tone hardened as he wiped the blood from his own mouth with the back of his hand. Cal took a handkerchief and stood nursing the cut to his brow. He went in close to Gray.

"You're getting too close as the culler, too personally involved, and personal is never good when it comes to what you do as a culler. Martin shouldn't be here. Jan—"

"Jan *what?*"

Cal eased off seeing the protectiveness, but also something else too. "Keep him closer, okay? He's... he's not you. He's not Martin."

"He's tougher than you think. Damn tougher."

"No he's not," he said gently. "His harmony runs *with* life, not against it. Just... just don't lose sight of that, okay? Of him?"

"You have the bollocks to warn me over not hurting Jan when you planted Baz here to make sure mine fucking hurt?"

It was getting into dark places again. He went to say something, but Craig came out and closed the door behind him, forcing Cal to break away from Gray.

"You two okay?" Craig flicked a look at Gray, then focused on Cal and checked out his cut. "This visit wasn't planned, Gray. I need time for a care plan to be arranged with all visits, for Martin's sake as well as your guests and my staff."

"My apologies," said Cal as Gray signed something on a table close by. "I asked to meet him."

Craig didn't say anything for a moment as he finished with his cut. "Gray knows the Queen Mother shouldn't get access through that door without a care plan. I shouldn't have allowed it, but…" Was he going to add something about Baz here? Trying to repair damage. Trust? "All respect to you and him, but Martin is under my care. This doesn't happen again."

Cal eased his hand away. "It won't. No."

Craig nodded, then looked at Gray. "That cut needs looking at. Come to the nurses' station."

"I'm fine. How's Mart?" Gray came back over, rechecking Cal's cut and this time not taking no for an answer.

"Scarily in a good mood." Craig signed something by the table-. "I caught his skill in the cell. That's new."

"One major fucking concern," added Gray.

Cal rubbed at his neck, then at his cut brow. Gray seemed to switch so quickly, looking a lot different from the Gray back there with Martin. "Not being funny here, but I thought Jack was the one trained to fight."

"I'll talk to Halliday," Craig said, going in close to Gray. "It doesn't always mean what it signifies."

"Which is *what* exactly?" Cal couldn't understand their quiet now, nor the upset he saw bringing Gray down to earth.

"When the MC first met Jack and Martin, their job was to get Jack and Martin to acknowledge each other's existence," said Craig, but Cal knew that. "The final step in recovery is personality blending."

"But that's something to work towards, then?"

"Yeah," said Gray quietly. "Only it won't be Jack. It will be half Martin, half Jack. Or from that in there, maybe more Martin, less Jack."

Craig brushed a hand at Gray's arm. "Perhaps to who

Jack was supposed to be from birth? Jack watched his mother cut herself from when he was a toddler. She suppressed a lot of his reactions and growth as a boy."

Gray tugged away, his gaze not letting Craig's fall.

"I know you don't want that, okay," said Craig softly. "And it's why these visits like this—" He flicked a look at Cal, the cut to his eye, at the cut Gray carried. "—they need to stop."

"That's Martin in there. He's not Jack. Maybe if he was treated more like Martin, like I've asked from the beginning, he'll fuck off. Because…" The muscles in Gray's jaw tensed. "Because I fell in love with Jack. He's the one who has every right to fuck up my world, where Martin can only try. We clear?"

Craig eased back. Away. And Cal kept an eye on Gray in that moment.

"You can't force Jack back, Gray. It has to come at his pace, his speed. And the more you push—"

Gray went close to Craig. "I respect everything you do, but you remember I've known Martin since Jack fashioned him into existence. I know exactly how to handle him. This, this here? That's trying to cure Jack when that's Martin in there."

And Gray used Martin to catch a spy? To get at Baz? That was enticement games, enough to touch Jack as well as Baz. That hadn't been part of any care plan Cal knew of. Gray was taking control, bit by bit. Everything into his own hands, dangerously so.

Craig looked away for a moment, just a moment. "Yeah, you've known them both for years, but sometimes, just sometimes, time distorts what a newcomer like me can easily see as unethical behaviour. You push it, Gray, you push Martin, I will take him out of here and sign an order that blocks you from getting near him again. We clear on that?"

As Gray fell silent, Cal eased in between them, turning Gray away. "Dinner, right?"

Gray looked back. Cal too, but he offered a nod to Craig. He liked the man. He had one huge set of balls. Gray just needed a minute to cool off and—

"Apologies." Gray pulled away from Cal. "Craig, I asked you to work here because of your specialist and objective point of view. I meant no disrespect."

Oh, but he had. Cal saw that. This was Gray's home, his rules. Always his rules. He'd subtly ensured Jack had been placed here all those months back to ensure he could shift and change everything to *his* rules. Always three sides ruled Gray: the spy, the Dom, the culler. And Martin had triggered the worst in him. Craig would be as lost as Baz in the culler's control, if he wasn't careful. Especially if he went against him.

"None taken." Although Craig's body language told a different story. He wouldn't let this go. He would pull Jack out of here, his look told Gray that.

This was going bad places.

"A favour, though." Gray seemed to ease down into the not-so-calm truce.

"Sure."

"Keep an eye on our newcomers. Ash in particular, the younger of the two. He's just come out of a bad place and I don't want him near Jan or here. Especially near Jan."

"Understood." Craig wrote something down. "I'll leave a note for tonight's shift. You remember I'm not on tonight? Halliday is sending over extra care staff from the psychiatric unit to cover Baz's old post."

Cal winced. He'd really stepped on a scorpion's pit here and damaged trust on all sides. That was why it was tense between them now. Craig no doubt felt responsible for hiring Baz and threatening Gray's home life; Gray no doubt not blaming Craig, but perhaps doubting his ability a little now to give the best care for Jack. Christ. "Craig, Gray. You listen now. I placed Baz here, and I'm sorry for the grief it's caused. I know Gray's checks with his staff, how thorough they are, so I made damn sure neither of you would pick up any flaws. That's what I do. That's my job, for government business." He'd really needed to know if and when Gray's attention would be shifted to the West Midlands. Not just because of Raif, because... because Gray really needed to stay away from the West Midlands and Light, for his own good.

Craig gave a hard sigh and seemed to back down. "No worries, but both of you...." He eyed up Cal. "I don't care what level you are. Martin is a psychiatric patient. Under MC care. Mine. Whatever spy games you both play, it stays away from these doors."

"Yeah." Cal offered a smile, but had Gray already crossed a line with Martin when it came to blowing Baz's cover? "And I apologise too. This won't happen again."

"Good." Craig looked at Gray.

Gray patted his arm. "Thank you. But please just keep an eye on Ash. On Jan for me."

Now Craig relaxed, but Gray knew how to fool people into a sense of false calm. "Always."

CHAPTER 34
REDUCED TO ASH

RAIF KEPT HIS back to Ash, giving Ash the space he needed to get ready for a bath that *could* have cleaned a rugby team from the look of it. Jan had run the water, then quietly made his leave. Something about his look to Ash, to the burn on Ash's shoulder and one on his side that looked older, spoke of hurt and understanding. Raif didn't push or interrupt Jan, just let Ash help sort the bath as he found towels from a steam room store cupboard a few doors down.

Caleb. Ferryman had given Jan his real first name, he didn't doubt that, and that pit of dread told Raif that he was invading life on a personal level with his boss. Dangerously so. He didn't like Gray; hated it more that Caleb's son was a culler. It made all of this very ill for him. Questioning would come from Gray at some point, Raif knew that, but for now at least, there was a grace period. Maybe they'd be out of here before Gray felt that harder bite to start asking questions.

What good it would do was the real question. Gray was MI5 on top of everything else. That added its own strangeness for Raif. He got to travel the world and let off steam. But MI5 spooks... all that time tied to UK shorelines, it drove the best into bad ways: dogs kept in cages and all that. It must have been why Gray was a culler. Perhaps his love for Jan made sure he kept close to home shores, not allowing Gray the choice of an international playground with MI6, so culling became his... stress-release point.

Fuck. Raif felt sick. What a mess.

"Hey."

He glanced back hearing Ash. His back turned to him, Ash glanced over his shoulder.

"You're scared."

Raif looked away. Ash still hadn't gotten undressed yet, just stood looking at the bath, his head God knows where.

"Worried," Raif said quietly. "We really shouldn't be here."

"You know something about Gray. Something perhaps to do with that work week surveillance that kept taking you away from me?"

Raif stiffened. He'd been that obvious even someone outside of MI6 had picked that up? But this was Ash. "No." He looked down at his hands. "I know a few things about Ferryman, about his son. I just didn't know that Gray was his son."

"Or the culler?"

Raif shook his head eventually, although he could tell from Ash's flat voice that he was still half lost to the depths of the bath water. "No. I didn't know he was the culler."

Quiet, then—"What you know, will it piss him off?"

Raif sighed. Light? What Raif had done? "Yeah. More

than." It would anger him, if the roles were reversed.

"And you don't want to stay around long enough to find out?"

Raif frowned. "I'm going nowhere, Ash. And Gray's allowed us here with a promise not to push for intel."

"He didn't promise that, though, did he?"

The bathroom fell quiet, and eventually Ash gave a shaky sigh. "Thank you. For… talent. For being here with me."

Raif didn't understand where that came from. "You weren't being an asshole then, Ash. You're scared."

"I wasn't saying it because I was an asshole. I'm saying it because I know you're scared too and that I don't like anyone putting you in a position where you're scared to breathe."

Raif dug his hands into jean pockets and let a smile creep up.

The sound of the tie to jogging pants being undone came, then water was disturbed, with a few quiet *fucks* as Ash no doubt eased down. Raif went over a moment later and crouched down by him.

Belt marks became angrier in the hot water, the burn on his shoulder blistered and sore. Ash looked really uncomfortable as the fresh burn on his ass no doubt played hell with him in the water. But the need was clear. To be clean.

"You okay?" Raif asked quietly.

Ash shook his head, and Raif shifted and brought down a shower head. He switched it on to cool and gently let it run through Ash's hair and the tangle of dried mud.

"Me and Chase." Ash kept his head down. "The games

we play. We're more than friends, mostly friends with... twisted benefits, you still know that, right?"

With Ash's hair now soaked, Raif switched off the shower and took hold of some shampoo. "Yeah, I know."

Ash hadn't moved to clean himself. "Do you? After we broke up, we'd still talk on the phone." He looked down at his hands. "Being lovers was nothing like being friends, though, how we'd grown up finding things out between us and having a laugh, nothing more. And when we realised that, we went back to who we are, all the play and cruel joking. But Johnny knew we still played about over the phone and in the pub with other guys in the mix too. So fucked up.... I wouldn't have touched Chase if I'd known Johnny had his heart. So how much did I fuck up Johnny by not opening my eyes? How fucking sick was Miles for watching all of that play out?"

Raif paused a moment to digest what that meant and, yeah, he'd figured Miles stuck around with both of them to see just where and when Chase and Ash played. Miles had missed Johnny's touch on Chase up until those last few weeks, though. So had Raif, but Raif had been busy with Ferryman back in the West Midlands. Had Johnny and Chase gone to a motel? Slept over at Johnny's? How much had that pissed Miles off with not having surveillance equipment at Johnny's, discounting the guy with weight issues, automatically putting him out of the picture? Yeah, Ash was right. This was fucked up. "I can't see Chase wanting to hurt you or Johnny, Ash." He started to wash his hair. "And Johnny saw you playing, right? He knew what you and Chase were about. He'd have accepted that long ago."

"But it still would have killed him." Ash fell still as Raif rubbed gently at his curls. "Miles said my dad had put a plastic bag over his head after he first raped Rhiannon. That the threat of my dad had kept his sickness buried. That Chase liking bugs as a kid had....” He sounded like he wanted to be sick again. “That we were all just the same side of the bad penny. Products of our time. He wanted to train us to be like him.”

Raif kept quiet as he rinsed Ash’s hair, the last traces of mud running to mix with the mud that he’d already washed off.

“Me and Chase…. I love him to bits, but we’re just good friends, Raif.” He sounded so strange. “Just… I need you to know that’s all we are. Friends. But I… I need you to know I’m not like Miles, too. I *don’t* want to be like *him* and—”

“Easy….” Raif took the body wash and started to clean Ash’s shoulders, staying away from the burn. “Your head’s taking you in one direction, your heart in the other. How you feel, how screwed up life is at the moment, it gets better. It—”

“Feels good for the right reasons sometimes?”

Raif smiled sadly. “Yeah. There’s a right kind of goodness out there.”

For a while Ash said nothing, just stared down and ran his thumb over Raif’s hand, like he’d traced Raif’s face in the shadows of his kitchen as if he couldn’t trust what he felt or saw, so he… touched. “Thank you,” Ash said quietly.

“Been here before,” Raif replied just as quietly. “You’re not being an asshole.”

“No.” He kept his head down. “I’m saying thank you, for your talent. For being the best at what you do. For your skill at tracking something down even when you’re constantly met by locked doors."

Oh…. So this was about Ash pushing him away three weeks ago, after Johnny's death. Raif had understood it. More than. Ash didn't ever have to apologise for grief. Hot and cold was who he was. Raif gave a hard sigh and pulled Ash into him, despite all the wet hair and soap. "Locked doors only mean there's something rare to be found behind them." He kissed his head. "And you keep breaking all those rules there, flitter."

"Not a fucking bat." But a hard kiss came at Raif's jaw, all that heat and drive that had driven Ash before, then was gone in the next second as Ash took the body wash. Almost like he'd left behind his head and just ran with touch. But he held on. He still held on.

"I'm… I'm gonna take a quick shower." Raif wanted Ash to know he'd have his privacy. "It's just through here." He pointed behind him. "Call if you need anything."

"Yeah. Same here," said Ash, quietly. And that was them. Only time would tell where this would take them, but Raif was used to watching. To waiting. And Ash had always been worth waiting for. He just didn't see it. Raif hadn't understood it either to begin with, but he did now. Soul-taking how having Ash nearly pulled away from him, having the door locked by someone else, could make him understand that. Those doors were always Ash and Raif's to play with, never anyone else's. Never anyone like Miles.

≈

Raif made his shower quick, just enough to scrub off all the dirt and grime. By the time he got out, Ash was drying himself too. He got a glance, then Ash came over and took his towel off him.

Raif frowned as Ash wiped him down, then started on his back. "You say thank you again, I'm gonna start shouting."

"That's okay. Because I need this." A deep breath came, a deeper sigh. "The scent of something good." A bite came at Raif's shoulder, one that had him groaning with the roughness to it. It was done to mark, to taste something… good. He'd make a fucking spectacular Dom if he could learn the care behind game-playing, behind trusting.

Raif eased around and snaked his arms around Ash. He closed his eyes and took in Ash's scent too. Yeah, this was the scent of so much possibility, of something really… good.

A knock came at the bathroom door and they both looked over.

"Jan here. I'll leave your clothes by the door. I'm going to head down and order some food. Is there anything in particular you'd like?"

Raif glanced at Ash. He'd seen the uneaten dinner left over from yesterday at Ash's. "Something filling. Like a roast?"

"Fuck," breathed Ash into his neck. He doubted Ash was hungry, but he seemed to relive a memory, one that hurt and made life lighter in the same breath. Had Chase been with him when he'd eaten that dinner yesterday? Raif tightened his hold.

"Sure. I'll find something," Jan called on through. "Can you find your way back downstairs?"

"Yeah." Ash pulled away slightly, now looking at the door. "Follow the disinfectant dispensers. The colour was white coming up here, yet cream going into the kitchen."

Raif raised an eyebrow as a snort came from Jan.

"You noticed that, huh?" said Jan.

"Yeah." Ash glanced at Raif. "I saw."

Jan went quiet for a moment. "Just try not to wander from the path and cross disinfectant dispensers, okay? It's kind of like a *Ghostbusters* thing: Gozer and all her hell dogs break loose if you cross disinfectant colours here and fall onto the wrong path."

Ash raised a brow at Raif. "Okay. We won't cross the disinfectant streams." And they both bit back a smile.

Upper-class and their fucked-up eccentricity....

≈

Ten minutes later they made it down the long staircase, and Ash looked around for the cream disinfectant dispensers. He thumbed over his shoulder to the right. "Strange to have so many around a home, right? I'm not the only one thinking that?"

Checking his watch, Raif followed him over and smiled. Ash looked so much better, all loose dark auburn hair, with a stray wild curl falling over those sea-green pools, and he smelled absolutely amazing. "Dunno, you seen the size of this place? There's a lot of scope to get lost, get dirty, and need a—"

From behind them, down the long reception hall, muffled shouts drifted through.

It didn't sound good wherever it came from and Raif tugged Ash away, mostly to break how he'd stilled, looking back at past ghosts and who came out of the woods, through the cloud of drugs. "Kitchen, c'mon."

A snarl came through, a "fuck" from Jan, which didn't sound right considering Jan didn't seem the type to swear; then Ash pulled out of the grip on his arm and went for the way they'd come.

"Ash. No." Raif hissed that, but Ash glanced back, looking just as pissed.

"I keep fucking standing still and waiting for the burn, Raif. No more. If there's trouble, I need to see where... why."

Not happy, Raif followed. This wasn't the place to go hunting and poking at facts.

~

The muffled scuffles got a little louder as Raif passed one huge-looking dining room, then headed into a corridor with clear-looking disinfectant dispensers. A few of them had been smashed along the way, and at the far end, a big man who could have almost matched Raif for size looked to be trying to hold Jan back a touch. Jan didn't look happy.

"What the hell's gone on, Craig?"

Yeah, Raif shared Jan's snap of anger. Ferryman and Gray both nursed fighting scars, and he didn't take kindly to how Ferryman nursed any kind of damage. As he started over, Jan pushed away from Craig, going over to Gray.

Gray let Jan in close enough to touch-feel over the wound. "Martin. He's picked up a few skills." That came from Gray, but Jan didn't seem to buy it as he glanced at Ferryman. Had Gray used his fists in the home before? That unease off Jan seemed to suggest so.

Gray made sure Jan looked at him. "Martin, nothing

more, okay. We fought. We're fine."

"What? You took *him* in there?" Grief touched Jan's voice. "No visitors, Gray, certainly not ones who come with a taste of Baz. It took months before Jack was ready to see me." Jan pulled more tissue from the first aid kit that sat on a table by them. Next to it, a clipboard kept it company, along with what looked like a printed personnel roster fastened on top. Jan started on Gray's wound. "You talk to Craig about visitors, then you come talk to *me* about *why* you go through the proper channels if you think he's being unreasonable."

A thud came from behind the door up ahead. "Fucking back off, you bastard." Jan didn't look up once, although he spoke to whoever hid behind the doors.

"What's wrong?" Ash followed Raif over, no doubt curious over *how* they had someone locked behind a door. Jan turned, looking a little startled, and that seemed to shift Craig.

"Hey, I'm Craig." The big man stepped around Jan, almost protectively, and Raif moved, doing the same with Ash. They stopped in front of each other, both warnings made clear as they stood their ground.

"You okay, Ferryman?" Raif kept that calm.

"Yes. We're good here. Ease down, Raif."

He did, but not much, not with Craig standing in front of him. "I'm Raif. This here, this is Ash." Raif offered his hand to control the tension levels. Craig, by the name tag, took it. "We heard the commotion, is all. We wanted to check that everything is okay."

Craig glanced back. "It is. Life's just a little… peachless at the moment." And Jan peered around his shoulder, giving him a very quirked brow. Craig returned it, smiled.

"What? I was going to add 'fucking' to that, then remembered Princess Peachy is too up himself to come out and say it."

The tension seemed to break a little, and Jan laughed, just softly. "Dinner." Jan scratched at his head just as another thud came from the room back down the corridor. Only one, but loud enough to have Gray look back and Jan try not to. "I was ordering dinner." He pointed back the way they had come. His polite way of saying *wrong place, wrong time, move on.* "This way." Jan tapped the nearest disinfectant dispenser. "You crossed streams and wandered into clear territory. Not a good place to be."

Ash glanced back as they were gently herded away. "Someone else staying here?"

Raif glanced back too. Craig had gone over into the small corridor, all to open a lock and look inside.

Someone started to whistle from inside and Raif caught sight of silver eyes that could give Ash a run for his money on uniqueness, then he caught sweat-streaked black hair.

"Aww, c'mon. I thought you two wanted to play." Another run of whistling came, like an owner calling his stray dogs to heel, then—"*Mary had one fit dad who liked a little flogging. So she tied him to a kitchen table, and kicked his fucking bollocks in.*" Those eyes seemed to grin a thousand and one ways. "Or Mary would have done, if she hadn't been slaughtered along the way, right, Ferryman, leaving little old Welsh all—"

Craig shut the slot, then came back out and stopped by Gray as Jan glanced back at Gray, then Ferryman. "I'll sort some pain meds in half-an-hour to help calm him down. He still looks like shite."

Ash tried to look around Jan, hearing that.

"He's…" Jan gently tugged at Ash's arm and seemed to struggle as he added to Raif. "He's a guest with issues, too. Hopefully not around for too long, but best to avoid unless you have a shotgun… full of sedatives, of course."

Ash glanced over, his *what the fuck* coming over clear enough. "Maybe it would be better all around if we went back to the Villa?"

Jan cocked a brow. "Villa? What Villa?"

"The safe house over at…" Ash struggled too now so Raif filled in the address.

"Oh really. You were over there, were you?" Jan turned around as he walked. "Gray?"

"Here" came the reply. And he was, following behind a few paces with Ferryman.

"My Villa is now a safe house? I specifically remember signing the documents that said my property had been sold and that the buyer was a young couple with kids." Jan gave a sniff. "Either you've gone straight on me and you have a wife and two kids now, or you lied about who bought my villa."

Quiet. "Option two. And this is something for more private discussion." Gray made a point of looking at Raif.

Jan didn't seem fazed. "Not when it's my property and it comes to finding out why you lied to me over who bought it." Jan held his arms out. "Something you *really* need to tell me?"

Gray wiped at his lip again, and this time Raif made a point of turning a deaf ear and throwing Ash a look to do the same. Because it told them not to listen now.

"It's no big secret, Jan. You needed a quick sale. It's also perfect for MI5 international delegates and overseas clients." That was mumbled under his breath, and that

Welsh crept back in, making it hard not to listen and not catch just how much Jan had caught him out here.

"Which means…?" Jan slowed, giving Gray time to walk to his side, so Jan at least wasn't forced to walk backwards anymore. "So, my Villa gets you what with tax breaks?"

"I've got no idea what you mean," said Gray.

"Oh let me help out here." Ferryman came up behind them both. "Gray gets liability premium insurance and a tax rebate each year that would see the cost of the Villa earned three times over in five years."

Jan stopped as Gray looked back at Ferryman, forcing Raif and Ash to a halt just a few paces away as they waited. "So, fiddling the lower class now, is it?"

Gray coughed, nearly choked at Jan. "What? No." Jan seemed to ease off seeing Gray cough a little more than necessary, showing illness more. "I paid you above the going price and took all the hassle from your shoulders. And I make sure you get back what you lose out on."

Jan folded his arms. "How, exactly?"

Gray went in close and seemed to forget that anyone else, bar him and Jan, were there, or he had that way of making Jan seem as though no one else existed around them. It certainly convinced Raif. This side to Gray was something new. There was more than humanity there. There was Jan and nothing else. Hands eased around Jan's waist, and Gray pulled him close, hip to hip, suit trousers to suit trousers. "I'm buying you dinner this afternoon." A kiss brushed Jan's cheek, then Jan turned into it, chased it like he had in the kitchen.

"Yeah?" Jan smiled goofily. "In order of having to do the right thing and use my Villa money to pay back what I owe in tax—so I technically gained nothing from that sale bar my dignity—dinner tonight better come on gold-rimmed plates, mate."

Gray sighed heavily. "You've been around Jack far too long."

Raif didn't like Gray as a spy, but the lover in him was an old soul, one Jan seemed tuned into on all levels. And this... this was a small glimpse into the good that he knew Ash could do with seeing.

"Food." Jan pushed away from Gray. "I could eat for three." He looked at Gray. "Nope, at least seven, I think. I'm gonna max out your credit card."

Raif caught Gray's smile as Gray headed back down the corridor.

"Where you going?" Jan didn't look happy, certainly not as Gray turned back and held up his own bank card.

"To order."

Jan looked from Gray to Ferryman, then patted his pockets down. "The asshole stole his own bank card on the back of that kiss."

Ferryman winked as he passed Jan, coming to Raif. "Always hold a spy as a lover with one hand, a thief with the other."

Gray was back over by Jan and, pulling him close again, he gave him a kiss. "They'll get here quicker if I growl down the phone and I'm—" A soft sigh came as he traced a hand discreetly over Jan's side. "—getting hungry too."

"You... you've been around Martin for far too long." Jan said it lightly, it was there in his voice, but Gray lost his smile. Jan missed it, or filed it away to discuss later. From the little bit that Raif knew of Jan, most probably the latter. He didn't seem to miss much going on in their home. Raif didn't either. Gray hadn't had much time on his own. He'd be wanting to get the Villa swept for surveillance equipment, find details on Miles... but he left Jan with Ferryman, and Raif had a feeling over why; Gray wanted Ferryman to meet just who he'd hurt with planting this Baz here.

As Gray pulled away, Jan looked at Ash. "Then it's on to the MC to discuss where we go from here, okay?"

Now Ash relaxed. "Thank you."

CHAPTER 35
SLEEPER

A FEW HOURS later, Ash eased himself past Raif as they were led through the corridors of what seemed like a Gothic-style architecture of a mansion. Yet once inside, to Ash it couldn't have cried more 'modern-day London office and business space' if it had run through London grabbing the latest technology and furniture on a theft spree.

Ash barely took it in, not the sports halls they passed, the luxury living quarters, and the people who nodded their way or held doors open for them; not the amount of technology that seemed visible through cracks in the doors... so maybe Ash did take a little more in, enough to leave him frowning at the business behind the place and just what went on here. This wasn't just a hospital. It wasn't just any hospital; something else went down here too.

The medical facilities cried that exclusivity. Here there were no A&E queues, no rush between beds from underpaid and overworked staff, just calm as people moved about.

Everything was so damn calm.

As they made it to the main reception desk, Dr Cohan came out, her look at her beeper almost saying she'd been called to let them know they were here. Another man came out behind her, and Ash couldn't take his eyes off him for a moment. He'd seen this man on the news often enough, mostly when it came to London murders or nationwide hunts.

The chief of the CID took Gray's hand first, gave him a light tap on the arm, then did the same with Jan, then he looked at Caleb.

"Shaun Brennan, sir." Brennan seemed to relax more when Caleb shook his hand. "It's a pleasure to meet you again."

That got a cocked brow off Gray, which Brennan ignored.

"You too, Shaun. Thank you for stepping in at such short notice to help here."

"Anytime. You know that, sir." Brennan finally looked at Ash and Raif. "You'll want to see Chase, right?"

It was a damn stupid statement, but it got Ash's emotions tumbling over each other.

"Dr Cohan will escort you through and explain the situation. Chase's parents have been called and a car has been sent to pick them up. We've made reservations for them at a hotel close by. Do you mind if you continue without us for a while?"

Ash nodded, and he tugged at Raif's sleeve. That was his way of saying to Gray that Raif wasn't here for questioning.

"Do you mind if I go with you too?" That came from Jan and Ash glanced back. "It gets tough through those doors."

Ash frowned, not understanding, in many ways not giving a fuck, which he knew was harsh. But he needed to see Chase now. "Of course."

Jan wasn't in the same league as the other three men, and it made Ash like the man. Jan offered normality, which seemed to bypass Ash at the moment and leave him fighting his way out of his corner.

Gray caught Jan's sleeve, forcing him to a stop. Jan gave the smallest smile, then eased the hold away.

"I'm good, Gray. It's okay."

And then they were pushing through some doors....

~

Ash went on through to Chase's room, not understanding the quiet from inside until he went and stood by Chase's bed.

A chair brushed the back of his legs, and somewhere Ash registered that Raif had gotten him a chair. He sat down before his heart slipped a few notches.

Two IVs assaulted Chase's forearm, a longer catheter targeting the more central veins of the body. It looked like fluids, drugs, and blood transfusions had recently been needed to support his circulation, mostly due to the small surgical bandage he had close to his heart. It's funny, but he always pictured life support as some sort of breathing tube through someone's nose and that hard push of breath in and out of the body by a machine, yet here the IVs seemed to be keeping him alive more. There was a breathing machine there and working, but it seemed to blur in and out of focus.

"Ash." Cohan came and sat on the foot of the bed as

417

Raif and Jan moved out of her way. "Chase hasn't regained consciousness. Because of the cardiac arrhythmia, he needed a pacemaker and defibrillator fitted. With the extent of the damage, tests show that he's most likely to not wake from the phenobarbital in a few days."

"What? Not at all?"

Cohan smiled gently. "It's all watching and waiting from here on in and providing the best care as his body stabilises."

"But there's no guarantee he'll wake up?"

Cohan shook her head and Ash groaned, pushing slowly to his feet. "His…" He stopped, looked down, and somehow let his hands go to his head, raking his hair constantly. "His parents can't afford this." He glanced at Raif. "They can't afford this and… Raif… what then? Who'll look after his heart? His heart… he's got such a goddamn soft heart. Take away all the games… he still sleeps with a stuffed fucking Batman, for Christ's sake."

"Easy, easy—"

"Don't fucking *easy* me." Ash pushed Raif away as he came over, sickness hitting his stomach over what had filled that toy and tried to hold Chase over the years. "Where will the money come from? What will these bastards do when it stops?" He shrugged, hating the money on display here and knowing he'd never see the likes of it in his lifetime. "I walked away from the factory. *I don't have enough saved to cover this. I—*"

"Calm it down."

Ash turned hearing Gray's voice and saw Jan had started to come over, but Gray now backed him away from getting involved, or was it more to back them both out of the hospital room? And it hit Ash then.

Gray.

He went over, but not even looking at him, Gray stopped him from getting close, more so to Jan.

"I'll work for you." Ash nodded and angrily shook Raif off as Raif gripped at his arm, trying to pull him away. "I don't know what the MC do, but I'll work my fucking bollocks off for you if you take care of him long-term. I don't care what: chauffeur, groundsman—fucking toilet cleaner if you need it, but—"

Jan tried to step forward but Gray denied that.

"Gray," Jan said quietly.

"For God's sake, please." Ash went closer. "He's here because of me. He's hurting because of me, and his heart..." Ash denied the tear as Gray denied looking at him. "If you knew him for just five minutes, you'd know it's the best part of him. Of both of us."

"Gray, for God's sake." Jan tried to get past but Gray made sure he took a step back.

"*What?*" said Jan, more snapped. "You're denying who I talk to now? Fucking move."

"*No.* Ash needs help, but not the sort he's asking for." Gray snarled that, making Jan jolt, then he looked at Ash. "You. No."

"Because I'm fucked up? Because I'm not army? I'm not a fighter—I'm not fucking worthy? I'm just the son of an ex-detective, a son who never did anything with his life but look after his dad and fuck about playing games? I've lost one of those friends because of me and Chase." Again Raif tried to take his arm, but Ash pulled away. "Leave me the fuck alone, Raif." And he was back with Gray. "I'll get help if it stops you pulling Jan away from me as though I'm going to fuck him over—which I damn well won't, but hey,

I know you don't trust me, but I sure as hell don't trust you either. But just let me find a way to pay for Chase's care, because I can't...." He had to stop. "I can't lose another friend, and I damn well won't skive off everything Raif has done for the army in order for me to take care of him."

"I have no employment positions for you. You abuse the Dom role. The MC is not your world—"

"*Gray.*" Jan pulled away from him as Gray gave a hard sigh. "It isn't fucking mine either, but you helped me."

"*But* if you'll calm the fuck down enough so that I can talk...." Gray looked hard at Jan first, then Ash. "You admit you need help?"

"Yes," Ash bit out, and Gray pulled back. Ash visibly took a deep breath. "Yes," he said a lot calmer. "Christ, yes, if it stops someone else getting hurt like this."

Gray nodded after a moment. "And you've worked in manufacturing for years now and you're familiar with car parts?"

"Yeah." Ash wasn't polite with that when he knew he should be.

"Then I'll have a word with a manager of two garages to see if he can add you to his books as a parts collector."

"Steve?" Jan's eyes widened a touch. "God yes! Jack was always saying he hated having to spend time away, collecting parts for jobs."

Gray nodded.

"You think he'll help?" Jan frowned. "And Jack would be okay with that." Jan glanced over at Chase and everything about him seemed to soften. "Yeah, Jack would be more than okay with that."

Ash hadn't a fucking clue who *Jack* was, but he loved him in that moment.

"But there is a condition."

Ash felt his heart slip again. Gray was looking at Raif.

"Name your terms." Raif didn't sound happy. Here it came. The catch.

Gray stepped up close to Raif. "When it's time, I'll ask one question, and you'll answer it."

"No." Ash didn't know what secret Raif held, but he didn't care at that moment either. "This is my problem, no one else's."

"Ash—"

"*No*," he snarled back at Raif. "He doesn't buy secrets on the back of Chase's hurt, on the back of you being hurt. No man with a fucking heart does."

Raif passed him the gentlest smile, then focused on Gray. "One question. One answer. When you're ready."

Gray nodded.

But Raif wasn't finished. "My conditions: long-term care for Chase, a job for Ash, and a place for him to stay here in London."

Gray's smile was wry. "Yes to the first. For the other two, only if you work on my books."

Raif frowned. Ash felt like hitting Gray. He was bargaining with Raif over a friend's life, one who was on life support—in this very fucking room.

"You mean I cross departments with intel and work for MI5 too?" It was stated matter-of-factly from Raif. Ash hadn't realised Ferryman had come in now and Ferryman seemed to straighten hearing that.

"No, you work for me. No one else."

"Why?" Ash frowned.

Gray didn't look over at Ferryman. "The price of being

fucked about."

Raif didn't answer, and Ash saw how everything turned slowly within him, like when they'd first met. Gray waited just as patiently.

"Additional condition for that to be considered," Raif said quietly, "being as you're adding to them each time. The little girl, Voodoo. Young Lucy who saw her mother killed? I want her here with me and getting help too if I decide to work for you."

Gray narrowed his eyes. "No promises on the latter. This isn't the place for a child."

"Then no promises on working for you. This isn't a place for me if I can't look after those I care for. Agreed?"

Gray pulled back a little. "More than."

"But I have your word you'll do everything you can to try and get her, plus every other condition we've asked for?"

He got a nod, and Raif nodded back.

"Wait, what?" Ash jerked Raif around to face him. "You don't get to decide what happens to me... to Chase. And you don't fucking whore yourself out like that to this bastard."

A big hand cupped the side of Ash's face, a thumb brushing at his cheek. "And you don't get to decide what I do when it comes to giving you, Chase, and Voodoo this."

Ash grabbed at his hand and made sure Raif didn't touch him anymore, but he kept hold of his hand as he let it fall to his side. "You get grief out of this, nothing else."

Raif smiled sadly. "I get a home. No locked doors. You. Now you tell me I get nothing."

Ash watched him for a moment. His turn now to let all

the details sink in and process. "My condition, being as everyone else gets a fucking say here."

Raif frowned, then smiled. "Name it."

"That London home. You get a key, with no pissing off at night unless it's for work. We pay equal rent, and we see where that takes us both."

Raif's eyes seemed to startle, but in the good kind of way. "Deal."

"I'll also need to message my dad's carers and let them know; my dad needs to know I'm not going back." And he meant that. He couldn't stomach going back there. Raif nodded, but Gray didn't.

"I'd like your father over at the manor for now."

Ash stiffened. "What the fuck for?"

"Because he has additional intel on Miles and is known for taking police equipment that I'd like one of my ops from MI5 to look at."

Did he think Miles was a tie to this I-dosing that Raif was looking into? Ash screwed his face. That seemed a long stretch, but who knew how these people worked?

"I'll send someone to pick him up." Gray had moved over to the wall and stood thumbing something into his phone. He went quiet for a moment. "Ferryman."

Caleb looked over at Gray.

"You're at the Victoria and Albert Museum tonight, right? They're showing the conservation of *Pentecost* by Botticelli."

"Seriously?" Jan's ear pricked up as he looked over. He'd moved over to Chase. "Birmingham Museums Trust let them borrow that painting, and they're showcasing its conservation?"

Caleb smiled at Jan. "You like art?"

Jan's eyes widened. "You're fucking kidding me, right?" He seemed to catch himself and rubbed at his neck. "Well, it's a hobby," he added with a blush, one that Gray smiled to as he worked on his phone. "But you're going there tonight?"

Caleb looked at Gray. "Yes, I am." Ash didn't like the look. It was one he and Chase would share before they lined up some... fun. Caleb was back with Jan. "I have a spare ticket. Would you like—?"

Jan snapped a glance to Gray, maybe tried to read him, but Gray wasn't giving anything away from what Ash could tell. "Gray's the collector, maybe—"

"Nottingham." Gray typed something into his phone. "I'm in Nottingham in a few hours." He didn't seem to like the news that came through, and Ash got a sick feeling, knowing why Raif had been given twenty-four hours to get out of town. Time was up, right? He'd go for the kill after all?

Gray put his phone away and came over. "Jan, it would be good to let Ferryman know how much of a bastard he's been the past week or so. And a good place to start is *Pentecost*. It isn't the best in the collection—"

Caleb coughed. "Yes, it is."

Gray smiled. "And I expect you to side with me one hundred percent and say fuck to any other so-called professional critique you may hear tonight, thus taking hours out of Ferryman's time to explain... just why that is."

Jan cocked a brow. "Well, the thing is with a professional art debate, and I know how you appreciate this, Gray: it's always good to take time to listen to both sides. And if I'm going with guidance and expertise, Ferryman outshines you by… how many years?"

"A decade." Gray flipped him the finger, not looking the gentleman now. "Plus one more."

"Language." That came from Jan, but there was a play between him and Gray now that put everyone outside, at such a far distance from this intimate closeness they shared. "Which bush was you dragged out from, Raoul?"

Gray's eyes came so alive then. "An alley, mate. Find all sorts of gems, their soft lovers, and hidden psychopathic bastards hiding away up there. And I wouldn't change it for the fucking world."

CHAPTER 36
MILES FROM HOME

ASH EASED BACK into the sofa, finding a place to hide away from a bad head for the first time as the low sound came from the wall-mounted flat screen TV. Gray's lounge and manor slept quiet enough in the soft lighting, the gentle sound of the fountain coming from outside and giving it that expensive, yet calm holiday feel. Jan had gone out an hour ago with Caleb, and the genuine love of art had seemed to bury some of the Baz anger as he'd held the door for Caleb. Gray himself had left over three hours ago, just half-an-hour after they got back, and although a little puzzled by it, Ash had secretly thanked him for pretty much shutting his manor down tonight for them. Maybe he'd calmed a little more because Craig had stopped by before going off shift to talk to Ash, and Ash had asked a few questions, just tested Craig out on terms like PTSD, what it meant. Raif had watched from the doorway, and Ash had tried not to look at him without carrying a heavy feel of... ugly inside. Ash knew there was something wrong inside him, so small steps. He was prepared to take small steps, and Craig seemed more than willing to help too. Ash would be seeing a man named Halliday this Wednesday. He'd booked the appointment for him, then.

Life still felt incredibly displaced, with even the images flickering on the huge screen not bringing any sense of realism through his skin, so the quiet of the manor helped as well.

It wasn't eased, though, with how Gray told them the man in the cell just down the hall had been moved out of the manor for the night, and that his cell could act as a panic room if they needed it.

With all the security outside, why the hell would they need a panic room? But then he supposed big homes like this had multiple levels of security.

Sat next to a barely touched whiskey, a few housing leaflets were stacked neatly on the glass coffee table, and occasionally the flick of a page came as one was turned over. Raif sat next to him, glasses on as he studied the estate agents' leaflets for in and around London. Ash took a swig from his beer. It had surprised him that Gray went so "normal" with alcohol. The whiskey Raif drank had come from some expensive make Ash hadn't recognised, but the beer could have come from any supermarket shelf. Two tastes always seemed catered for here, the former being Gray's, the latter maybe Jan's. Although he couldn't picture Jan preferring a beer, maybe a nice brand of expensive wine. Or was he stereotyping again?

"Christ, the prices to some of those London homes." Ash rubbed at his head, the throbbing having eased, but it left behind a dull ache that saw the lights kept low, the TV lower. "This Gray's going to just give you one?"

Raif licked a finger and gave Ash a very sweet school-teacher look over his glasses as he flicked over another leaflet. The homes he searched had two or three bedrooms, and Ash buried the grief over knowing he was thinking about a little girl too. He hoped that if Gray pulled anything off, that would be the one thing he gave Raif.

"You're never given anything from MI5. You have to work for it." He turned another leaflet over. "Besides, whatever Gray pays out, he gets back twice-fold in taxes from MI5, especially when it comes to spies and intelligence."

"He never said that, though. That you were working for MI5."

Raif flicked through another one. "They never do out in the open, Ash." He hovered over one that came with a modest price tag. "And you can guarantee it'll be nothing like this place or the Villa earlier."

Ash took another sip of his beer and pulled his legs up to him. "To be honest, I'd be happy with a caravan."

Raif looked over, his touch stilling on the list of homes. "You mean that, don't you?"

Thing is, he did. This manor... the Villa, they were a different life, different bloody existence. Even the usual two-up two-downs around here came with a gross price tag that cried out extravagance he couldn't afford, and wouldn't even if he had the money. He'd... lingered for too long. Give him a caravan he could hook up to a car, petrol in his tank, and coasting from town to town would be enough for him now. It's what they'd been planning most of his life but had never really gotten around to it. Ash felt like he needed to now.

Hating how cold the beer was, Ash laid it to rest on the table, pushed the leaflets back, then before he thought it over, he rested his head on Raif's shoulder.

"Voodoo would love the sea," mumbled Raif distantly.

"Chase too, if he wants to come."

Ash slipped his arms around Raif's chest. The grief in Raif's voice tore at him. What Lucy had been through, it was his fault. She'd lost her mother, Raif had lost his wife because of him, had lost his own son long before that, yet… yet he was still here. Hurting. "Yeah," he replied gently. "Voodoo would love the sea."

A noise from behind them forced Ash to twist his head back as Raif looked up too. It sounded like static from a radio, and a few moments later, Ray could be heard talking in the hall. His voice was low, but he came into the lounge after he'd finished.

"Ash, your dad's just been allowed into the grounds. He has an escort and will be here in five minutes."

Raif pushed up and Ash followed suit. Gray had said he'd had someone go and pick him up, but….

But?

"You sure you're okay with him being here?" Raif stopped him for a moment. "This is still raw."

He nodded, then shook his head. "I don't fucking know, Raif. He made us all."

"I don't excuse anything he's done, but from how he was yesterday, if he'd known where it would take you, he would rather have walked away and let you grow up on your own. So he tried his best to right it when he did see the damage, Ash. When he did remember."

Ash rubbed at his head. "Yeah… maybe. But he'll always forget eventually."

They headed into the reception hall, but Ray stopped him from going anywhere near the door, leaving them by the staircase. "Just precaution, but I answer, okay?"

Layers of security. Ash didn't want to live here. You

couldn't breathe, not without someone checking to see if you'd taken a deep enough breath in case you decapitated someone—Jan—in the process. Yeah, he'd noticed how his path would be blocked to Jan at times. He'd seen so many enemies for so long now, but at least he could tell the difference between an enemy and Gray's genuine concern for Jan's safety.

Maybe Gray had every right to keep pulling Jan away from him.

Ray tugged out a radio again as he checked through the slim window just left of the door. "Contact. Registration plates match." Ray paused. "Positive ID on driver and passenger. Allowing access in ten, nine…."

Ray opened the door on *one* and withdrew his gun, stepping back and aiming it at the door as—

Ash cried out as his dad came through, choking and spluttering as he scratched at the cable tie around his throat and how Miles kept the chokehold.

"Don't fucking move," snarled Ray at Miles.

"*What the fuck?*" That came off Ash as Miles inched his dad in the door and slammed it shut with his foot.

Miles had been left in the woods with Frank. With Raif's friend. Where Miles might have been able to take his dad down, Frank wouldn't have been so easy, not with how Ash had seen Frank take Miles down. What the hell had gone wrong?

"Drop it. Fucking drop it," Miles said to Ray, levelling his own gun. He kept his back to the wall. He was a big man himself and used to handling Ash's dad.

How…. How the hell had he gotten through the gates… the security?

"Run." Raif looked at him.

"What?"

"*Fucking run, Ash*," he whispered harshly. "Panic room." His eyes desperately seemed to ask the same as Ash on just exactly how things had taken such a bad turn.

Miles looked over in that moment, and Ash cried out, covering his head as a shot was fired, slamming into an oil-on-canvas painting behind them. Raif tugged him back into the lounge, then Ash was up and running as Raif shoved him forward.

He didn't understand how it had all gone wrong so quickly. Why it had all gone wrong so quickly.

~

Raif hissed as another shot whipped by his ear, deafening him for a moment. "Fucking cunt." He'd taken up position behind the wall and briefly kept checking Miles's position as Ash bolted from the lounge via the far exit. Ash had noticed the disinfectant first, so he'd know where to go now to get to the clear dispensers.

In the hall, Miles had pushed Ash's dad at Ray, then a shot rang out, then one more just inches from Ray's head as he twisted and tried to protect Ash's dad. A kick to Ray's jaw saw him hit the floor before he could help, and blood covered the floor as Ray hit it, not moving.

As the gun raised in Raif's direction, his only option was to use Ash's escape exit and double back to the reception hall. Ash would bolt for the panic room, so he was safer than Ash's dad at the moment.

The sound of Ash's bare feet on marble chased through the lounge, and Raif followed. Then as Ash seemed to twist and turn through a few corridors, following the change of disinfectant dispensers, Raif followed suit and used their colours to double-back on to the hall to find a firearm.

Miles was nowhere to be seen, but Ray was just pulling himself to his knees and tugging Ash's dad onto his back. Keeping low, Raif made it over.

"Take the gun." Ray pushed it at him, then fumbled in his jacket. He came out with a penknife and grabbed at the cable tie. "If I can't get this off, I'll need to get air into his system." Ray looked at him. "Help Ash. Go. Unless you know how to cut his throat and get a tube in?"

He didn't, so Raif was up and taking Ray's radio and gun with him.

As he ran back through the lounge, chasing the colours of the disinfectant, he flicked the radio. It would still be locked into the security station that Ray had used. "Breach. Man armed, dangerous. Assistance needed."

Only static answered his call and Raif swore under his breath. Keeping the gun raised, body low, he twisted through the halls and dining room, hating how bloody quiet everything had gone.

Where the fuck was Gray, the rest of his fucking security? Raif pressed his back up against a door, then gently eased it open. This was Gray's home. His turf. And if Miles had come here, it stood to bloody reason that Gray should be close behind. Or what bloody use as a culler was he?

The studio he glanced into came with the fine scent of fresh rain and woodland, with a classic designed bedroom suite that cried Gray. The photos on the wall showed the stunning form of a tanned man bound in all sorts of positions, and the hint of BDSM equipment spoke of something more personal going on in this studio. Raif shut the door quickly and scratched a mark in the panelling. The clear message to let anyone know that he'd checked this one.

Raif made it to the hall where the panic room was homed, and a shot ringing out and a cry off Ash said Miles had found it too. Had he followed the run of broken dispensers? Putting that down to Ash's temper and him breaking things when life didn't go his way? Probably. But it would lead him back to the panic room. Shit.

Raif paused and quickly checked the cylinder of Ray's six-shooter. No shots had been fired, which meant the four he'd heard had come from Miles. He'd carried a six shooter too.

Which meant Miles had two bullets left.

That was okay. Raif had six. And each one would find Miles's fucking head if he touched Ash.

A cry came from down the hall, off to the left, and Raif flattened his back against the cool of the corridor. Breathing calmed, he cast a quick look around to see Miles just outside the panic room, aiming the gun his way, Ash at his side and struggling with an arm around his throat.

"Come out, come out, wherever you fucking are. I heard your boots, you big fucker" came the coldness. "Put your gun down. I really don't want to hurt Ash here, but I will unless you put the fucking gun down and come out, you cunt."

Yeah. That would get them both killed.

"Okay. Some enticement.... Y'know, Voodoo... she didn't even hide?"

The grip on Raif's gun tightened.

"Kept such a tight hold on that butterfly case, right up until she watched me stuff it in her mother's fat hip, she did." A snort. "Do you think little Lucy will have dreams about it? About how I fucked her mother. How I'd have taken my cock and stuffed it in Lucy's pretty little butterfly opening—"

Ash snarled and there was a struggle as Raif rounded the corner and aimed the gun at Miles.

"Let him fucking go."

Miles grinned and tightened his arm around Ash's throat. "Aww, Ashy. You finally grow up and go good for someone other than your old man? Look at how his feelings for you bleed on through." He got a kiss to the side of his head. "Pity it's come so late in the game, huh?" He focused his aim on Raif and pulled the trigger.

Ash kicked back with a cry, knocking his aim off as the gun fired. "You don't fucking touch him."

"One bullet left." Raif had ducked instinctively, now he aimed his gun again. "You shoot me, you have Ash there. And he's got a kick to him, that kid. You then take all the bullets that the security is packing here. Just where do you think you'll fucking go with Ash, you asshole?"

Sweat dripping down his temple, Miles licked at the side of Ash's face. He aimed the gun at Ash's head, and Raif instantly backed off. "How about here? Really fuck with his pretty head?"

"Drop it."

"Nah. Kid needs a new lesson for his shit. Besides... he knows where you're keeping Chase for me."

"He's fucking on life support, you *fuck*." Ash tried to dig into the arm around his throat, but a harder dig in of the gun stopped him.

Miles's eyes darkened, his gaze seeming to show a whole new level of breath control. "Life support...? Ash, sometimes you say the fucking sexiest things."

Ash's eyes widened slightly, then—"*Sick, you fucking sick cunt. You*—"

"Shush, shush-shush," whispered Miles, and Raif hated how he ended it with a kiss to Ash's neck. "Breath and death-play at its best...." Miles seemed to hug Ash a little tighter and not in any way that said it would kill him. "You ever fucked someone when they're cold and not breathing, Ash? Fuck." His hand started to shake, and Ash frowned over at Raif. "They're so fucking still, so cold around my cock. Never felt anything like it, Ashy. Fucking a cooling body. And I've got Chase in that permanent state now. Can fuck him till my dick's content. And you... teach you to like it too. You'll like it. You'll love to love it. You'll—"

"Yeah? We done now," said a new voice.

Raif flicked a look down the bend of the corridor off to his right, to the nurses' station— and who stood there now.

Gray.

"And just who the fuck are you?" Miles didn't shift his gun, but his look went down the corridor too.

A sniff came. "Homeowner. And a pissed off one at that. Tell me, have you seen the change in law lately on just how homeowners are allowed to defend themselves in their own homes?"

CHAPTER 37
GRAY

"YEAH?" MILES SMIRKED at Gray. "You feel you need to defend yourself against me? I'm scaring you, am I, buttercup? And here's me, just here to take a few things."

Gray leaned against the wall, messing with his phone. Always messing with his fucking phone, no gun in sight. Raif stiffened seeing it.

Not looking up, Gray pointed to the corner of the hall above Miles. "You know you've just confessed to theft, well, more kidnap with the intent to rape, on camera, right? Not the brightest sperm in the bank, are we?"

Raif glanced up. CCTV and full audio. So what? Gun. Why the hell wasn't he holding his gun, fuck the cameras. Gray was a culler by fucking nature.

"And necrophilia? Seriously?" added Gray. "You got any idea just how fucked up that is?"

Miles forced the gun into Ash's temple so hard Ash cried out. "About as fucked up as this kid. He'll love it eventually. And you, you're in my way, so move, luv. Or I'll kill him."

"No, you won't; it's not in your profile. You want him as your understudy." Gray slipped his phone in his pocket and kept his hand there, looking so fucking casual. "But just for clarification here, besides the people you've already murdered, you'll rape a young man on life support? Well, after you've taken him off life support?"

Miles smirked. "Kinks, we all have them. What's yours, I wonder."

The light on the camera flicked off.

"You've got no fucking idea, my friend." Gray pointed to the door behind Miles. "But let's try some mercy here, considering the view from certain sources is that I've been lacking it lately. Go in there, how you die, it will be messy. So this is me being a gentleman with the offer of... humanity. A quick kill out here."

Christ. That room wasn't empty, or the door was tapped to set an explosion off if opened. So if Miles went in there with Ash... "No." Raif couldn't believe this shit and flicked a look at Gray. "You fucking cunt." Was he playing tag-team with another culler? With explosives? Each culler had a signature mark. Was fire Gray's?

"Ah, but I know Ash," said Miles, and he reached behind for the handle, just the gun to Ash's temple keeping him still. "Gay sex without the ties: he always takes the back door to avoid any emotional bullshit. I'll trust the fucker in him, thanks, and good old Raif's reaction to you there too. Ash knows there's safety in here."

Ash snarled as Gray shrugged. "And if I lied when I told him to run into there and use it as a panic room, all to reduce the mess over cleaning up my manor after I kill you?"

Miles gave a soft laugh. "Cocky fucker, aren't you? But

see, Ash here, he avoids cops like the clap. If he's running this way, I know there's a reason and that it's away from real hard trouble."

Gray gave such a stunning smile. "Then by all means. Take the door behind you. Run."

"Yeah, right." The door behind Miles clicked open, but it opened too easily for it to have been done solely by Miles. Then Ash had the breath pulled out of him as he was tugged back into the small hall.

Raif tensed, but no explosion came. So what...?

Miles and Ash stumbled backward, then the second door clicked open as Miles blindly fumbled for it and pushed in, letting the door open wide.

The smell of heat and sweat made Raif twist his head away slightly as he rushed to follow them in, not wanting the door to shut—then everything moved so bloody quickly.

A kick to the back of Miles's knee saw him lose his footing and cry out, then a run of several punches to the ribs caused him to lose his grip on Ash even quicker. Twisted viciously around, Miles hit the padded cell wall, then a headbutt saw him hit the floor.

"Fucking *loving* these new skills." The man's hair was longer than Jan's, wilder, jet black like the darkness loitering around outside: a blackbird, caged. He wore no shirt, leaving the tanned, supple twists to his abs on full display. Jogging pants hung loose and low on his hips.

Silver eyes looked almost apologetic as he grabbed Miles to his feet by his hair, then Blackbird dusted him down as Raif moved in and dragged Ash back behind him.

"Fuck me, sorry, mate. Thought you were Craig there. All his, y'know, 'you don't smack visitors when Gray brings his old man in.""

Miles wiped blood from his nose, looking dazed, and he got a vicious head-butt again, this time Blackbird pulling him in hard with a drag on his shirt.

"I *was* expecting *you* then, though." Miles got a pat to his cheek off Blackbird as Miles grunted and tried to catch the blood pouring from his nose.

Blackbird's nose bled too, but the smile there only cried relief, cried more as he licked at Miles's broken nose….

Ash bolted from the cell as Gray came in. Wearing black leather gloves, he picked up Miles's firearm. It seemed to take Blackbird's attention, and Raif couldn't for the life of him figure out just what the hell passed between Gray and that silver gaze.

"Oh… Now just what in the hell are you whoring me out to, Welsh? What buttons you pushing now?"

Gray put the gun in a plastic cover. "Thirty seconds. Play profiler for me, pet."

Silver eyes came alive as Blackbird looked at the gloves. "Oh, now that's fucking interesting. You're *really* whoring me out." He focused on Miles. "So, now then, what are we all doing here?" Black nodded back to what Gray held. "That's a police-issued weapon he's just bagged, and not one of Welsh's here. He likes his Glocks." Silver eyes briefly fixed on Raif's, then as Miles groaned and tried to push Blackbird away, a few more vicious head-butts saw Miles nearly lose his footing and consciousness.

"Talking." A smile was given as Blackbird dusted Miles's clothes down again. "Oh, manners. Forgot them for a moment. I'm Martin, pleased to meet you." He went in close. "And you are?" No answer came, but he didn't look like he expected one. "Considering Gray would have killed you straight out if you were a cop killer, therefore making you a cop by default by the firearm—does that mean you've gone rogue, fluttering away like a butterfly in the breeze as he catches a new scent, being as I'm being allowed playtime with you?"

Raif kept his aim on-target, and it left him seriously questioning why he hadn't pulled the trigger. "He inserts butterflies into open wounds, then comes all over it. He raped a single mother after he'd killed her, forced her daughter to watch. He wants to fuck a young man he put in a coma."

"No fucking way." Blackbird—Martin's—eyes lit up.

"The bastard's psychotic."

"No. He's not delusional. Know your disorders, mate. There's no room for voices in with all that ego. You're a psychopath, right?" Martin grinned at Miles. "Fuck me, me too. Wanna play tag with these fuckers and compare head and eye counts as we play marbles and dance with them in the dining room?" He winced. "You're on your own with fucking the dead, though. Necrophilia is just sick, mate. Really fucked up and sick."

Miles stilled, seemed to see something in Martin's eyes, and a slow smile crept up as Raif tensed. Blood dripped from his chin as he spoke. "I'll leave you the tosser in the suit, leave him dead for you to fuck, how's that?"

Martin ran fingers over Miles's mouth, for a moment briefly closing his eyes. "Tempting."

And his smile said just that. "But I'm kind of a possessive bastard at heart, one who loves the guy in the suit there all warm-blooded and heated when we play. He's at his best then, and me, so am I."

He pulled Miles closer, losing all play. "And I really,

really don't like fucking peers threatening mine, and they are fucking mine to play with. Not yours, not Baz's, not the grey-haired cunt who tried to play father for a while."

Raif caught Gray's look in that moment, how Miles's scent had disrupted and called out two different types of animal, but two animals who would always feed on the same meat that threatened to poison theirs.

A vicious kick to the side of his knee broke Miles's kneecap, twisting the leg inwards, then a slight shift of stance saw Miles kiss the floor, cupping a bloodied ear.

Martin wore no boots, and the kicking that came now would have been over sooner more than later if he had, but the hell of it was, that *thug off a leash* was there, that knowing how this way took longer, and Martin enjoyed it. Head, ribs, stamps on the groin that left Miles gargling blood, it was… terrifyingly beautiful. Terrifying because it didn't stop, beautiful because Raif never wanted it to. And that was Raif's MI6 side, the one that wouldn't see it stop.

Martin played to the full until Gray suddenly shifted, grabbing an arm around Martin's throat and twisting him away.

Martin skidded to a stop, snarled, then went to shift back in for some more.

He stilled when Gray pulled a hunting knife from his jacket.

The colder control was there with Gray in that moment. No fancy words, no playing with guessing games….

He kept his look on Martin as he moved over Miles, pulled his head back to expose his neck—then slit Miles's throat, slow, ear to fucked-up ear.

"Fuck yeah." Martin shifted before warm blood even touched floor, going in for Gray. He cupped Gray's face, pulling him in, then forcing him back with a kiss that threatened a blooding of its own.

Gray instantly burned with it, hands grabbing Martin's hips, knife lost somewhere in the mix as he dragged him close, lips fighting lips, hips and heat still pushing Gray dangerously back close to the wall.

It confused the hell out of Raif because Gray was Jan's... Jan, Gray's... yet here...?

Gray spun Martin, forcing him against the padding of the cell, but still chasing that rough kiss, the rougher play that didn't even register Raif was there. Just dogs caught in the midst of the kill and not sure whether to fight, feast, or fuck.

Then Gray grabbed Martin's hair and exposed his throat.

As the bloodied knife went against it, Martin stilled. It was a move that saw one animal say another had crossed feeding territory, and it wasn't liked, or it should have been, but then Gray dropped his head to Martin's, closing his eyes.

"You feel that, Jack? That knife?" There was so much gentleness in how Gray played the knife against throat. "You still with me?"

Martin frowned along with Raif as Gray traced it down Martin's throat, the tip grazing over Adam's apple, to the curve of his throat, over a pec... gently circling the nipple.

Eyes still screwed closed, grip still tight on his hair, Gray slammed Martin's head into the wall. *You fucking hear, stunner? You fucking feel me now...?*

Martin hissed, body arched into Gray, hands now above his head, seeking something to hold as the rest of his body naturally sought out Gray's, to run with the play of knife on his body as Gray pulled back and ran the tip over his abs.

"'M here, mukka…" Something conflicted with the heat that Martin rode. It infected Gray too, that return frown looking heartbroken, lost. "Don't… please. Head… fucking hurts."

Gray pulled away and the knife dropped to the floor.

And in that moment, Martin jolted, focused on the knife, then eased down and picked it up.

He matched Gray's height a moment later as he looked down at what he held. "Still hurting him, Welsh? Still pushing this and making him hold on tighter to me? Still think you have what it takes to win?"

Gray seemed to have lost all fight. There was no move to take back the knife, nor fight to get away, just… quiet.

"Getting tired of playing those games now, Welsh?" Martin had lost his heat too, then he shifted in close, crowding Gray, and the kiss was just as hard, just as brutal as last time as the knife went to Gray's throat.

Only there was no fight from Gray there now. No return of heat. Nothing.

Martin pulled away this time, his smile wry as he looked down at the knife.

He handed it over to Gray in the next moment, handle first.

"This slow suicide of yours…." Martin tilted his head slightly. "It's fucking stunning, Welsh. And it's coming. You're gonna fall, and you'll fall so badly."

A long look at Martin, Gray took the knife, then walked away. He took out his phone as he did. "Housecleaning" was all he said in a flat tone. Then he started removing his shoes, jacket, shirt and gloves. He tossed them back into the cell and Raif was left to stare at Martin, Ash now just as quiet as he came in the doorway.

They both knew Gray had known Miles would come here tonight. Miles had been set up.

Martin smiled back at them, *knowing* that. But it was there too with the next words that fell from his mouth. "I got my ten out of ten off Gray for my bitch-in-training part tonight." He winked at Raif. "How do you think your skills ranked with him, hm?"

Yeah, Raif knew Miles hadn't been the only one set up tonight. That had been another test for Raif's skills on Gray's part, not just for Martin, but also to see what he'd do seeing Ash taken hostage. Would he stand by and allow Gray to kill?

Martin headed for the door. His intent was clear enough with how the door offered the open invitation. But Martin jolted as he reached the frame, then hit the floor in the next breath. He started to chuckle, then rubbed at his ankle, his laugh sounding more and more drowsy with each passing second.

"Bastard's got one hell of a mean streak, hmm?" He looked back at them. "I see why Jack loves the fucker so much."

The anger in Ash's eyes saw Ash didn't wait to see Martin pass out, but Raif did. Just to make sure.

CHAPTER 38
SCARS AND SCAPEGOATS

THEY BOTH CAUGHT up with Gray in the kitchen as he finished pulling on a fresh white shirt, like butter would rather privately run down those abs and cry *fuck yes* over telling anyone he wasn't innocent. A storeroom stood close by, the door ajar, and the fresh packaging on the table said Gray had taken the spare clothes from there. He took the packaging and tossed it in the bin as Raif followed Ash into the kitchen.

Raif could no more stop Ash going for Gray than he could have stopped what had happened tonight.

He couldn't stop Gray's reaction either.

As Ash went to shove at his shoulders, Gray twisted Ash's arm behind his back and forced him face-first down onto the table.

"Easy, easy, please." Raif went straight over, his hand on Gray's arm, needing to get him off Ash but not pushing for it at the same time.

There was something wrong in Gray's eyes. He was still wired by what had gone on in the cell.

"You knew he would come, you bastard." Ash struggled to move. "You set us fucking up."

"My home, *my fucking lovers.*" Gray grabbed Ash's hair, pulling his head up off the table enough to strain the muscles in his throat. "Miles's psychological profiling said he wouldn't stop until he found you once he'd been triggered. Your backpacking trip, you saying you wanted to leave, it triggered him that first time. It would have triggered him again with you leaving…"

Gray pulled Ash up off the table and sent him stumbling away. "I knew he'd come, yes."

Raif steadied Ash but Ash shook him off. "Fucking bollocks. You arranged for him to come. He was already in custody. So you put him at risk?" He pointed at Raif. "You put Chase at more risk? You put the people *you* care for— over the people *I* care for? *What kind of a fucking bastard are you?*"

Raif agreed. "This didn't need to happen. Even with him in custody, you could have finished this in the West Midlands. I checked Ash's mobile and took out the tracking device. It's how he traced me to Voodoo's. Even if Miles got free, he wouldn't know to come here. I'm not stupid."

"No," said Gray, "you're not."

Raif pulled back when he added nothing else. He knew what that silence meant. "So you let him go?" He frowned. "You brought him here specifically to… to—"

"What?" Gray looked at him.

To feed and play, to stay and look after his own, but… but more so to feed and play with that down there in the cell, on their own turf. With Ferryman taking Jan out and knowing full well what was going down right here. Gray's warning to him too. Christ. That level of vicious control, of reasserting bloodied pecking order and that *don't fuck with mine again, ever...* even with his own father. Raif wanted out of here now.

This, this is what cullers were all about. Feed... play... fuck about with their prey, on their terms, no distraction, no interruption or tolerance of a collar around their throats, from anyone.

Gray seemed to read that. "I merely cut the bullshit and fed his need to be here."

"And Raif's friend, Frank. He went along with that?" That came off Ash, and Gray raised a brow, that arrogance over "you don't fucking question me now, boy" look. But it only seemed to push Ash more. "I'm not your family. I'm not your fucking pet in cell eight. I'm not your staff. I abuse BDSM safe, sane, consensual guidelines and make a lousy Dom. So I walk out that door now, I won't keep your *fucking* secrets—"

Yeah, that was why he loved Ash. That lack of fear, that same look of control as Gray, even if it was just in emerging territory and yet had a few more years to grow as Gray's had done.

"I walk out that door, I'll tell Craig, or whatever his fucking name is. I'll shout it from the fucking Met office roof about your killing fest and make sure you lose that black-haired killer in your cells. So you cut the bullshit now too; you talk to me." Ash wasn't even shouting. "Because, yeah, I know if I walk out that door and do all that, you'll still look after Chase all in order to keep Raif close. So you be fucking straight with me now over how you made Frank give up Miles and you stop me fucking up your world like you've tried to do with mine. Because that's me playing with you. And I will *fucking* play with you now."

449

Jesus. Raif looked away. Ash was deadly serious, only the quiet off Gray—it wasn't a good sign. Life was clear cut for him, black and white, where the two colours rarely mixed, by the look of it. But Ash was in crossover territory now. It meant Gray would do one of two things: shut him up for asking questions or shut him up for staring him down. Neither would be good for Ash.

But after a moment, Gray cocked the faintest smile. And, yeah, Raif knew in that moment that Frank had gone along with whatever Gray had said if he'd pulled the same on him. He also knew Ash was granted permission to come and play if he fucking dared.

"Frank is staff," Gray said quietly. "Come all his faults, all his flaws; especially his flaws."

Ah. Frank was a smoker. Knowing Gray, he knew Frank's brand. Either Gray had burned his intent onto Frank, or Gray had threatened to plant evidence of Frank being on scene at Lucy's. MI6 wouldn't like that. Not another operative caught in a murder case. Frank would have gone along with Gray's orders. Raif, in his own way, had too. He'd not shot Miles when he had the chance. He'd watched everything play out. Frank wouldn't have been given a choice. Frank would no doubt have been told to leave behind evidence that would lead Miles to this address too.

"And those flaws led Miles here, right?" Ash worked with Gray's quiet too. "With us here? Jan?"

"To this address, with you here." That coldness again. "Never Jan. Like you've said, he's family, something you've yet to learn about, Ash."

The bastard.

Ash clenched his fists at his sides, no doubt thinking the

same as Raif here. "And because you trust no fucker with his life?"

"I don't trust *you*." Gray looked at Ash. "Martin's tough enough and sound enough in mind to take what I dish out, but you...."

"*You fub*—" He went for Gray again, but he played into how Gray would always shut down the opposition, no matter how well they thought they could play. Gray again made him kiss the table, culling the anger down to mere grunts and snarled out anger as he twisted Ash's arm behind his back and dug an elbow into the back of his neck. "I'm not Miles," shouted Ash, trying to struggle free. "I'm not into raping men after I've killed them, and you damn well don't treat me like a fucking nutcase when the fucker in that cell just beat the shit out of someone before you slaughtered them. My life's worth more than that. Raif's life's worth more than—"

"Jan's?" Gray said quietly, waiting for Ash to stop struggling. Ash did, that fight still there in his eyes, and Gray pulled him up and shoved him away. "Not in this lifetime," said Gray as Ash skidded to a stop and turned back to face him. "He's seen enough. So choose his life over yours? Every fucking time. People around here seem to be forgetting that."

"But you... you...." Ash fought anger and hate. "You couldn't guarantee that all... all this would go to plan."

"There's no guarantee of anything when it comes to handling serial killers, Ash." Raif took a seat next to him and Ash frowned over. "You can only anticipate and plan, and trust in the killer's instinct to do just that: try and kill." Yeah, he felt old now. Really fucking old.

"You're not pissed at what he's done?" Anger bit deep in his eyes. "You're okay with all of this... bullshit? He tested you out too." He looked at Gray. "And did he jump through the right fucking hoops for you when it came to protecting you and yours?"

"You're alive, Ash," Raif said quietly. "That's all that matters to me, and—"

"Everything okay?" Ray came in the kitchen, and Ash fell quiet as Ray made a point of looking at Ash. The moment came now for Ash to face the same choice Raif had a moment ago: do or die. Ash could cause Gray a lot of trouble—he had every right to—or he could taste what family meant, with all the silence, lies, and poison that came with it, yes, but also a passion that would see someone looked after and protected until bodies were broken and bled. And yeah, Raif knew Gray would test Ash too. That this was his test now. Do or die. Do was wiser, because Gray wouldn't let him walk out of his home and threaten that.

Ash looked Gray over, the muscles tensing in his jaw as he did, then Ray found his attention, and....

Raif breathed a long sigh seeing Ash push all of the fight away, bury it for more private discussion later. But private being the key word here. Like Gray, Ash wouldn't run out on caring for Chase. They both had a humane side that pulled them back, and Ash's quiet acknowledged that now. He'd toe the line as family, for family.

Gray looked away for a moment, then he moved over to Ray. He took time checking Ray's cuts and bruises to his face, then Ash jerked, as if suddenly remembering what the hell had gone on before Gray had killed Miles. "My fucking dad...."

"It's okay, Ash." Ray raised his hands. "He's in the lounge with paramedics. They don't think his wounds are serious enough for a stay at hospital, but they will get someone in to watch over him here tonight."

"You said he'd need a cut to his throat." Raif looked at him.

"I lied," said Ray.

As easy as that.

Ash shifted past them, and Raif let him go this time, knowing he needed time with his dad if ever they were to try and recognise the hurt done. If his dad even remembered the hurt done.

He stayed focused on Gray.

"Housecleaning is on scene." Ray rubbed at his neck, and Gray moved over to the sink and got him a glass of water and some pain meds. Ray took the water and swallowed the tablets whole.

"You okay?" asked Gray.

Ray nodded. "Paramedics gave the all clear. Good thing I get paid for this shit."

"You were the only one on staff I'd allow to do this without the backup." Gray snorted a smile, then patted his shoulder. "Still happy you volunteered? Take a few days off. Get some rest."

"You're making me sound old." The sir had gone, and Raif wondered just how much Ray had seen in this house. How long he'd been here.

"Yeah, I'm asking you to take time off because I think you're... old, Ray."

Ray let a slow smile creep up, then he rubbed at Gray's arm. "Craig's back on scene and wanting to know why he got a call off Paul tonight to say Paul wasn't needed for a few hours, along with the new carer. Craig knows something's gone down. You know you'll lose Jack and

Martin if he sees what's gone on. You know you'll have to face Jan and explain to him just how that's happened."

Gray gave a hard sigh, and Ray turned away. "I've asked him to wait in the Oval whilst housecleaning finishes."

"Thank you." Gray paused. "Ray."

"Hmm?" He glanced back.

"Get Martin cleaned and back in his room and ask Craig to run the usual vital checks when Martin's ready. Especially for any head wounds and concussion."

"Will do. I'll also let Craig know I mixed up the dates and thought Craig was on scene tonight." He half shrugged, then pointed at his own bruises. "And Martin of course loved my screw-up, hence why Martin's out and looking rough."

Gray smiled down at his feet, then looked at Ray. He'd just agreed to a cover-up. "Thank you."

Ray left, leaving Raif watching Gray. After a moment, Raif got to his feet and made to head out too. He paused by the door, scratching his head, then turned back to Gray.

"This Martin," he said quietly, "quite a coincidence how Ash was told he'd been taken away for the night and to now use that room as a panic room." Raif dug his hands in his pockets as Gray held his gaze. "Tables moved, care staff fooled into taking the night off." Raif gave a sniff. "Cullers. You didn't just plan to catch a killer. You wanted to have as much fun in the process with Martin as you slaughtered Miles too."

Noise from down the corridor drew Gray's attention again. Jan's voice drifted through, getting close, and Gray seemed tuned into that more.

Raif knew Jan came in the hall behind him now, along with someone else, but not yet close enough to hear.

"Yeah, a lot of planning there, with one flaw that could see you lose Martin tonight."

Gray cocked a brow.

"His door is on remote to his cell. You unlocked it to allow Miles in despite the warning you gave on not doing that. The remote is tied to your mobile, as is the CCTV and where Martin would be in that cell. You needed Martin to stay locked up until just the right moment. So how will you explain to Craig on how Miles got into that cell without someone—you or Jan—allowing it?"

Jan pushed past Raif, glancing at him briefly, no doubt taking everything in Raif had just said, then buffeting Gray slightly as he went and took him back a step.

Gray didn't even look at Raif now, not as Jan went nose to nose with him, again taking him back a little. Nothing was said, just a whole host of emotion in Jan's eyes. Anger, hurt, frustration, downright fear.... Then his face screwed slightly, an angered tear running free, and that seemed to stir the look in Gray's eyes back to normality a little.

"What the fuck are you doing, Raoul? Where's that fucking head of yours going? We can't lose him, Gray. Not from here. And Jack's skill or not, it's still Jack in there," Jan mumbled so softly, tracing a hand over his cheek. "And Jack... he was so fucking scared of falling. Remember? How he stood in the hall, nearly wanting to crawl inside you to get away from falling into Martin? You promised you'd hold him through it, until we got him back. You...." Jan rested his head against Gray's and Gray closed his eyes, his hand ghosting up to Jan's neck. "Fuck. I walk out that door, you bastard," breathed Jan, "I walk out that door, I need to know you'll both be here when I get back. Don't shut me out. Not like Vince did."

Yeah, Jan was damn smart. He knew he'd been taken out

of here for a reason, especially with all the paramedics on scene.

Gray pushed Jan away, just a little, but rough enough to jolt Jan. "It's not Jack in there."

Jan pushed back harder at Gray, this time startling him, then he went back in. "You listen now; whatever's in there, *Jack* trusted you. Don't ever forget that. Don't ever fucking forget he fell with an open heart, and he's... he's not so fucking tough, Gray. He's... he's such a soft loveable soul.... Every time you touch Martin, you touch Jack, and he's had enough, you hear me? You don't touch Jack. You don't ever fuck about with that or I swear I'll fight you every step of the fucking way for him, we clear?"

Jan's fire seemed to slip, and he brushed his cheek discreetly against Gray's, a touch that instantly stilled Gray. "Did you ask him tonight, Gray? Did you ask Jack? Did the Dom get permission to touch his sub's soul?"

Hurt crept in blue eyes.

"No. I know. So when you can't ask Jack's permission, when it comes to deciding anything about what's locked in those cells, beyond that—" He pushed Gray away again, hard. "—you ask mine. You get fucking permission from me. Always."

Gray reacted so differently, glancing away, then closing his eyes as he pulled Jan back in. A gentle swipe of thumb came at Jan's cheek. Only this one seemed to say sorry in so many ways when words hurt too much. Yeah, Raif saw it. A Dom had been pulled up for breaking the most barest of guidelines: he'd touched his sub without permission, maybe not in the sense that most Dom's would ever experience, but it was a bad touch all the same.

"I just need to feel him, Jan. So fucking badly now. Trust

me, please. I keep seeing Jack. I need to keep pushing for Jack."

"I know." Jan kissed his cheek. "But you need to trust me too. I saw Jack in the psychiatric unit when Craig and Halliday got him back, and after that... Christ, he was so scared of fucking up, of being taken back there. He needs peace here, we all fucking do, Gray. Don't give them any reason to take him from us, please."

"Jack's going nowhere." That look belonging back in the cell crept into Gray's eyes. "No one moves him from this manor. Period."

Giving them a moment, Raif went over, causing Gray to look up, even though Jan stayed close in the curve of his neck, and Gray turned slightly, putting Jan out of Raif's path, his own body square on to anything that threatened who he held.

Some undercurrent flowed here, good, bad... whether it was healthy for Jan and Gray, Gray and Martin, this Jack he had yet to meet, Raif still wasn't sure. But they fought to hold on to something that was locked away in that padded cell, no matter how frayed those threads were becoming, and they took care of their own, no matter how tough it got. Always.

Raif offered his hand over. "It's a pleasure to work for you, sir."

Gray stilled, frowned, then shook his hand.

"And on that note, I apologise for accidentally unlocking Martin's door. With Craig and no sign of staff there, I assumed the room had been emptied and needed to check for it when it came to finding Ash. Unlocking doors is my speciality, and access wasn't that hard to work. My mistake. Please have Ray explain to Craig that I'm new on scene and learning the… Peachless ropes too. I'm sure Craig will understand Martin's fight at seeing an open door and a newcomer."

Gray frowned.

Everyone had scars, but sometimes scapegoats were needed to give them time to heal. He understood that more than anyone.

Raif left them alone at that and felt a gentle pat on his arm off Caleb. He hadn't even known the older man was there. But Caleb didn't follow him out, instead he stood watching from a distance how Gray pulled Jan in close.

For Raif, though, he needed Ash away from here now. Miles was the wrong influence in every hardcore way, but bring in Gray, stand Ash in his shadow…? There was a hell living here he didn't want rubbing off on Ash.

CHAPTER 39
NO

NEVER FEELING MORE tired, Raif found Ash in the lounge. But he sat alone, looking down at his hands, with no sign that he'd spoken to his father.

"He forgot," Ash said quietly. "He knew something had happened, and I could see him trying to remember, to say sorry, but... but...."

Raif went over and sat down next to him. He took Ash's hand in his and drew it into his lap.

"I let Ray arrange for someone to take him home. He wasn't happy that he was here." Ash looked up. "How much of a bastard does that make me? I never went with him. Didn't even see him to the car."

"It makes you someone who needs a break, nothing more, Ash." He went quiet for a moment. "We all need a break sometimes, just to regroup."

Raif brushed his thumb over Ash's hand. It was long, thin, a musician's hand, yet Ash played no instrument, only played the best in Raif. Maybe the worst too. He'd stood in that cell and watched Miles be slaughtered for him. "Ash,

I'm no good with words, I've told you that, but I love you so fucking much. I need you to know that, okay? Doesn't matter what you can and can't give me. I need you to know."

Ash frowned, then Raif looked away as Ash pulled his hand free. Raif heard scribbling on paper a moment later, and he found a leaflet tucked into his hand.

"I like the look of this one," Ash said quietly.

Raif looked it over but didn't really see it. "Only like? Maybe we need to look for another home?"

Ash tapped the paper then got to his feet. "That one's ours."

Raif gave a heavy sigh. "Why this in particular?"

"Sez so on the back." Ash had moved over to the windows, sounding so distracted.

Raif turned the paper over and caught the note there.

Doesn't matter which house. I'd leave the door unlocked to any when it comes to you.

Raif brushed his thumb over that one word. Unlocked. Ash could have told him that he loved him and it wouldn't have made his hands shake so much in that moment.

Raif eased to his feet and went over to the window. Coming in close behind Ash, he slipped his arms around him and rested his chin down on Ash's shoulder. "Okay, maybe that house is perfect."

Ash cocked a look at him. "You sure? Because I've fucked up about every home I've come into contact with lately."

Raif briefly closed his eyes. "Not mine. I trust you to come through, Ash."

Quiet, then—"Enough to give me your name? I'm going

to need it for council tax purposes." Ash looked back again and his look called out *liar* in every way. He needed this one final detail to move forward. "Your *real* name."

Raif smiled and brushed a kiss against his cheek. He knew he was entitled now. "It's Raif."

Ash narrowed his eyes.

"Acronym: Richard Alex Ianto-Foland."

"Ianto?" Ash scrunched his face. "Your parents really didn't like you, did they?" Then he nodded and gave the faintest smile back. "Mind if I stick with Raif?"

Raif let out a long breath, then took Ash's scent in again. "Coming from you… no." He slipped his hands in Ash's jeans pockets. "You… you get to call me whatever the fuck you like."

∽

Daylight cut through the windows, although the sights and sounds from around the manor called early afternoon. Raif hadn't found much sleep, neither had Ash. They'd let a few movies play out in the darkness of one of Gray's guest rooms, their quiet maybe listening for where the next game of Gray's would come from.

It had been too late to go to a hotel, so a night in the manor it had been. They sorted their things now, tugging dirty clothes into the cases Jan had given them, along with Ash slipping on some trainers from Jan. Ash had taken them, not really liking what seemed to be a payoff, but not turning it down either.

A knock had come a few hours ago, and the rattle of tray said breakfast had been served, but neither of them had ventured out of the bed to find out. Sometimes locked doors were safer.

Now it had the feel of intruding on someone else's home, when the homeowners were here to catch him, and Raif felt... uneasy. Enough for Ash to offer a quiet smile over as he dressed over by the window.

He felt the unease too.

"You think we'll get a hotel subsidy whilst we wait for a house?" Ash said quietly as he tugged his T-shirt out of his jeans. "We don't have to stay here until then, right?"

Raif shook his head and threw Ash his jacket. "When you're ready."

Ash slipped the jacket on as Raif zipped up his own. "Oh I'm more than fucking ready."

A knock at the door had them both falling quiet, their gazes resting on the door.

"Raif?"

Ash frowned. That was Jan. "It's Ash. What's up, Jan?"

Quiet, then—"Can you get Raif to head on down to the kitchen? There's someone here to see him."

Raif finished flattening the collar to his jacket. No one knew he was here. He flicked a look at Ash, letting him know that, but the glance he got back saw Ash head over and open the door. Whoever was down there, Raif wouldn't be facing them alone, not in this manor.

That was fine by him.

Jan smiled as Ash headed out, and Raif managed to find one for Jan. He was the only "normal" in this place, if you could count sleeping in the arms of a culler as normal, but he understood it. More than.

"That way," said Jan, and he let Raif and Ash lead as they made their way down the hall, eventually to find the stairs. Raif knew the disinfectant signs now.

All the hustle and bustle from last night had quieted down by the time they reached the kitchen, and Raif pushed on through to find a woman and a man sitting at the table, Gray and everyone else nowhere in sight, but the air felt a little more tense than it had before, for some reason. No doubt Craig had all of Gray's attention now, and Craig was far from stupid. Maybe he'd buy the lies for a while, but what then?

Giving a frown, and pushed in a little more by Jan, Raif went still seeing the iPad sat on the table; at the little girl who sat sitting down staring at it.

"Lucy." His heart slipped all the way to his toes, and Ash's hand slipped a hold into his a moment later and grounded him with a rough squeeze.

A man, looking tall and spider-like with his limbs, rose from the table and came over. Raif barely registered the offer of hand.

Spider came in close, now speaking very quietly in his ear. "With Lucy, the name Voodoo is a trigger for her, please avoid using it. Don't touch her yet either—see if she'll reach for you. Although the iPad is there and is one of her favourites, she's not made any attempt to interact with that. Eating is basic, very basic, and sometimes she'll ask for toast for the lady in the shed. Nothing more."

Raif looked at Spider, the mole on his face, at the mention of Kerry. Of toast.

"I'm Philip Halliday." Philip gave him a nod. "I'll be working with you, Lucy, and Ash over the next coming months. Also with Chase when he regains consciousness."

When. He knew Ash would have been grateful for that. Raif nodded, this time making sure that Philip knew he'd taken in everything he'd just said, plus the name. "She's here to stay?"

Halliday offered a smile. "Her father has automatic parental responsibility, but he's in agreement she needs the best care. He'd like visitation rights if she wants to. Same with her staying here. It's her decision. If not, don't let it hurt. She'll be staying with me at Clearwater, the MC psychiatric unit, and there's plenty of room for you to stay or visit too. Her father has only chosen to visit."

Raif looked back at Ash. He was focused purely on Lucy, on all the detachment going on at the table. Did he see an echo of himself there? Ash found him a moment later.

"Whatever she needs, Raif. Whatever you need. Staying at the psychiatric unit is fine with me if that's what you call."

For how hard he found it to say "I trust you," everything else about Ash said that for him. Maybe Raif had missed that, maybe Ash didn't see it yet, or maybe "I trust you," would always hold more value in Ash's world. Raif would take whatever was on offer. Raif brushed Ash's hand, then went and crouched by the table, by Lucy.

"Hey, sweetheart." He resisted every urge to pick her up and scrunch her into the biggest cuddle. "Do you remember me?" It seemed such a strange question; he'd only seen her a week ago, but he wanted to see if she'd say his name, if she'd look at him.

She didn't.

"I bet it was a long journey in that car, hey, pumpkin? Longer than donkey ears and Pinocchio's nose, all rolled into one: a dononcchio."

Long black hair covered her face, knotty, like it hadn't

been brushed in a while, but that was nothing new. Even brushed it had that gypsy wildness.

"Well me and Ash, you remember Ash, right?" He glanced back briefly to catch the look in Ash's eyes. "We're going to be here for whenever you need us, okay? You call, we'll run. You laugh and we'll be there quicker than a bucket full of kittens trying to escape to milk island. But if you say my name…" Raif tilted his head slightly. "You bet your Xbox and all your Roblox money that I'll be there."

He always got it wrong, calling Xboxes PlayStations, PlayStations iPads, and it usually won a smile, a giggle, a call of stupid, but in the nicest way.

But today there was nothing. He knew the damage the mind could take, had seen it on the field, both with MI6 and army, with grown men. He knew how small and often could sometimes be the best way to heal, especially the often, the contact, just letting them know you were there. "Oh, baby. We're always going to be here for you, okay?"

He looked over at Halliday, knowing Ash would be okay with this. "She needs specialist care. Can we all stay at Clearwater?"

Halliday nodded, smiled. "Of course."

"I'll just get our things." Ash turned to leave and Raif stood, taking Lucy with him in his arms, but only when he cleared it with Halliday to try.

He still got no reaction off Lucy, but he'd damn well be there, holding her like this until he did.

≈

All of their gear, for how little it was, was packed in the boot of a Mercedes-Benz. Lucy had untangled herself from

Raif, and when he caught sight of Gray resting against his Rolls, Raif looked across to Halliday, knowing something remained outstanding.

"I'll just be a minute."

Ash frowned over the car at him, then caught sight of Gray before Ash got in the car to sit by Lucy.

Raif got a nod off Halliday, then he went over to Gray, and Gray softened a lot about his manner seeing Lucy staring blankly out of the car window.

"I have a lifetime of thank yous to give, and it seems never enough time to do it." Raif offered his hand over to Gray. "All of those surrounding Ash, Chase, and that little lass over there."

Gray looked down at his hand for a moment, then shook it. "I'll be in touch."

Raif nodded. "I don't doubt that. Can I just ask for time to see this little one back to playing with her iPad?"

Gray looked Lucy over, his gaze so much different than what Raif saw in the cell, understanding held in them so clearly now. He smiled as he watched Lucy. "You don't ever need to ask."

"But you want your question answering."

Gray looked across to the woods that surrounded his manor. "I'd like my question answering, yes." He focused back on Raif.

"Which is?"

"My father… why didn't he want our paths to cross in the West Midlands?"

Raif thought it over for a long moment, Gray watching, waiting, and it's that waiting that made him say the next word. "No."

"No?"

Gray wasn't told that often, he could see that, but Raif looked back at Lucy, then at Gray, then Light crept into his thoughts, more haunted them.

"Sometimes, Gray, it's not what's said, but who it's spoken to." Raif offered a sad smile. "If your father won't tell you, if lives have been taken, if a young girl's mind has been taken—and he still won't tell you about us and the West Midlands, then you need to step back and question if it's what he needs to say, or who he has to tell it to, that's stopping him."

Gray pulled back a touch, so Raif went in a little closer, more so respectful of privacy and knowing how anyone could listen in.

"Please don't ask me again." He frowned. "I won't tell you because I saw you in that cell, what you're capable of, and you need to listen to why neither I nor your father will tell you what you want to know now. I need you to trust me when I say 'no, I can't tell you this.' I need you to back off completely from asking about it. Not just for your sake now."

Raif eased away, giving a sniff. "Now you can take away everything you've done for me, but I hope you don't. I hope what went on in that cell isn't all you are." He looked down at his feet briefly. "So, are we good with that?" Raif held out his hand again, and from the corner of his eyes, he caught Caleb standing by the lamppost, leaning against it. "Are we good with all of this? How I've answered your question, but perhaps not in the way you wanted?"

Gray was focused on his father too, which was how it should stay.

After a moment, Gray shook his hand again. "You

answered. Thank you for your honesty. I'm good with that. We're good."

He hoped for Gray's sanity that was true, because Raif hid just how much he shook. When he'd started out with MI6, he'd played a part in killing Gray's mother, maybe Gray suspected that. But the real nail in the coffin, the one that had Raif looking back at Lucy, at what happened in that cell...?

He'd taken Gray's son from him too.

At the age of four, new identity, new nationality, new name. Only something had gone wrong. Dark web headlong into depravity wrong.

The investigation into the I-dosing, into dark web play that had already seen one dead girl that Raif had found, it concerned Gray's son, Light. There were... concerns.

The call had come from Caleb to start the investigation in the West Midlands because his grandson's name had come up a few months ago when it came to potentially handling that stolen equipment. Whoever made the call to get Gray here, they knew that too. Cal hadn't lied, he was protecting his family: Gray's. But those behind who'd called Gray in? Gray was no natural father. He'd made it clear that if anyone got near his son, threatened the normality he'd given him by walking away and leaving him alone, he'd kill them. And if Raif had touched a nerve over the military equipment that had gone missing, over I-dosing teenagers, then what better silencing weapon than Gray when it came to MI6 investigating those cullers. There was a private war going on here, one that Gray was too focused on Martin to see, and it was starting to push heavily into home shores, into his own son's life.

And if Gray's boy was involved with the likes of the dark web, then what would that mean for him? Few got involved with the dark web unless they liked life far more twisted than most. Was the son turning out to be like the father, even though the father had done everything he could to keep this life away from him? That Cal and Raif had also tried to ensure it wouldn't attract him?

There were more than... concerns with the eighteen-year-old... Especially with those late-night runs that Light kept on taking, all the chemicals that were delivered to Light's on a Friday night.

Cal didn't want to risk Gray finding out either way. That was the heavy concern that Raif saw in the older man's eyes. In his silence, Gray would tear his own boy down, in ways that kept Martin knee-deep in his own personal dark web hell and locked away in that cell.

And if Gray knew the order had come from Caleb himself to give Gray's boy a new nationality, denying him his Welsh heritage, yes, but also denying Gray his option of finding his son if ever he felt the pull to see him? How that order had come from Caleb to keep Gray's boy under surveillance? Gray would go for the throat, going through everyone to get at Caleb and Raif, including a little girl.

Raif had denied Gray intelligence on his own boy on the back of trying to make sure Lucy stayed safe. Yeah, the anger there would be more than justified from Gray.

So Caleb had played the only card he had once he knew Gray had been put on to Raif's trail: it was why Raif had been forced into Gray's world. Better face the devil than turn your back. Or from what went down in that cell, face the two devils.

That sinking feeling hit Raif as Gray looked back at the house.

Martin poisoned the air here, and Gray breathed it in so

deeply.

His fall would come.

It had started already.

It just remained to be seen who'd be left holding him when the dust cleared. Cal was just trying to make sure his grandson didn't get caught in the fallout.

Jan came out from within the reception hall, standing away from Caleb, further back, and resting against the doorframe. Gray's reaction was just as instinctive as he shifted and went over to him.

That quiet whisper went to Jan's ear, that discreet touch to Jan's abs, and Jan turned into the kiss that brushed his cheek, chasing the kiss with a soft blush to his nose.

There was goodness here too, though, and it centred on everything that Gray touched now, how Jan had as much pull on Gray as all the badness did.

Jan opened the door for Gray, giving a look around as Gray headed on in. He had a fight on his hands. Maybe he knew that already. All Raif understood in that moment? It took the kind of balls Raif didn't have for such a soft-hearted soul to go in after Gray and shut the door.

Ballsy. Yeah, Jan was a ballsy bastard, more subtle in his ways, so quiet in approach, but there to stay and hold his ground. The four-way dynamic: Jan, Martin, Gray... whoever this Jack was, it was startling. Dangerous, but fucking potent.

Caleb watched from the outside too, his lean into the lamppost saying he'd be watching for a lot longer. But maybe, just maybe, there was a matched hope that Jan carried enough lightness in soul to stop whatever walk into darkness lingered behind those doors for Gray. It gave Cal enough time to ensure his grandson wouldn't also take that walk into darkness, wouldn't walk headlong into Gray and catch the infection.

Family. It broke the best of people, but what stayed beyond those walls was a far cry away from the best of anything, so Raif shared a look with Cal.

Raif would be here watching too.

He knew Gray's son.

And if the father wasn't bad enough, there were more than… concerns when it came to Gray's son.

FINAL THOUGHTS &
ABOUT THE AUTHOR

THANK YOU! Gray's son... my lord. I can't wait for you to meet him if you haven't already in *Fractured* (Don't... 6)!! The next novel is going to be so tough on the soul, but it wouldn't be in the Don't world if it wasn't tough. But Gray's son... I don't think I've loved portraying a character so much.

And Jack... it's been hard to write this novel without him being here. Martin's a force unto himself, but the more I wrote, the more I needed Jack there in the story. I've really missed him. He will be back, there's no doubt about that, but how that comes about, what state of mind dominates, wins... loses... that's always going to be the question. How Gray wins... loses... falls... that's in there too: their fates are always so closely intertwined, right along with Martin's.

That leaves Jan. He's gotten so much stronger, always retaining who he is, even though he's still left fighting everything on his own sometimes. The one question I always wanted to look at, though, is if he's ever forced to face Gray and Martin together, playing together... would he have the draw it takes to keep Gray grounded? And that's coming too....

Tough times ahead. I think Jan knows that. Martin definitely does, and he's loving it! Gray... he's caught in the spiral now, running more on blind instinct, and that's never known him to fall on safe shores.

For those who have been with me long enough they might recognise a little bit about Ash and Raif! They're from the prequel to this story: *Ash* (Don't... Book 4.5), where we got to meet them for the first time, away from the Don't... world. I've always loved Raif's night-walking life and thought it would be a perfect addition to the Don't world and how Gray's world works. Ash is something different too, bringing in that emerging Dom who's got all the youth to screw it up along the way. Having Raif as his sub just offered so much scope and heat for their relationship. Having Ash have that darker side to his character offered so much more. Their story continues into Don't 6: *Fractured*, and we'll get to see how Lucy and Chase are doing too.

As usual, I have one hell of a team who backs me up with everything I write, and they each bring something special to the table. Thanks to Dilo Keith, erotica author and BDSM consultant, who always shows stunning patience and stays with me to continue to provide absolutely excellent conceptual and technical guidance into the BDSM lifestyle. Also, as ever, to Vicki Howard, who is a tireless dark content consultant and general good friend who always pushes me forward when I feel like stepping back. So many thank yous and you're awesomes to Elaine Slansky: my dark web and computer go-to lady! You know about some of the wickedest avenues for plots, and you read and reread until I know you're ready for throwing things at me!!! And to the utterly gorgeous Kimberly Sewald, Lisa, Barbara, Becky, and Jenn Boltz (how many times did you read this script, guys!? You're AWESOME). And special and stunning thanks also to Dr. Katerina Schmidt, who's been my medical source for Chase's care, all the meds and procedures he'd need. Your love for the Don't world, like with Vicky, Elaine, Dilo, Kim, Lisa, Barbara, and Jenn is… wow! There's also a quiet thanks and huge hug to author Joseph Lance Tonlet. Such a gorgeous dark mind to pick and prod at! And yeah, I still wish I'd written your *Brother's LaFon*, Joe!

But deepest, deepest thanks, as always, go to you, reading this. It's stunning how you stay with me and keep on reading. I love my writing a lot darker than most authors, and it's so good to know I get the best of readers who stop by and take a seat with me. You're utterly, utterly amazing! Thank you! So very much.

Reviews help authors survive, so if you'd love to review, that would be—stunning!

Visit Jack at: http://www.jacklpyke.com.

Love always,
Jack.

～

JACK L. PYKE

Jack L. Pyke blames her dark writing influences on living close to one of England's finest forests. Having grown up hearing a history of kidnappings, murders, strange sightings, and sexual exploits her neck of the woods is renowned for, Jack takes that into her writing, having also learnt that human coping strategies for intense situations can sometimes make the best of people have disastrously bad moments. Redeeming those flaws is Jack's drive, and if that drive just happens to lead to sexual tension between two or more guys, Jack's the first to let nature take its course.

ALSO BY JACK L. PYKE

DON'T... SERIES

Don't (Don't... book 1)
Antidote (Don't... book 2)
Breakdown (Don't... book 3)
Backlash (Don't... book 4)
Ash (Don't... book 4.5)
Psychopaths & Sinners (Don't... book 5)
Fractured (Don't... book 6)

NOVELS

Broken Ink

NOVELLAS

Lost in the Echo
Shaded Chains

ANTHOLOGIES

Being Me
Love is Love

JACK L. PYKE

Made in the USA
Las Vegas, NV
21 January 2023

65998388R10272